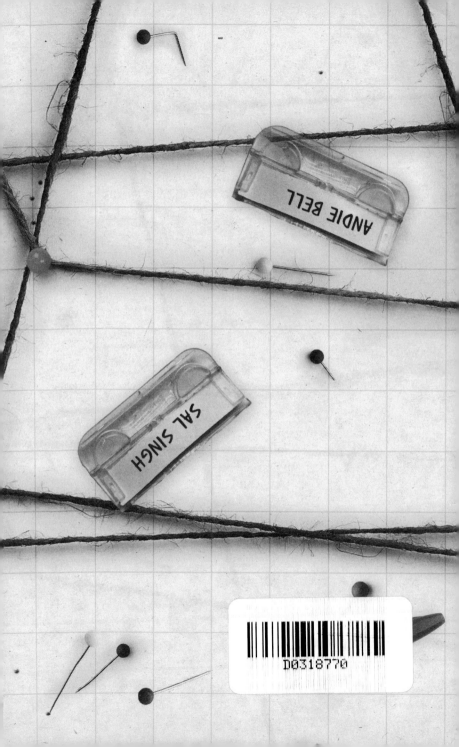

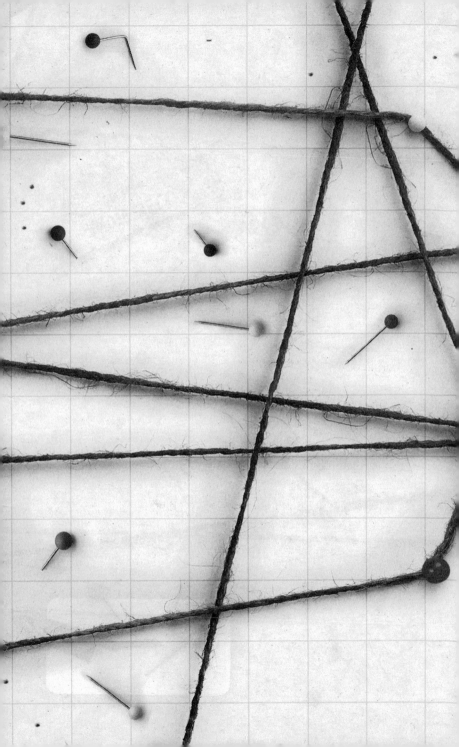

A Good Girl's Guide to Murder

A Good Girl's Guide to Murder

HOLLY JACKSON

First published in Great Britain in 2019
by Electric Monkey, part of Farshore

An imprint of HarperCollins*Publishers*
1 London Bridge Street, London SE1 9GF

farshore.co.uk

HarperCollins*Publishers*
Macken House, 39/40 Mayor Street Upper,
Dublin 1, D01 C9W8, Ireland

Text copyright © 2019 Holly Jackson
The moral rights of the author have been asserted

ISBN 978 1 4052 9318 1
Printed and bound in the UK using 100% renewable electricity
at CPI Group (UK) Ltd
55

This book is produced from independently certified FSC™ paper
to ensure responsible forest management.

For more information visit: www.harpercollins.co.uk/green

To Mum and Dad,
this first one is for you.

PART I

QAG

Recognising
Academic
Achievement

EXTENDED PROJECT QUALIFICATION 2017/18

Candidate number	Candidate's full name
4169	Pippa Fitz-Amobi

Part A: Candidate proposal

To be completed by the candidate

- The courses of study or area(s) of interest to which the topic relates:

English, Journalism, Investigative Journalism, Criminal Law

Working title of Extended Project.

Present the topic to be researched in the form of a statement/question/hypothesis.

Research into the 2012 missing persons investigation of Andie Bell in Little Kilton.

A detailed report on how both print/televised media and social media have become invaluable players in police investigations, using Andie Bell as a case study. And the implications of the press in their presentations of Sal Singh and his alleged guilt.

- My initial resources will be:

Interview with missing persons expert, interview with a local journalist reporting on the case, newspaper articles, interviews with members of the community. Textbooks and articles on police procedure, psychology and the role of media.

Pippa, as previously discussed, this is an incredibly sensitive topic to pick – a terrible crime that happened in our own town. I know you cannot be persuaded away but the project has been accepted only on the condition that <u>no ethical lines are crossed</u>. I think you need to find a more focused angle for your report as you work through your research, without concentrating too much on sensitive issues.

And let me be clear, there is to be **NO CONTACT** made with either of the families involved in this case. This will be considered an ethical violation and your project will be disqualified. And don't work too hard. Have a nice summer.

Candidate declaration

I certify that I have read and understood the regulations relating to unfair practice as set out in the notice to candidates.

Signature: *Pippa Fitz-Amobi*

Date: 18/07/2017

One

Pip knew where they lived.

Everyone in Little Kilton knew where they lived.

Their home was like the town's own haunted house; people's footsteps quickened as they walked by and their words strangled and died in their throats. Shrieking children would gather on their walk home from school, daring one another to run up and touch the front gate.

But it wasn't haunted by ghosts, just three sad people trying to live their lives as before. A house not haunted by flickering lights or spectral falling chairs, but by dark spray-painted letters of *Scum Family* and stone-shattered windows.

Pip had always wondered why they didn't move. Not that they had to; they hadn't done anything wrong. But she didn't know how they lived like that.

Pip knew a great many things; she knew that hippopotomonstrosesquipedaliophobia was the technical term for the fear of long words, she knew that babies were born without kneecaps, she knew verbatim the best quotes from Plato and Cato, and that there were more than four thousand types of potato. But she didn't know how the Singhs found the strength to stay here. Here, in Kilton, under the weight of so many widened eyes, of the comments whispered just loud enough to be heard, of neighbourly small talk never stretching into long talk any more.

It was a particular cruelty that their house was so close to Little Kilton Grammar School, where both Andie Bell and Sal Singh had gone, where Pip would return for her final year in a few weeks when the August-pickled sun dipped into September.

Pip stopped and rested her hand on the front gate, instantly braver than half the town's kids. Her eyes traced up the path to the front door. It might only look like a few feet but there was a rumbling chasm between where she stood and over there. It was possible that this was a very bad idea; she had considered that. The morning sun was hot and she could already feel her knee pits growing sticky in her jeans. A bad idea or a bold idea. And yet, history's greatest minds always advised bold over safe; their words good padding for even the worst ideas.

Snubbing the chasm with the soles of her shoes, she walked up to the door and, pausing for just a second to check she was sure, knocked three times. Her tense reflection stared back at her: the long dark hair sun-dyed a lighter brown at the tips, the pale face, despite a week just spent in the south of France, the sharp muddy green eyes braced for impact.

The door opened with the clatter of a falling chain and a double-locked click.

'Hello?' he said, holding the door half open, his hand folded over the side. Pip blinked to break her stare, but she couldn't help it. He looked so much like Sal: the Sal she knew from all those television reports and newspaper pictures.

The Sal fading from her adolescent memory. Ravi had his brother's messy black side-swept hair, thick arched eyebrows and oaken-hued skin.

'Hello?' he said again.

'Um . . .' Pip's put-on-the-spot charmer reflex kicked in too late. Her brain was busy processing that, unlike Sal, he had a dimple in his chin, just like hers. And he'd grown even taller since she last saw him. 'Um, sorry, hi.' She did an awkward half-wave that she immediately regretted.

'Hi?'

'Hi, Ravi,' she said. 'I . . . you don't know me . . . I'm Pippa Fitz-Amobi. I was a couple of years below you at school before you left.'

'OK . . .'

'I was just wondering if I could borrow a jiffy of your time? Well, not a jiffy . . . Did you know a jiffy is an actual measurement of time? It's one one-hundredth of a second, so . . . can you maybe spare a few sequential jiffies?'

Oh god, this is what happened when she was nervous or backed into a corner; she started spewing useless facts dressed up as bad jokes. And the other thing: nervous Pip turned four strokes more posh, abandoning middle class to grapple for a poor imitation of upper. When had she ever seriously said 'jiffy' before?

'What?' Ravi asked, looking confused.

'Sorry, never mind,' Pip said, recovering. 'So I'm doing my EPQ at school and –'

'What's EPQ?'

'Extended Project Qualification. It's a project you work on independently, alongside A levels. You can pick any topic you want.'

'Oh, I never got that far in school,' he said. 'Left as soon as I could.'

'Er, well, I was wondering if you'd be willing to be interviewed for my project.'

'What's it about?' His dark eyebrows hugged closer to his eyes.

'Um . . . it's about what happened five years ago.'

Ravi exhaled loudly, his lip curling up in what looked like pre-sprung anger.

'Why?' he said.

'Because I don't think your brother did it – and I'm going to try to prove it.'

Production Log – Entry 1

Interview with Ravi Singh booked in for Friday afternoon (take prepared questions).

Type up transcript of interview with Angela Johnson.

The production log is intended to chart any obstacles you face in your research, your progress and the aims of your final report. My production log will have to be a little different: I'm going to record all the research I do here, both relevant and irrelevant, because, as yet, I don't really know what my final report will be, nor what will end up being relevant. I don't know what I'm aiming for. I will just have to wait and see what position I am in at the end of my research and what essay I can therefore bring together. [This is starting to feel a little like a diary???]

I'm hoping it will *not* be the essay I proposed to Mrs Morgan. I'm hoping it will be the truth. What really happened to Andie Bell on the 20th April 2012? And – as my instincts tell me – if Salil 'Sal' Singh is not guilty, then who killed her?

I don't think I will actually solve the case and discover the person who murdered Andie. I'm not a police officer with access to a forensics lab (obviously) and I am also not deluded. But I'm hoping that my research will uncover facts and accounts that will lead to reasonable doubt about Sal's guilt, and suggest that the police were mistaken in closing the case without digging further.

So my research methods will actually be: interviewing those close to the case, obsessive social media stalking and wild, WILD speculation.

[DON'T LET MRS MORGAN SEE ANY OF THIS!!!]

The first stage in this project then is to research what happened to Andrea Bell – known as Andie to everyone – and the circumstances surrounding her disappearance. This information will be taken from news articles and police press conferences from around that time.

[Write your references in now so you don't have to do it later!!!]

Copied and pasted from the first national news outlet to report on her disappearance:

'Andrea Bell, 17, was reported missing from her home in Little Kilton, Buckinghamshire, last Friday.

She left home in her car – a black Peugeot 206 – with her mobile phone, but did not take any clothes with her. Police say her disappearance is "completely out of character".

Police have been searching woodland near the family home over the weekend.

Andrea, known as Andie, is described as white, five feet six inches tall, with long blonde hair. It is thought that she was wearing dark jeans and a blue cropped jumper on the night she went missing.'[1]

After everything happened, later articles had more detail as to when Andie was last seen alive and the time window in which she is believed to have been abducted.

Andie Bell was 'last seen alive by her younger sister, Becca, at around 10:30 p.m. on the 20th April 2012.'[2]

This was corroborated by the police in a press conference on Tuesday 24th April: 'CCTV footage taken from a security camera outside STN Bank on Little Kilton High Street confirms that Andie's car was seen driving away from her home at about 10:40 p.m.'[3]

According to her parents, Jason and Dawn Bell, Andie was 'supposed to pick (them) up from a dinner party at 12:45 a.m.' When Andie didn't show up or answer any of their phone calls, they started ringing her friends to see if anyone knew of her whereabouts. Jason Bell 'called the police to report his daughter missing at 3:00 a.m. Saturday morning.'[4]

So whatever happened to Andie Bell that night, happened between 10:40 p.m. and 12:45 a.m.

Here seems a good place to type up the transcript from my telephone interview yesterday with Angela Johnson.

1 www.gbtn.co.uk/news/uk-england-bucks-54774390 23/04/12

2 www.thebuckinghamshiremail.co.uk/news/crime-4839 26/04/12

3 www.gbtn.co.uk/news/uk-england-bucks-69388473 24/04/12

4 Forbes, Stanley, 2012, 'The Real Story of Andie Bell's Killer,' Kilton Mail, 1/05/12, pp. 1–4.

Transcript of interview with Angela Johnson from the Missing Persons Bureau

Angela: Hello.

Pip: Hi, is this Angela Johnson?

Angela: Speaking, yep. Is this Pippa?

Pip: Yes, thanks so much for replying to my email.

Angela: No problem.

Pip: Do you mind if I record this interview so I can type it up later to use in my project?

Angela: Yeah, that's fine. I'm sorry I've only got about ten minutes to give you. So what do you want to know about missing persons?

Pip: Well, I was wondering if you could talk me through what happens when someone is reported missing? What's the process and the first steps taken by the police?

Angela: So, when someone rings 999 or 101 to report someone as missing, the police will try to get as much detail as possible so they can identify the potential risk to the missing person and an appropriate police response can be made. The kinds of details they will ask for in this first call are name, age, description of the person, what clothes they were last seen wearing, the circumstances of their disappearance, if going missing is out of character for this person, details of any vehicle involved. Using this information, the police will determine whether this is a high-, low- or medium-risk case.

Pip: And what circumstances would make a case high-risk?

Angela: If they are vulnerable because of their age or a disability, that would be high-risk. If the behaviour is out of character, then it is likely an indicator that they have been exposed to harm, so that would be high-risk.

Pip: Um, so, if the missing person is seventeen years old and it is deemed out of character for her to go missing, would this be considered a high-risk case?

Angela: Oh, absolutely, if a minor is involved.

Pip: So how would the police respond to a high-risk case?

Angela: Well, there would be immediate deployment of police officers to the location the person is missing from. The officer will have to acquire further details about the missing person, such as details of their friends or partners, any health conditions, their financial information in case they can be found when trying to withdraw money. They will also need a number of recent photographs of the person and, in a high-risk case, they may take DNA samples in case they are needed in subsequent forensic examination. And, with consent of the homeowners, the location will be searched thoroughly to see if the missing person is concealed or hiding there and to establish whether there are any further evidential leads. That's the normal procedure.

Pip: So immediately the police are looking for any clues or suggestions that the missing person has been the victim of a crime?

Angela: Absolutely. If the circumstances of the disappearance are suspicious, officers are always told 'if in doubt, think murder.' Of course, only a very small percentage of missing person cases turn into homicide cases, but officers are instructed to document evidence early on as though they were investigating a homicide.

Pip: And after the initial home address search, what happens if nothing significant turns up?

Angela: They will expand the search to the immediate area. They might request telephone information. They'll question friends, neighbours, anyone who may have relevant information. If it is a young person, a teenager, who's missing, a reporting parent cannot be assumed to know all of their child's friends and acquaintances. Their peers are a good port of call to establish other important contacts, you know, any secret boyfriends, that sort of thing. And a press strategy is usually discussed because appeals for information in the media can be very useful in these situations.

Pip:	So, if it's a seventeen-year-old girl who's gone missing, the police would have contacted her friends and boyfriend quite early on?
Angela:	Yes of course. Enquiries will be made because, if the missing person has run away, they are likely to be hiding out with a person close to them.
Pip:	And at what point in a missing persons case do police accept they are looking for a body?
Angela:	Well, timewise, it's not . . . Oh, Pippa, I have to go. Sorry, I've been called into my meeting.
Pip:	Oh, OK, thanks so much for taking the time to talk to me.
Angela:	And if you have any more questions, just pop me an email and I'll get to them when I can.
Pip:	Will do, thanks again.
Angela:	Bye.

I found these statistics online:

> **80% of missing people are found in the first 24 hours. 97% are found in the first week. 99% of cases are resolved in the first year. That leaves just 1%.**
>
> **1% of people who disappear are never found.**
> **But there's another figure to consider: just 0.25% of all missing person cases have a fatal outcome.[5]**

And where does this leave Andie Bell? Floating incessantly somewhere between 1% and 0.25%, fractionally increasing and decreasing in tiny decimal breaths.

But by now, most people accept that she's dead, even though her body has never been recovered. And why is that?

Sal Singh is why.

---

5 www.findmissingperson.co.uk/stats

Two

Pip's hands strayed from the keyboard, her index fingers hovering over the *w* and *h* as she strained to listen to the commotion downstairs. A crash, heavy footsteps, skidding claws and unrestrained boyish giggles. In the next second it all became clear.

'Joshua! Why is the dog wearing one of my shirts?!' came Victor's buoyant shout, the sound floating up through Pip's carpet.

Pip snort-laughed as she clicked save on her production log and closed the lid of her laptop. It was a time-honoured daily crescendo from the moment her dad returned from work. He was never quiet: his whispers could be heard across the room, his whooping knee-slap laugh so loud it actually made people flinch, and every year, without fail, Pip woke to the sound of him *tiptoeing* the upstairs corridor to deliver Santa stockings on Christmas Eve.

Her stepdad was the living adversary of subtlety.

Downstairs, Pip found the scene mid-production. Joshua was running from room to room – from the kitchen to the hallway and into the living room – on repeat, cackling as he went.

Close behind was Barney, the golden retriever, wearing Pip's dad's loudest shirt: the blindingly green patterned one he'd bought during their last trip to Nigeria. The dog skidded elatedly across the polished oak in the hall, excitement whistling through his teeth.

And bringing up the rear was Victor in his grey Hugo Boss three-piece suit, charging all six and a half feet of himself after the dog and the boy, his laugh in wild climbing scale bursts. Their very own Amobi home-made Scooby-Doo montage.

'Oh my god, I was trying to do homework,' Pip said, smiling as she jumped back to avoid being mowed down by the convoy. Barney stopped for a moment to headbutt her shin and then scarpered off to jump on Dad and Josh as they collapsed together on the sofa.

'Hello, pickle,' Victor said, patting the sofa beside him.

'Hi, Dad, you were so quiet I didn't even know you were home.'

'My Pipsicle, you are too clever to recycle a joke.'

She sat down next to them, Josh and her dad's worn-out breaths making the sofa cushion swell and sink against the backs of her legs.

Josh started excavating in his right nostril and Dad batted his hand away.

'How were your days then?' he asked, setting Josh off on a graphic spiel about the football games he'd played earlier.

Pip zoned out; she'd already heard it all in the car when she picked Josh up from the club. She'd only been half listening, distracted by the way the replacement coach had stared bewilderedly at her lily-white skin when she'd pointed out which of the nine-year-olds was hers and said: 'I'm Joshua's sister.'

She should have been used to it by now, the lingering looks while people tried to work out the logistics of her family, the numbers and hedged words scribbled across their family tree. The giant Nigerian man was quite evidently her stepfather and Joshua her half-brother. But Pip didn't like using those words, those cold technicalities. The people you love weren't algebra: to be calculated, subtracted, or held at arm's length across a decimal point. Victor and Josh weren't just three-eighths hers, not just forty per cent family, they were fully hers. Her dad and her annoying little brother.

Her *'real'* father, the man that lent the Fitz to her name, died in a car accident when she was ten months old. And though Pip sometimes nodded and smiled when her mum would ask whether she remembered the way her father hummed while he brushed his teeth, or how he'd laughed when Pip's second spoken word was 'poo,' she didn't remember him. But sometimes remembering isn't for yourself, sometimes you do it just to make someone else smile. Those lies were allowed.

'And how's the project going, Pip?' Victor turned to her as he unbuttoned the shirt from the dog.

'It's OK,' she said. 'I'm just looking up the background and typing up at the moment. I did go to see Ravi Singh this morning.'

'Oh, and?'

'He was busy but he said I could go back on Friday.'

'I *wouldn't*,' Josh said in a cautionary tone.

'That's because you're a judgemental pre-pubescent boy who still thinks little people live inside traffic lights.' Pip looked at him. 'The Singhs haven't done anything wrong.'

Her dad stepped in. 'Joshua, try to imagine if everyone judged you because of something your sister had done.'

'All Pip ever does is homework.'

Pip executed a perfect arm-swung cushion lob into Joshua's face. Victor held the boy's arms down as he squirmed to retaliate, tickling his ribs.

'Why's Mum not back yet?' asked Pip, teasing the restrained Josh by floating her fluffy-socked foot near his face.

'She was going straight from work to Boozy Mums' book club,' Dad said.

'Meaning . . . we can have pizza for dinner?' Pip asked. And suddenly the friendly fire was forgotten and she and Josh were in the same battalion again. He jumped up and hooked his arm through hers, looking imploringly at their dad.

'Of course,' Victor said, patting his backside with a grin. 'How else am I to keep growing this junk in my trunk?'

'Dad,' Pip groaned, admonishing her past self for ever teaching him that phrase.

Production Log – Entry 2

What happened next in the Andie Bell case is quite confusing to glean from the newspaper reports. There are gaps I will have to fill with guesswork and rumours until the picture becomes clearer from any later interviews; hopefully Ravi and Naomi – who was one of Sal's best friends – can assist with this.

Using what Angela said, presumably after taking statements from the Bell family and thoroughly searching their residence, the police asked for details of Andie's friends.

From some seriously historical Facebook stalking, it looks like Andie's best friends were two girls called Chloe Burch and Emma Hutton. I mean, here's my evidence:

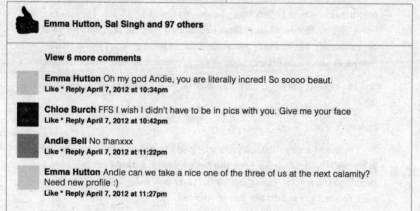

Emma Hutton, Sal Singh and 97 others

View 6 more comments

Emma Hutton Oh my god Andie, you are literally incred! So soooo beaut.
Like * Reply April 7, 2012 at 10:34pm

Chloe Burch FFS I wish I didn't have to be in pics with you. Give me your face
Like * Reply April 7, 2012 at 10:42pm

Andie Bell No thanxxx
Like * Reply April 7, 2012 at 11:22pm

Emma Hutton Andie can we take a nice one of the three of us at the next calamity? Need new profile :)
Like * Reply April 7, 2012 at 11:27pm

Write a comment...

This post is from two weeks before Andie disappeared. It looks like neither Chloe nor Emma live in Little Kilton any more. [Maybe private-message them and see if they'll do a phone interview?]

Chloe and Emma did a lot on that first weekend (21st and 22nd) to help spread the Thames Valley Police's Twitter campaign: #FindAndie.

I don't think it's too big of a leap to assume that the police contacted Chloe and Emma either on the Friday night or on Saturday morning. What they said to the police, I don't know. Hopefully I can find out.

We do know that police spoke to Andie's boyfriend at the time. His name was Sal Singh and he was attending his final year at Kilton Grammar alongside Andie.

At some point on the Saturday the police contacted Sal.

'DI Richard Hawkins confirmed that officers had questioned Salil Singh on Saturday 21st April. They questioned him as to his whereabouts for the previous night, particularly the period of time in which it is believed Andie went missing.'[6]

That night, Sal had been hanging out at his friend Max Hastings' house. He was with his four best friends: Naomi Ward, Jake Lawrence, Millie Simpson and Max.

Again, I need to check this with Naomi next week, but I think Sal told the police that he left Max's house at around 12:15 a.m. He walked home and his father (Mohan Singh) confirmed that 'Sal returned home at approximately 12:50 a.m.' [7] Note: the distance between Max's house (Tudor Lane) and Sal's (Grove Place) takes about 30 minutes to walk – says Google.

The police confirmed Sal's alibi with his four friends over the weekend.

Missing posters went up. House-to-house enquiries started on the Sunday.[8]

On the Monday, 100 volunteers helped the police carry out searches in the local woodland. I've seen the news footage; a whole ant line of people in the woods, calling her name. Later in the day, forensic teams were spotted going into the Bell residence.[9]

And on the Tuesday, everything changed.

I think chronologically is the best way to consider the events of that day and those that followed, even though we, as a town, learned the details out of order and jumbled.

Mid-morning: Naomi Ward, Max Hastings, Jake Lawrence and Millie

6. www.gbtn.co.uk/news/uk-england-bucks-78355334 05/05/12

7. www.gbtn.co.uk/news/uk-england-bucks-78355334 05/05/12

8. Forbes, Stanley, 'Local Girl Still Missing,' Kilton Mail, 23/04/12, pp. 1–2.

9 www.gbtn.co.uk/news/uk-england-bucks-56479322 23/04/12

Simpson contacted the police from school and confessed to providing false information. They said that Sal had asked them to lie and that he actually left Max's house at around 10:30 p.m. on the night Andie disappeared.

I don't know for sure what the correct police procedure would have been but I'm guessing that at that point, Sal became the number-one suspect.

But they couldn't find him: Sal wasn't at school and he wasn't at home. He wasn't answering his phone.

It later transpired, however, that Sal had sent a text to his father that morning, though he was ignoring all other calls. The press would refer to this as a 'confession text'.[10]

That Tuesday evening, one of the police teams searching for Andie found a body in the woods.

It was Sal.

He had killed himself.

The press never reported the method by which Sal committed suicide but by the power of high school rumour, I know (as did every other student at Kilton at the time).

Sal walked into the woods near his home, took a load of sleeping pills and placed a plastic bag over his head, secured by an elastic band around his neck. He suffocated while unconscious.

At the police press conference later that night no mention of Sal was made. The police only revealed that bit of information about CCTV imaging placing Andie as driving away from her home at 10:40 p.m.[11]

On the Wednesday, Andie's car was found parked on a small residential road (Romer Close).

It wasn't until the following Monday that a police spokeswoman revealed the following: 'I have an update on the Andie Bell investigation. As a result of recent intelligence and forensic information, we have strong reason to suspect that a young man named Salil Singh, aged 18, was involved in Andie's abduction and murder. The evidence would have been sufficient to arrest and charge the suspect had he not died before

---

10. www.gbtn.co.uk/news/uk-england-bucks-78355334 05/05/12

11. www.gbtn.co.uk/news/uk-england-bucks-69388473 24/03/12

proceedings could be initiated. Police are not looking for anyone else in relation to Andie's disappearance at this time but our search for Andie will continue unabated. Our thoughts go out to the Bell family and our deepest sympathies for the devastation this update has caused them.'

Their sufficient evidence was as follows:

They found Andie's mobile phone on Sal's body.

Forensic tests found traces of Andie's blood under the fingernails of his right middle and index fingers.

Andie's blood was also discovered in the boot of her abandoned car. Sal's fingerprints were found around the dashboard and steering wheel alongside prints from Andie and the rest of the Bell family.[12]

The evidence, they said, would have been enough to charge Sal and – police would have hoped – to secure a conviction in court. But Sal was dead, so there was no trial and no guilty conviction. No defence either.

In the following weeks, there were more searches of the woodland areas in and around Little Kilton. Searches using cadaver dogs. Police divers in the River Kilbourne. But Andie's body was never found.

The Andie Bell missing persons case was administratively closed in the middle of June 2012.[13] A case may be 'administratively closed' only if the 'supporting documentation contains sufficient evidence to charge had the offender not died before the investigation could be completed'. The case 'may be reopened whenever new evidence or leads develop'.[14]

Off to the cinema in 15 minutes: another superhero film that Josh has emotionally blackmailed us to see. But there's just one final part to the background of the Andie Bell/Sal Singh case and I'm on a roll.

Eighteen months after Andie Bell's case was administratively closed, the police filed a report to the local coroner. In cases like this, it is up to the coroner to decide whether further investigation into the death is required, based on their belief that the person is likely to be dead and that sufficient time has elapsed.

The coroner will then apply to the Secretary of State for Justice, under the Coroners Act 1988 Section 15, for an inquest with no body.

---

12 www.gbtn.co.uk/news/uk-england-bucks-78355334 09/05/12

13 www.gbtn.co.uk/news/uk-england-bucks-87366455 16/06/12

14 The National Crime Recording Standards (NCRS) https://www.gov.co.uk/government/uploads/ system/uploads/attachment_data/file/99584773/ncrs.pdf

Where there is no body, an inquest will rely mostly on evidence provided by the police, and whether the senior officers of the investigation believe the missing person is dead.

An inquest is a legal enquiry into the medical cause and circumstances of death. It cannot 'blame individuals for the death or establish criminal liability on the part of any named individual.'[15]

At the end of the inquest, January 2014, the coroner returned a verdict of 'unlawful killing' and Andie Bell's death certificate was issued.[16] An unlawful killing verdict literally means 'the person was killed by an "unlawful act" by someone' or, more specifically, death by 'murder, manslaughter, infanticide or death by dangerous driving.'[17]

This is where everything ends.

Andie Bell has been legally declared dead, despite her body never having been found. Given the circumstances, we can presume that the 'unlawful killing' verdict refers to murder. After Andie's inquest, a statement from the Crown Prosecution Service said: 'The case against Salil Singh would have been based on circumstantial and forensic evidence. It is not for the CPS to state whether Salil Singh killed Andie Bell or not, that would have been a jury's job to decide.'[18]

So even though there has never been a trial, even though no head juror has ever stood up, sweaty palmed and adrenaline-pumped, and declared: 'We the jury find the defendant guilty,' even though Sal never had the chance to defend himself, he is guilty. Not in the legal sense, but in all the other ways that truly matter.

When you ask people in town what happened to Andie Bell, they'll tell you without hesitation: 'She was murdered by Salil Singh.' No *allegedly*, no *might have*, no *probably*, no *most likely*.

He did it, they say. Sal Singh killed Andie.

But I'm just not so sure . . .

[Next log – possibly look at what the prosecution's case against Sal might have looked like if it went to court. Then start pecking away and putting holes in it.]

15 http://www.inquest.uk/help/handbook/7728339

16 www.dailynewsroom.co.uk/AndieBellInquest/report57743 12/01/14

17 http://www.inquest.uk/help/handbook/verdicts/unlawfulkilling

18 www.gbtn.co.uk/news/uk-england-bucks-95322345 14/01/14

Three

It was an emergency, the text said. An SOS emergency. Pip knew immediately that that could only mean one thing.

She grabbed her car keys, yelled a perfunctory goodbye to Mum and Josh and rushed out of the front door.

She stopped by the shop on her way to buy a king-size chocolate bar to help mend Lauren's king-size broken heart.

When she pulled up outside Lauren's house, she saw that Cara had had the exact same idea. Yet Cara's post-break-up first-aid kit was more extensive than Pip's; she had also brought a box of tissues, crisps and dip, and a rainbow array of face mask packets.

'Ready for this?' Pip asked Cara, hip-bumping her in greeting.

'Yep, well prepared for the tears.' She held up the tissues, the corner of the box snagging on her curly ash-blonde hair.

Pip untangled it for her and then pressed the doorbell, both of them wincing at the scratchy mechanical song.

Lauren's mum answered the door.

'Oh, the cavalry are here,' she smiled. 'She's upstairs in her room.'

They found Lauren fully submerged in a duvet fort on the bed; the only sign of her existence was a splay of ginger hair poking out of the bottom. It took a full minute of coaxing and

22

chocolate bait to get her to surface.

'Firstly,' Cara said, prising Lauren's phone from her fingers, 'you're banned from looking at this for the next twenty-four hours.'

'He did it by text!' Lauren wailed, blowing her nose as an entire snot-swamp was cannon-shot into the woefully thin tissue.

'Boys are dicks, thank god I don't have to deal with that,' Cara said, putting her arm round Lauren and resting her sharp chin on her shoulder. 'Loz, you could do so much better than him.'

'Yeah.' Pip broke Lauren off another line of chocolate. 'Plus Tom always said "pacifically" when he meant "specifically".'

Cara clicked eagerly and pointed at Pip in agreement. 'Massive red flag that was.'

'I *pacifically* think you're better off without him,' said Pip.

'I *atlantically* think so too,' added Cara.

Lauren gave a wet snort of laughter and Cara winked at Pip; an unspoken victory. They knew that, working together, it wouldn't take them long to get Lauren laughing again.

'Thanks for coming, guys,' Lauren said tearfully. 'I didn't know if you would. I've probably neglected you for half a year to hang out with Tom. And now I'll be third-wheeling two best friends.'

'You're talking crap,' Cara said. 'We are all best friends, aren't we?'

'Yeah,' Pip nodded, 'us and those three boys we deign to share in our delightful company.'

The others laughed. The boys – Ant, Zach and Connor – were all currently away on summer holidays.

But of her friends, Pip had known Cara the longest and, yes, they were closer. An unsaid thing. They'd been inseparable ever since six-year-old Cara had hugged a small, friendless Pip and asked, 'Do you like bunnies too?' They were each other's crutch to lean on when life got too much to carry alone. Pip, though only ten at the time, had helped support Cara through her mum's diagnosis and death. And she'd been her constant two years ago, as a steady smile and a phone call into the small hours when Cara came out. Cara's wasn't the face of a best friend; it was the face of a sister. It was home.

Cara's family were Pip's second. Elliot – or Mr Ward as she had to call him at school – was her history teacher as well as tertiary father figure, behind Victor and the ghost of her first dad. Pip was at the Ward house so often she had her own named mug and pair of slippers to match Cara's and her big sister Naomi's.

'Right.' Cara lunged for the TV remote. 'Rom-coms or films where boys get violently murdered?'

It took roughly one and a half soppy films from the Netflix backlog for Lauren to wade through denial and extend a cautionary toe towards the acceptance stage.

'I should get a haircut,' she said. 'That's what

24

you're supposed to do.'

'I've always said you'd look good with short hair,' said Cara.

'And do you think I should get my nose pierced?'

'Ooh, yeah.' Cara nodded.

'I don't see the logic in putting a nose-hole in your nose-hole,' said Pip.

'Another fabulous Pip quotation for the books.' Cara feigned writing it down in mid-air. 'What was the one that cracked me up the other day?'

'The sausage one,' Pip sighed.

'Oh yeah,' Cara snorted. 'So, Loz, I was asking Pip which pyjamas she wanted to wear and she just casually says: "It's sausage to me." And then didn't realise why that might be a strange answer to my question.'

'It's not that strange,' said Pip. 'My grandparents from my first dad are German. "It's sausage to me" is an everyday German saying. It just means I *don't care*.'

'Or you've got a sausage fixation,' Lauren laughed.

'Says the daughter of a porn star,' Pip quipped.

'Oh my god, how many times? He only did one nude photoshoot in the eighties, that's it.'

'So, on to boys from this decade,' Cara said, prodding Pip on the shoulder. 'Did you go and see Ravi Singh yet?'

'Questionable segue. And yes, but I'm going back to interview him tomorrow.'

'I can't believe you've already started your EPQ,'

Lauren said with a mock dying-swan dive back on to the bed. 'I want to change my title already; famines are too depressing.'

'I imagine you'll be wanting to interview Naomi sometime soon.' Cara looked pointedly at Pip.

'Certainly, can you please warn her I may be coming around next week with my voice recorder app and a pencil?'

'Yeah,' Cara said, then hesitated. 'She'll agree to it and everything but can you go easy on her? She still gets really upset about it sometimes. I mean, he was one of her best friends. In fact, probably her *best* friend.'

'Yeah, of course,' Pip smiled, 'what do you think I'm going to do? Pin her down and beat responses out of her?'

'Is that your tactic for Ravi tomorrow?'

'I think not.'

Lauren sat up then, with a snot-sucking sniff so loud it made Cara visibly flinch.

'Are you going to his house then?' she asked.

'Yeah.'

'Oh, but . . . what are people going to think if they see you going into Ravi Singh's house?'

'It's sausage to me.'

Production Log – Entry 3

I'm biased. Of course I am. Every time I reread the details from the last two logs, I can't help but hosting imaginary courtroom dramas in my head: I'm a swaggering defence attorney jumping up to object, I shuffle my notes and wink at Sal when the prosecution falls into my trap, I run up and slap the judge's bench yelling, 'Your honour, he didn't do it!'

Because, for reasons I don't even quite know how to explain to myself, I want Sal Singh to be innocent. Reasons carried with me since I was twelve years old, inconsistencies that have nagged at me these past five years.

But I do have to be aware of confirmation bias. So I thought it would be a good idea to interview someone who is utterly convinced of Sal's guilt. Stanley Forbes, a journalist at the *Kilton Mail*, just responded to my email saying I could ring any time today. He covered a lot of the Andie Bell case in the local press and was even present at the coroner's inquest. To be honest, I think he's a crappy journalist and I'm pretty sure the Singhs could sue him for defamation and libel about a dozen times over. I'll type the transcript up here straight after.

Oooooh booooooyyyyyyy . . .

Transcript of interview with Stanley Forbes from the Kilton Mail newspaper

Stanley: Yep.

Pip: Hi, Stanley, this is Pippa, we were emailing earlier.

Stanley: Yep, yeah, I know. You wanted to pick my brains about the Andie Bell/Salil Singh case, right?

Pip: Yes that's right.

Stanley: Well, shoot.

Pip: OK, thanks. Erm, so firstly, you attended Andie's coroner inquest, didn't you?

Stanley: Sure did, kid.

Pip: As the national press didn't elaborate much further than reporting the verdict and the CPS's later statement, I was wondering if you could tell me what kind of evidence was presented to the coroner by the police?

Stanley: A whole bunch of stuff.

Pip: Right, could you tell me some of the specific points they made?

Stanley: Err, so the main investigator on Andie's case outlined the details of her disappearance, the times and so on. And then he moved on to the evidence that linked Salil to her murder. They made a big deal about the blood in the boot of her car; they said this suggested that she was murdered somewhere and her body was put in the boot to be transported to wherever she was disposed of. In the closing remarks the coroner said something like 'it seems clear that Andie was the victim of a sexually motivated murder and considerable efforts were made to dispose of her body.'

Pip: And did DI Richard Hawkins or any other officer provide a timeline of what they believed were the events of that night and how Sal allegedly killed her?

Stanley: Yeah, I do kinda remember that. Andie left home in her car and at some point on Salil's walk home, he intercepted her. With either him or her driving, he took her to a secluded place and murdered her. He hid her body in the boot and then drove somewhere to hide or dispose of her body. Mind you, well enough so that it hasn't been found in five years, must have been a pretty big hole. And then he ditched the car on that road where it was found, Romer Close I think it was, and he walked home.

Pip: So, because of the blood in the boot, the police believed that Andie was killed somewhere and then hidden in a different location?

Stanley: Yep.

Pip: OK. In a lot of your articles about the case, you refer to Sal as a 'killer', a 'murderer' and even a 'monster.' You are aware that without a conviction, you are supposed to use the word 'allegedly' when reporting crime stories.

Stanley: Not sure I need a child to tell me how to do my job. Anyway, it's obvious that he did it and everyone knows it. He killed her and the guilt drove him to suicide.

Pip: OK. So for what reasons are you convinced of Sal's guilt?

Stanley: Almost too many to list. Evidence aside, he was the boyfriend, right? And it's always the boyfriend or the ex-boyfriend. Not only that, Salil was Indian.

Pip: Um . . . Sal was actually born and raised in Britain, though it is notable that you refer to him as Indian in all of your articles.

Stanley: Well, same thing. He was of Indian heritage.

Pip: And why is that relevant?

Stanley: I'm not like an expert or anything, but they have different ways of life to us, don't they? They don't treat women quite like we do, their women are like their possessions. So I'm guessing maybe Andie decided she didn't want to be with him or something and he killed her in a rage because, in his eyes, she belonged to him.

Pip: Wow . . . I . . . Err . . . you . . . Honestly, Stanley, I'm pretty

	surprised you haven't been sued for defamation.
Stanley:	That's 'cause everyone knows what I'm saying is true.
Pip:	Actually, I don't. I think it's very irresponsible to label someone a murderer without using 'suspected' or 'allegedly' when there's been no trial or conviction. Or calling Sal a monster. Speaking of word use, it's interesting to compare your recent reporting of the Slough Strangler. He murdered five people and pleaded guilty in court, yet in your headline you referred to him as a 'lovesick young man'. Is that because *he's* white?
Stanley:	That's got nothing to do with Salil's case. I just call it how it is. You need to chill out. He's dead, why does it matter if people call him a murderer? It can't hurt him.
Pip:	Because his family aren't dead.
Stanley:	It's starting to sound like you actually think he's innocent. Against all the expertise of senior police officers.
Pip:	I just think there are certain gaps and inconsistencies in the supposed case against Sal.
Stanley:	Yeah, maybe if the kid hadn't offed himself before getting arrested, we would have been able to fill the gaps.
Pip:	Well, that was insensitive.
Stanley:	Well it was insensitive of him to kill his pretty blonde girlfriend and hide her remains.
Pip:	Allegedly!
Stanley:	You want more proof that that kid was a killer, fangirl? We weren't allowed to print it, but my source in the police said they found a death threat note in Andie's school locker. He threatened her and then he did it. Do you really still think he can be innocent?
Pip:	Yes I do. And I think you're a racist, intolerant, dickhead, mindless bottom-feeder –

(Stanley hangs up the phone)

Yeah, so, I don't think Stanley and I are going to be best friends.

However, his interview has given me two bits of information I didn't have before. The first is that police believe Andie was killed somewhere before being put in the boot of her car and driven to a second location to be disposed of.

The second bit of intel lovely Stanley gave me is this 'death threat'. I've not seen it mentioned in any articles or in any of the police statements. There must be a reason: maybe the police didn't think it was relevant. Or maybe they couldn't prove it was linked to Sal. Or maybe Stanley made it up. In any case, it's worth remembering when I interview Andie's friends later on.

So now that I (sort of) know what the police's version of events were for that night, and what the prosecution's case might have looked like, it's time for a *MURDER MAP*.

After dinner because Mum's going to call up in about three. . . two . . . yep . . .

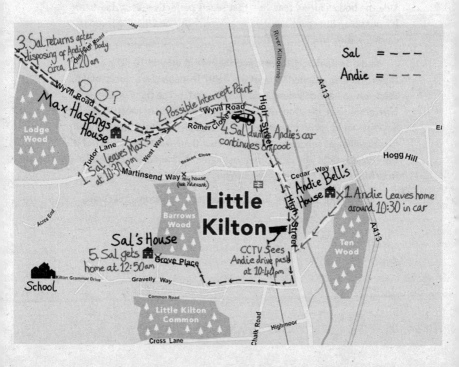

So professional-looking. But it does help to visualize the police's version of events. I had to make a couple of assumptions when creating it. The first is that there are several ways to walk from Max's to Sal's; I picked the one that heads back through the high street because Google said it was the quickest and I'm presuming most people prefer to walk on well-lit streets at night.

It also provides a good intercept point somewhere along Wyvil Road where Andie potentially pulled over and Sal got in the car. Thinking like a detective, there are actually some quiet residential roads and a farm on Wyvil Road. These quiet, secluded places – circled – could potentially be the site of the murder (according to the police's narrative).

I didn't bother guessing where Andie's body was disposed of because, like the rest of the world, I have no clue at all where that is. But given that it takes about eighteen minutes to walk from where the car was dumped on Romer Close back to Sal's house in Grove Place, I have to presume he'd have been back in the vicinity of Wyvil Road around 12:20 a.m. So if the Andie and Sal intercept happened at around 10:45 p.m., this would have given Sal one hour and thirty-five minutes to murder her and hide the body. I mean, timewise, that seems perfectly reasonable to me. It's possible. But there are already a dozen 'why' and 'how' questions elbowing their way in.

Andie and Sal both leave where they are at around 10:30 p.m., so they must have planned to meet up, right? It seems too coincidental for them not to have communicated and planned it. The thing is, the police have never once mentioned a phone call or any texts between Andie and Sal that would account as a meet-up arrangement. And if they planned this together, at school for example, where there would be no record of the conversation, why didn't they just agree that Andie would pick Sal up from Max's house? It seems weird to me.

I'm rambling. It's 2 a.m. and I just ate half a Toblerone, that's why.

Four

There was a song in her. A sickly beat troubling the skin on her wrists and neck, a crackling chord as she cleared her throat and the jagged trill of her breath. Next, the terrible realization that once she noticed her breathing she couldn't, for the life of her, un-notice it.

She stood before the front door and willed it open. Every second grew syrupy and thick as the door stared her down, the minutes unrolling themselves into forever. How long had it been since she'd knocked? When Pip could stand it no longer, she picked the sweating Tupperware of fresh muffins out from under her arm and turned to walk away. The ghost house was closed to visitors today and the disappointment burned.

Only a few steps away, she heard the sound of scraping and clicking and turned back to see Ravi Singh in the doorway, his hair ruffled and his face drawing tight in confusion.

'Oh,' Pip said in a high-pitched voice that wasn't her own. 'Sorry, I thought you told me to come back Friday. Today's Friday.'

'Um, yeah, I did,' Ravi said, scratching his head with his eyes somewhere around Pip's ankles. 'But . . . honestly, though . . . I thought you were just taking the piss. A prank. I wasn't expecting you to actually come back.'

'That's, um, unfortunate.' Pip tried her best to not look

hurt. 'No prank, I promise. I'm serious.'

'Yeah, you seem like the serious type.' The back of his head must have been exceptionally itchy. Or maybe Ravi Singh's itchy head was the equivalent of Pip's useless facts: armour and shield when the knight inside was squirming.

'I'm irrationally serious,' Pip smiled, holding the Tupperware box out to him. 'And I made muffins.'

'Like bribery muffins?'

'That's what the recipe said, yeah.'

Ravi's mouth twitched, not quite a smile. Pip only then appreciated how hard his life must be in this town, the spectre of his dead brother reflected in his own face. It was no wonder smiling was hard for him.

'So I can come in?' Pip said, tucking up her bottom lip and over-stretching her eyes in her best pleading expression, the one her dad said made her look constipated.

'Yes, fine,' he said after an almost devastating pause. 'Only if you stop making that face.' He stepped back to let her in the house.

'Thank you, thank you, thank you,' Pip said quickly and tripped over the front step in her eagerness.

Raising an eyebrow, Ravi shut the door and asked if she'd like a cup of tea.

'Yes please.' Pip stood awkwardly in the hallway, trying to take up as little space as possible. 'Black please.'

'I've never trusted someone who takes their tea black.' He gestured for her to follow him through into the kitchen.

The room was wide and exceptionally bright; the outside wall was one giant panel of sliding glass doors that opened into a long garden exploding with the blush of summer and fairy-tale winding vines.

'How do you take it then?' Pip asked, resting her rucksack down on one of the dining chairs.

'Milk till it's white and three sugars,' he said over the sputtering-inferno sounds of the kettle.

'Three sugars? *Three?*'

'I know, I know. Clearly I'm not sweet enough already.'

Pip watched Ravi clatter around the kitchen, the boiling kettle excusing the silence between them. He dug through an almost empty jar of teabags, tapping his fingers on the side as he went about pouring and sugaring and milking. The nervous energy was contagious, and Pip's heart quickened to match his tapping fingers.

He brought the two mugs over, holding Pip's by the scorching base so she could take it by the handle. Her mug was adorned with a cartoon smile and the caption: *When's the best time to visit the dentist? Tooth hurty.*

'Your parents aren't in?' she asked, setting the mug down on the table.

'Nope.' He took a sip and Pip noted, thankfully, that he wasn't a slurper. 'And if they were, you wouldn't be. We try not to talk about Sal too much; it upsets Mum. It upsets everyone actually.'

'I can't even imagine,' Pip said quietly. It didn't matter that

five years had passed; this was still raw for Ravi – it was written all over his face.

'It's not just that he's gone. It's that . . . well, we're not allowed to grieve for him, because of what happened. And if I were to say "I miss my brother", it makes me some kind of monster.'

'I don't think it does.'

'Me neither, but I'm guessing you and I are in the minority there.'

Pip took a sip of her tea to fill the silence but it was far too hot and her eyes prickled and filled.

'Crying already? We haven't even got to the sad parts.' Ravi's right eyebrow peaked up on his forehead.

'Tea hot,' Pip gasped, her tongue feeling fluffy and scorched.

'Let it cool down for *a jiffy*, or, you know, *one one-hundredth of a second*.'

'Hey, you remembered.'

'How could I possibly forget that introduction of yours? So what questions did you want to ask me?'

Pip looked down at the phone in her lap and said, 'Firstly, do you mind if I record us, so I can type it up accurately later?'

'Sounds like a fun Friday night.'

'I'll take that as you don't mind.' Pip opened the zip on her metallic brass-coloured rucksack and pulled out her bundle of notes.

'What are those?' He pointed.

'Pre-prepared questions.' She shuffled the papers

to straighten the stack.

'Oh, wow, you're really into this, aren't you?' He looked at her with an expression that quivered somewhere between quizzical and sceptical.

'Yep.'

'Should I be nervous?'

'Not yet,' said Pip, fixing him with one last look before pressing the red record button.

Production Log – Entry 4

Transcript of interview with Ravi Singh

Pip: So, how old are you?

Ravi: Why?

Pip: Just trying to get all the facts straight.

Ravi: OK, Sergeant, I just turned twenty.

Pip: (Laughs) [Side note: OH MY GOD, MY LAUGH IS ATROCIOUS ON AUDIO. I'M NEVER LAUGHING AGAIN!] And Sal was three years older than you?

Ravi: Yes.

Pip: Do you remember your brother acting strangely on Friday the twentieth of April 2012?

Ravi: Wow, straight in there. Um, no, not at all. We had an early dinner at, like, seven before my dad dropped him at Max's, and he was just chatting along, like normal Sal. If he was secretly planning a murder, it wasn't at all obvious to us. He was . . . chirpy, I'd say was a good description.

Pip: And what about when he returned from Max's?

Ravi: I had already gone up to bed. But the next morning, I remember him being in a really good mood. Sal was always a morning person. He got up and made breakfast for us all and it wasn't until just after that he got a phone call from one of Andie's friends. That's when we all found out she was missing. From that point, obviously, he wasn't chirpy any more, he was worried.

Pip: So neither Andie's parents nor the police rang him during Friday night?

Ravi: Not that I know of. Andie's parents didn't really know Sal. He'd never met them or been to their house. Andie usually

	came around here or they hung out at school and parties.
Pip:	How long had they been together?
Ravi:	Since just before Christmas the year before, so about four months. Sal did have a couple of missed calls from one of Andie's best friends at, like, 2 a.m. that night. His phone was on silent, though, so he slept through them.
Pip:	So what else happened on that Saturday?
Ravi:	Well, after finding out Andie was missing, Sal literally sat on the phone, calling her every few minutes. It went to voicemail each time, but he figured if she'd pick up for anyone, it'd be him.
Pip:	Wait, so Sal was calling Andie's phone?
Ravi:	Yeah, like a million times, throughout that weekend and on the Monday too.
Pip:	Doesn't sound like the kind of thing you'd do if you knew you had murdered the person and they would never pick up.
Ravi:	Especially if he had her phone hidden somewhere on him, or in his room.
Pip:	An even better point. So what else happened that day?
Ravi:	My parents told him not to go to Andie's house, because the police would be busy searching it. So he just sat at home, trying to call her. I asked him if he had any idea where she'd be, and he was stumped. He said something else I always remembered. He said that everything Andie did was deliberate, and maybe she'd run off on purpose to punish someone. Obviously by the end of the weekend he realized that probably wasn't the case.
Pip:	Who would Andie be wanting to punish? Him?
Ravi:	I don't know, I didn't push it. I didn't know her well; she only came around a handful of times. I mean, I presumed the 'someone' Sal was talking about was Andie's dad.
Pip:	Jason Bell? Why?

Ravi: I just overheard some stuff when she was here. I figured
           she didn't have the best relationship with her dad. I can't
           remember anything specifically.

[Phew, he says 'specifically' not 'pacifically'.]

Pip: Specifics are what we need. So when did the police contact
           Sal?

Ravi: It was that Saturday afternoon. They called him and asked if
           they could come over for a chat. They arrived at, like, three
           or four-ish. Me and my parents came into the kitchen to give
           them a bit of space, so we didn't hear any of it really.

Pip: And did Sal tell you what they asked him?

Ravi: A bit. He was a little freaked out that they recorded it and st–

Pip: The police recorded it? Is that normal?

Ravi: I don't know, you're the sergeant. They said it was routine and
           just asked him questions about where he was that night, who
           he was with. And about his and Andie's relationship.

Pip: And what was their relationship like?

Ravi: I'm his brother; I didn't see all that much of it. But, yeah,
           Sal liked her a lot. I mean, he seemed pretty chuffed he was
           with the prettiest, most popular girl in the year. Andie always
           seemed to bring drama, though.

Pip: What kind of drama?

Ravi: I don't know, I think she was just one of those people who
           thrives on it.

Pip: Did your parents like her?

Ravi: Yeah, my parents were cool with her. She never gave them a
           reason not to be.

Pip: And so what else happened after the police interviewed him?

Ravi: Err, his friends came around in the evening, you know to check
           if he was OK.

Pip: And is that when he asked his friends to lie to the police and

	give him an alibi?
Ravi:	I guess so.
Pip:	Why do you think he did that?
Ravi:	I mean, I don't know. Maybe he was rattled after the police interview. Maybe he was scared he would be a suspect so he tried to cover himself. I don't know.
Pip:	Presuming Sal's innocence, do you have any idea where he could have been between leaving Max's at 10:30 and getting home at 12:50?
Ravi:	No, because he also told us that he started walking home from Max's at like 12:15. I guess maybe he was alone somewhere so he knew that if he told the truth he'd have no alibi. It looks bad, doesn't it?
Pip:	I mean, lying to the police and asking his friends to as well does look bad for Sal. But it's not absolute proof that he had anything to do with Andie's death. So what happened on the Sunday then?
Ravi:	On the Sunday afternoon, me, Sal and his friends volunteered to help put up some missing posters, handing them out to people in town. On the Monday, I didn't see much of him at school, but it must have been pretty hard for him because all anyone was talking about was Andie's disappearance.
Pip:	I remember.
Ravi:	Police were about too; I saw them looking through Andie's locker. Yeah, so that night he was a little down. He was quiet, but he was worried, that's what you'd expect. His girlfriend was missing. And the next day –
Pip:	You don't have to talk about the next day if you don't want to.
Ravi:	(Small pause) It's OK. We walked into school together and I went off to registration, leaving Sal behind in the car park. He wanted to sit outside for a minute. That was the last time I ever saw him. And all I said was 'see you later'. I . . . I knew police were at the school; rumour was that they were talking

to Sal's friends. And it wasn't until like two-ish that I saw my mum had been trying to ring me, so I went home and my parents told me that the police really needed to speak to Sal and had I seen him. I think officers had been searching his bedroom. I tried calling Sal too, but it just rang out. My dad showed me this text he got, the last time they'd heard from Sal.

Pip: Do you remember what it said?

Ravi: Yeah, it said: *it was me. I did it. I'm so sorry.* And . . . (small pause) it was later that evening when the police came back. My parents went to answer the door and I stayed in here listening. When they said they'd found a body in the woods, I was so sure for a second that it was Andie they were talking about.

Pip: And . . . I don't want to be insensitive, but the sleeping pills . . .

Ravi: Yeah, they were Dad's. He was taking phenobarbitals for his insomnia. He blamed himself afterwards. Doesn't take anything any more. He just doesn't sleep much.

Pip: And had you ever before thought that Sal could be suicidal?

Ravi: Never, not once. Sal was literally the happiest person there was. He was always laughing and messing around. It's cheesy but he was the kind of person that lit up a room when he walked into it. He was the best at everything he ever did. He was my parents' golden child, their straight-A student. Now they're left with just me.

Pip: And, sorry, but the biggest question then: do you think Sal killed Andie?

Ravi: I . . . No, no I don't. I can't think that. It just doesn't make sense to me. Sal was one of the nicest people on the planet, you know. He never lost his temper ever, no matter how much I wound him up. He was never one of those boys that got in fights. He was the greatest big brother anyone could have and he always came to my rescue when I needed it. He was the best person I ever knew. So, I have to say no. But then, I don't

	know, the police seem so sure and the evidence . . . yeah, I know it looks bad for Sal. But I still can't believe he had it in him to do that.
Pip:	I understand. I think those are all the questions I need to ask for now.
Ravi:	(Sits back and lets out a long sigh) So, Pippa —
Pip:	You can call me Pip.
Ravi:	Pip then. You said this is for a school project?
Pip:	It is.
Ravi:	But why? Why did you choose this? OK, maybe you don't believe Sal did it, but why would you want to prove it? What's it to you? No one else in this town has trouble believing my brother was a monster. They've all moved on.
Pip:	My best friend, Cara, she's Naomi Ward's sister.
Ravi:	Oh, Naomi, she was always nice to me. Always over at our house, following Sal around like a puppy. She was one hundred per cent in love with him.
Pip:	Oh, really?
Ravi:	I always thought so. The way she laughed at everything he said, even the unfunny stuff. Don't think he felt the same way back, though.
Pip:	Hm.
Ravi:	So you're doing this for Naomi? I still don't get it.
Pip:	No, it's not that. What I meant was . . . I knew Sal.
Ravi:	You did?
Pip:	Yeah. He was often over at the Wards' house when I was too. One time, he let us watch a fifteen film with them, even though Cara and I were only twelve. It was a comedy and I can still remember how much I laughed. Laughed until it hurt, even when I didn't quite get it, because Sal's laugh was so contagious.

Ravi:	High and giggly?
Pip:	Yeah. And when I was ten, he accidentally taught me my first swear word. *Shit*, by the way. And another time, he taught me how to flip pancakes because I was useless at it but too stubborn to let someone do it for me.
Ravi:	He was a good teacher.
Pip:	And when I was in my first year at school, these two boys were picking on me because my dad is Nigerian. And Sal saw. He came over and just said, very calmly, 'When you two get expelled for bullying, the next grammar school is half an hour away, if you even get in. Starting from scratch at a completely new school, think about it.' They never picked on me again. And afterwards Sal sat with me and gave me his KitKat to cheer me up. Since then, I've . . . well, never mind.
Ravi:	Hey, come on, share. I let you have your interview – even though your bribery muffins taste like cheese.
Pip:	Since then, he's always been a hero to me. I just can't believe he did it.

Production Log – Entry 5

I've just spent two hours researching this: I think I can send a request to the Thames Valley Police for a copy of Sal's police interview under the Freedom of Information Act.

There are certain exemptions to disclosing information under the FOIA, like if the requested material relates to an ongoing investigation, or if it would infringe on Data Protection laws by divulging personal information about living people. But Sal is dead, so surely they'd have no reason to withhold his interview? I may as well see if I can access other police records from the Andie Bell investigation too.

On another note: I can't get these things Ravi said about Jason Bell out of my head. That Sal first thought Andie had run away to punish someone and that her relationship with her father was strained.

Jason and Dawn Bell got divorced not long after Andie's death certificate was issued (this is common Little Kilton knowledge but I corroborated it with a quick Facebook investigation). Jason moved away and is now living in a town about fifteen minutes from here. It wasn't long after their divorce that he starts appearing in pictures with a pretty blonde lady who looks a little too young for him. It appears they are married now.

I've been on YouTube watching hours and hours of footage from the early press conferences after Andie went missing. I can't believe I never noticed it before, but there's something a bit off about Jason. The way he squeezes his wife's arm just a little too hard when she starts crying about Andie, the way he shifts his shoulder in front of her so he can push her back from the microphone when he decides she's said enough. The voice breaks that sound a little forced when he says: 'Andie, we love you so much' and 'Please come home, you won't be in trouble.' The way Becca, Andie's sister, shrinks under his gaze. I know this isn't very *objective detective* of me, but there's something in his eyes – a coldness – that concerns me.

And then I noticed THE BIG THING. On the Monday 23rd April evening press conference, Jason Bell says this: 'We just want our girl back.

We are completely broken and don't know what to do with ourselves. If you know where she is, please tell her to call home so we know she's safe. Andie *was* such a huge presence in our home, it's too quiet without her.'

Yeah. He said 'was'. *WAS*. PAST TENSE. This was before any of the Sal stuff had happened. Everyone thought Andie was still alive at this point. But Jason Bell said WAS.

Was this just an innocent mistake, or was he using the past tense because he already knew his daughter was dead? Did Jason Bell slip up?

From what I can tell, Jason and Dawn were at a dinner party that night and Andie was supposed to pick them up. Could he have left the party at some point? And if not, even if he has a solid alibi, that doesn't mean he can't somehow be involved in Andie's disappearance.

If I'm creating a persons of interest list, I think Jason Bell is going to have to be the first entry.

Persons of Interest

Jason Bell

Five

Something felt a little off, like the air in the room was stale and slowly thickening and thickening until she was breathing it down in giant gelatinous clots. In all her years of knowing Naomi, it had never felt quite like this.

Pip gave Naomi a reassuring smile and made a passing joke about the amount of Barney dog-fluff attached to her leggings. Naomi smiled weakly, running her hands through her flicky ombré blonde hair.

They were sitting in Elliot Ward's study, Pip on the swivelling desk chair and Naomi across from her in the oxblood-leather armchair. Naomi wasn't looking at Pip; she was staring instead at the three paintings on the far wall. Three giant canvases of the family, immortalized forever in rainbow tinted strokes. Her parents walking in the autumn woods, Elliot drinking from a steaming mug, and a young Naomi and Cara on a swing. Their mum had painted them when she was dying, her final mark upon the world. Pip knew how important these paintings were to the Wards, how they looked to them in their happiest and saddest times. Although she remembered there used to be a couple more displayed in here too; maybe Elliot was keeping them in storage to give the girls when they grew up and moved out.

Pip knew Naomi had been going to therapy since her mum

died seven years ago. And that she had managed to wade through her anxiety, neck just above the water, to graduate from university. But a few months ago she had a panic attack at her new job in London and quit to move back in with her dad and sister.

Naomi was fragile and Pip was trying her hardest not to tread on any cracks. In the corner of her eye she could see the ever-scrolling timer on her voice recorder app.

'So, can you tell me what you were all doing at Max's that night?' she said gently.

Naomi shifted, eyes moving down to circle her knees.

'Um, we were just, like, drinking, talking, playing some Xbox, nothing too exciting.'

'And taking pictures? There's a few on Facebook from that night.'

'Yeah, taking silly pictures. Just messing around really,' Naomi said.

'There aren't any pictures of Sal from that night, though.'

'No, well, I guess he left before we started taking them.'

'And was Sal acting strangely before he left?' said Pip.

'Um, I . . . no, I don't think he was really.'

'Did he talk about Andie at all?'

'I, err . . . yeah, maybe a bit.' Naomi shuffled in her seat and the leather made a loud, rumbling sound as she unstuck herself from it. Something Pip's little brother would have found very funny and, under other circumstances, she might have too.

'What did he say about her?' Pip asked.

'Um.' Naomi paused for a moment, picking at a ripped cuticle by her thumb. 'He, erm . . . I think maybe they were having a disagreement. Sal said he wasn't going to talk to her for a bit.'

'Why?'

'I don't remember specifically. But Andie was . . . she was a bit of a nightmare. She was always trying to pick fights with Sal over the smallest things. Sal preferred to give her the silent treatment rather than argue.'

'What kind of things were these fights about?'

'Like the stupidest things. Like him not texting her back quick enough. Things like that. I . . . I never said it to him, but I always thought Andie was trouble. If I had said something, I don't know, maybe everything would have turned out differently.'

Looking at Naomi's downcast face, at the telling tremble of her upper lip, Pip knew she needed to bring them up from this particular rabbit hole, before Naomi closed up entirely.

'Had Sal said at any point in the evening that he would be leaving early?'

'No, he didn't.'

'And what time did he leave Max's?'

'We're pretty sure it was close to ten thirty.'

'And did he say anything before he left?'

Naomi shuffled and closed her eyes for a moment, the lids pressed so tightly that Pip could see them vibrating, even from

49

across the room. 'Yeah,' she said. 'He just said that he wasn't really feeling it and was going to walk home and get an early night.'

'And what time did you leave Max's?'

'I didn't, I . . . me and Millie stayed over in the spare room. Dad came and got me in the morning.'

'What time did you go up to bed?'

'Um, I think it was a bit before half twelve. Not sure really.'

There was a sudden triad of knocks on the study door and Cara poked her head in, squeaking when her messy topknot got caught on the frame.

'Bugger off, I'm recording,' Pip said.

'Sorry, emergency, two secs,' Cara said, lingering as a floating head. 'Nai, where the hell have all those Jammie Dodger biscuits gone?'

'I don't know.'

'I literally saw Dad unpack a full packet yesterday. Where have they gone?'

'I don't know, ask him.'

'He's not back yet.'

'Cara,' Pip said, raising her eyebrows.

'Yep, sorry, buggering off,' she said, unhooking her hair and closing the door behind her again.

'Um, OK,' Pip said, trying to recover their lost tangent. 'So when did you first hear that Andie was missing?'

'I think Sal texted me Saturday, maybe late morning-ish.'

'And what were your initial thoughts about where

50

she might be?'

'I don't know.' Naomi shrugged; Pip wasn't sure she'd ever seen her shrug before. 'Andie was the kind of girl who knew lots of people. I guess I thought she was hanging with some other friends we didn't know, not wanting to be found.'

Pip took a preparatory deep breath, glancing at her notes; she needed to handle the next question carefully. 'Can you tell me about when Sal asked you to lie to the police about what time he left Max's?'

Naomi tried to speak, but she couldn't seem to find the words. A strange, underwater silence mushroomed in the small space. Pip's ears rang with the weight of it.

'Um,' Naomi said finally, her voice breaking a little. 'We went around on Saturday evening to see how he was doing. And we were talking about what happened and Sal said he was nervous because the police had already been asking him questions. And because he was her boyfriend, he thought he was going to be a target. So he just said did we mind saying he left Max's a little later than he did, like quarter past twelve-ish, so the police would stop looking at him and actually concentrate on finding Andie. It wasn't, um, it didn't seem wrong to me at the time. I just thought he was trying to be sensible and help get Andie back quicker.'

'And did he tell you where he was between ten thirty and twelve fifty?'

'Um. I can't remember. No, maybe he didn't.'

'Didn't you ask? Didn't you want to know?'

51

'I can't really remember, Pip. Sorry,' she sniffed.

'That's OK.' Pip realized she'd leaned right forward with her last question; she shuffled her notes and sat back again. 'So the police called you on the Sunday, didn't they? And you told them that Sal left Max's at twelve fifteen?'

'Yeah.'

'So why did you four change your mind and decide to tell the police on Tuesday about Sal's false alibi?'

'I . . . I think it's because we'd had some time to think about it, and we knew we could get in trouble for lying. None of us thought Sal was involved in what happened to Andie, so we didn't see the problem in telling police the truth.'

'Had you discussed with the other three that that's what you were going to do?'

'Yeah, we called each other that Monday night and agreed.'

'But you didn't tell Sal that you were going to talk to the police?'

'Um,' she said, her hands racing through her hair again. 'No, we didn't want him to be upset with us.'

'OK, last question.' Pip watched as Naomi's face ironed out with evident relief. 'Do you think Sal killed Andie that night?'

'Not the Sal I knew,' she said. 'He was the best, the nicest person. Always cheeky and making people laugh. And he was so nice to Andie too, even though she maybe didn't deserve it. So I don't know what happened or if he did it, but I don't want to believe he did.'

'OK, done,' Pip smiled, pressing the stop button on her phone. 'Thanks so much for doing that, Naomi. I know it's not easy.'

'That's OK.' She nodded and stood up from the chair, the leather squeaking against her legs.

'Wait, one more thing,' Pip said. 'Are Max, Jake and Millie around to be interviewed?'

'Oh, Millie's off the grid travelling around Australia and Jake's living with his girlfriend down in Devon – they just had a baby. Max is in Kilton, though; he just finished his master's and is back applying for jobs, like me.'

'Do you think he'd mind giving me a short interview?' Pip said.

'I'll give you his number and you can ask him.' Naomi held the study door open for her.

In the kitchen they found Cara trying to fit two pieces of toast in her mouth simultaneously and a just-returned Elliot in an eyesore pastel yellow shirt, wiping down the kitchen surfaces. He turned when he heard them come in, the ceiling lights picking up small wisps of grey in his brown hair and flashing across his thick-rimmed glasses.

'You done, girls?' He smiled kindly. 'Excellent timing, I've just popped the kettle on.'

Pippa Fitz-Amobi
EPQ   12/08/2017

Production Log – Entry 7

Just got back from Max Hastings' house. It felt strange being there, like walking through some kind of crime-scene reconstruction; it looks just the same as it does in those Facebook photos Naomi and co. took of that fateful night five years ago. The night that forever changed this town. Max still looks the same too: tall, blonde floppy hair, mouth slightly too wide for his angular face, somewhat pretentious. He said he remembered me, though, which was nice.

After speaking to him . . . I don't know, I can't help but think something's going on here. Either one of Sal's friends is misremembering about that night, or one of them is lying. But why?

Transcript of interview with Max Hastings

Pip: All right, recording. So, Max you're twenty-three, right?

Max: Wrong actually. I'm twenty-five in about a month.

Pip: Oh.

Max: Yeah, when I was seven I had leukaemia and missed lots of school, so I got held back a year. I know, I'm a miracle boy.

Pip: I had no idea.

Max: You can have my autograph later.

Pip: OK, so, jumping straight in, can you describe what Sal and Andie's relationship was like?

Max: It was fine. It wasn't like the romance of the century or anything. But they both thought the other was good-looking, so I guess it worked.

Pip: There wasn't more depth to it?

Max: Don't know, I never really paid attention to high-school romances.

Pip: So how did their relationship start?

Max: They just got drunk and hooked up at a party at Christmas. It carried on from there.

Pip: Was that a – what are they called – oh, a calamity party?

Max: Holy shit, I forgot we used to call our house parties 'calamities'. You know about those?

Pip: Yeah. People at school still throw them, tradition apparently. Legend is that you were their originator.

Max: What, kids are still throwing messy house parties and calling them calamities? That's so cool. I feel like a god. Do they still do the next host triathlon bit?

Pip: I've never been. Anyway, did you know Andie before she started a relationship with Sal?

Max: Yeah, a bit, from school and calamities. We sometimes spoke, yeah. But we weren't ever, like, friend friends, I didn't really know her. Like an acquaintance.

Pip: OK, so on Friday the twentieth of April, when everyone was at your house, do you remember if Sal was acting strangely?

Max: Not really. Maybe a little quiet, if anything.

Pip: Did you wonder why at the time?

Max: Nope, I was pretty drunk.

Pip: And that night, did Sal talk about Andie at all?

Max: No, he didn't mention her once.

Pip: He didn't say they were having a disagreement at the time or –

Max: No he just didn't bring her up.

Pip: How well do you remember that night?

Max: I remember all of it. Spent most of it playing Jake and Millie on *Call of Duty*. I remember 'cause Millie was going on about equality and stuff, and then she didn't win once.

Pip: This was after Sal left?

Max:	Yeah, he left really early.
Pip:	Where was Naomi when you were playing video games?
Max:	M.I.A.
Pip:	Missing? She wasn't there?
Max:	Um, no . . . err . . . she went upstairs for a while.
Pip:	By herself? Doing what?
Max:	I don't know. Taking a nap. Taking a dump. Fuck knows.
Pip:	For how long?
Max:	I don't remember.
Pip:	OK, and when Sal left what did he say?
Max:	He didn't really. He just slipped out quietly. I didn't really notice him going at the time.
Pip:	So the next evening, after you'd all learned that Andie was missing, you went round to see Sal?
Max:	Yeah 'cause we figured he would be pretty bummed out.
Pip:	And how did he ask you all to lie and give him an alibi?
Max:	He just came out and said it. Said it was looking bad for him and asked if we could help out and just change the times a bit. It wasn't a biggie. He didn't phrase it like: give me an alibi. That's not how it was. It was just a favour for a friend.
Pip:	Do you think Sal killed Andie?
Max:	He had to have done it, didn't he? I mean, if you're asking if I thought my friend was capable of murder, the answer would be no way. He was like this sweet little agony aunt. But he did it because, you know, the blood and stuff. And the only way that Sal would ever kill himself, I think, is if he'd done something really bad. So, it all fits unfortunately.
Pip:	OK, thanks, those are all my questions.

There are some inconsistencies between their two versions of events.

Naomi said that Sal did talk about Andie and told all his friends they were having a disagreement. Max says he didn't mention her once. Naomi says Sal told everyone that he was heading home early because he wasn't 'feeling it'. Max says he slipped out quietly.

Of course, I am asking them to remember a night over five years ago. Certain lapses in memory are to be expected.

But then there's this thing Max said, that Naomi was M.I.A. Though he said he didn't remember how long Naomi was gone for, he had just before indicated that he spent 'most' of the night with Millie and Jake and for that particular activity Naomi wasn't there. Let's just say I can infer that she was 'upstairs' for at least an hour. But why? Why would she be upstairs alone at Max's house instead of with her friends? Unless Max just accidentally told me that Naomi left the house for a period of time that night and he's trying to cover for her.

I can't believe I'm actually going to type this, but I'm starting to suspect that Naomi could have had something to do with Andie. I've known her eleven years. I've lived almost my whole life looking up to her as a big sister, so I might learn how to be one too. Naomi's kind; the sort of person who'd give you an encouraging smile when you're mid-story and everyone else has stopped listening. She's mild-tempered, she's delicate, calm. But could she be unstable? Is it in her to be violent?

I don't know, I'm getting ahead of myself. But there's also what Ravi said, that he thought Naomi was in love with his brother. It's pretty clear from her answers too that she didn't particularly like Andie. And her interview, it was just so awkward, so tense. I know I was asking her to relive some bad memories but the same goes for Max and his was a breeze. Then again . . . was Max's interview too easy? Was he just a bit too aloof?

I don't know what to think but I can't help it, my imagination just threw off its leash and stuck its middle finger up at me. I'm now picturing a scene: Naomi kills Andie in a jealous rage. Sal stumbles across the scene, confounded and distraught. His best friend has killed his girlfriend.

But he still cares for Naomi so he helps her dispose of Andie's body and they agree to never speak of it. But he can't hide from the terrible guilt of what he helped conceal. The only escape he can think of is death.

Or maybe I'm making a something out of a nothing?

Most likely. Either way, I think she has to go on the list.

I need a break.

Persons of Interest

Jason Bell

Naomi Ward

Six

'OK, so now we just need frozen peas, tomatoes and thread,' Pip's mum said, holding the shopping list out at arm's length so she could decipher Victor's scribbles.

'That says bread,' said Pip.

'Oh yes, you're right,' Leanne giggled, 'that could have made for some interesting sandwiches this week.'

'Glasses?' Pip pulled a packaged loaf off the shelf and chucked it in the basket.

'Nope, I'm not admitting defeat yet. Glasses make me look old,' Leanne said, opening the freezer section.

'That's OK, you are old,' said Pip, for which she received a cold whack on the arm with a bag of frozen peas. As she dramatically feigned her demise to the fatal pea wound, she caught sight of him watching her. Dressed in a white T-shirt and jeans. Laughing quietly into the back of his hand.

'Ravi,' she said, crossing the aisle over to him. 'Hi.'

'Hi,' he smiled, scratching the back of his head, just as she thought he might.

'I've never seen you in here before.' *Here* was Little Kilton's only supermarket, pocket-sized and tucked in by the train station.

'Yeah, we usually shop out of town,' he said. 'But milk emergency.' He held up a vat-size bottle of semi-skimmed.

'Well, if only you had your tea black.'

'I'll never cross to the dark side,' he said, looking up as Pip's mum came over with her filled basket. He smiled at her.

'Oh, Mum, this is Ravi,' Pip said. 'Ravi, my mum, Leanne.'

'Nice to meet you,' Ravi said, hugging the milk to his chest and stretching out his right hand.

'You too,' Leanne said, shaking his offered palm. 'Actually, we've met before. I was the agent who sold your parents' house to them, gosh, must be fifteen years ago. I remember you were about five at the time and always wore a Pikachu onesie with a tutu.'

Ravi's cheeks glowed. Pip held in her nose-laugh until she saw that he was smiling.

'Can you believe that trend never caught on?' he chuckled.

'Yeah, well, Van Gogh's work was unappreciated in his own time as well,' Pip said as they all wandered over to the till.

'You go on ahead of us,' Leanne said, gesturing to Ravi, 'we'll take much longer.'

'Oh, really? Thanks.'

Ravi strode up to the till and gave the woman working there one of his perfect smiles. He placed the milk down and said, 'Just that, please.'

Pip watched the woman, and saw the creases crawl through her skin as her face folded with disgust. She scanned the milk, staring at Ravi with cold and noxious eyes. Fortunate, really, that looks couldn't actually kill. Ravi was looking down at his feet like he hadn't noticed but Pip knew he had.

Something hot and primal stirred in Pip's gut. Something that, in its infant stages, felt like nausea, but it kept swelling and boiling until it even reached her ears.

'One pound forty-eight,' the lady spat.

Ravi pulled out a five-pound note but when he tried to give her the money, she shuddered and withdrew her hand sharply. The note fell in an autumnal glide to the floor and Pip ignited.

'Hey,' she said loudly, marching over to stand beside Ravi. 'Do you have a problem?'

'Pip, don't,' Ravi said quietly.

'Excuse me, Leslie,' Pip read out snidely from her name tag, 'I asked if you had a problem?'

'Yeah,' the woman said, 'I don't want him touching me.'

'I think it's safe to say he doesn't want you touching him either, Leslie; stupidity might be catching.'

'I'm going to call my manager.'

'Yeah, you do that. I'll give them a sneak peek of the complaint emails I'll drown your head office in.'

Ravi put the five-pound note down on the counter, picked up his milk and strode silently towards the exit.

'Ravi?' Pip called, but he ignored her.

'Whoa.' Pip's mum stepped forward now, hands up in the surrender position as she came to stand between Pip and the reddening Leslie.

Pip turned on her heels, trainers screaming against the over-polished floor. Just before she reached the door, she called back: 'Oh, but, Leslie, you should really see someone about getting that arsehole removed from your face.'

Outside she could see Ravi thirty feet away pacing quickly down the hill. Pip, who didn't run for anything, ran to catch him.

'Are you OK?' she said, stepping in front of him.

'No.' He carried on round her, the giant milk bottle sloshing at his side.

'Did I do something wrong?'

Ravi turned, dark eyes flashing. He said, 'Look, I don't need some kid I hardly know fighting my battles for me. I'm not your problem, Pippa; don't try to make me your problem. You're only going to make things worse.'

He kept walking and Pip watched him go until the shade from a cafe awning dimmed and took him away. Standing there, breathing hard, she felt the rage retreat back into her gut where it slowly simmered out. She was hollow when it left her.

Production Log – Entry 8

Let it never be said that Pippa Fitz-Amobi is not an opportunistic interviewer. I was at Cara's house again today with Lauren. The boys joined us later too, though they insisted the football be on in the background. Cara's dad, Elliot, was chattering on about something when I remembered: he knew Sal pretty well, not just as his daughter's friend but as Sal's teacher. I've already got character assessments from Sal's friends and brother (his generational peers, I might say) but I thought maybe Cara's dad would have some further adult insights. Elliot agreed to it; I didn't give him much choice.

Transcript of interview with Elliot Ward

Pip: So for how many years had you taught Sal?

Elliot: Err, let's see. I started teaching at Kilton Grammar in 2009. Salil was in one of the first GCSE classes I took so . . . almost three full years, I think. Yeah.

Pip: So Sal took history for GCSE and A level?

Elliot: Oh, not only that, Sal was hoping to study history at Oxford. I don't know if you remember, Pip, but before I started teaching at the school I was an associate professor at Oxford. I taught history. I moved jobs so I could be around to take care of Isobel when she was sick.

Pip: Oh yeah.

Elliot: So actually, in the autumn term of that year before everything happened, I spent a lot of time with Sal. I helped him with his personal statement before he sent his uni applications off. When he got his interview at Oxford I helped him prepare for it, both in school and outside. He was such a bright kid. Brilliant. He got his offer from them too. When Naomi told me I bought him a card and some chocolate.

Pip: So Sal was very intelligent?

Elliot: Yeah, oh absolutely. Very, very smart young man. It's such a
          tragedy what happened in the end. Such a waste of two young
          lives. Sal would have got A stars across the board, no question.

Pip: Did you have a class with Sal on that Monday after Andie
          disappeared?

Elliot: Erm, gosh. I think so actually. Yes, because I remember talking
          to him after and asking if he was OK about everything. So yes, I
          must have done.

Pip: And did you notice him acting strangely at all?

Elliot: Well, it depends on your definition of strange. The whole school
          was acting strangely that day; one of our students was missing
          and it was all over the news. I suppose I remember him seeming
          quiet, maybe a bit tearful about the whole thing. Definitely
          seemed worried.

Pip: Worried for Andie?

Elliot: Yes, possibly.

Pip: And what about on the Tuesday, the day he killed himself. Do
          you remember seeing him at school that morning at any point?

Elliot: I . . . no, I didn't because on that day I had to call in sick. I had
          a bug so I dropped the girls off in the morning and had a day at
          home. I didn't know until the school rang me in the afternoon
          about this whole Naomi/Sal alibi thing and that the police had
          interviewed them at school. So, the last time I saw Sal would
          have been that Monday lesson time.

Pip: And do you think Sal killed Andie?

Elliot: (Sighs) I mean, I can understand how easy it is to convince
          yourself he didn't; he was such a lovely kid. But, considering
          the evidence, I don't see how he couldn't have done it. So, as
          wrong as it feels, I guess I think he must have. There's no other
          explanation.

Pip: And what about Andie Bell? Did you teach her too?

Elliot:	No, well, um, yes, she was in the same GCSE history class as Sal, so I had her that year. But she didn't study history any further so I'm afraid I didn't really know her that well.
Pip:	OK, thanks. You can go back to peeling potatoes now.
Elliot:	Thanks for your permission.

Ravi hadn't mentioned that Sal had an offer from Oxford University. There might be more he hasn't told me about Sal, but I'm not sure Ravi will ever speak to me again. Not after what happened a couple of days ago. I didn't mean to hurt him; I was trying to help. Maybe I should go around and apologize? He'll probably just slam the door on me. [But anyway, I can't let that distract me, not again.]

If Sal was so intelligent and Oxford-bound, then why was the evidence that linked him to Andie's murder so obvious? So what if he didn't have an alibi for the time of Andie's disappearance? He was clever enough to have got away with it, that much is clear now.

PS. we were playing Monopoly with Naomi and . . . maybe I overreacted before. She's still on the persons of interest list, but a murderer? There's just no way. She refuses to put houses down on the board even when she has the two dark blues because she thinks it's too mean. I hotel-up as soon as I can and laugh when others roll into my death trap. Even I have more of a killer's instinct than Naomi.

Seven

The next day, Pip was doing one final read-through of her information request to the Thames Valley Police. Her room was sweltering and stagnant, the sun trapped and sulking in there with her, even though she'd pushed open the window to let it out.

She heard distant knocking downstairs as she verbally approved her own email, 'Yep, good,' and pressed the send button; the small click that began her twenty-working-day wait. Pip hated waiting. And it was a Saturday, so she had to wait for the wait to begin.

'Pips,' came Victor's shout from downstairs. 'Front door for you.'

With each step down the stairs, the air became a little fresher; from her bedroom's first-ring-of-hell heat into quite bearable warmth. She took the turn after the stairs as a sock-skid across the oak but stopped in her tracks when she saw Ravi Singh outside the front door. He was being talked at enthusiastically by her dad. All the heat returned to her face.

'Um, hi,' Pip said, walking towards them. But the fast tap-tap of claws on wood grew behind her as Barney barged past and got there first, launching his muzzle into Ravi's groin.

'No, Barney, down,' Pip shouted, rushing forward. 'Sorry, he's a bit friendly.'

'That's no way to talk about your father,' said Victor.

Pip raised her eyebrows at him.

'Got it, got it, got it,' he said, walking away and into the kitchen.

Ravi bent down to stroke Barney, and Pip's ankles were fanned with the dog-tail breeze.

'How do you know where I live?' Pip asked.

'I asked in the estate agents your mum works in,' he straightened up. 'Seriously, your house is a palace.'

'Well, the strange man who opened the door to you is a hot-shot corporate lawyer.'

'Not a king?'

'Only some days,' she said.

Pip noticed Ravi looking down and, though his lips twitched trying to contain it, he broke into a big smile. That's when she remembered what she was wearing: baggy denim dungarees over a white T-shirt with the words *TALK NERDY TO ME* emblazoned across her chest.

'So, um, what brings you here?' she said. Her stomach lurched, and only then did she realize she was nervous.

'I . . . I'm here because . . . I wanted to say sorry.' He looked at her with his big downturned eyes, his brows bunching over them. 'I got angry and said some things I shouldn't have. I don't really think you're just some kid. Sorry.'

'It's OK,' Pip said, 'I'm sorry too. I didn't mean to step in and fight your battles for you. I just wanted to help, just wanted her to know that what she did wasn't OK. But sometimes my mouth starts saying words without checking them with my brain first.'

'Oh, I don't know about that,' he said. 'That arsehole comment was pretty inspired.'

'You heard?'

'Feisty Pip was pretty loud.'

'I've been told other kinds of Pip are pretty loud too, school-quiz Pip and grammar-police Pip among them. So . . . are we OK?'

'We're OK.' He smiled and looked down at the dog again. 'Me and your human are OK.'

'I was actually just about to head out on a dog walk, do you want to come with?'

'Yeah, sure,' he said, ruffling Barney's ears. 'How could I say no to that handsome face?'

Pip almost said, *Oh please, you'll make me blush*, but she bit it back.

'OK, I'll just grab my shoes. Barney, stay.'

Pip scooted into the kitchen. The back door was open and she could see her parents pottering around the flowers and Josh, of course, playing with his football.

'I'm taking Barns, see you in a bit,' she called outside and her mum waved a gardening-gloved hand to let her know she'd heard.

Pip slipped on her not-allowed-to-be-left-in-the-kitchen trainers that were left in the kitchen and grabbed the dog lead on her way back to the front door.

'Right, let's go,' she said, clipping the lead to Barney's collar and shutting the front door behind them.

At the end of her drive they crossed the road and into the woods opposite. The stippled shade felt nice on Pip's hot face. She let Barney off the lead and he was gone in a golden flash.

'I always wanted a dog.' Ravi grinned as Barney circled back to hurry them on. He paused, his jaw moving as he chewed on some silent thought. 'Sal was allergic, though, that's why we never . . .'

'Oh.' She wasn't quite sure what else to say.

'There's this dog at the pub I work at, the owner's dog. She's a slobbery Great Dane called Peanut. I sometimes *accidentally* drop leftovers for her. Don't tell.'

'I encourage *accidental* droppage,' she said. 'Which pub do you work at?'

'The George and Dragon, over in Amersham. It's not what I want to do forever. Just saving up so I can get myself as far away from Little Kilton as I can.'

Pip felt an unutterable sadness for him then, rising up her tightened throat.

'What do you want to do forever?'

He shrugged. 'I used to want to be a lawyer.'

'Used to?' She nudged him. 'I think you could be great at that.'

'Hmm, not when the only GCSEs I got spell out the word DUUUDDEE.'

He'd said it like a joke, but she knew it wasn't. They both

knew how awful school had been for Ravi after Andie and Sal died. Pip had even witnessed some of the worst of the bullying. His locker painted in red dripping letters: *Like brother like brother*. And that snowy morning when eight older boys had pinned him down and upturned four full bins over his head. She would never forget the look on sixteen-year-old Ravi's face. Never.

That's when, with the clarity of cold slush pooling in her stomach, Pip realized where they were.

'Oh my god,' she gasped, covering her face with her hands. 'I'm so sorry, I didn't even think. I completely forgot these are the woods where they found Sal –'

'That's OK.' He cut her off. 'Really. You can't help it that these happen to be the woods outside your house. Plus, there's nowhere in Kilton that doesn't remind me of him.'

Pip watched for a while as Barney dropped a stick at Ravi's feet and Ravi raised his arm in mock-throws, sending the dog backwards and forwards and back, until he finally let go.

They didn't speak for a while. But the silence wasn't uncomfortable; it was charged with the offcuts of whatever thoughts they were working on alone. And, as it turned out, both their minds had wandered to the same place.

'I was wary of you when you first knocked on my door,' Ravi said. 'But you really don't think Sal did it, do you?'

'I just can't believe it,' she said, stepping over an old fallen tree. 'My brain hasn't been able to leave it alone. So, when this project thing came up at school, I jumped at the excuse to re-examine the case.'

'It is the perfect excuse to hide behind,' he said, nodding. 'I didn't have anything like that.'

'What do you mean?' She turned to him, fiddling with the lead round her neck.

'I tried to do what you're doing, three years ago. My parents told me to leave it alone, that I was only going to make things harder for myself, but I just couldn't accept it.'

'You tried to investigate?'

He gave her a mock salute then, barking, 'Yes, Sergeant.' Like he couldn't let himself be vulnerable, couldn't let himself be serious long enough to expose a chink in his armour.

'But I didn't get anywhere,' he carried on. 'I couldn't. I called Naomi Ward when she was at university, but she just cried and said she couldn't talk about it with me. Max Hastings and Jake Lawrence never replied to my messages. I tried contacting Andie's best friends, but they hung up as soon as I said who I was. Murderer's brother isn't the best intro. And, of course, Andie's family were out of the question. I was too close to the case, I knew it. I looked too much like my brother, too much like the "murderer". And I didn't have the excuse of a school project to fall back on.'

'I'm sorry,' Pip said, wordless and embarrassed by the unfairness of it.

'Don't be.' He nudged her. 'It's good to not be alone in this, for once. Go on, I want to hear your theories.' He picked up Barney's stick, now foamy with dribble, and threw it into the trees.

Pip hesitated.

'Go on.' He smiled into his eyes, one eyebrow cocked. Was he testing her?

'OK, I have four working theories,' she said, the first time she'd actually given voice to them. 'Obviously the path of least resistance is the accepted narrative of what happened: that Sal killed her and his guilt or fear of being caught led him to take his own life. The police would argue that the only reasons there are gaps in the case are because Andie's body hasn't been recovered and Sal isn't alive to tell us how it happened. But my first theory,' she said, holding up one finger, making sure it wasn't the swear-y one, 'is that a third party killed Andie Bell, but Sal was somehow involved or implicated, such as an accessory after the fact. Again his guilt leads him to suicide and the evidence found on him implicates him as the perpetrator, even though he isn't the one who killed her. The actual killer is still at large.'

'Yeah, I thought of that too. I still don't like it. Next?'

'Theory number two,' she said, 'a third party killed Andie, and Sal had no involvement or awareness at all. His suicide days later wasn't motivated by a murderer's guilt, but maybe a multitude of factors, including the stress of his girlfriend's disappearance. The evidence found on him – the blood and the phone – have an entirely innocent explanation and are unrelated to her murder.'

Ravi nodded thoughtfully. 'I still don't think Sal would do

that, but OK. Theory three?'

'Theory three.' Pip swallowed, her throat feeling dry and sticky. 'Andie is murdered by a third party on the Friday. The killer knows that Sal, as Andie's boyfriend, would make for the perfect suspect. Especially as Sal seems to have no alibi for over two hours that night. The killer murders Sal and makes it look like a suicide. They plant the blood and the phone on his body to make him look guilty. It works just as they planned it.'

Ravi stopped walking for a moment. 'You think it's possible that Sal was actually murdered?'

She knew, looking into his sharpened eyes, that this was the answer he'd been looking for.

'I think it's a theoretical possibility,' Pip nodded. 'Theory four is the most far-fetched of the lot.' She took a large breath and did it in one. 'No one killed Andie Bell, because she isn't dead. She faked her disappearance and then lured Sal out into the woods, murdered him and dressed it up as a suicide. She planted her own phone and blood on him so that everyone believed she was dead. Why would she do this? Maybe she needed to disappear for some reason. Maybe she feared for life and needed to make it look like she was already dead. Maybe she had an accomplice.'

They were quiet again, while Pip caught her breath and Ravi ticked over her answers, his upper lip puffed out in concentration.

They had come to the end of their circuit round the woods; the bright sun-stroked road was visible through the trees ahead. She called Barney over and put him on the lead. They crossed the road and wandered over to Pip's front door.

There was an awkward moment of silence and Pip wasn't sure whether she should invite him inside or not. He seemed to be waiting for something.

'So,' Ravi said, scratching his head with one hand, the dog's with the other, 'the reason I came over is . . . I want to make a deal with you.'

'A deal?'

'Yeah, I want in on this,' he said, a small tremor in his voice. 'I never had a chance, but you actually might. You're an outsider to the case, you have this school project excuse to open doors. People might actually talk to you. You might be my chance to find out what really happened. I've waited so long for a chance.'

Her face felt full and hot again, the shaking edge in his voice making something tug inside her chest. He was really trusting her to help; she'd never have thought this would happen at the start of the project. Partners with Ravi Singh.

'I can agree to that,' she smiled, holding out her hand.

'Deal,' he said, taking her hand in his warm, clammy one, although he forgot to shake it. 'OK, I've got something for you.' He reached into his back pocket and pulled out an old iPhone cradled in his palm.

'Um, I've actually already got one, thanks,' Pip said.

'It's Sal's phone.'

Eight

'What do you mean?' Pip stared at him, open-mouthed.

Ravi answered by holding up the phone and shaking it gently.

'That's Sal's?' Pip said. 'How do you have it?'

'The police released it to us a few months after they closed Andie's investigation.'

A cautious electricity sparked up the back of Pip's neck. 'Can I . . .' she said, 'can I look at it?'

'Of course,' he laughed, 'that's why I brought it round, you plonker.'

Unchecked, the excitement charged through her, nimble and dizzying.

'Holy pepperoni,' she said, flustered and hurrying to unlock the door. 'Let's go and look at it at my workstation.'

She and Barney bolted over the threshold, but a third set of feet didn't follow. She spun back round.

'What's funny?' she said. 'Come on.'

'Sorry, you're just very entertaining when you're extra serious.'

'Quick,' she said, beckoning him through the hallway and to the stairs. 'Don't drop it.'

'I'm not going to drop it.'

Pip jogged up the steps, Ravi following far too slowly

behind. Before he got there, she did a hasty check of her bedroom for potential embarrassment. She dived for a pile of just-laundered bras by her chair, scooped them up and shoved them in a drawer, slamming it shut just as Ravi walked in. She pointed him into her desk chair, too flappy to sit herself.

'Workstation?' he asked.

'Yep,' she said, 'while some people might work in their bedrooms, I sleep in my workstation. It's very different.'

'Here you go then. I charged it last night.'

He handed her the phone and she took it in her cupped palms with as much deliberate dexterity and care as she did yearly when unwrapping her first father's German-market Christmas baubles.

'Have you looked through it before?' she asked, sliding to unlock more carefully than she'd ever unlocked her own phones, even at their newest.

'Yeah, of course. Obsessively. But go ahead, Sergeant. Where would *you* look first?'

'Call log,' she said, tapping the green phone button.

She looked through the missed call list first. There were dozens from the 24th April, the Tuesday he had died. Calls from *Dad*, *Mum*, *Ravi*, *Naomi*, *Jake* and unsaved numbers that must have been the police trying to locate him.

Pip scrolled back further, to the date of Andie's disappearance. Sal had two missed calls that day. One was from *Max-y Boy* at 7:19 p.m., probably a *when-are-you-coming-over* call from Max. The other missed call, she read with a skipped heartbeat, was from *Andie<3* at 8:54 p.m.

'Andie rang him that night,' Pip said to herself and Ravi. 'Just before nine.'

Ravi nodded. 'Sal didn't pick up, though.'

'Pippa!' Victor's jokey-but-serious voice sailed up the stairs. 'No boys in bedrooms.'

Pip felt her cheeks flood with heat. She turned so Ravi couldn't see and yelled back, 'We're working on my EPQ! My door is open.'

'OK, that will do!' came the reply.

She glimpsed back at Ravi and saw he was chuckling at her again.

'Stop finding my life amusing,' she said, looking back at the phone.

She went through Sal's outgoing calls next. Andie's name repeated over and over again in long streams. It was broken up in places with the odd call to home, or Dad, and one to Naomi on Saturday. Pip took a few moments to count all the 'Andie's: from 10:30 a.m. on the Saturday until 7:20 a.m. on the Tuesday, Sal called her 112 times. Each call lasted two or three seconds; straight to voicemail.

'He called her over a hundred times,' Ravi said, reading her face.

'Why would he ring her so many times if he'd supposedly killed her and had her phone hidden somewhere?' said Pip.

'I contacted the police years ago and asked them that very question,' Ravi said. 'The officer told me it was clear that Sal was making a conscious effort to look innocent, by ringing the victim's phone so many times.'

'But,' Pip countered, 'if they thought he was making an effort to appear innocent and evade capture, why didn't he dispose of Andie's phone? He could have put it in the same place as her body and it never would have connected him to her death. If he was trying to not get caught, why would he keep the one biggest bit of evidence? And then feel desperate enough to end his life with this vital evidence on him?'

Ravi shot two clicking gun-hands at her. 'The policeman couldn't answer that either.'

'Did you look at the last texts Andie and Sal sent each other?' she asked.

'Yeah, have a look. Don't worry, they aren't sexty or anything.'

Pip exited on to the home screen and opened the messages app. She clicked on the Andie tab, feeling like a time-hopping trespasser.

Sal had sent two texts to Andie after she disappeared. The first on the Sunday morning: *andie just come home everyones worried*. And on Monday afternoon: *please just ring someone so we know youre safe*.

The message preceding them was sent on the Friday she went missing. At 9:01 p.m. Sal texted her: *im not talking to you till youve stopped*.

Pip showed Ravi the message she'd just read. 'He said that just after ignoring her call that night. Do you know what they could have been fighting about? What did Sal want Andie to stop?'

'No idea.'

'Can I just type this out in my research?' she said, reaching over him for her laptop. She parked herself on her bed and typed out the text, grammar mistakes and all.

'Now you need to look at the last text he sent my dad,' Ravi said. 'The one they said is his confession.'

Pip flicked over to it. At 10:17 a.m. on his final Tuesday morning, Sal said to his father: *it was me. i did it. i'm so sorry.* Pip's eyes flicked over it several times, picking up a little more each read through. The pixelated building blocks of each letter were a riddle, the kind you could only solve if you stopped looking and started seeing.

'You see it too, don't you?' Ravi was watching her.

'The grammar?' Pip said, looking for the agreement in Ravi's eyes.

'Sal was the cleverest person I knew,' he said, 'but he texted like an illiterate. Always in a rush, no punctuation, no capital letters.'

'He must have had autocorrect turned off,' Pip said. 'And yet, in this last text, we have three full stops and an apostrophe. Even though it's all in lower case.'

'And what does that make you think?' asked Ravi.

'My mind doesn't make small jumps, Ravi,' she said. 'Mine takes Everest-sized leaps. It makes me think that someone else wrote that text. Someone who added in the punctuation themselves because that's how they were used to writing in

79

texts. Maybe they checked quickly and thought it looked enough like Sal because it was all lower case.'

'That's what I thought too, when we first got it back. The police just sent me away. My parents didn't want to hear it either,' he sighed. 'I think they're terrified of false hope. I am too, if I'm honest.'

Pip scoured through the rest of the phone. Sal hadn't taken any photos on the night in question, and none since Andie disappeared. She checked in the deleted folder to be sure. The reminders were all about essays he had to hand in, and one about buying his mum's birthday present.

'There's something interesting in the notes,' Ravi said, rolling over on the chair and opening the app for her.

The notes were all quite old: Sal's home Wi-Fi password, a listed abs workout, a page of work experience placements he could apply to. But there was just one later note, written on Wednesday 18th April 2012. Pip clicked into it. There was one thing typed on the page: *R009 KKJ*.

'Car number plate, right?' Ravi said.

'Looks it. He wrote that down in his notes two days before Andie went missing. Do you recognize it?'

Ravi shook his head. 'I tried to Google it, see if I could find the owner, but no luck.'

Pip typed it up in her log anyway, and the exact time the note was last edited.

'That's everything,' Ravi said, 'that's all I could find.'

Pip gave the phone one last wistful look before handing it back.

'You seem disappointed,' he said.

'I just hoped there'd be something more substantial we could chase up on. Inconsistent grammar and lots of phone calls to Andie certainly make him appear innocent, but they don't actually open any leads to pursue.'

'Not yet,' he said, 'but you needed to see it. Have you got anything to show me?'

Pip paused. Yes, she did, but one of those things was Naomi's possible involvement. Her protective instinct flared up, grabbing hold of her tongue. But if they were going to be partners, they had to be all in. She knew that. She opened up her production log documents, scrolled to the top and handed the laptop to Ravi. 'This is everything so far,' she said.

He read through it quietly and then handed the computer back, a thoughtful look on his face.

'OK, so the Sal alibi route is a dead end,' he said. 'After he left Max's at ten thirty, I think he was alone because that explains why he panicked and asked his friends to lie for him. He could have just stopped on a bench on his walk home and played *Angry Birds* or something.'

'I agree,' said Pip. 'He was most likely alone and therefore has no alibi; it's the only thing that makes sense. So that line of enquiry is lost. I think the next step should be to find out as much as we can about Andie's life and, in the process, identify anyone who might have had motive to kill her.'

'Read my mind, Sarge,' he said. 'Maybe you should start with Andie's best friends, Emma Hutton and Chloe Burch.

They might actually speak to you.'

'I've messaged them both. Haven't heard back yet, though.'

'OK, good,' he said, nodding to himself and then to the laptop. 'In that interview with the journalist, you talked about inconsistencies in the case. What other inconsistencies do you see?'

'Well, if you'd killed someone,' she said, 'you'd scrub yourself down multiple times, fingernails included. Especially if you were lying about alibis and making fake calls to look innocent, wouldn't you think to, oh, I don't know, wash the frickin' blood off your hands so you don't get caught red-handed, literally.'

'Yeah, Sal definitely wasn't that stupid. But what about his fingerprints in her car?'

'Of course his fingerprints would be found in her car; he was her boyfriend,' said Pip. 'Fingerprints can't be accurately dated.'

'And what about hiding the body?' Ravi leaned forward. 'I think we can guess, living where we do, that she's buried somewhere in the woods in or just out of town.'

'Exactly,' Pip nodded. 'A hole deep enough that she's never been found. How did Sal have enough time to dig a hole that big with his bare hands? It would even be a push with a shovel.'

'Unless she isn't buried.'

'Yeah, well, I think it takes a little more time and a lot more hardware to dispose of a body in other ways,' said Pip.

'And this is the path of least resistance, you said.'

'It is, supposedly,' she said. 'Until you start asking *where*, *what* and *how*.'

Nine

They probably thought she couldn't hear them. Her parents, bickering in the living room downstairs. She had long ago learned that the word 'Pip' was one that travelled exceptionally well through walls and floors.

Listening through the crack of her bedroom door, it wasn't hard to catch hold of snatches and shape them into a gist. Her mum wasn't happy that Pip was spending so much of her summer on schoolwork. Her dad wasn't happy that her mother had said that. Then her mum wasn't happy because her dad had misunderstood what she meant. She thought that obsessing over the Andie Bell thing would be unhealthy for her. Her dad wasn't happy that her mum wouldn't give Pip the space to make her own mistakes, if that's what they were.

Pip grew bored of the sparring match and closed her bedroom door. She knew their cyclical argument would burn itself out soon, without neutral intervention. And she had an important phone call to make.

She had private-messaged both of Andie's best friends last week. Emma Hutton replied a few hours ago with a phone number, saying she didn't mind answering 'just a few' questions at eight o'clock tonight. When Pip told Ravi this, he'd texted back with a whole page of shock-face and fist-bump emojis.

She glanced at the clock on her computer dashboard and the glance became a stare. The clock stood stubbornly at 7:58 p.m.

'Oh, come on,' she said when, even after twenty Mississippis, the eight in the :58 hadn't sprung into the leg of a nine.

When it did, an age later, Pip said, 'Close enough,' and pressed the record button on her app. She dialled Emma's number, her skin prickling with nerves. It picked up on the third ring.

'Hello?' said a high and sweet voice.

'Hi, Emma, this is Pippa here.'

'Oh yeah, hi. Hold on, let me just go up to my room.'

Pip listened impatiently to the sound of Emma's feet skipping up a flight of stairs.

'OK,' she said. 'So, you said you're doing a project about Andie?'

'Sort of, yeah. About the investigation into her disappearance and the media's role in it. A kind of case study.'

'OK,' Emma said, sounding uncertain. 'I'm not sure how much help I can be with that.'

'Don't worry, I just have a few basic questions about the investigation as you remember it,' Pip said. 'So firstly, when did you find out she was missing?'

'Um . . . it was around one o'clock that night. Her parents rang both me and Chloe Burch; we were Andie's best friends. I said how I hadn't seen her or heard from her and told them I would call around a bit. I tried Sal Singh that night but he didn't pick up until the next morning.'

'Did the police contact you at all?' asked Pip.

'Yeah, Saturday morning. They came around asking questions.'

'And what did you tell them?'

'Just the same as I said to Andie's parents. That I had no idea where she was; she hadn't told me she was going anywhere. And they were asking about Andie's boyfriend, so I told them about Sal and that I'd just rung and told him she was missing.'

'What did you tell them about Sal?'

'Well, only that at school that week they were kind of fighting. I definitely saw them bickering on the Thursday and Friday, which was out of the ordinary. Usually Andie bickered at him and he didn't get involved. But this time he seemed super mad about something.'

'What about?' Pip said. It was suddenly clearer to her why the police might have thought it prudent to interview Sal that afternoon.

'I don't know, honestly. When I asked Andie she just said that Sal was being "a little bitch" about something.'

Pip was taken aback. 'OK,' she said. 'So Andie didn't have plans to see Sal on the Friday?'

'No, she didn't have plans to do anything actually; she was supposed to stay at home that night.'

'Oh, how come?' Pip sat up a little straighter.

'Um, I don't know if I should say.'

'Don't worry –' Pip tried to hide the desperation in her

voice – 'if it's not relevant it won't go in my project. It just might help me better understand the circumstances of her disappearance.'

'Yeah, OK. Well, Andie's little sister, Becca, had been hospitalized for self-harming several weeks before. Her parents had to go out, so they told Andie she had to stay in and take care of Becca.'

'Oh,' was all Pip could think to say.

'Yeah, I know, poor girl. And still Andie left her. Only looking back now can I understand how difficult it must have been having Andie as an older sister.'

'What do you mean by that?'

'Erm, it's just, I don't want to speak ill of the dead, you know, but . . . I've had five years to grow up and reflect on everything and when I think back to those times I don't like the person I was at all. The person I was with Andie.'

'Was she a bad friend to you?' Pip didn't want to say too much; she needed to keep Emma talking.

'Yes and no. It's really difficult to explain,' Emma sighed. 'Andie's friendship was very destructive, but at the time, I was addicted to her. I wanted to be her. You're not going to write any of this, are you?'

'No, of course not.' Small lie.

'OK. So Andie was beautiful, she was popular, she was fun. Being her friend, being someone she chose to spend her time with, it made you feel special. Wanted. And then she would flip and use the things you were most self-conscious about to cut you down and hurt you. And still we both remained by her side, waiting for the next time she would pick us up and make us feel good again. She could be amazing and awful, and you never knew which side of Andie was turning up at your door. I'm surprised my self-esteem even survived.'

'Was Andie like this with everyone?'

'Well, yeah, to me and Chloe. Andie wouldn't let us go over to her house much, but I saw the way she was with Becca too. She could be so cruel.' Emma paused. 'I'm not saying any of this because I mean that Andie deserved what she got. No, no that's not what I mean at all, no one deserves to be murdered and put in a hole. I only mean that, appreciating now the kind of person Andie was, I can understand why Sal snapped and killed her. She could make you feel so high and then so low; it was bound to end in tragedy, I think.'

Emma's voice slipped into a wet sniff and Pip knew the interview was over. Emma couldn't hide the fact that she was crying, and she didn't try to.

'OK, those are all the questions I have. Thank you so much for your help.'

'That's OK,' Emma said. 'Sorry, I thought I was over everything. Guess not.'

'No, I'm sorry for making you go over it all. Um, actually, I've also messaged Chloe Burch for an interview, but she hasn't got back to me yet. Are you two still in contact?'

'No, not really. Like, I'll message her on her birthday, but . . . we definitely drifted after Andie and then leaving school.

I think we both wanted it that way really, a clean break from the people we had been back then.'

Pip thanked her again and hung up the phone. She exhaled and just stared at it for a minute. She knew that Andie had been pretty and popular, that much social media had made perfectly clear. And like everyone that's ever been to high school, she knew that popular people sometimes had their hard edges. But she hadn't expected this. That Emma could still resent herself after all this time for loving her tormentor.

Was this the real Andie Bell, hiding behind that perfect smile, behind those sparkling pale blue eyes? Everyone in her orbit so dazzled by her, so blinded, that they didn't notice the darkness that might lurk beneath. Not until it was too late.

Production Log – Entry 11

UPDATE: I researched to see if I could find the owner of the car with the number plate Sal had written down in his notes: *RO09 KKJ*. Ravi was right. We'd need to know the make and model of the car to send a request to the DVLA. I guess that particular lead is dead.

OK, back to the task at hand. I just got off the phone with Chloe. I tried a different tactic this time; I didn't need to go over the same things I'd learned from Emma and I didn't want to hinder the interview with any dormant Andie emotional issues.

But I stumbled into some anyway . . .

Transcript of interview with Chloe Burch

[I'm getting bored of typing out the interview intros; they're all the same and I always sound awkward. Skipping from now on straight to juicy bits.]

Pip: OK, so my first question is how would you describe Andie and Sal's relationship?

Chloe: Yeah, good, he was nice to her and she thought he was hot. Sal always seemed really calm and chilled; I thought he would mellow Andie out a bit.

Pip: Why would Andie have needed mellowing out?

Chloe: Oh, just because she always had some drama going on.

Pip: And did Sal mellow her?

Chloe: (Laughs) No.

Pip: But were they quite serious about each other?

Chloe: I don't know, I guess so. Define serious?

Pip: Well, excuse the question, but were they sleeping together?

[Yes, I do cringe hearing this back. But I need to know everything.]

Chloe:	Wow, school projects have changed since I left. Why on earth would you need to know that?
Pip:	Did she not tell you?
Chloe:	Of course she told me. And no, they weren't, actually.
Pip:	Oh. Was Andie a virgin?
Chloe:	No, she wasn't.
Pip:	So who was she sleeping with?
Chloe:	(Small pause) I don't know.
Pip:	You didn't know?
Chloe:	Andie liked her secrets, OK? They made her powerful. She got a thrill out of me and Emma not knowing certain things. But she'd dangle them in front of us because she liked us to ask. Like where she got all that money from; she would just laugh and wink when we asked.
Pip:	Money?
Chloe:	Yeah. That girl was always shopping, always had a load of cash on her. And, in our final year, she told me she was saving up to get lip fillers and a nose job. She never told Emma that, just me. But she was generous with it too; she'd buy us make-up and stuff, and always let us borrow her clothes. But then she'd pick her moment at the party to say something like: "Oh, Chlo, looks like you've stretched that. I'll have to give it to Becca now." Sweet girl.
Pip:	Where did her money come from? Did she have a part-time job?
Chloe:	No. I told you, I didn't know. I just presumed her dad was giving it to her.
Pip:	Like an allowance?
Chloe:	Yeah, maybe.
Pip:	So when Andie first went missing, was there any part of you that thought she had run away to punish someone? Maybe her father?

Chloe: Andie had things too good to want to run away.

Pip: But was there tension in Andie's relationship with her dad?

[As soon as I say the word 'dad' Chloe's tone flips.]

Chloe: I don't see how that can be relevant to your project. Look, I
           know I've been flippant about her and, yeah, she had her flaws,
           but she was still my best friend who got murdered. I don't think
           it's right to be talking about her personal relationships and her
           family, however many years later.

Pip: No, you're right, sorry. I just thought if I knew what Andie
           was like and what was happening in her life, I could better
           understand the case.

Chloe: Yeah OK, but none of that is relevant. Sal Singh killed her. And
           you're not going to get to know Andie from a few interviews. It
           was impossible to know her, even when you were her best friend.

[I inelegantly try to apologize and bring us back on topic, but it is clear
Chloe is done. I thank her for her help before she hangs up.]

Grrr, so frustrating. I thought I was actually getting somewhere, but,
no, I blundered into a giant minefield of raw emotion with both of Andie's
friends and ruined it. I guess even though they think they've moved on,
they still haven't quite broken free of Andie's hold. Maybe they are even
still keeping some of her secrets. I certainly struck a nerve when I brought
up Andie's dad; is there a story there?

I just read the transcript another few times and . . . maybe there's
something else hidden here. When I asked Chloe who Andie was sleeping
with, what I'd meant to ask was who Andie had slept with *before* Sal, any
past relationships. But I accidentally phrased it in the past continuous:
'who was she sleeping with?' This, in context, means that what I
accidentally asked was: who else was Andie sleeping with *at the same time*
as her relationship with Sal? But Chloe didn't correct me. She just said
she didn't know.

I'm grasping at straws, I know. Of course, Chloe could have been
answering the question I'd meant to ask. This could be nothing. I know I
can't solve this case by being particular about grammar, that's not how
the real world works unfortunately.

But now I've got the scent of it, I can't let it go. Was Andie secretly seeing someone else? Did Sal find out and that's why they were arguing? Does this explain Sal's last text to Andie before she disappeared: *im not talking to you till youve stopped*?

I'm not a police officer, this is still just a school project, so I can't make them tell me anything. And these are the kinds of secrets you only share with your best friends, not some random girl doing her EPQ.

Oh My God. I've just had a horrible but maybe brilliant idea. Horrible and certainly immoral and probably stupid. And definitely, definitely wrong. And even so, I think I should do it. I can't come out of this thing entirely squeaky clean if I actually want to find out what happened to Andie and Sal.

I'm going to catfish Emma, pretending to be Chloe.

I have that pay-as-you-go SIM I used on holiday last year. If I put that in my phone, I can text Emma pretending that I'm Chloe with a new number. It might work; Emma said they lost contact so she might not realize. And it might not work. But I have nothing to lose, and maybe secrets to gain and a killer to find.

> Hey Em, it's Chloe, I got a new number recently. So this kid from Kilton just rang me asking questions about Andie for a project. Did she call you too? Xxx

Omg hi .
Yeah she did a couple of days ago. It made me get a bit emosh about everything again tbh Xx

> Yeah well Andie had that effect on us. You didn't tell her anything about Andie's love life did you? Xx

I presume you mean her secret older guy, not Sal?

> Yeah

No I didn't tell her

> Yeah, me neither. I always wondered if Andie had told you who it was though?

Nah, you know she didn't. Only thing she said was that she could ruin him if she wanted to, right?

Yeah she liked her secrets

I'm not even sure he existed tbh

She might have just made it up to seem more mysterious.

Yeah maybe.
This girl was asking about Andie's dad as well, do you think she knows?

Maybe. It's not hard to work it out now, he married the whore not long after they got divorced.

Yeah, but does she know that Andie knew at the time?

Don't see how she could, we were the only ones that knew. And Andie's dad obviously. Anyway, why does it matter if she knows?

Yeah you're right. I guess I still feel protective of Andie's secrets, you know?

I think it'd be good for you to try to let go more. I def feel better for distancing myself from everything Andie related.

Yeah I'll try. Hey I've gotta go, I've got work early. But we really should meet for a catch up some time soon?

Yeah would love to! Let me know when you're free and down in London. 👍

I will do. Bye xxxxx

Holy pepperoni.

I have never sweated so much in my whole damn life. I'm in shock that I managed to pull that off. I almost lost it a couple of times but . . . I actually did it.

I do feel bad, though. Emma is so nice and trusting. But it's good that I feel guilty; it shows I haven't quite lost my moral compass. I might still be a good girl yet . . .

And just like that, we have two more leads.

Jason Bell was already on the persons of interest list, but now he goes on in *bold* as number-one suspect. He was having an affair and Andie knew about it. More so than that, Jason knew that Andie knew. She must have approached him about it, or maybe she's the one who caught him. That's definitely filled in some of the gaps about why their relationship was strained.

And, now I think about it, was all this secret money Andie had given to her by her dad BECAUSE she knew? Was she, maybe, blackmailing him? No, that's pure conjecture; I need to consider the money as separate intel until I can confirm where it came from.

The second lead and the biggest reveal of the night then: Andie was secretly seeing an older man during her relationship with Sal. So secret that she never told her friends who it was, only that she could ruin him. My mind goes immediately to that place: a married man. Could *he* have been the source of the secret money? I have a new suspect. One who would certainly have motive to silence Andie for good.

This is not the Andie I expected to find in my investigation, so removed from that public image of a beautiful blonde victim. A victim loved by her family, a victim adored by her friends, a victim who was taken too soon by her '*cruel, murderous*' boyfriend. Maybe that Andie was a fictional character all along, designed to bucket-collect people's sympathy, to exchange their coins for newspapers. And now that I'm scratching, that image is starting to peel away at the corners.

I need to call Ravi.

Persons of Interest

Jason Bell

Naomi Ward

Secret Older Guy (how much older?)

Ten

'I hate camping,' Lauren grunted, tripping over the crumpled canvas.

'Yeah, well, it's my birthday and I like it,' Cara said, reading over the instructions with her tongue tucked between her teeth.

It was the final Friday of the summer holidays and the three of them were in a small clearing in a beech forest on the outskirts of Kilton. Cara's choice for her early eighteenth birthday celebration: to sleep without a roof and squat-piss behind dark trees all night. It wouldn't have been Pip's choice either; she certainly didn't see the logic in retrogressive toilet and sleeping arrangements. But she knew how to pretend well enough.

'It's technically illegal to camp outside of a registered campsite,' Lauren said, kicking the canvas in retaliation.

'Well, let's hope the camping police don't check Instagram, because I've announced it to the world. Now shush,' Cara said, 'I'm trying to read.'

'Um, Cara,' Pip said tentatively, 'you know this isn't a tent you brought, right? It's a marquee.'

'Same difference,' she said. 'And we have to fit us and the three boys in.'

'But it comes with no floor.' Pip jabbed her finger at the picture on the instructions.

'*You* come with no floor.' Cara butt-shoved her away. 'And my dad packed us a separate groundsheet.'

'When are the boys getting here?' Lauren asked.

'They texted they were leaving about two minutes ago. And no,' Cara snapped, 'we're not waiting for them to put it up for us, Lauren.'

'I wasn't suggesting that.'

Cara cracked her knuckles. 'Dismantling the patriarchy, one tent at a time.'

'Marquee,' Pip corrected.

'Do you want me to hurt you?'

'No-quee.'

Ten minutes later, a full ten-by-twenty-foot white marquee stood on the forest floor, looking as out of place as anything could. It had been easy once they worked out the frame was a pop-up. Pip checked her phone. It was half seven already and her weather app said that sunset would be in fifteen minutes, though they'd have another couple of twilight-lit hours before darkness fell.

'This is going to be so fun.' Cara stood back to admire their handiwork. 'I love camping. I'm gonna have gin and strawberry laces until I puke. I don't want to remember a thing tomorrow.'

'Admirable goals,' Pip said. 'Do you two want to go and grab the rest of the food from the car? I'll lay out our sleeping bags and put up the sides.'

Cara's car was parked in the tiny concrete car park about

200 yards from their chosen spot. Lauren and Cara toddled off that way through the trees, the woods lit with that final orange nightly glow before they begin to darken.

'Don't forget the torches,' she called, just as she lost sight of them.

Pip attached the large canvas sides to the marquee, swearing when the Velcro betrayed her and she had to start one side from scratch. She wrestled with the groundsheet, glad when she heard the twig-snap tread of Cara and Lauren returning. But when she went to look outside for them no one was there. It was just a magpie, mocking her from the darkening treetops, laughing its scratchy, bony laugh. She begrudgingly saluted it and got to work laying their three sleeping bags in a row, trying not to think about the fact that Andie Bell could very well be buried somewhere in these woods, deep underground.

The sound of branches breaking underfoot grew louder as she laid out the last one, and a din of guffawing and shrieking that could only mean the boys had arrived. She waved at them and the returning arm-laden girls. Ant, who – as his name suggested – hadn't grown much since they'd first made friends aged twelve, Zach Chen, who lived four doors down from the Amobis, and Connor, who Pip and Cara knew from primary school. He'd been paying a bit too much attention to Pip recently. Hopefully it would burn out quickly, like that time he was convinced he had a real future as a cat psychologist.

'Hey,' said Connor, carrying a cool box with Zach. 'Oh damn, the girls got the best sleeping spots. We've been *pipped* to the post.'

Not, surprisingly, the first time Pip had heard that joke.

'Hilarious, Con,' she said flatly, brushing the hair out of her eyes.

'Aw,' Ant chimed in, 'don't feel too bad, Connor. Maybe if you were a piece of homework she'd want to do you.'

'Or Ravi Singh,' Cara whispered just to her with a wink.

'Homework is far more rewarding than boys,' Pip said, digging an elbow into Cara's ribs. 'And you can talk, Ant, you have the sex life of an argonaut mollusc.'

'Which means?' Ant gesticulated his hand in a rolling wave.

'Well,' said Pip, 'an argonaut mollusc's penis snaps off during intercourse, so it can only ever have sex once in its whole life.'

'I can confirm this,' Lauren said, who'd had a failed dalliance with Ant last year.

The group fell about laughing and Zach gave Ant a conciliatory whack on the back.

'Absolutely savage,' Connor chortled.

A silver-tinted darkness had taken over the woods, enclosing on all sides the small bright marquee that glowed like a lantern amongst the sleeping trees. They had two battery-powered yellow lamps on inside and three torches between them.

Lucky they had moved to sit inside the marquee, Pip noted then, as it had just started to rain, quite heavily, although the tree cover protected their patch from most of it.

They were sitting in a circle around the snacks and drinks, the two ends of the marquee rolled up to alleviate the boy smell.

Pip had even allowed herself to get to the bottom of one beer, sitting with her navy star-crossed sleeping bag rolled up to her waist. Although she was much more interested in the crisps and sour cream dip. She didn't much like drinking, didn't like feeling that loss of control.

Ant was halfway through his ghost story, the torch under his chin making his face distorted and grotesque. It just happened to be a story about six friends, three boys and three girls, who were camping in a marquee in the woods.

'And the birthday girl,' he said theatrically, 'is finishing off a whole packet of strawberry laces, the red sweets sticking to her chin like trails of blood.'

'Shut up,' Cara said, mouth full.

'She tells the handsome guy with the torch to shut up. And that's when they hear it: a scraping sound against the side of the marquee. There's something or someone outside. Slowly fingernails start dragging through the canvas, ripping a hole. "You guys having a party?" a girl's voice asks. And then she tears through the hole and, with one swipe of her hand, slits the throat of the guy in the check shirt. "Missed me?" she shrieks, and the surviving friends can finally see who it is: the rotting zombie corpse of Andie Bell, out for revenge –'

'Shut up, Ant.' Pip shoved him. 'That isn't funny.'

'Why's everyone laughing then?'

'Because you're all sick. A murdered girl isn't fair game

for your crappy jokes.'

'But she's fair game for a school project?' Zach interjected.

'That's entirely different.'

'I was just about to get to the part about Andie's secret older lover slash killer,' Ant said.

Pip winced and shot him a blistering look.

'Lauren told me,' he said quietly.

'Cara told me,' Lauren jumped in, slurring the edges of her words.

'Cara?' Pip turned to her.

'I'm sorry,' she said, tripping over the words because she was the wrong side of eight measures of gin. 'I didn't know it was supposed to be secret. I only told Naomi and Lauren. And I told them not to tell anyone.' She swayed, pointing accusatorily at Lauren.

It was true; Pip hadn't specifically told her to keep it secret. She thought she didn't have to. Not a mistake she would make again.

'My project isn't to provide you with gossip.' She tried to flatten out her voice when it spiked with annoyance, looking from Cara to Lauren to Ant.

'Doesn't matter,' Ant said. 'Like, half of our year knows you're doing a project about Andie Bell. And why are we talking about homework on our last Friday night of freedom? Zach, bring out the board.'

'What board?' Cara asked.

'I bought a Ouija board. Cool, huh?' Zach said, dragging

his rucksack over. He pulled out a tacky plastic-looking board adorned with the alphabet and a planchette with a little plastic window you could see the letters through. He laid them out in the middle of the circle.

'Nope,' Lauren said, crossing her arms. 'No way. That's way over the scary boundary. Stories are fine, but no board.'

Pip lost interest in the boys trying to convince Lauren so they could play whatever prank it was they had planned. Probably about Andie Bell again. She reached over the Ouija board to grab another bag of crisps and that's when she saw it.

A white light flash from within the trees.

She sat up on her heels and squinted. It happened again. In the distant dark a small rectangular light turned into view and then disappeared. Like the glow of a phone screen extinguished by the lock button.

She waited but the light didn't come back. There was only darkness out there. The sound of rain in the air. The silhouettes of sleeping trees against the gloom of the moon.

Until one of the dark tree figures shifted on two legs.

'Guys,' she said quietly. A small kick to Ant's shin to shut him up. 'No one look now, but I think there's someone in the trees. Watching us.'

Eleven

'Where?' Connor mouthed, his eyes narrowing as they held Pip's.

'My ten o'clock,' she whispered. Fear like a blistering frost dripped into her stomach. Wide eyes spread like a contagion around the circle.

And then with an eruption of sound Connor grabbed a torch and sprang to his feet.

'Hey, pervert,' he yelled with unlikely courage. He sprinted out of the marquee and into the darkness, the light beam swinging wildly in his hand as he ran.

'Connor!' Pip called after him, disentangling herself from her sleeping bag. She grabbed the torch out of a dumbfounded Ant's hands and took off after her friend into the trees. 'Connor, wait!'

Shut in on all sides by black spidery shadows, snatches of lit trees jumped out at Pip as the torch shook in her hands and her feet pounded the mud. Drops of rain hung in the beam.

'Connor,' she screamed again, chasing the only sign of him up ahead, a vein of torchlight through the stifling darkness.

Behind her she heard more feet crashing through the forest, someone shouting her name. One of the girls screaming.

A stitch was already starting to split in her side as she tore on, the adrenaline swallowing any last dregs of beer that might have dulled her. She was sharp and she was ready.

'Pip,' someone shouted in her ear.

Ant had caught up with her, the torch on his phone guiding his feet through the trees.

'Where's Con?' he panted.

There was no air left in her. She pointed at the flickering light ahead and Ant overtook her.

And still there was the sound of feet behind her. She tried to look around but could only see a pinpoint of growing white light.

She faced forwards, and a flash from her torch threw two hunched figures at her. She swerved and fell to her knees to avoid crashing into them.

'Pip, you OK?' Ant said breathlessly, offering his hand.

'Yeah.' She sucked at the humid air, a cramp now twisting into her chest and gut. 'Connor, what the hell?'

'I lost him,' Connor gasped, his head by his knees. 'I think I lost him a while back.'

'It was a man? Did you see him?' Pip asked.

Connor shook his head. 'No, I didn't see it was a man, but it had to be, right? I only saw that they were wearing a dark hood. Whoever it was ducked out of the way while my torch was down, and I stupidly kept following the same path.'

'Stupidly chased them in the first place,' Pip said angrily. 'By yourself.'

'Obviously!' Connor said. 'Some pervert in the woods at midnight, watching us and probably touching himself.

Wanted to beat the crap out of him.'

'That was needlessly dangerous,' she said. 'What were you trying to prove?'

There was a flash of white in Pip's periphery and Zach emerged, pulling up just before he collided with her and Ant.

'What the hell?' was all he said.

Then they heard the scream.

'Shit,' Zach said, turning on his heels and sprinting back the way he'd just come.

'Cara! Lauren!' Pip shouted, gripping her torch and following Zach, the other two beside her. Through the dark trees again, their nightmare fingers catching her hair. Her stitch ripping deeper with each step.

Half a minute later, they found Zach using his phone to light up where the two girls stood together, arm in arm, Lauren in tears.

'What happened?' Pip said, wrapping her arms round them both, all shivering even though the night was warm. 'Why did you scream?'

'Because we got lost and the torch smashed and we're drunk,' Cara said.

'Why didn't you stay in the marquee?' Connor said.

'Because you all left us,' Lauren cried.

'OK, OK,' Pip said. 'We've all overreacted a bit. Everything's fine; we just need to head back to the marquee. They've run off now, whoever it was, and there are six of us, OK? We're all fine.' She wiped the tears from Lauren's chin.

*

It took them almost fifteen minutes, even with the torches, to find their way back to the marquee; the woods were a different planet at night. They even had to use the map app on Zach's phone to see how far they were from the road. Their steps quickened when they caught sight of distant snatches of white canvas between the trunks and the soft yellow glow of the battery lanterns.

No one spoke much as they did a speedy clean-up of the empty drink cans and food packets into a bin bag, clearing space for their sleeping bags. They dropped all the sides of the marquee, safe within its four white canvas walls, their only view of the trees distorted through the mock plastic sheet windows.

The boys were already starting to joke about their midnight sprint through the trees. Lauren wasn't ready for jokes yet.

Pip moved Lauren's sleeping bag between hers and Cara's and helped her into it when she could no longer bear to watch her drunkenly fumble with the zip.

'I'm guessing no Ouija board then?' Ant said.

'Think we've had enough scares,' said Pip.

She sat next to Cara for a while, forcing water down her friend's throat while she distracted her by talking idly about the fall of Rome. Lauren was already asleep, Zach too on the other side of the marquee.

When Cara's eyelids began to wilt lower with each blink, Pip crept back to her own sleeping bag. She saw that Ant and

106

Connor were still awake and whispering, but she was ready for sleep, or at least to lie down and hope for sleep. As she slid her legs inside, something crinkled against her right foot. She pulled her knees up to her chest and reached inside, her fingers closing round a piece of paper.

Must have been a food packet that fell inside. She pulled it out. It wasn't. It was a clean white piece of printer paper folded in half.

She unfolded the paper, eyes skipping across it.

In a large formal font printed across the page were the words: *Stop digging, Pippa.*

She dropped it, eyes following as it fell open. Her breath time-travelled back to running in the dark, snapshots of trees in the flashing torchlight. Disbelief staled to fear. Five seconds there and the feeling crisped at the edges, burning into anger.

'What the hell?' she said, picking up the note and storming over to the boys.

'Shh,' one of them said, 'the girls are asleep.'

'Do you think this is funny?' Pip said, looking down at them as she brandished the folded note. 'You are unbelievable.'

'What are you talking about?' Ant squinted at her.

'This note you left me.'

'I didn't leave you a note,' he said, reaching up for it.

Pip pulled away. 'You expect me to believe that?' she said. 'Was this whole stranger-in-the-woods thing a set-up too? Part of your joke? Who was it, your friend George?'

'No, Pip,' Ant said, staring up at her. 'Honestly don't know what you're talking about. What does the note say?'

'Save me the innocent act,' she said. 'Connor, care to add anything?'

'Pip, you think I would have chased that pervert so hard if it was just a bloody prank? We didn't plan anything, I promise.'

'You're saying neither of you left me this note?'

They both nodded.

'You're full of shit,' she said, turning back to the girls' side of the marquee.

'Honestly, Pip, we didn't,' Connor said.

Pip ignored him, clambering into her sleeping bag and making more noise about it than was necessary.

She laid down, using her scrunched-up jumper as a pillow, the note left open on the groundsheet beside her. She turned to watch it, ignoring four more whispered 'Pip's from Ant and Connor.

Pip was the last one awake. She could tell by the breathing. Alone in wakefulness.

From the ashes of her anger a new creature was born, creating itself from the cinders and dust. A feeling that fell between terror and doubt, between chaos and logic.

She said the words in her head so many times that they became rubbery and foreign-sounding.

Stop digging, Pippa.

It couldn't be. It was just a cruel joke. Just a joke.

She couldn't look away from the note, her eyes sleeplessly

tracing back and forward over the curves of the black printed letters.

And the forest in the dead of night was alive around her. Crackling twigs, wingbeats through the trees and screams. Fox or deer, she couldn't tell, but they shrieked and cried and it was and wasn't Andie Bell, screaming through the crust of time.

Stop digging, Pippa.

PART II

Twelve

Pip was fidgeting nervously under the table, hoping that Cara was too busy jabbering to notice. It was the first time ever that Pip had to keep things from her and the nerves were puppet-stringing Pip's fiddling hands and the knot in her stomach.

Pip had gone over after school on the third day back, when teachers stopped talking about what they were going to teach and actually started teaching. They were sitting in the Wards' kitchen pretending to do homework, but really Cara was unspooling into an existential crisis.

'And I told him that I still don't know what I want to study at uni, let alone where I want to go. And he's all "time's ticking, Cara" and it's stressing me out. Have you had the talk with your parents yet?'

'Yeah, a few days ago,' Pip said. 'I've decided on King's College, Cambridge.'

'English?'

Pip nodded.

'You are the worst person to vent to about life plans,' Cara snorted. 'I bet you already know what you want to be when you grow up.'

'Of course,' she said. 'I want to be Louis Theroux and Heather Brooke and Michelle Obama all rolled into one.'

'Your efficiency offends me.'

A loud train whistle erupted from Pip's phone.

'Who's that?' Cara asked.

'It's just Ravi Singh,' Pip said, scanning the text, 'seeing if I have any more updates.'

'Oh, we're texting each other now, are we?' Cara said playfully. 'Should I be saving a date next week for the wedding?'

Pip threw a ballpoint pen at her. Cara dodged expertly.

'Well, do you have any Andie Bell updates?' she said.

'No,' Pip said. 'Absolutely nothing new.'

The lie made the knot in her gut squeeze tighter.

Ant and Connor were still denying authorship of the note in her sleeping bag when she'd asked them at school. They'd suggested maybe it was Zach or one of the girls. Of course, their denial wasn't solid proof it hadn't been them. But Pip had to consider the other possibility: *what if*? What if it was actually someone involved in the Andie Bell case trying to scare her into giving up the project? Someone who had a lot to lose if she kept going.

She told no one about the note: not the girls, not the boys when they asked what it said, not her parents, not even Ravi. Their concern might stop her project dead in its tracks. And she had to take control of any possible leaks. She had secrets to hold to her chest and she would learn from the master, Miss Andrea Bell.

'Where's your dad?' asked Pip.

'Duh, he came in, like, fifteen minutes ago to say

he was off tutoring.'

'Oh yeah,' Pip said. Lies and secrets were distracting. Elliot had always tutored three times a week; it was part of the Ward routine and Pip knew it well. Her nerves were making her sloppy. Cara would notice before long; she knew her too well. Pip had to calm down; she was here for a reason. And being skittish would get her caught out.

She could hear the buzz and thud of the television in the other room; Naomi was watching some American drama that involved a lot of *pew-pewing* from silenced guns and shouts of 'Goddamit'.

Now was Pip's perfect moment to act.

'Hey, can I borrow your laptop for two secs?' she asked Cara, relaxing her face so it wouldn't betray her. 'Just want to look up this book for English.'

'Yep, sure,' Cara said, passing it across the table. 'Don't close my tabs.'

'Won't,' Pip said, turning the laptop so Cara couldn't see the screen.

Pip's heartbeat bolted into the tops of her ears. There was so much blood behind her face she was sure she must be turning red. Leaning down to hide behind the screen, she clicked up the control panel.

She'd been up until three last night, that *what if* question haunting her, chasing away sleep. So she had trawled through the internet, looking at badly worded forum questions and wireless printer instruction manuals.

Anyone could have followed her there into the woods. That was true. Anyone could have watched her, lured her and her friends out of the marquee so they could leave their message. True. But there was one name on her persons of interest list, one person who would have known exactly where Pip and Cara were camping. Naomi. She'd been stupid to discount her because of the Naomi she thought she knew. There could well be another Naomi. One who may or may not be lying about leaving Max's for a period of time the night Andie died. One who may or may not have been in love with Sal. One who may or may not have hated Andie enough to kill her.

After hours of stubborn research, Pip had learned that there was no way to see the previous documents a wireless printer had printed. And no one in their right mind would save a note like that on their computer, so attempting to look through Naomi's would be pointless. But there was something else she could do.

She clicked into *Devices and Printers* on Cara's laptop and hovered the mouse over the name of the Ward family printer, which someone had nicknamed *Freddie Prints Jr.* She right-clicked into *Printer Properties* and on to the advanced tab.

Pip had memorized the steps from a 'how to' webpage with cartoon illustrations. She checked the box next to *Keep Printed Documents*, clicked apply and it was done. She closed down the panel and clicked back on to Cara's homework.

'Thanks,' she said, passing the laptop back, certain that her heart was loud enough to hear, a boom box sewn on the outside of her chest.

'No problemo.'

Cara's laptop would now keep track of everything that came through their printer. If Pip received another printed message, she could find out for definite if it had come from Naomi or not.

The kitchen door opened with an explosion from the White House and federal agents screaming to 'Get out of here!' and 'Save yourself!' Naomi stood in the door frame.

'God, Nai,' Cara said, 'we're working in here, turn it down.'

'Sorry,' she whispered, as though it compensated for the loud TV. 'Just getting a drink. You OK, Pip?' Naomi looked at her with a puzzled expression and only then did Pip realize she had been staring.

'Err . . . yep. You just made me jump,' she said, her smile just a little too wide, carving uncomfortably into her cheeks.

Production Log – Entry 13

Transcript of second interview with Emma Hutton

Pip: Thanks for agreeing to talk again. This is a really short follow-up, I promise.

Emma: Yeah, no that's fine.

Pip: Thanks. OK, so firstly I've been asking around about Andie and I've heard certain rumours I wanted to run by you. That Andie may have been seeing someone at the same time as Sal. An older guy perhaps? Had you ever heard anything like that?

Emma: Who told you that?

Pip: Sorry, they asked me to keep them anonymous.

Emma: Was it Chloe Burch?

Pip: Again, sorry, I was asked not to say.

Emma: It had to be her; we were the only ones who knew.

Pip: So it's true? Andie was seeing an older man during her relationship with Sal?

Emma: Well, yeah, that's what she said; she never told us his name or anything.

Pip: Did you have any indication about how long it had been going on for?

Emma: Like, not long at all before she went missing. I think she started talking about it in March. That's just a guess, though.

Pip: And you knew nothing about who it was?

Emma: No, she liked teasing us that we didn't know.

Pip: And you didn't think it was relevant to tell the police?

Emma: No because, honestly, those are the only details we ever knew.

And I kind of thought Andie had made him up for some drama.

Pip: And after the whole Sal thing happened, you never thought to tell the police that that could be a possible motive?

Emma: No, 'cause again I wasn't convinced he was real. And Andie wasn't stupid; she wouldn't have told Sal about him.

Pip: But what if Sal found out anyway?

Emma: Hmm, I don't think so. Andie was good at keeping secrets.

Pip: OK, moving on to my final question, I was wondering if you knew whether Andie had ever fallen out with Naomi Ward. Or whether they had a strained relationship?

Emma: Naomi Ward, Sal's friend?

Pip: Yeah.

Emma: No, not to my knowledge.

Pip: Andie never mentioned any tension with Naomi or said bad things about her?

Emma: No. Actually, now you mention it, she definitely was hating on one of the Wards, but it wasn't Naomi.

Pip: What do you mean?

Emma: You know Mr Ward, the history teacher? I don't know if he's still at Kilton Grammar. But yeah, Andie did not like him. I remember her referring to him as an arsehole, among other stronger words.

Pip: Why? When was this?

Emma: Um, I couldn't say specifically but I think it was around that Easter. So, not long before everything happened.

Pip: But Andie wasn't taking history?

Emma: No, it must have been something like he'd told her that her skirt was too short for school. She always hated that.

Pip: OK that's everything I needed to ask. Thanks again for all your help, Emma.

Emma: No worries. Bye.

NO. Just no.

First Naomi, who I can't even look in the eye any more. And now Elliot? Why are questions about Andie Bell returning answers about the people close to me?

OK, Andie insulting a teacher to her friends in the lead-up to her death looks like an utter coincidence. Yes. It could be entirely innocent.

But – and it's quite a big but – Elliot told me he hardly knew Andie or had anything to do with her in the last two years of her life. So why did she call him an arsehole if they had nothing to do with each other? Was Elliot lying, and for what reason?

I would be a hypocrite if I didn't speculate wildly, as I have before, just because I'm close to Elliot. So even though it physically pains me: could this innocuous clue, in fact, indicate that Elliot Ward was the secret older man? I mean, I first thought the 'secret older guy' would be someone in their mid to late twenties. But maybe my instincts were wrong; maybe it refers to someone much older. I baked the cake for Elliot's last birthday, so I know he's now forty-seven, which would have made him forty-two in the year of Andie's disappearance.

Andie told her friends she could 'ruin' this man. I thought this meant that the guy – whoever he was – was married. Elliot wasn't; his wife had died a couple of years before. But he was a teacher at her school, in a position of trust. If there was some inappropriate relationship, Elliot could have faced jail time. That certainly can be covered under 'ruining' someone.

Is he the type of person who would do that? No, he isn't. And is he the kind of man a seventeen-year-old beautiful blonde student would lust after? I don't think so. I mean, he's not hideous and he has a certain greying professorial look but . . . just no. I can't see it.

I can't believe I'm even allowing myself to think this. Who will be next on the persons of interest list? Cara? Ravi? Dad? Me?

I think I should just grit my teeth and ask Elliot so I can bite down on some actual facts. Otherwise I may end up suspecting everybody I know who may have spoken to Andie at some point in their lives. And paranoia does not suit me.

But how do you casually ask a grown man you've known since you were six why they lied about a murdered girl?

Persons of Interest

Jason Bell

Naomi Ward

Secret Older Guy

Elliot Ward

Thirteen

Her writing hand must have had its own mind, an independent circuitry from the one contained in her head.

Mr Ward was speaking, 'But Lenin did not like Stalin's policy towards Georgia after the Red Army invasion in 1921,' and Pip's fingers moved in harmony, scribbling it all down with dates underlined too. But she wasn't really listening.

There was a war going on inside her, the two sides of her head squabbling and pecking at each other. Should she ask Elliot about Andie's comments, or was that a risk to the investigation? Was it rude to ask probing questions about murdered students, or was it an entirely forgivable Pippism?

The bell rang for lunch and Elliot called over the scraping chairs and zipping bags, 'Read chapter three before our next lesson. And if you want to be really keen, you can Trotsky on over to chapter four as well.' He chuckled at his own joke.

'You coming, Pip?' Connor said, standing up and swinging his rucksack on to his back.

'Um, yeah I'll come find you lot in a minute,' she said. 'I need to ask Mr Ward something first.'

'You need to ask Mr Ward something, eh?' Elliot had overheard. 'That's ominous. I hope you haven't started thinking about the coursework already.'

'No, well, yes I have,' Pip said, 'but that's not what

I want to ask you about.'

She waited until they were the only two left in the classroom.

'What is it?' Elliot glanced down at his watch. 'You have ten of my minutes before I start panicking about the panini queue.'

'Yeah, sorry,' Pip said, grasping for her stash of courage but it leaked out of reach. 'Um . . .'

'Everything OK?' Elliot said, sitting back on his desk, his arms and legs crossed. 'You worrying about university applications? We can go over your personal statement some time if –'

'No, it's not that.' She took a breath and blew out her top lip. 'I . . . when I interviewed you before you said you didn't have anything to do with Andie in the last two years of school.'

'Yes, correct.' He blinked. 'She didn't take history.'

'OK, but –' the courage trickled back all at once and her words raced each other out – 'one of Andie's friends said that, excuse the language, Andie referred to you as an arsehole and other unsavoury words sometime in the weeks before she went missing.'

The why question was evidently there hiding beneath her words; she didn't need to speak it.

'Oh,' Elliot said, rubbing the dark hair back from his face. He looked at her and sighed. 'Well, I was hoping this wouldn't come up. I don't see what good it can do to dwell on it now. But I can see you're being very thorough with your project.'

Pip nodded, her long silence beckoning an answer.

Elliot shuffled. 'I don't feel too comfortable about it, saying unpleasant things about a student who has lost their life.' He glanced up at the open classroom door and scooted over to shut it. 'Um, I didn't have much to do with Andie at school but I knew of her, of course, as Naomi's dad. And . . . it was in that capacity, through Naomi, that I learned some things about Andie Bell.'

'Yes?'

'No soft way of saying it but . . . she was a bully. She was bullying another girl in their year. I can't remember her name now, something Portuguese-sounding. There was some sort of incident, a video online that Andie had posted.'

Pip was both surprised and not at all. Yet another path opening up in the maze of Andie Bell's life. Palimpsest upon palimpsest, the original concept of Andie only just peeking out through all the overlaying scribbles.

'I knew enough to understand that Andie would be in trouble with both the school and the police for what she'd done,' Elliot continued. 'And I . . . I thought it was a shame because it was the first week back after Easter and her A-level exams were coming up. Exams that would determine her entire future.' He sighed. 'What I should have done, when I found out, was tell the head teacher about the incident. But the school has a no-tolerance policy on bullying or cyber-bullying and I knew Andie would be expelled immediately. No A levels, no university and I, well, I just couldn't do it. Even though she was a bully, I couldn't live with myself knowing I'd play a part in ruining a student's future.'

'So what did you do?' Pip asked.

'I looked up her father's contact details and I called him, the first day of term after the Easter holidays.'

'You mean the Monday of the week Andie disappeared?'

Elliot nodded. 'Yes, I suppose it was. I phoned Jason Bell and I told him everything I'd learned and said that he needed to have a very serious talk with his daughter about bullying and consequences. And I suggested restricting her online access. I said I was trusting him to sort this out, otherwise I would have no choice but to inform the school and have Andie expelled.'

'And what did he say?'

'Well, he was thankful that I was giving his daughter a second chance she possibly didn't deserve. And he promised he would sort it out and talk to her. I'm guessing now that when Mr Bell did speak to Andie he mentioned that I was the source of the information. So, if I was the target of some choice words from Andie that week, I'm not entirely surprised, I must say. Disappointed is all.'

Pip took a deep breath, one glazed with undisguised relief.

'What's that for?'

'I'm just glad you weren't lying for a worse reason.'

'Think you've read too many mystery novels, Pip. Why not some historical biographies instead?' He smiled gently.

'They can be just as disturbing as fiction.' She paused. 'You'd never told anyone before, had you . . . about

Andie's bullying?'

'Of course not. It seemed pointless after everything that happened. Insensitive too.' He scratched his chin. 'I try not to think about it because I get lost in butterfly-effect theories. What if I had just told the school and Andie was expelled that week? Would it have changed the outcome? Would the conditions that led to Sal killing her not have been in place? Would those two still be alive?'

'That's a rabbit hole you shouldn't go down,' Pip said. 'And you definitely don't remember the girl that who bullied?'

'No, sorry,' he said. 'Naomi would remember; you could ask her about it. Not sure what this has to do with use of media in criminal investigations, though.' He looked at her with a slightly scolding look.

'Well, I'm yet to decide on my final title,' she smiled.

'OK, well, don't go falling down your own rabbit hole.' He wagged his finger. 'And now I'm running away from you because I'm desperate for a tuna melt.' He smiled and dashed out into the corridor.

Pip felt lighter, the bulk of doubt disappearing, just as Elliot now had through the door. And instead of misplaced speculation leading her astray, she now had another real lead to follow. And one less name on her list. It was a good trade to make.

But the lead was taking her back to Naomi again. And Pip would have to look her in the eyes like she didn't think there was something dark hiding behind them.

Production Log – Entry 15

Transcript of second interview with Naomi Ward

Pip: OK, recording. So, your dad told me that he found out Andie was bullying another girl in your year. Cyber-bulling. He thought there was some online video involved. Do you know anything about this?

Naomi: Yeah, like I said, I thought Andie was trouble.

Pip: Can you tell me more about it?

Naomi: There was a girl in our year, called Natalie da Silva, and she was pretty and blonde too. They looked quite similar actually. And I guess Andie felt threatened by her because ever since the start of our final year Andie started spreading rumours about her and finding ways to humiliate her.

Pip: If Sal and Andie didn't start seeing each other until that December, how did you know all this?

Naomi: I was friends with Nat. We had biology together.

Pip: Oh. And what kind of rumours was Andie starting?

Naomi: The kind of disgusting things only a teenage girl could think up. Things like her family was incestuous, that Nat watched people undress in the changing rooms and touched herself. Those kinds of things.

Pip: And you think Andie did this because Nat was pretty and she felt threatened by that?

Naomi: I actually think that was the extent of her thought process. Andie wanted to be the girl in the year that all the boys wanted. Nat was competition so Andie had to take her down.

Pip: So did you know about this video at the time?

Naomi: Yeah, it got shared all over social media. I think it wasn't taken down until a few days later when someone reported it as inappropriate content.

Pip: When was this?

Naomi: It was during the Easter holidays. Thank god it wasn't during the school term; that would have been even worse for Nat.

Pip: OK, so what was it?

Naomi: So, as far as I know, Andie had been hanging out with some friends from school, including her two minions.

Pip: Chloe Burch and Emma Hutton?

Naomi: Yeah and some other kids. Not Sal or any of us. And there was this guy, Chris Parks, who everyone knew Nat fancied. I don't know all the details, but Andie either used his phone or told him what to do, and they were sending flirty texts to Nat. And she was responding 'cause she liked Chris and thought it was him. And then Andie slash Chris asked Nat to send a video of her topless, with her face in it so he'd know it was really her.

Pip: And Nat did it?

Naomi: Yeah. A little naive, but she thought she was talking to just Chris. The next we all know, the clip is online and Andie and loads of other people are sharing it on their profiles. The comments were so horrible. And practically everyone in the year saw it before it got taken down. Nat was inconsolable. She even skipped the first two days back at school after Easter because she was so humiliated.

Pip: Sal knew Andie was doing this?

Naomi: Well, I mentioned it to him. He didn't approve obviously, but he just said, 'It's Andie's drama. I don't want to get involved.' Sal was just too laid-back about some things.

Pip: Was there anything else that happened between Nat and Andie?

Naomi:	Yeah, actually. Something I think is just as bad, but hardly anyone knew about it. I might have been the only one Nat told 'cause she was crying in biology right after it happened.
Pip:	What?
Naomi:	So in that autumn term the school was doing a sixth-form play. I think it was *The Crucible*. After auditions Nat was given the main part.
Pip:	Abigail?
Naomi:	Maybe, I don't know. And apparently Andie had wanted that part and she was really pissed off. So after the parts were posted, Andie corners Nat and she told her . . .
Pip:	Yes?
Naomi:	Sorry, I forgot to mention some context. Nat's brother, Daniel, who was, like, five years older than us, he had worked at the school part-time as a caretaker when we were like fifteen or sixteen. Only for a year while he was looking for other jobs.
Pip:	OK?
Naomi:	OK, so Andie corners Nat and says to her that when her brother was still working at the school he had sex with Andie even though she was only fifteen at the time. And Andie tells Nat to drop out of the play or she will go to the police and say she was statutorily raped by Nat's brother. And Nat dropped out because she was scared of what Andie would do.
Pip:	Was it true? Did Andie have a relationship with Nat's brother?
Naomi:	I don't know. Nat didn't know for sure either, that's why she dropped out. But I don't think she ever asked him.
Pip:	Do you know where Nat is now? Do you think I could talk to her?
Naomi:	I'm not really in contact with her, but I know she's back at home with her parents. I heard some stuff about her, though.
Pip:	What stuff?

Naomi: Um, I think at uni she was involved in some kind of fight. She got arrested and charged with ABH and I think she spent some time in prison.

Pip: Oh god.

Naomi: I know.

Pip: Can you give me her number?

Fourteen

'Did you get all dressed up to come and see me, Sarge?' Ravi said, leaning against his front door frame in a green plaid flannel shirt and jeans.

'Nope, I came straight from school,' said Pip. 'And I need your help. Put some shoes on –' she clapped her hands – 'you're coming with me.'

'Are we going on a mission?' he said, staggering back to slip on some old trainers discarded in the hallway. 'Do I need to bring my night-vision goggles and utility belt?'

'Not this time,' she smiled, starting down the garden path as Ravi closed the front door, following behind her.

'Where we going?'

'To a house where two potential Andie-killer suspects grew up,' Pip said. 'One of them just out of prison for committing an *"assault occasioning actual bodily harm"*,' she used quotation fingers around her words. 'You're my back-up as we're going to speak to a potentially violent person of interest.'

'Back-up?' he said, catching up to walk alongside her.

'You know,' Pip said, 'so there's someone there to hear my screams of help if they're required.'

'Wait, Pip.' He closed his fingers round her arm and pulled them both to a stop. 'I don't want you doing something that's actually dangerous. Sal wouldn't have wanted that either.'

'Oh, come on.' She shrugged him off. 'Nothing gets in between me and my homework, not even a little danger. And I'm just going to, very calmly, ask her a few questions.'

'Oh, it's a her?' Ravi said. 'OK then.'

Pip swung her rucksack to whack him on the arm.

'Don't think I didn't notice that,' she said. 'Women can be just as dangerous as men.'

'Ouch, tell me about it,' he said, rubbing his arm. 'What have you got in there, bricks?'

When Ravi stopped laughing at Pip's squat and bug-faced car, he clicked his seat belt into place and Pip keyed the address into her phone. She started the car and told Ravi everything she'd learned since they last spoke. Everything except the dark figure in the forest and the note in her sleeping bag. This investigation meant everything to him, and yet, she knew he would tell her to stop if he thought she was putting herself in danger. She couldn't put him in that position.

'Andie sounds like a piece of work,' he said when Pip was done. 'And yet it was so easy for everyone to believe that Sal was the monster. Wow, that was deep.' He turned to her. 'You can quote me on that in your project if you want.'

'Certainly, footnote and everything,' she said.

'Ravi Singh,' he said, drawing his words with his fingers, 'deep unfiltered thoughts, Pip's bug-faced car, 2017.'

'We had an hour-long EPQ session on footnotes today,' Pip said, eyes back on the road. 'As if they think I don't already know. I came out of the womb knowing how to do academic references.'

'Such an interesting superpower; you should call up Marvel.'

The mechanical and snobby voice on Pip's phone interrupted, telling them that in 500 yards they would reach their destination.

'Must be this one,' Pip said. 'Naomi told me it was the one with the bright blue door.' She indicated and pulled up on to the kerb. 'I rang Natalie twice yesterday. The first time she hung up after I said the words "school project". The second time she wouldn't pick up at all. Let's hope she'll actually open the door. You coming?'

'I'm not sure,' he said, pointing at his own face, 'there's that whole *murderer's brother* thing. You might get more answers if I'm not there.'

'Oh.'

'How about I stand on the path there?' He gestured to the slabs of concrete that divided the front garden up to the house, at the point where they turned sharply left to lead to the front door. 'She won't see me, but I'll be right there, ready for action.'

They stepped out of the car and Ravi handed over her rucksack, making exaggerated grunting sounds as he lifted it.

She nodded at him when he was in position and then strolled up to the front door. She prodded the bell in two short bursts, fiddling nervously with the collar of her blazer as a dark, shadowy figure appeared in the frosted glass.

The door opened slowly and a face appeared in the crack. A young woman with white-blonde hair cropped closely to her head and eyeliner raccoon-dripped around her eyes. The face beneath it all looked eerily Andie-like: similar big blue eyes and plump pale lips.

'Hi,' Pip said, 'are you Nat da Silva?'

'Y-yes,' she said hesitantly.

'My name's Pip,' she swallowed. 'I was the one who called you yesterday. I'm friends with Naomi Ward; you knew her at school, didn't you?'

'Yeah, Naomi was a friend. Why? Is she OK?' Nat looked concerned.

'Oh, she's fine,' Pip smiled. 'She's back home at the moment.'

'I didn't know.' Nat opened the door a little wider. 'Yeah, I should catch up with her sometime. So . . .'

'Sorry,' Pip said. She looked down at full-length Natalie, noticing the electronic tag buckled round her ankle. 'So, as I said when I called, I'm doing a school project and I was wondering if I could ask you some questions?' She looked quickly back up into Nat's face.

'What about?' Nat shifted the tagged foot back behind the door.

'Um, it's about Andie Bell.'

'No thanks.' Nat stood back and tried to shut the door but Pip stepped forward to block it with her foot.

'Please. I know the awful things she did to you,' she said. 'I can understand why you wouldn't want to but –'

'That bitch ruined my life.' Nat spat, 'I'm not wasting one more breath on her. Move!'

That's when they both heard the sound of a rubber sole skidding over concrete and a whispered, 'Oh crap.'

Nat glanced up and her eyes widened. 'You,' she said quietly. 'You're Sal's brother.'

It wasn't a question.

Pip turned now, her eyes falling on Ravi behind her, standing sheepishly next to the uneven slab that must have tripped him up.

'Hi,' he said, ducking his head and raising his hand, 'I'm Ravi.'

He came to stand beside Pip and as he did Nat's grip on the door loosened and she let it swing back open.

'Sal was always nice to me,' she said, 'even when he didn't have to be. The last time I spoke to him, he was offering to give up his lunch breaks to tutor me in politics because I was struggling. I'm sorry you don't have your brother any more.'

'Thank you,' Ravi said.

'It must be hard for you too,' Nat carried on, her eyes still lost in another world, 'how much this town worships Andie Bell. Kilton's saint and sweetheart. And that bench dedication she has: *Taken too soon*. Not soon enough, it should say.'

'She wasn't a saint,' Pip said gently, trying to coax Nat out from behind the door. But Nat wasn't looking at her, only at Ravi.

He stepped up. 'She bullied you?'

'Sure did,' Nat laughed bitterly, 'and she's still ruining my life, even from the grave. You've checked out my hardware.' She pointed to her ankle tag. 'Got this because I punched one of my housemates at university. We were deciding on bedrooms and this girl started pulling a stunt, exactly like Andie would've, and I just lost it.'

'We know about the video she put up of you,' Pip said. 'She should have faced charges over it; you were still a minor at the time.'

Nat shrugged. 'At least she was punished in some way that week. Some divine providence. Thanks to Sal.'

'Did you want her dead, after what she'd done to you?' Ravi asked.

'Of course I did,' Nat said darkly. 'Of course I wanted her gone. I skipped two days of school because I was so upset. And when I went back on the Wednesday, everyone was looking at me, laughing at me. I was crying in the corridor and Andie walked by and called me a slut. I was so angry that I left her a nice little note in her locker. I was too scared to ever say anything to her face.'

Pip glanced sideways at Ravi, at his tensed jaw and furrowed brows, and she knew he'd picked up on it too.

'A note?' he said. 'Was it a . . . was it a threatening note?'

'Of course it was a threatening note,' Nat laughed. '*You stupid bitch, I'm going to kill you*, something like that.

Sal got there first, though.'

'Maybe he didn't,' Pip said.

Nat turned and looked Pip in the face. Then she burst into loud and forced laughter, a mist of spit landing on Pip's cheek.

'Oh, this is too good,' she hooted. 'Are you asking me whether *I* killed Andie Bell? I had the motive, right, that's what you're thinking? You want my fucking alibi?' She laughed cruelly.

Pip didn't say anything. Her mouth was filling uncomfortably with saliva but she didn't swallow. She didn't want to move at all. She felt Ravi brushing against her shoulder, his hand skimming just past hers, disturbing the air around it.

Nat leaned towards them. 'I didn't have any friends left because of Andie Bell. I had no place to be on that Friday night. I was in playing Scrabble with my parents and my sister-in-law, tucked in by eleven. Sorry to disappoint you.'

Pip didn't have time to swallow. 'And where was your brother? If his wife was home with you?'

'He's a suspect too, is he?' Her voice darkened with a growl. 'Naomi must have been talking then. He was out at the pub drinking with his cop friends that night.'

'He's a police officer?' Ravi said.

'Just finished his training that year. So yeah, no murderers in this house, I'm afraid. Now fuck off, and tell Naomi to fuck off too.'

Nat stepped back and kicked the door shut in their faces.

Pip watched the door vibrating in its frame, her eyes so transfixed that it looked for a moment like the very particles of air were rippling from the slam. She shook her head and turned to Ravi.

'Let's go,' he said gently.

Back in the car, Pip allowed herself to just breathe for a few slow seconds, to arrange the haze of her thoughts into actual words.

Ravi found his first: 'Am I in trouble for, well, literally tripping into the interrogation. I heard raised voices and –'

'No.' Pip looked at him and couldn't help but smile. 'We're lucky you did. She only talked because you were there.'

He sat up a little straighter in his seat, his hair crushed against the roof of the car. 'So the death threat that journalist told you about,' he said.

'Came from Nat,' Pip finished, turning the key in the ignition.

She pulled the car off the kerb and drove about twenty feet up the road, out of sight of the Da Silva house, before stopping again and reaching for her phone.

'What are you doing?'

'Nat said her brother is a police officer.' She thumbed on to the browser app and started typing her search. 'Let's look him up.'

It came up as the first item when she searched: *Thames Valley Police Daniel da Silva*. A page on the national police website, telling her that PC Daniel da Silva was a constable on the local policing team covering Little Kilton. A quick check to his LinkedIn profile said he had been so since the end of 2011.

'Hey, I know him,' Ravi said, leaning over her shoulder, jabbing his finger at the picture of Daniel.

'You do?'

'Yeah. Back when I started asking questions about Sal, he was the officer who told me to give it up, that my brother was guilty beyond doubt. He does *not* like me.' Ravi's hand crept up to the back of his head, losing his fingers in his dark hair. 'Last summer, I was sitting on the tables outside the cafe. This guy –' he gestured to the photo of Daniel – 'made me move along, said I was "loitering". Funny that he didn't think all the other people outside were loitering, just the brown kid with the murderer for a brother.'

'What a contemptible arsehole,' she said. 'And he shut down all your questions about Sal?'

Ravi nodded.

'He's been a police officer in Kilton since just before Andie disappeared.' Pip stared down at her phone into Daniel's forever-smiling snapshot face. 'Ravi, if someone *did* frame Sal and make his death look like suicide, wouldn't it be easier for someone with knowledge of police procedure?'

'That it would, Sarge,' he said. 'And there's the rumour that Andie slept with him when she was fifteen, which is what she used to blackmail Nat out of the play.'

'Yes, and what if they started up again later, after Daniel was married and Andie was in her final year?

He could be the secret older guy.'

'What about Nat?' he said. 'I sort of want to believe her when she says she was home with her parents that night because she'd lost all her friends. But . . . she's also proven to be violent.' He weighed up his hands in a conceptual see-saw. 'And there's certainly motive. Maybe a brother-and-sister killer tag team?'

'Or a Nat-and-Naomi killer tag team,' Pip groaned.

'She did seem pretty angry that Naomi had talked to you,' Ravi agreed. 'What's the word count on this project, Pip?'

'Not enough, Ravi. Not nearly enough.'

'Should we just go and get ice cream and give our brains a rest?' He turned to her with that smile of his.

'Yes, we probably should.'

'As long as you're a cookie dough kinda gal. Quote, Ravi Singh,' he said dramatically into an invisible microphone, 'a thesis on the best ice-cream flavour, Pip's car, Septemb--'

'Shut up.'

'OK.'

<u>Production Log – Entry 17</u>

I can't find anything on Daniel da Silva. Nothing that gives me any further leads. There's hardly anything to learn from his Facebook profile, other than he got married in September 2011.

But if he was the secret older guy, Andie could have *ruined* him in two different ways: she could have told his new wife he was cheating and destroyed his marriage, OR she could have filed a police report about statutory rape from two years before. Both circumstances are just rumour at this point but, if true, they certainly would give Daniel a motive for wanting her dead. Andie could have blackmailed him; it's definitely not out of character for her to have been blackmailing a Da Silva.

There's nothing about his professional life online either, other than an article written by Stanley Forbes three years ago about a car collision on Hogg Hill that Daniel responded to.

But *if* Daniel is our killer, I'm thinking he might have disturbed the investigation somehow in his capacity as a police officer. A man on the inside. Perhaps when searching the Bell residence he could have stolen or tampered with any evidence that would lead back to him. Or his sister?

It's also worth noting the way he reacted to Ravi asking questions about Sal. Did he shut Ravi down to protect himself?

I've looked through all the newspaper reports on Andie's disappearance again. I've stared at pictures of the police searches until it feels like my eyes are growing scratchy little legs to climb out of their sockets and splat against the laptop screen, like grotesque little moths. I don't recognize Da Silva as any of the investigating officers.

Although there is one picture I'm not sure about. It was taken on the Sunday morning. There are some police officers in high-vis standing round the front of Andie's house. One of them is walking through the front door, his back to the camera. His hair colour and length matches Da Silva's when I cross-reference social media pictures of him from around that time.

It could be him.

It could be.

On to the list he goes.

Production Log – Entry 18

It's here!

I can't believe it's really here.

The Thames Valley Police have responded to my Freedom of Information request. Their email:

Dear Miss Fitz-Amobi,

FREEDOM OF INFORMATION REQUEST REFERENCE NO: 3142/17

I write in connection with your request for information dated 19/08/17, received by the Thames Valley Police for the following information:

I'm doing a project at school about the Andrea Bell investigation and I would like to request the following:

1. *A transcript of the interview conducted with Salil Singh on 21/04/2012*

2. *A transcript of any interviews conducted with Jason Bell*

3. *Records of the findings from the searches of the Bell residence on 21/04/2012 and 22/04/2012*

I would be very grateful if you could help with any of these requests.

Result

Requests 2 and 3 have been refused citing exemptions Section 30 (1) (a) (Investigations) and Section 40 (2) (Personal Information) of the FOIA. This email serves as a partial Refusal Notice under Section 17 of the Freedom of Information Act (2000).

Request 1 has been upheld, but the document contains redactions as per Section 30 (1) (a) (b) and Section 40 (2). The transcript is attached below.

Reasons for decision

Section 40 (2) provides an exemption for information that is the personal data of an individual other than the requester and where the disclosure of that personal data would be in breach of any of the principles of the Data Protection Act 1988 (DPA).

Section 30 (1) provides an exemption from the duty to disclose information that a public authority has held at any time for certain investigations or proceedings.

If you are not satisfied with this response, you have a right of complaint to the Information Commissioner. I should draw your attention to the attached sheet which details your right of complaint.

Yours sincerely,

Gregory Pannett

I have Sal's interview! Everything else was refused. But in their refusal they still confirmed that Jason Bell was at least interviewed in the investigation; maybe the police had their suspicions too?

The attached transcript:

Salil Singh Recorded Interview
Date: 21/04/2012
Duration: 11 minutes
Location: Interviewee's residence
Conducted by officers from the Thames Valley Police

Police: This interview is being tape recorded.
It is the 21st of April 2012 and I make it just 3:55 p.m.
My name is redacted Sec 40 (2) and I'm based at
 redacted Sec 40 (2) with the Thames Valley Police.
Also present is my colleague redacted Sec 40 (2) .
Could you please state your full name?

SS: Oh, sure, Salil Singh.

Police: And can you confirm your date of birth for me?

SS: 14th February 1994.

Police: A Valentine's baby, eh?

SS: Yeah.

Police: So, Salil, let us just get some introduction bits out of
the way first. Just so you understand, this is a voluntary
interview and you are free to stop it or ask us to leave at
any time. We are interviewing you as a significant witness
in the missing persons inquiry of Andrea Bell.

SS: But, sorry for interrupting, I told you I didn't see her after
school, so I didn't witness anything.

Police: Yes, sorry the terminology is a bit confusing. A significant
witness is also someone who has a particular relationship
to a victim, or in this case a possible victim. And as we
understand it, you are Andrea's boyfriend, correct?

SS: Yeah. No one calls her Andrea. She's Andie.

Police: OK, sorry. And how long have you and Andie been
together?

SS: Since just before Christmas last year. So around 4
months. Sorry, you said Andie was a possible victim?
I don't understand.

Police:	It's just standard procedure. She is a missing person but because she is a minor and this is out of character, we cannot wholly rule out that Andie has been a victim of a crime. Of course we hope otherwise. Are you OK?
SS:	Um, yeah, I'm just worried.
Police:	That's understandable, Salil. So the first question I'd like to ask you is when was the last time you saw Andie?
SS:	At school, like I said. We talked in the car park at the end of the day, and then I walked home and she was walking home as well.
Police:	And at any time up until that Friday afternoon, had Andie ever indicated to you a desire to run away from home?
SS:	No, never.
Police:	Did she ever tell you about any problems she was having at home, with her family?
SS:	I mean yeah we obviously talked about stuff like that. Never anything major, just normal teenager stuff. I always thought that Andie and redacted Sec 40 (2) But there wasn't anything recent that would make her want to run away, if that's what you're asking. No.
Police:	Can you think of any reason why Andie would want to leave home and not be found?
SS:	Um. I'm not sure, I don't think so.
Police:	How would you describe your relationship with Andie?
SS:	What do you mean?
Police:	Is it a sexual relationship?
SS:	Erm, yeah sort of.
Police:	Sort of?
SS:	I, we haven't actually, you know, gone all the way.
Police:	You and Andie haven't had sex?

SS: No.

Police: And would you say your relationship is a healthy one?

SS: I don't know. What do you mean?

Police: Do you argue often?

SS: No not argue. I'm not confrontational, which is why we are OK together.

Police: And were you arguing in the days before Andie went missing?

SS: Um, no. We weren't.

Police: So in written statements from ▮▮redacted Sec 40 (2)▮▮ taken this morning, they both separately allege that they saw you and Andie arguing at school this week. On the Thursday and the Friday. ▮▮redacted Sec 40 (2)▮▮ claims it's the worst she has seen you both argue since the start of your relationship. Do you know anything about this, Salil? Any truth to it?

SS: Um, maybe a bit. Andie can be a hot-head, sometimes it's hard not to answer back.

Police: And can you tell me what you were arguing about in this instance?

SS: Um, I don't, I don't know if . . . No, it's private.

Police: No, you don't want to tell me?

SS: Erm, yeah, no. I don't want to tell you.

Police: You may not think it's relevant, but even the smallest detail could help us find her.

SS: Um. No, I still can't say.

Police: Sure?

SS: Yeah.

Police: OK, let's move on then. So did you have any plans to meet up with Andie last night?

SS: No, none. I had plans with my friends.

Police: Because ▮redacted Sec 40 (2)▮ said that when Andie left the house at around 10:30 p.m., she presumed Andie was going to see her boyfriend.

SS: No, Andie knew I was at my friend's house and wasn't meeting her.

Police: So where were you last night?

SS: I was at my friend ▮redacted Sec 40 (2)▮ house. Do you want to know times?

Police: Yeah, sure.

SS: I think I got there at around 8:30, my dad dropped me. And I left at around quarter past 12 to walk home, my curfew is 1 a.m. when I'm not staying over somewhere. I think I got in just before 1, you can check with my dad, he was up.

Police: And who else was with you at ▮redacted Sec 40 (2)▮ house?

SS: ▮redacted Sec 40 (2)▮
        ▮redacted Sec 40 (2)▮

Police: And did you have any contact with Andie that evening?

SS: No, I mean she tried to call me at 9ish, but I was busy and didn't pick up. I can show you my phone?

Police: ▮redacted Sec 40 (2)▮
        And have you had any contact with her at all, since she went missing?

SS: Since I found out this morning, I've called her like a million times. It keeps going to voicemail. I think her phone is off.

Police: OK and ▮redacted Sec 40 (2)▮ did you want to ask . . .

Police: . . . Yeah. So, Salil, I know you've said you don't know, but where do you think Andie could be?

SS: Um, honestly, Andie never does anything that she doesn't want to do. I think she could just be taking a break somewhere, her phone off so she can just ignore the world for a bit. That's what I'm hoping this is.

Police: What might Andie need a break from?

SS: I don't know.

Police: And where do you think she could be taking this break?

SS: I don't know. Andie keeps a lot to herself, maybe she has some friends we don't know about. I don't know.

Police: OK, so is there anything else you might want to add that could help us find Andie?

SS: Um, no. Um, if I can, I'd like to help in any searches, if you're doing them.

Police: **redacted Sec 30 (1) (b)**
redacted Sec 30 (1) (b)
OK then, I've asked everything we need to at the moment. I'm going to end the interview there, it's 4:06 p.m. and I shall stop the tape.

OK, deep breath. I've read it over six times, even out loud. And now I have this horrible, sinking feeling in my gut, like being both unbearably hungry and unbearably full.

This does not look great for Sal.

I know it's sometimes hard to read nuances from a transcript, but Sal was *very* evasive with the police about what he and Andie were arguing about. I don't think anything is too private that you wouldn't tell the police if it could help find your missing girlfriend.

If it was potentially about Andie seeing another man, why didn't Sal just tell the police? It could have led them to the possible real killer right at the start.

But what if Sal was covering up something worse? Something that would have given him real motive to kill Andie. We know he's lying elsewhere in this interview; when he tells the police what time he left Max's.

It would crush me to have come all this way just to find out that Sal really is guilty. Ravi would be devastated. Maybe I should never have started this project, should never have spoken to him. I'm going to have to show him the transcript, I told him just yesterday that I was expecting a reply any day now. But I don't know how he's going to take it. Or . . . maybe I could lie and say it hasn't arrived yet?

Could Sal really have been guilty all along? Sal as the killer has always been the path of least resistance, but was it so easy for everyone to believe because it's also true?

But no: *The note.*

Somebody warned me to stop digging.

Yes, the note could have been someone's idea of a prank, and if the note was a joke, then Sal could be the real killer. But it doesn't feel right. Someone in this town has something to hide and they're scared because I'm on the right path to chasing them down.

I just have to keep chasing, even when the path is resisting me.

Persons of Interest

Jason Bell

Naomi Ward

Secret Older Guy

Nat da Silva

Daniel da Silva

Fifteen

'Take my hand,' Pip said, reaching down and cupping her fingers round Joshua's.

They crossed the road, Josh's palm sticky in her right hand, Barney's lead grating in the other as the dog pulled ahead.

She let go of Josh when they reached the pavement outside the cafe and crouched to loop Barney's lead round the leg of a table.

'Sit. Good boy,' she said, stroking his head as he looked up at her with a tongue-lolling smile.

She opened the door to the cafe and ushered Josh inside.

'I'm a good boy too,' he said.

'Good boy, Josh,' she said, absently patting his head as she scanned the sandwich shelves. She picked out four different flavours, brie and bacon for Dad, of course, and cheese and ham *'without the icky bits'* for Josh. She took the bundle of sandwiches up to the till.

'Hi, Jackie,' she said, smiling as she handed over the money.

'Hello, sweetheart. Big Amobi lunch plans?'

'We're assembling garden furniture and it's getting tense,' Pip said. 'Need sandwiches to placate the hangry troops.'

'Ah, I see,' said Jackie. 'Would you tell your mum I'll pop by next week with my sewing machine?'

'I shall do, thanks.' Pip took the paper bag from her and

turned back to Josh. 'Come on then, squirt.'

They were almost at the door when Pip spotted her, sitting at a table alone, her hands cupped round a takeaway coffee. Pip hadn't seen her in town for years; she'd presumed she was still away at university. She must be twenty-one by now, maybe twenty-two. And here she was just feet away, tracing her fingertips over the furrowed words *caution hot beverage,* looking more like Andie than she ever had before.

Her face was slimmer now, and she'd started dying her hair lighter, just like her sister's had been. But hers was cut short and blunt above her shoulders where Andie's had hung down to her waist. Yet even though the likeness was there, Becca Bell's face did not have the composite magic of her sister's, a girl who had looked more like a painting than a real person.

Pip knew she shouldn't; she knew it was wrong and insensitive and all those words Mrs Morgan had used in her '*I'm just concerned about the direction of your project*' warnings. And even though she could feel the sensible and rational parts of herself rallying in her head, she knew that a small sliver of Pip had already made the decision. That flake of recklessness inside contaminating all other thoughts.

'Josh,' she said, handing him the sandwich bag, 'can you go and sit outside with Barney for a minute? I'll be two seconds.'

He looked pleadingly up at her.

'You can play on my phone,' she said, digging it out of her pocket.

'Yes,' he said in hissed victory, taking it and scrolling

150

straight to the page where the games were, bumping into the door on his way out.

Pip's heart kicked up in an agitated protest. She could feel it like a turbulent clock in the base of her throat, the ticking fast-forward in huddling pairs.

'Hi. Becca, isn't it?' she said, walking over and placing her hands on the back of the empty chair.

'Yeah. Do I know you?' Becca's eyebrows dropped in scrutiny.

'No, you don't.' She tried to don her warmest smile but it felt stretchy and tight. 'I'm Pippa, I live in town. Just in my last year at Kilton Grammar.'

'Oh, wait,' Becca said, shuffling in her seat, 'don't tell me. You're the girl doing a project about my sister, aren't you?'

'Wh-wh–' Pip stammered. 'How did you know?'

'I'm, err.' She paused. 'I'm kind of seeing Stanley Forbes. Kind of not.' She shrugged.

Pip tried to hide her shock with a fake cough. 'Oh. Nice guy.'

'Yeah.' Becca looked down at her coffee. 'I just graduated and I'm doing an internship over at the *Kilton Mail*.'

'Oh, cool,' Pip said. 'I actually want to be a journalist too. An investigative journalist.'

'Is that why you're doing a project about Andie?' She went back to tracing her finger round the rim of the cup.

'Yes,' Pip nodded. 'And I'm sorry for intruding and you can absolutely tell me to go away if you want. I just wondered

151

whether you could answer some questions I have about your sister.'

Becca sat forward in her chair, her hair swinging about her neck. She coughed. 'Um, what kind of questions?'

Far too many; they all rushed in at the same time and Pip spluttered.

'Oh,' she said. 'Like, did you and Andie get an allowance from your parents as teenagers?'

Becca's face scrunched in a wrinkled, bemused look. 'Um, that's not what I was expecting you to ask. But no, not really. They kind of just bought us stuff as and when we needed it. Why?'

'Just . . . filling in some gaps,' Pip said. 'And was there ever tension between your sister and your dad?'

Becca's eyes dropped to the floor.

'Erm.' Her voice cracked. She wrapped her hands round the cup and stood, the chair screaming as it scraped against the tiled floor. 'Actually, I don't think this is a good idea,' she said, rubbing her nose. 'Sorry. It's just . . .'

'No, I'm sorry,' Pip said, stepping back, 'I shouldn't have come over.'

'No, it's OK,' Becca said. 'It's just that things are finally settled again. Me and my mum, we've found our new normal and things are getting better. I don't think dwelling on the past . . . on Andie stuff, is healthy for either of us. Especially not my mum. So, yeah.' She shrugged. 'You do your project if that's what you want to do, but I'd prefer it if you left us out of it.'

'Absolutely,' Pip said. 'I'm so sorry.'

'No worries.' Becca's head dipped in a hesitant nod as she walked briskly past Pip and out of the cafe door.

Pip waited several moments and then followed her out, suddenly enormously glad she had changed out of the grey T-shirt she'd been wearing earlier, otherwise she'd now certainly be modelling giant dark grey pit-rings.

'All right,' she said, unhooking Barney's lead from the table, 'let's get home.'

'Don't think that lady liked you,' Josh said, his eyes still down on the cartoon figures dancing across her phone screen. 'Were you being unfriendly, hippo pippo?'

<u>Production Log – Entry 19</u>

I know, I pushed my luck trying to question Becca. It was wrong. I just couldn't help myself; she was right there, two steps away from me. The last person to see Andie alive, other than the killer of course.

Her sister was murdered. I can't expect her to want to talk about it, even if I am trying to find the truth. And if Mrs Morgan finds out, my project will be disqualified. Not that I think that would stop me at this point.

But I am lacking a certain insight into Andie's home life and, of course, it's not even in the realm of possibility or acceptability to try to speak to her parents.

I've been stalking Becca on Facebook back to five years ago, pre-murder. Other than learning that her hair used to be mousier and her cheeks fuller, it looks like she had one really close friend in 2012. A girl called Jess Walker. Maybe Jess will be detached enough to not be as emotional about Andie, yet close enough that I can get some of the answers I desperately need.

Jess Walker's profile is very neat and informative. She's currently at university in Newcastle. Just scrolled back to five years ago (it took forever) and nearly all of her photos were taken with Becca Bell back then, until they abruptly aren't.

Crap crap fudging bugger monkeypoo crapola arse chops . . .

I just accidentally liked one of her photos from five years ago.

Damn it. Could I look any more like a stalker??? I've un-liked it now but she'll still get the notification. Grr, laptop/tablet hybrids with touch screens are ABSOLUTELY HAZARDOUS to the casual Facebook prowler.

It's too late now anyway. She'll know I've been poking my nose into her life half a decade ago. I'll send her a private message and see if she'd be willing to give me a phone interview.

STUPID CLUMSY THUMBS.

Production Log – Entry 20

Transcript of interview with Jess Walker (Becca Bell's friend)

[We talk a bit about Little Kilton, about how the school has changed since she left, which teachers are still there, etc. It's a few minutes until I can steer the conversation back to my project.]

Pip: So I wanted to ask you, really, about the Bells, not just Andie. What kind of family they were, how did they get on? Things like that.

Jess: Oh, well I mean, that's a loaded question right there. (She sniffs.)

Pip: What do you mean?

Jess: Um, I don't know if dysfunctional is quite the right word. People use that as a funny kind of accolade. I'd mean it in the proper sense. Like they weren't quite normal. I mean, they were normal enough; they seemed normal unless you spent a lot of time there, like I did. And I picked up on a lot of little things that you wouldn't have noticed if you didn't live among the Bells.

Pip: What do you mean by not quite normal?

Jess: I don't know if that's a good way of describing it. There were just a couple of things that weren't quite right. It was mainly Jason, Becca's dad.

Pip: What did he do?

Jess: It was just the way he spoke to them, the girls and Dawn. If you only saw it a couple of times, you'd think he was just trying to be funny. But I saw it often, very often, and I think it definitely affected the environment in that house.

Pip: What?

Jess: Sorry, I'm talking in circles, aren't I? It's quite difficult to explain. Um. He would just say things to them, always little digs about how they looked and stuff. The total opposite of how you should talk to your teenage daughters. He'd pick up on things he knew they were self-conscious about. He said things to Becca about her weight and would laugh it off as a joke. He'd tell Andie she needed to put on make-up before she left the house, that her face was her money-maker. Jokes like this all the time. Like how they looked was the most important thing in the world. I remember when I was over for dinner one time Andie was upset that she didn't get any offers from the universities she'd applied to, only one from her back-up, that local one. And Jason said, 'Oh, it doesn't matter, you're only going to university to find a rich husband anyway.'

Pip: No?!

Jess: And he did it to his wife too; he'd say really uncomfortable things when I was there. Like how she was looking old, joking around counting wrinkles on her face. Saying that he'd married her for her looks and she'd married him for his money and only one of them was upholding their deal. I mean, they would all laugh when he did it, like it was just family teasing. But seeing it happen so many times, it was . . . unsettling. I didn't like being there.

Pip: And do you think it affected the girls?

Jess: Oh, Becca never, ever wanted to talk about her dad. But, yes, it was obvious it played havoc with their self-esteem. Andie started caring so much about what she looked like, about what people thought of her. There would be screaming matches when her parents said it was time to go out and Andie wasn't ready, hadn't done her hair or make-up yet. Or when they refused to buy her a new lipstick she said she *needed*. How that girl could ever have thought she was ugly is beyond me. Becca became obsessed with her flaws; she started skipping meals. It affected them in different ways, though: Andie got louder, Becca got quieter.

Pip: And what was the relationship between the sisters like?

Jess: Jason's influence was all over that as well. He made everything in that house a competition. If one of the girls did something

	good, like got a good grade, he would use it to put the other one down.
Pip:	But what were Becca and Andie like together?
Jess:	I mean, they were teenage sisters, they fought like hell and then a few minutes later it was forgotten. Becca always looked up to Andie, though. They were really close in age, only fifteen months between them. Andie was in the year just above us at school. And when we turned sixteen Becca started, I guess, trying to copy Andie. I think because Andie always seemed so confident, so admired. Becca started trying to dress like her. She begged her dad to start teaching her to drive early so that as soon as she was seventeen she could take her test and get a car, like Andie had. She started wanting to go out like Andie too, to house parties.
Pip:	You mean the ones called calamity parties?
Jess:	Yeah, yeah. Even though it was people in the year above that threw them, and we hardly knew anyone, she convinced me to go one time. I think it was in March, so not too long before Andie's disappearance. Andie hadn't invited her or anything, Becca just found out where the next one was being hosted and we turned up. We walked there.
Pip:	How was it?
Jess:	Ugh, awful. We just sat in the corner all night, not talking to anyone. Andie completely blanked Becca; I think she was angry she'd turned up. We drank a bit and then Becca completely disappeared on me. I couldn't find her anywhere among all the drunk teenagers and I had to walk home, tipsy, all by myself. I was really angry at Becca. Even more angry the next day when she finally answered her phone and I found out what happened.
Pip:	What happened?
Jess:	She wouldn't tell me but I mean it was pretty obvious when she asked me to go and get the morning-after pill with her. I asked and asked and she just would not tell me who she'd slept with. I think she might have been embarrassed. That upset me at the time, though. Especially as she had considered it important

enough to completely abandon me at a party I never wanted to go to. We had a big fight and, I guess, that was the start of the wedge in our friendship. Becca skipped some school and I didn't see her for a few weekends. And that's when Andie went missing.

Pip: Did you see the Bells much after Andie disappeared?

Jess: I visited a few times but Becca didn't want to talk much. None of them did. Jason had an even shorter temper than usual, especially the day the police interviewed him. Apparently, on the night Andie disappeared, the alarm had gone off at his business offices during the dinner party. He'd driven round to check it out but he'd already drunk quite a lot of alcohol, so he was nervous talking to the police about it. Well, this is what Becca told me anyway. But, yeah, the house was just so quiet. And even months later, after it was presumed Andie was dead and never coming home, Becca's mum insisted on leaving Andie's room as it was. Just in case. It was all really sad.

Pip: So, when you were at that calamity party in March, did you see what Andie was up to, who she was with?

Jess: Yeah. You know, I never actually knew that Sal was Andie's boyfriend until after she went missing; she'd never had him over at the house. I knew she had a boyfriend, though, and, after that calamity party, I had presumed it was this other guy. I saw them alone at that party, whispering and looking pretty close. Several times. Never once saw her with Sal.

Pip: Who? Who was the guy?

Jess: Um, he was this tall blonde guy, kind of long hair, spoke like he was posh.

Pip: Max? Was his name Max Hastings?

Jess: Yeah, yeah, I think that was him.

Pip: You saw Max and Andie alone at the party?

Jess: Yep, looking pretty friendly.

Pip: Jess, thanks so much for talking with me. You've been a big help.

Jess:	Oh, that's OK. Hey, Pippa, do you know how Becca's doing now?
Pip:	I saw her just the other day actually. I think she's doing well, she's got her degree and she's interning at the Kilton newspaper. She looks well.
Jess:	Good. I'm glad to hear that.

I'm struggling to even process the amount I've learned from that one conversation. This investigation shifts tonally each time I peek behind another screen in Andie's life.

Jason Bell is looking darker and darker the more I dig. And I now know that he left his dinner party for a while on *that* night. From what Jess said, it sounds like he was emotionally abusive to his family. A bully. A chauvinist. An adulterer. It's no wonder Andie turned out the way she did in a toxic environment like that. It seems Jason wrecked his children's self-esteem so much that one became a bully like him and the other turned to self-harming. I know from Andie's friend Emma that Becca had been hospitalized in the weeks before Andie's disappearance and that Andie was supposed to be watching her sister that very night. It seems like Jess didn't know about the self-harming; she just thought Becca had been skipping school.

So Andie wasn't the perfect girl and the Bells weren't the perfect family. Those family photographs may speak a thousand words but most of them are lies.

Speaking of lies: Max. Max bloody Hastings. Here's a direct quote from his interview when I asked how well he knew Andie: *'We sometimes spoke, yeah. But we weren't ever, like, friend friends; didn't really know her. Like an acquaintance.'*

An acquaintance that you were seen cuddling up to at a party? So much so that a witness presumed YOU were Andie's boyfriend?

And there's this as well: even though they were in the same school year, Andie had a summer birthday and Max had been held back a year because of his leukaemia AND has a September birthday. When you look at it like this, there is almost a two-year age gap between them. From Andie's perspective, Max WAS technically an older guy. But was he a secret older guy? Right up close and personal behind Sal's back.

I've tried looking Max up on Facebook before; his profile is basically barren, just holiday and Christmas pictures with his parents and birthday wishes from uncles and aunties. I remember thinking before that it didn't seem fitting but I shrugged it off.

Well, I'm not shrugging any more, Hastings. And I've made a discovery. In some of Naomi's pictures online, Max isn't tagged as *Max Hastings* but as *Nancy Tangotits*. I thought it was some kind of private joke before but NO, *Nancy Tangotits* is Max's actual Facebook profile. The *Max Hastings* one must be a tame decoy he kept in case universities or potential employers decided to look up his online activities. It makes sense, even some of my friends have started changing their profile names to make them unsearchable as we draw closer to uni-application season.

The real Max Hastings – and all his wild, drunken photos and posts from friends – has been hiding as Nancy. This is what I presume, at least. I can't actually get on to see anything: Nancy has his privacy settings set on full throttle. I can only see photos or posts that Naomi is also tagged in. It's not giving me much to work with: no secret pictures of Max and Andie kissing in the background, none of his photos from the night she disappeared.

I've already learned my lesson here. When you catch someone lying about a murdered girl, the best thing to do is to go and ask them why.

Persons of Interest

Jason Bell

Naomi Ward

Secret Older Guy

Nat da Silva

Daniel da Silva

Max Hastings (Nancy Tangotits)

Sixteen

The door was different now. It had been brown the last time she was here, over six weeks ago. Now it was covered in a streaky layer of white paint, the dark undercoat still peering through.

Pip knocked again, harder this time, hoping it would be heard over the droning murmur of a vacuum cleaner running inside.

The drone clicked off abruptly, leaving a slightly buzzy silence in its wake. Then sharp footsteps on a hard floor.

The door opened and a well-dressed woman with cherry-red lipstick stood before her.

'Hi,' Pip said. 'I'm a friend of Max's, is he in?'

'Oh, hi,' the woman smiled, revealing a smear of red on one of her top teeth. She stood back to let Pip through. 'He certainly is, come in . . .'

'Pippa,' she smiled, stepping inside.

'Pippa. Yes, he's in the living room. Shouting at me for vacuuming while he's playing some death match. Can't pause it, apparently.'

Max's mum walked Pip down the hall and through the open archway into the living room.

Max was spread out on the sofa, in tartan pyjama bottoms and a white T-shirt, his hands gripped round a controller as he furiously thumbed the X button.

His mum cleared her throat.

Max looked up.

'Oh, hi, Pippa Funny-Surname,' he said in his deep, refined voice, his eyes returning to his game. 'What are you doing here?'

Pip almost grimaced in reflex, but she fought it with a fake smile. 'Oh, nothing much.' She shrugged nonchalantly. 'Just here to ask you how well you *really* knew Andie Bell.'

The game was paused.

Max sat up, stared at Pip, then his mum, then back to Pip.

'Um,' his mum said, 'would anyone like a cup of tea?'

'No, we don't.' Max stood. 'Upstairs, Pippa.'

He strode past them and up the grand stairs in the hallway, his bare feet thundering on the steps. Pip followed, flashing a polite wave back at his mother. At the top, Max held open his bedroom door and gestured her inside.

Pip hesitated, one foot suspended above the vacuum-tracked carpet. Should she really be alone with him?

Max jerked his head impatiently.

His mum was just downstairs; she should be safe. She planted the foot and strode into his room.

'Thank you for that,' he said, closing the door. 'My mum didn't need to know I've been talking about Andie and Sal again. The woman is a bloodhound, never lets anything go.'

'Pit bull,' Pip said. 'It's pit bulls that don't let things go.'

Max sat back on his maroon bedspread. 'Whatever.

What do you want?'

'I said. I want to know how well you really knew Andie.'

'I already told you,' he said, leaning back on his elbows and shooting a glance up past Pip's shoulder. 'I didn't know her that well.'

'Mmm.' Pip leaned back against his door. 'Just acquaintances, right? That's what you said?'

'Yeah, I did.' He scratched his nose. 'I'll be honest, I'm starting to find your tone a tad annoying '

'Good,' she said, following Max's eyes as they looked over again to a noticeboard on the far wall, littered with posters and pinned-up notes and photographs. 'And I'm starting to find your lies a tad intriguing.'

'What lies?' he said. 'I didn't know her well.'

'Interesting,' Pip said. 'I've spoken to a witness who went to a calamity party that you and Andie attended in March 2012. Interesting because she said she saw you two alone several times that night, looking pretty comfortable with each other.'

'Who said that?' Another micro-glance over to the noticeboard.

'I can't reveal my sources.'

'Oh my god.' He laughed a deep throaty laugh. 'You're deluded. You know you're not actually a police officer, right?'

'You're avoiding the question,' she said. 'Were you and Andie secretly seeing each other behind Sal's back?'

Max laughed again. 'He was my best friend.'

'That's not an answer.' Pip folded her arms.

'No. No, I wasn't seeing Andie Bell. Like I said, I didn't know her that well.'

'So why did this source see you together? In a manner that made her think you were actually Andie's boyfriend?'

While Max rolled his eyes at the question, Pip stole her own glance at the noticeboard. The scribbled notes and bits of paper were several layers deep in places, with hidden corners and curled edges. Glossy photos of Max skiing and surfing were pinned on top. A *Reservoir Dogs* poster took up most of the board.

'I don't know,' he said. 'Whoever it was, they were mistaken. Probably drunk. An unreliable source, you might say.'

'OK.' Pip shuffled away from the door. She took a few steps to the right, then paced back a couple, so Max wouldn't realize as she moved herself incrementally towards the noticeboard. 'So let's get this straight.' She paced again, positioning herself nearer and nearer. 'You're saying you never spoke one-on-one with Andie at a calamity party?'

'I don't know if never,' Max said, 'but it's not like you're implying.'

'OK, OK.' Pip looked up from the floor, just a couple of feet from the board now. 'And why do you keep looking over here?' She twisted on her heels and started flipping through the papers pinned to the board.

'Hey, stop.'

She heard the bed groan as Max got to his feet.

Pip's eyes and fingers scanned over to-do lists, scribbled names of companies and grad schemes, leaflets and old photos of a young Max in a hospital bed.

Heavy bare-footed steps behind her.

'That's my private stuff!'

And then she saw a small white corner of paper, tucked underneath *Reservoir Dogs*. She pulled and ripped the paper out just as Max grabbed her arm. Pip spun towards him, his fingers digging into her wrist. And they both looked down at the piece of paper in her hand.

Pip's mouth fell open.

'Oh for fuck's sake.' Max let her arm go and ran his fingers through his untamed hair.

'Just acquaintances?' she said shakily.

'Who do you think you are?' Max said. 'Going through my stuff.'

'Just acquaintances?' Pip said again, holding the printed photo up to Max's face.

It was Andie.

A photo she'd taken of herself in a mirror. Standing on a red and white tiled floor, her right hand raised and clutched round the phone. Her mouth was pushed out in a pout and her eyes looked straight out of the page; she was wearing nothing but a pair of black pants.

'Care to explain?' Pip said.

'No.'

'Oh, so you want to explain it to the police first? I get it.'
Pip glared at him and feigned walking towards the door.

'Don't be dramatic,' Max said, returning her glare with his
glassy blue eyes. 'It has nothing to do with what happened to
her.'

'I'll let them decide that.'

'No, Pippa.' He blocked her way to the door. 'Look, this is
really not how it looks. Andie didn't give me that picture. I
found it.'

'You found it? Where?'

'It was just lying around at school. I found it and I kept it.
Andie never knew about it.' There was a hint of pleading in his
voice.

'You found a nude picture of Andie just lying around at
school?' She didn't even try to hide her disbelief.

'Yes. It was just hidden in the back of a classroom. I swear.'

'And you didn't tell Andie or anyone that you'd found it?'
said Pip.

'No, I just kept it.'

'Why?'

'I don't know,' his voice scrambled higher. 'Because she's
hot and I wanted to. And then it seemed wrong to throw it
away after . . . What? Don't judge me. She took the photo; she
clearly wanted it to be seen.'

'You expect me to believe that you just found this naked
picture of Andie, a girl you were seen getting close to at parties –'

Max cut her off. 'Those are completely unrelated. I wasn't

talking to Andie because we were together and neither do I have that picture because we were together. We weren't together. We never had been.'

'So you *were* alone talking to Andie at that calamity party?' Pip said triumphantly.

Max held his face in his hands for a moment, his fingertips pressing into his eyes.

'Fine,' he said quietly, 'if I tell you, will you please just leave me alone? And no police.'

'That depends.'

'OK, fine. I knew Andie better than I said I did. A lot better. Since before she started with Sal. But I wasn't *seeing* her. I was buying from her.'

Pip looked at him in confusion, her mind ticking back over his last words.

'Buying . . . drugs?' she asked softly.

Max nodded. 'Nothing super hard, though. Just weed and a few pills.'

'H-holy pepperoni. Hold on.' Pip held up her finger to push the world back, give her brain space to think. 'Andie Bell was dealing drugs?'

'Well, yeah, but only at calamities and when we went out to clubs and stuff. Just to a few people. A handful at most. She wasn't like a proper dealer.' Max paused. 'She was working with an actual dealer in town, got him an inside into the school crowd. It worked out for both of them.'

'That's why she always had so much cash,' Pip said, the

puzzle piece slotting in with an almost audible click in her head. 'Did she use?'

'Not really. Think she only did it for the money. Money and the power it gave her. I could tell she enjoyed that.'

'And did Sal know she was selling drugs?'

Max laughed. 'Oh no,' he said, 'no, no, no. Sal always hated drugs, that wouldn't have gone down well. Andie hid it from him; she was good at secrets. I think the only people who knew were those who bought from her. But I always thought Sal was a little naive. I'm surprised he never found out.'

'How long had she been doing this?' Pip said, feeling a crackle of sinister excitement spark through her.

'A while.' Max looked up at the ceiling, his eyes circling as though he were turning over his own memories. 'Think the first time I bought weed off her was early 2011, when she was still sixteen. That was probably around when it started.'

'And who was Andie's dealer? Who did she get the drugs from?'

Max shrugged. 'I dunno, I never knew the guy. I only ever bought through Andie and she never told me.'

Pip deflated. 'You don't know anything? You never bought drugs in Kilton after Andie was killed?'

'Nope.' He shrugged again. 'I don't know anything more.'

'But were other people at calamities still using drugs? Where did they get them?'

'I don't know, Pippa,' Max over-enunciated. 'I told you what you wanted to hear. Now I want you to leave.'

He stepped forward and whipped the photo out of Pip's hands. His thumb closed over Andie's face, the picture crumpling in his tight and shaking grip. A crease split down the middle of Andie's body as he folded her away.

Seventeen

Pip tuned out of the others' conversation and into the background soundtrack of the cafeteria. A bass of scraping chairs and guffaws from a group of teenage boys whose voices fluctuated at will from deep tenor into squeaky soprano. The tuneful scrape of lunch trays sliding along the bench, picking up salad packs or bowls of soup, harmonized by the rustle of crisp packets and weekend gossip.

Pip spotted him before the others and waved him over to their table. Ant waddled over, two packaged sandwiches cradled in his arms.

'Hey, guys,' he said, sliding on to the bench beside Cara, already tearing into sandwich number one.

'How was practice?' Pip asked.

Ant looked up at her warily, his mouth slightly open, revealing the churned produce of his chewing. 'Fine,' he swallowed. 'Why are you being nice to me? What do you want?'

'Nothing,' Pip laughed. 'I'm just asking how football was.'

'No,' Zach butted in, 'that's far too friendly for you. Something's up.'

'Nothing's up.' She shrugged. 'Only the national debt and global sea levels.'

'Probably hormones,' Ant said.

Pip wound the invisible crank by her hand, jerkily raising her middle finger up at him.

They were on to her already. She waited a full five minutes for the group to have a conversation about the latest episode of that zombie programme they all watched, Connor stuffing his ears and humming loudly and tunelessly because he was yet to watch it.

'So, Ant,' Pip tried again, 'you know your friend George from football?'

'Yes, I think I know my friend George from football,' he said, clearly finding himself rather too amusing.

'He's in the crowd that still do calamity parties, isn't he?'

Ant nodded. 'Yeah. Actually I think the next party is at his house. His parents are abroad for an anniversary or something.'

'This weekend?'

'Yeah.'

'Do you . . .' Pip sat forward, resting her elbows on the table. 'Do you think you could get us all invited?'

Every single one of her friends turned to gawp at her.

'Who are you and what have you done with Pippa Fitz-Amobi?' Cara said.

'What?' She felt herself getting defensive, about four useless facts simmering to the surface, ready to fire. 'It's our last year at school. I thought it would be fun for us all to go. This is the opportune time, before coursework deadlines and mock-exams creep up.'

'Still sounds Pip-ish to me,' Connor smiled.

'You want to go to a house party?' Ant said pointedly.

'Yes,' she said.

'Everyone will be smashed, people getting off, throwing up, passing out. A lot of mess on the floor,' Ant said. 'It's not really your scene, Pip.'

'Sounds . . . cultural,' she said. 'I still want to go.'

'OK, fine.' Ant clapped his hands together. 'We'll go.'

Pip stopped by Ravi's on her way home from school. He set a black tea down in front of her, informing her there was no need to wait a jiffy for it to cool because he'd thought ahead and poured in some cold water.

'OK,' he finally said, his head bouncing in a part-shaking part-nodding movement as he tried to process the image of Andie Bell – cute, button-faced blonde – as a drug dealer. 'OK, so you're thinking the man who supplied her could be a suspect?'

'Yes,' she said. 'If you have the depravity to peddle drugs to kids, I definitely think you could be the sort inclined to murder.'

'Yeah, I see the logic,' he nodded. 'But how are we going to find this drug dealer, though?'

She plonked down her mug and sharpened her eyes on his. 'I'm going undercover,' she said.

Eighteen

'It's a house party, not a pantomime,' Pip said, trying to wrestle her face out of Cara's grip. But Cara held on tight: facial hijack.

'Yeah, but you're lucky – you have a face that can pull off eyeshadow. Stop wriggling, I'm almost done.'

Pip sighed and went limp, submitting to the forced preening. She was still sulking that her friends had made her change out of her dungarees and into a dress of Lauren's that was short enough to be mistaken for a T-shirt. They'd laughed a lot when she'd said that.

'Girls,' Pip's mum called up the stairs, 'you'd better hurry up. Victor's started showing Lauren his dance moves down here.'

'Oh jeez,' Pip said. 'Am I done? We need to go and rescue her.'

Cara leaned forward and blew on her face. 'Yep.'

'Cracking,' said Pip, grabbing her shoulder bag and checking, once again, that her phone was at full charge. 'Let's go.'

'Hello, pickle!' her dad said loudly as Pip and Cara made their way downstairs. 'Lauren and I have decided that I should come to your kilometre party too.'

'Calamity, Dad. And over my dead brain cells.'

Victor strolled over, wrapped his arm round her shoulders and squeezed. 'Little Pipsy going to a house party.'

'I know,' Pip's mum said, her smile wide and glistening. 'With alcohol and boys.'

'Yes.' He let go and looked down at Pip, a serious expression on his face and his finger raised. 'Pip, I want you to remember to be, at least, a little irresponsible.'

'Right,' Pip announced, grabbing her car keys and strolling to the front door. 'We're going now. Farewell, my backwards and abnormal parents.'

'Fare thee well,' Victor said dramatically, gripping on to the banister and reaching for the departing teenagers, like the house was a sinking ship and he the heroic captain going down with it.

Even the pavement outside was pulsing with the music. The three of them strolled up to the front door and Pip raised her fist to knock. As she did, the door swung inward, opening a gateway into a writhing cacophony of deep-bass tinny tunes, slurred chattering and poor lighting.

Pip took a tentative step inside, her first breath already tainted with the muggy metallic smell of vodka, undertones of sweat and the slightest hint of vomit. She caught sight of the host, Ant's friend George, trying to mesh his face with a girl's from the year below, his eyes open and staring. He looked their way and, without breaking the kiss, waved to them behind his partner's back.

Pip couldn't let herself be complicit in such a greeting, so she ignored it and started down the corridor. Cara and Lauren walked beside her, Lauren having to step over Paul-from-politics who was slumped against the wall, lightly snoring.

'This looks . . . like some people's idea of fun,' Pip muttered as they entered the open-plan living room and the chaos of teenage bustle hosted there: bodies grinding and thrashing to the music, towers of precariously balanced beer bottles, drunken meaning-of-life monologues yelled across the room, wet carpet patches, unsubtle groin scratches and couples pushed up against the condensation-dripping walls.

'You're the one who was so desperate to come,' Lauren said, waving to some girls she took after-school drama class with.

Pip swallowed. 'Yeah. And present Pip is always pleased with past Pip's decisions.'

Ant, Connor and Zach spotted them then and made their way over, manoeuvring through the staggering crowd.

'All right?' Connor said, giving Pip and the others clumsy hugs. 'You're late.'

'I know,' Lauren said. 'We had to re-dress Pip.'

Pip didn't see how dungarees could be embarrassing by association, yet the jerky robot dance moves of Lauren's drama friends were totally acceptable.

'Are there cups?' Cara said, holding up a bottle of vodka and lemonade.

'Yeah, I'll show you,' Ant said, taking Cara off towards the kitchen.

When Cara returned with a drink for her, Pip took frequent imaginary sips as she nodded and laughed along with the conversation. When the opportunity presented itself, she sidled over to the kitchen sink, poured out the cup and filled it with water.

Later, when Zach offered to refill her cup for her, she had to pull the stunt again and got cornered talking to Joe King, who sat behind her in English. His only form of humour was to say a ridiculous statement, wait for his victim to pull a confused face and then say: 'I'm only *Joe*-King.'

After the joke's third resurgence, Pip excused herself and went to hide in a corner, thankfully alone. She stood there in the shadows, undisturbed, and scrutinized the room. She watched the dancers and the over-enthusiastic kissers, searching for any signs of shifty hand trades, pills or gurning jaws. Any over-wide pupils. Anything that might give her a possible lead to Andie's drug dealer.

Ten whole minutes passed and Pip didn't notice anything dubious, other than a boy called Stephen smashing a TV remote and hiding the evidence in a flower vase. Her eyes followed him as he wandered through to a large utility room and towards the back door, reaching for a pack of cigarettes from his back pocket.

Of course.

Outside with the smokers should have been the first place

on her list to scout out. Pip made her way through the mayhem, protecting herself from the worst of the lurchers and staggerers with her elbows.

There were a handful of people outside. A couple of dark shadows rolling around on the trampoline at the bottom of the garden. A tearful Stella Chapman standing by the garden waste bin wailing down the phone at someone. Another two girls from her year on a children's swing having what looked like a very serious conversation, punctuated by hands-slapped-to-mouths gasps. And Stephen Thompson-or-Timpson who she used to sit behind in maths. He was perched on a garden wall, a cigarette prone in his mouth as he searched double-handed in his various pockets.

Pip wandered over. 'Hi,' she said, plonking herself down on the wall next to him.

'Hi, Pippa,' Stephen said, taking the cigarette from his mouth so he could talk. 'What's up?'

'Oh nothing much,' Pip said. 'Just came out here, looking for Mary Jane.'

'Dunno who she is, sorry,' he said, finally pulling out a neon green lighter.

'Not a who.' Pip turned to give him a meaningful look. 'You know, I'm looking to blast a roach.'

'Excuse me?'

Pip had spent an hour online that morning researching Urban Dictionary for its current street names.

She tried again, lowering her voice to a whisper. 'You

know, looking for some herb, the doob, a bit of hippie lettuce, giggle smoke, some skunk, wacky tobaccy. You know what I mean. Ganja.'

Stephen burst into laughter. 'Oh my god,' he cackled, 'you are so smashed.'

'Certainly am.' She tried to feign a drunken giggle, but it came off as rather villainous. 'So do you have any? Some shwag grass?'

When he stopped hooting to himself, he turned to look her up and down for a drawn-out moment. His eyes very obviously stalling over her chest and pasty legs. Pip squirmed inside; a gloopy cyclone of disgust and embarrassment. She mentally threw a reproach into Stephen's face, but her mouth had to remain shut. She was undercover.

'Yeah,' Stephen said, biting his bottom lip. 'I can roll us a joint.' He searched his pockets again and pulled out a small baggy of weed and a packet of rolling papers.

'Yes please,' Pip nodded, feeling anxious and excited and a little sick. 'You get rolling there; roll it like a . . . um, croupier with a dice.'

He laughed at her again and licked one edge of the paper, trying to hold eye contact with her while his stubby pink tongue was out. Pip looked away. It crossed her mind that maybe she had gone too far this time for a homework project. Maybe. But this wasn't just a project any more. This was for Sal, for Ravi. For the truth. She could do this for them.

Stephen lit the joint and took two long sucks on its end before passing it to Pip. She took it awkwardly between her middle and index fingers and raised it to her lips. She turned her head sharply so that her hair flicked over her face, and pretended to take a couple of drags on the joint.

'Mmm, lovely stuff,' she said, passing it back. 'Spliffing you could say.'

'You look nice tonight,' Stephen said, taking a drag and offering the joint again.

Pip tried to take it without her fingers touching his. Another pretend puff but the smell was cloying and she coughed over her next question.

'So,' she said, giving it back, 'where might I score me some of this?'

'You can share with me.'

'No, I mean, who do you buy it from? You know, so I can get in on that too.'

'Just this guy in town.' Stephen shuffled on the wall, closer to Pip. 'Called Howie.'

'And where does Howie live?' Pip said, passing back the weed and using the movement as an excuse to shift away from Stephen.

'Dunno,' Stephen said. 'He doesn't deal from his house. I meet him at the station car park, down the end with no cameras.'

'In the evening?' Pip asked.

'Usually, yeah. Whatever time he texts me.'

'You have his number?' Pip reached down to her bag for her own phone. 'Can I have it?'

Stephen shook his head. 'He'd be mad if he knew I was just handing it out. You don't need to go to him; if you want something, you can just pay me and I'll get it for you. I'll even discount.' He winked.

'I'd really rather buy direct,' Pip said, feeling the heat of annoyance creeping up her neck.

'No can do.' He shook his head, eyeing her mouth.

Pip looked away quickly, her long dark hair a curtain between them. Her frustration was too loud, gorging itself on all other thoughts. He wasn't going to budge, was he?

And then the spark of an idea pushed its way through.

'Well, how can I buy through you?' she said, taking the joint from his hands. 'You don't even have my number.'

'Ah, and what a shame that is,' Stephen said, his voice so slimy it practically dripped out of his mouth. He reached into his back pocket and pulled out his phone. Jabbing his finger at the screen, he entered his passcode and handed her the unlocked phone. 'Put your digits in there,' he said.

'OK,' said Pip.

She opened the phonebook application and shifted her shoulders, facing Stephen so he couldn't see the screen. She typed *how* into the contacts search bar and it was the only result to pop up. *Howie Bowers* and his phone number.

She studied the sequence of numbers. Damn, she'd never be able to remember the whole thing. Another idea flickered into life. Maybe she could take a picture of the screen; her own phone was on the wall just beside her. But Stephen was right there, staring at her, chewing his finger. She needed some kind of distraction.

She lurched forward suddenly, launching the joint across the lawn. 'Sorry,' she said, 'I thought there was a bug on me.'

'Don't worry, I'll get it.' Stephen jumped down from the wall.

Pip had just a few seconds. She grabbed her phone, swiped left into the camera and positioned it above Stephen's screen.

Her heart was thudding, her chest closing uncomfortably around it.

The camera flicked in and out of focus, wasting precious time.

Her finger hovered over the button.

The shot cleared and she took the picture, dropping her phone into her lap just as Stephen turned.

'It's still lit,' he said, jumping back up on the wall, sitting far too close to her.

Pip held out Stephen's phone to him. 'Um, sorry, I don't think I want to give you my number actually,' she said. 'I've decided that drugs aren't for me.'

'Don't be a tease,' Stephen said, closing his fingers round both his phone and Pip's hand. He leaned into her.

'No, thank you,' she said, scooting back. 'Think I'm going to go inside.'

And then Stephen put his hand on the back of her head,

grabbed her forward and lunged for her face. Pip twisted out of the way and shoved him back. She pushed so hard that he was deseated and fell three feet from the garden wall, sprawled on the wet grass.

'You stupid slut,' he said, picking himself up and wiping off his trousers.

'You degenerate, perverted, reprobate ape. Sorry, apes,' Pip shouted back. 'I said no.'

That was when she realized. She didn't know how or when it had happened, but she looked up and saw that they were now alone in the garden.

Fear flushed through her in an instant, her skin bristling with it.

Stephen climbed back over the wall and Pip turned, hurrying towards the door.

'Hey, it's OK, we can talk for a bit more,' he said, grabbing her wrist to pull her back.

'Let me go, Stephen.' She spat the words at him.

'But –'

Pip grabbed his wrist with her other hand and squeezed, digging her nails into his skin. Stephen hissed and let go and Pip did not hesitate. She ran towards the house and slammed the door, flicking the lock behind her.

Inside, she wound her way through the crowd on the makeshift Persian-rug dance floor, being jostled this way and that. She searched through the flailing body parts and sweaty laughing faces. Searching for the safety of Cara's face.

It was musty and hot, inside the crush of all these bodies. But Pip was shaking, an aftershock of cold quaking through her, knocking her bare knees.

Production Log – Entry 22

Update: I waited in my car for four hours tonight. At the far end of the station car park. I checked, no cameras. Three separate waves of commuters getting in from London Marylebone came and went, Dad among them. Luckily he didn't spot my car.

I didn't see anyone hanging around. No one who looked like they were there to buy or sell drugs. Not that I really know what that looks like; I never would have guessed Andie Bell was the kind.

Yes, I know I managed to get Howie Bowers' number from Stephen-the-creep. I could just ring Howie and see whether he'd be willing to answer some questions about Andie. That's what Ravi thinks we should do. But – let's be real – he's not going to give me anything that way. He's a drug dealer. He's not going to admit it to a stranger on the phone like he's casually discussing the weather or trickle-down economics.

No. The only way he'll talk to us is if we have the appropriate leverage first.

I'll return to the station tomorrow evening. Ravi has work again, but I can do this alone. I'll just tell my parents I'm doing my English coursework over at Cara's house. The lying gets easier the more I have to do it.

I need to find Howie.

I need this leverage.

I also need sleep.

Nineteen

Pip was thirteen chapters in, reading by the harsh silver light from the torch on her phone, when she noticed a lone figure crossing under a street lamp. She was in her car, parked down the far end of the station car park, every half-hour marked with the screech and growl of London or Aylesbury-bound trains.

The street lamps had flickered on about an hour ago, when the sun had retreated, staining Little Kilton a darkening blue. The lights were that buzzy orange-yellow colour, illuminating the area with an unsettling industrial glow.

Pip squinted against the window. As the figure passed under the light, she saw it was a man in a dark green jacket with a furred hood and bright orange lining. His hood was up over a mask made of shadows, with only a downward-lit triangle nose for a face.

She quickly switched off her phone torch and put *Great Expectations* down on the passenger seat. She shifted her own seat back so she could crouch on the car floor, hidden from sight by the door, the top of her head and her eyes pressed up against the window.

The man walked over to the very outer boundary of the car park and leaned against the fence there, in a gloomy space just between two orange-lit pools from the lamps. Pip watched him, holding her breath because it fogged the window and blocked her view.

With his head down, the man pulled a phone out of one of his pockets. As he unlocked it and the screen lit up, Pip could see his face for the first time: a bony face full of sharp lines and edges and neatly kept dark stubble. Pip wasn't the best with ages but, at a guess, the man was in his late twenties or early thirties.

True, this wasn't the first time tonight she thought she'd found Howie Bowers. There had been two other men she'd ducked and hid to watch. The first got into a banged-up car straight away and drove off. The second stopped to smoke, long enough for Pip's heart to pick up. But then he'd stubbed out the cigarette, blipped a car and also headed off.

But something hadn't felt right about those last two sightings: the men had been dressed in work suits and smart coats, clearly dawdlers of a train-load from the city. But this man was different. He was in jeans and a short parka, and there was no doubt that he was waiting for something. Or someone.

His thumbs were working away on his phone screen. Possibly texting a client to tell them he was waiting. Typical Pippism, getting ahead of herself. But she had one sure way to confirm that this lurking parka-wearing man was Howie. She pulled out her phone, trying to hide its illumination by holding it low and turning it to face into her thigh. She scrolled down in her contacts to the entry for Howie Bowers and pressed the call button.

Her eyes back to the window, thumb hovering over the red hang-up button, she waited. Her nerves spiking with every half second.

Then she heard it.

Much louder than the outgoing call sound from her own phone.

A mechanical duck started quacking, the sound coming from the hands of the man. She watched as he pressed something on his phone and raised it to his ear.

'Hello?' came a distant voice from outside, muffled by her window. Fractionally later the same voice spoke through the speakers of her phone. Howie's voice, it was confirmed.

Pip pressed the hang-up button and watched as Howie Bowers lowered his phone and stared at it, his thick but remarkably straight eyebrows lowering, eclipsing his eyes in shadows. He thumbed the phone and raised it to his ear again.

'Crap,' Pip whispered, snatching her phone up and clicking it on to silent. Less than a second later, the screen lit up with an incoming call from Howie Bowers. Pip pressed the lock button and let the call silently ring out, her heart drumming painfully against her ribs. That was close, too close. Stupid not to withhold her number, really.

Howie put his phone away then and stood, head down, hands back in pockets. Of course, even though she now knew this man was Howie Bowers, she didn't have confirmation that he had been the man who'd supplied Andie with drugs.

The only fact was that Howie Bowers was now currently dealing to kids at school, the same crowd that Andie had introduced her dealer to. It could be coincidence. Howie Bowers might not be the man Andie had worked with all that time ago. But in a small town like Kilton you couldn't put too much trust in coincidences.

Just then, Howie raised his head and nodded pointedly. Then Pip heard it, sharp clicking footsteps against the concrete drawing closer and louder. She didn't dare move to look for who was approaching, the clicks jolting through her with each step. And then the person crossed into view.

It was a tall man wearing a long beige coat and polished black shoes, their sheen and sharp clicking a sign of their newness. His hair was dark and cropped close to his head. As he arrived at Howie's side, he spun to lean against the fence beside him. It took a few moments of straining her eyes to focus her gaze before Pip gasped.

She knew this man. Knew his face from the staff pictures on the *Kilton Mail* website. It was Stanley Forbes.

Stanley Forbes, an outsider to Pip's investigation who had now cropped up twice. Becca Bell said she was kind of seeing him and now here he was, meeting with the man who had possibly supplied Becca's sister with drugs.

Neither of the men had spoken yet. Stanley scratched his nose and then pulled out a thick envelope from his pocket. He shoved the packet into Howie's chest and only then did she notice that his face was flushed and his hands shaking.

Pip raised her phone and, checking the flash was off, took a few pictures of the meeting.

'This is the last time, do you hear me?' Stanley spat, making no effort to keep his voice down. Pip could just about hear the edges of his words through the glass of the car window. 'You can't keep asking for more; I don't have it.'

Howie spoke far too quietly and Pip only heard the mumbled start and end of his sentence: 'But . . . tell.'

Stanley rounded on him. 'I don't think you would dare.'

They stared into each other's faces for a tense and lingering moment, then Stanley turned on his heels and walked quickly away, his coat flicking out behind him.

When he was gone Howie looked through the envelope in his hands before stuffing it in his coat. Pip took another few pictures of him with it in his hands. But Howie wasn't going anywhere yet. He stood against the fence, tapping away at his phone again. Like he was waiting for someone else.

A few minutes later, Pip saw someone approaching. Huddling back in her hiding spot, Pip watched as the boy strode over to Howie, raising his hand in a wave. She recognized him too: a boy in the year below her at school, a boy who played football with Ant. Called Robin something.

Their meeting was just as brief. Robin pulled out some cash and handed it over. Howie counted the money and then produced a rolled-up paper bag from his coat pocket. Pip took five quick pictures as Howie handed the bag to Robin and pocketed the cash.

Pip could see their mouths moving, but she couldn't hear the secret words they exchanged. Howie smiled and clapped the boy on the back. Robin, stuffing the bag into his rucksack, wandered back up the car park, calling a low 'See you later', as he passed behind Pip's car, so close it made her jump.

Ducking below the door frame, Pip scrolled through the pictures she'd taken; Howie's face was clear and visible in at least three of them. And Pip knew the name of the boy she'd caught him selling to. It was textbook leverage, if anyone had ever written a textbook on how to blackmail a drug dealer.

Pip froze. Someone was walking just behind her car, moving with shuffling footsteps, whistling. She waited twenty seconds and then looked up. Howie was gone, heading back towards the station.

And now came the moment of indecision. Howie was on foot; Pip couldn't follow him in her car. But she really, really did not want to leave the bug-faced safety of her little car to follow a criminal without a reinforced Volkswagen shield.

Fear started to uncurl in her stomach, winding up around her brain with one thought: Andie Bell went out in the dark on her own, and she never came back. Pip stifled the thought, breathed back the fear and climbed out of the car, shutting the door as carefully as she could. She needed to learn as much as she could about this man. He could be the one who supplied Andie, the one who really killed her.

Howie was about forty paces ahead of her. His hood was down now and its orange lining was easy to spot in the dark.

Pip kept the distance between them, her heart getting in four beats between each of her steps.

She drew back and increased the gap as they passed through the well-lit roundabout outside the station. She wouldn't get too close. She followed Howie as he turned right down the hill, past the town's mini-supermarket. He crossed the road and turned left along High Street, the other end from school and Ravi's house.

She trailed behind him, all the way up Wyvil Road, over the bridge that crossed the rail tracks. Beyond the bridge, Howie turned off the road on to a small path that carved across a grass verge through a yellowing hedge.

Pip waited for Howie to get a little further ahead before she followed him down the path, emerging on to a small and dark residential road. She kept going, her eyes on the orange-furred hood fifty feet ahead of her. Darkness was the easiest of disguises; it made the familiar unknown and strange. It was only when Pip passed a street sign that she realized what road they were on.

Romer Close.

Her heart reacted, now getting in six beats between her feet. Romer Close, the very road where Andie Bell's car was found abandoned after her disappearance.

Pip saw Howie swerving up ahead and she darted to hide behind a tree, watching as he headed towards a small bungalow, pulled out his keys and let himself in. As the door clicked shut, Pip emerged from her hiding place and approached

Howie's house. Number twenty-nine Romer Close.

It was a squat semi-detached house, with tan bricks and a mossy slate roof. Both windows at the front were covered by thick blinds, the left one now cracking with streaks of yellow as Howie turned on the lights inside. There was a small gravel plot just outside the front door where a faded maroon car sat.

Pip stared at it. There was no delay in her recognition this time. Her mouth fell open and her stomach jumped to her throat, filling her mouth with the regurgitated taste of the sandwich she'd eaten in the car.

'Oh my god,' she whispered.

She stepped back from the house, pulling out her phone. She skipped through her recent calls and dialled Ravi's number.

'Please tell me you're off shift,' she said when he picked up.

'I just got home. Why?'

'I need you to come to Romer Close right now.'

Twenty

Pip knew from her murder map that it would take Ravi about eighteen minutes to walk from his house to Romer Close. He was four minutes faster, running when he spotted her.

'What is it?' he said, slightly out of breath and brushing the hair back off his face.

'*It* is a lot of things,' Pip said quietly. 'I'm not quite sure where to start so I just will.'

'You're freaking me out.' His eyes flicked over her face, searching.

'I'm freaking me out too.' She paused to take a large breath, and hopefully force her figurative stomach back down her windpipe. 'OK, you know I was looking for the drug dealer, from my lead at the calamity party. He was there tonight, dealing in the car park and I followed him home. He lives here, Ravi. The road where Andie's car was found.'

Ravi's eyes wandered up to trace the outline of the dark street. 'But how do you even know he's the guy that supplied Andie?' he asked.

'I didn't for sure,' she said. 'I do now. But wait there's another thing I have to tell you first and I don't want you to be mad.'

'Why would I be mad?' He looked down at her, his soft face hardening around the eyes.

'Um, because I lied to you,' she said, her gaze down on her own feet instead of Ravi's face. 'I told you that Sal's police interview hadn't arrived yet. It did, over two weeks ago.'

'What?' he said quietly. A look of unconcealed hurt clouded his face, wrinkling his nose and forehead.

'I'm sorry,' Pip said. 'But when it arrived and I read through it, I thought you'd be better off not seeing it.'

'Why?'

She swallowed. 'Because it looked really bad for Sal. He was evasive with the police and outright told them he didn't want to say why he and Andie were arguing on that Thursday and Friday. It looked like he was trying to hide his own motive. And I was scared that maybe he'd actually killed her and I didn't want to upset you.' She chanced to look up at his eyes. They were drawn and sad.

'You think Sal is guilty after all this?'

'No, I don't. I just doubted it for a while, and I was scared what it would do to you. I was wrong to do that, I'm sorry. It wasn't my place. But I was also wrong to ever doubt Sal.'

Ravi paused and looked at her, scratching the back of his head. 'OK,' he said. 'It's OK, I get why you did it. So what's going on?'

'I just found out exactly why Sal was so weird and evasive in his police interview, and why he and Andie were arguing. Come on.'

She beckoned him to follow and walked back over to

Howie's bungalow. She pointed.

'This is the drug dealer's house,' she said. 'Look at his car, Ravi.'

She watched Ravi's face as his eyes flicked up and down over the car. From windscreen to bonnet and headlight to headlight. Until they dropped to the number plate and there they stayed. Backwards and forwards and back.

'Oh,' he said.

Pip nodded. 'Oh indeed.'

'Actually, I think this is a "holy pepperoni" moment.'

And both their eyes fell back on the number plate: *R009 KKJ*.

'Sal wrote that number plate in the notes on his phone,' Pip said. 'On Wednesday the eighteenth of April at about seven forty-five p.m. He must have been suspicious, maybe he'd heard rumours at school or something. So he followed Andie that evening and must have seen her with Howie and this car. And what she was doing.'

'That's why they were arguing in the days before she went missing,' Ravi added. 'Sal hated drugs. Hated them.'

'And when the police asked him about their arguing,' Pip continued, 'he wasn't being evasive to hide his own motive. He was protecting Andie. He didn't think she was dead. He thought she was alive and coming back and he didn't want to get her in trouble with the police by telling them she was dealing drugs. And the final text he sent her on that Friday night?'

'*I'm not talking to you until you've stopped,*' Ravi quoted.

'You know something?' Pip smiled. 'Your brother has never looked more innocent than right now.'

'Thanks.' He returned the smile. 'You know, I've never said this to a girl before, but . . . I'm glad you came knocking on my door out of the blue.'

'I distinctly remember you telling me to go away,' she said.

'Well, it appears you're hard to get rid of.'

'That I am.' She bowed her head. 'Ready to do some knocking with me?'

'Wait. No. What?' He looked at her, appalled.

'Oh, come on,' she said, striding towards Howie's front door, 'you're finally going to get some action.'

'Gah, so hard not to point out all the innuendoes. Wait, Pip,' Ravi said, bounding after her. 'What are you doing? He's not going to talk to us.'

'He will,' Pip said, waving her phone above her head. 'I have leverage.'

'What leverage?' Ravi caught up with her just before the front door.

She turned and flashed him a scrunched-up, crinkly-eyed smile. And then she took his hand. Before Ravi could take it away, she knocked it three times against the door.

He widened his eyes and raised his finger in a silent telling-off.

They heard shuffling and coughing from inside. A few seconds later, the door was roughly pulled open.

Howie stood there, blinking at them. He'd taken his coat off now and was wearing a stained blue T-shirt, his feet bare. He appeared with a smell of stale smoke and damp, mouldering clothes.

'Hello, Howie Bowers,' Pip said. 'Please may we buy some drugs?'

'Who the hell are you?' Howie spat.

'I'm the hell person who took these lovely photos earlier tonight,' Pip said, scrolling on to the pictures of Howie and holding the phone up to face him. She swiped with her thumb so he saw the whole range. 'Interestingly I know this boy you sold drugs to. His name's Robin. I wonder what would happen if I called his parents right now and told them to search his rucksack. I wonder if they'd find a small paper bag of treats. And then I wonder how long it would take for the police to come knocking round here, especially once I give them a call to help them along.'

She let Howie digest it all, his eyes darting between the phone, Ravi and Pip's eyes.

He grunted. 'What do you want?'

'I want you to invite us in and answer some of our questions,' Pip said. 'That's all, and we won't go to the police.'

'What about?' he said, picking something from his teeth with his fingernails.

'About Andie Bell.'

A look of badly performed confusion stretched into Howie's face.

'You know, the girl you supplied with drugs to sell on to schoolkids. The same girl who was murdered five years ago. Remember her?' Pip said. 'Well, if you don't, I'm sure the police will remember.'

'Fine,' Howie said, stepping back over a pile of plastic bags, holding the door open. 'You can come in.'

'Excellent,' Pip said with a look back to Ravi over her shoulder. She mouthed, 'Leverage,' to him and he rolled his eyes. But as she went to enter the house Ravi pulled her back behind him, crossing the threshold first. He stared Howie down until the man drew back from the door and moved down the tiny corridor.

Pip followed Ravi inside, closing the door behind her.

'This way,' Howie said gruffly, disappearing into the living room.

Howie fell back into a tattered armchair, an open can of beer waiting for him on the armrest. Ravi stepped over to the sofa and, pushing away a pile of clothes, took the seat opposite Howie, straight-backed and as close to the edge of the sofa cushion as it was possible to be. Pip sat beside him, crossing her arms.

Howie pointed his beer can at Ravi. 'You're the brother of the guy that murdered her.'

'Allegedly,' both Pip and Ravi said at the same time.

The tension in the room flailed between the three of them, like invisible sticky tendrils that licked from one person to the other as eye contact shifted.

'You understand that we'll go to the police with these pictures if you don't answer our questions about Andie?' Pip said, eyeing the beer that probably wasn't Howie's first since returning home.

'Yes, darling,' Howie laughed a teeth-whistle laugh. 'You've made that clear enough.'

'Good,' she said. 'I'll keep my questions nice and clear too. When did Andie first start working with you and how did it come about?'

'I don't remember.' He took a large glug of beer. 'Maybe early 2011. And she was the one who came to me. All I know is I had this ballsy teenager strolling up to me in the car park, telling me she could get me more business if I gave her a cut. Said she wanted to make money and I told her that I had similar interests. Don't know how she found out where I sold.'

'So you agreed when she offered to help you sell?'

'Yeah, obviously. She was promising an in with the younger crowd, kids I couldn't really get to. It was win-win.'

'And then what happened?' Ravi said.

Howie's cold eyes alighted on Ravi, and Pip could feel him tensing where their arms almost touched.

'We met up and I set her some ground rules, like about keeping the stash and money hidden, about using codes rather than names. Asked what kind of stuff she thought kids at her school would be into. I gave her a phone to use for business stuff and that was it really. I sent her out into the big

200

wide world.' Howie smiled, his face and stubble unnervingly symmetrical.

'Andie had a second phone?' Pip asked.

'Yeah, obviously. Couldn't be arranging deals on a phone her parents pay for, could she? I bought her a burner phone, pre-paid in cash. Two actually. I got the second one when the credit on the first ran out. Gave it to her only a few months before she got killed.'

'Where did Andie keep the drugs before she sold them on?' said Ravi.

'That was part of the ground rules.' Howie sat back, speaking into his can. 'I told her this little business venture of hers would go nowhere if she didn't have somewhere to hide the stash and her second phone without her parents finding it. She assured me she had just the place and no one else knew about it.'

'Where was it?' Ravi pressed.

He scratched his chin, 'Um, think it was some kind of loose floorboard in her wardrobe. She said her parents had no idea it existed and she was always hiding shit there.'

'So, the phone is probably still hidden in Andie's bedroom?' Pip said.

'I don't know. Unless she had it on her when she . . .' Howie made a gurgling sound as he crossed his finger sharply across his throat.

Pip looked over at Ravi before her next question, a muscle tensing in his jaw as he ground his teeth, concentrating so hard on not dropping his eyes from Howie. Like he thought he could hold him in place with his stare.

'OK,' she said, 'so which drugs was Andie selling at house parties?'

Howie crushed the empty can and threw it on the floor. 'Started just weed,' he said. 'By the end she was selling a load of different things.'

'She asked *which* drugs Andie sold,' said Ravi. 'List them.'

'Yeah, OK.' Howie looked irked, sitting up taller and picking at a textured brown stain on his T-shirt. 'She sold weed, sometimes MDMA, mephedrone, ketamine. She had a couple of regular buyers of Rohypnol.'

'Rohypnol?' Pip repeated, unable to hide her shock. 'You mean roofies? Andie was dealing roofies at school parties?'

'Yeah. They're for, like, chilling out, though, too, not just what most people think.'

'Did you know who was buying Rohypnol from Andie?' she said.

'Um, there was this posh kid, I think she said. Dunno.' Howie shook his head.

'A posh kid?' Pip's mind immediately drew a picture of him: his angular face and sneering smile, his floppy yellow hair. 'Was this posh kid a blonde guy?'

Howie looked blankly at her and shrugged.

'Answer or we go to the police,' Ravi said.

'Yeah, it could have been that blonde guy.'

Pip cleared her throat to give herself some thinking time.

'OK,' she said. 'How often would you and Andie meet?'

'We met whenever we needed to, whenever she had orders to collect or cash to give me. I'd say it was probably about once a week, sometimes more, sometimes less.'

'Where did you meet?' Ravi said.

'Either at the station, or she sometimes came over here.'

'Were you . . .' Pip paused. 'Were you and Andie involved romantically?'

Howie snorted. He sat up suddenly, swatting something near his ear. 'Fuck no, we weren't,' he said, his laughter not wholly covering the annoyance creeping up his neck in red patches.

'Are you sure about that?'

'Yes, I'm sure.' The cover of amusement was cast aside now.

'Why are you getting defensive then?' Pip said.

'Course I'm defensive, there's two kids in my house berating me about stuff that happened years ago and threatening cops.' He kicked out at the crumpled beer can on the floor and it sailed across the room, clattering into the blinds just behind Pip's head.

Ravi jumped up from the sofa, stepping in front of her.

'What are you going to do about it?' Howie leered at him, staggering to his feet. 'You're a fucking joke, man.'

'All right, everyone, calm down,' Pip said, standing up too. 'We're almost finished here; you just have to answer honestly.

Did you have a sexual relationship with –'

'No, I already said no, didn't I?' The flush reached his face, peeking out above the line of his beard.

'Did you want to have a sexual relationship with her?'

'No.' He was shouting now. 'She was just business to me and me to her, OK? It wasn't more complicated than that.'

'Where were you the night she was killed?' Ravi demanded.

'I was passed out drunk on *that* sofa.'

'Do you know who killed her?' said Pip.

'Yeah, his brother.' Howie pointed aggressively at Ravi. 'Is that what this is, you want to prove your murdering scum brother was innocent?'

Pip saw Ravi stiffen, looking down at the jagged hilltop knuckles on his fists. But then he caught her eyes and shook the hardness out of his face, tucking his hands into his pockets.

'OK, we're done here,' Pip said, laying her hand on Ravi's arm. 'Let's go.'

'No, no, I don't think so.' In two giant leaps Howie darted over to the door, blocking their way out.

'Excuse me, Howard,' Pip said, her nervousness cooling into fear.

'No, no, no,' he laughed, shaking his head. 'I can't let you leave.'

Ravi stepped up to him. 'Move.'

'I did what you asked,' Howie said, turning to Pip. 'Now you have to delete those pictures of me.'

Pip relaxed a little. 'OK,' she said. 'Yes, that's fair.'

She held up her phone and showed Howie as she deleted every single picture from the car park, until she swiped right on to a photo of Barney and Josh both asleep in the dog bed. 'Done.'

Howie moved aside and let them pass.

Pip pulled open the front door and as she and Ravi stepped outside into the brisk night air Howie spoke one last time.

'You go around asking dangerous questions, girl, you're going to find some dangerous answers.'

Ravi yanked the door shut behind them. He waited until the house was at least twenty paces behind them before saying, 'Well that was fun, thanks for the invite to my first blackmailing.'

'Welcome,' she said. 'My first time too. But it was effective; we found out that Andie had a second phone, Howie had complicated feelings for her and Max Hastings had a taste for Rohypnol.' She raised her phone and clicked on to the photo app. 'Just recovering those photos in case we need future Howie leverage.'

'Oh, fantastic,' he said. 'Can't wait. Maybe then I can add blackmail as a special skill to my CV.'

'You know you use humour as a defence mechanism when you're rattled?' Pip smiled at him, letting him through the hedge gap ahead of her.

'Yeah, and you get bossy and posh.'

He looked back at her for a long moment and she broke first. They started laughing and then they just couldn't stop. The adrenaline comedown descended into hysterics. Pip fell into him, wiping away tears, snatching staccato breaths between cackles. Ravi stumbled, his face creased, laughing so hard he had to bend over and hold his gut.

They laughed until Pip's cheeks ached and her stomach felt tight and sore.

But the after-laugh sighs just set them off again.

<u>Production Log – Entry 23</u>

I should really be concentrating on my university applications; I have about a week to finish off my personal statement before the deadline for Cambridge. Just a small break right now from tooting my horn and shaking my tail feathers at admissions officers.

So Howie Bowers doesn't have an alibi for the night Andie disappeared. By his own admission he was 'passed out drunk' at his house. Without corroboration, this could be a total fabrication. He is an older guy and Andie could have *ruined* him by turning him in to the police for dealing. His relationship with Andie had criminal foundations and, judging by his defensive reaction, possibly some sexual undertones. And her car – the car that police believe was driven with her body in the boot – was found on his street.

I know Max has an alibi for the night Andie disappeared, the same alibi Sal asked his friends to give him. But let me think out loud here. Andie's abduction window was between 10:40 p.m. and 12:45 a.m. There is a possibility that Max could have worked with the upper limit of that time frame. His parents were away, Jake and Sal had left his house and Millie and Naomi went to sleep in the spare room 'a bit before half twelve'. Max could have left the house at that time without anyone knowing. Maybe Naomi could have too. Or together?

Max has a naked picture of a murder victim he claims he was never romantically involved with. He is technically an older guy. He was involved in Andie's drug dealing and regularly bought roofies from her. Posh ol' Max Hastings isn't looking so wholesome any more. Maybe I need to follow this Rohypnol line of intel, see if there is any other evidence of what I'm starting to suspect. (How could I not? He was buying *roofies* for crying out loud).

Though they are both looking simultaneously suspicious, there's no Max/Howie tag team going on here. Max only bought drugs in Kilton through Andie, and Howie only knew vaguely of Max and his buying habits via Andie.

But I think the most important lead we got from Howie is Andie's second burner phone. That is *priority number one*. That second phone most likely has all the details of the people she was selling drugs to. Maybe confirmation of the nature of her relationship with Howie. And if Howie wasn't the Secret Older Guy, maybe Andie was using her burner phone to contact this man, to keep it secret. The police had Andie's actual phone after they found Sal's body; if there were any evidence of a secret relationship on it, the police would have followed it up.

If we find that phone, maybe we find her secret older guy, maybe we find her killer and this will all be over. As it stands, there are three possible candidates for Secret Older Guy: Max, Howie or Daniel da Silva (italicized on POI list). If the burner phone confirms any one of them, I think we'd have enough to go to the police.

Or it could be someone we haven't found yet, someone waiting in the wings, preparing for their starring role in this project. Someone like Stanley Forbes, maybe? I know there's no direct link between him and Andie so he doesn't make the *POI* list. But doesn't it seem a little fluky that he's the journalist who wrote scathing articles about Andie's 'killer boyfriend' and now he's dating her little sister *and* I saw him giving money to the same drug dealer who had supplied Andie? Or are these coincidences? I don't trust coincidences.

Persons of Interest

Jason Bell

Naomi Ward

Secret Older Guy

Nat da Silva

Daniel da Silva

Max Hastings

Howie Bowers

Twenty-One

'Barney-Barney-Barney plops,' Pip sang, both the dog's front paws in her hands as they danced around the dining table. Then her mum's old CD got stuck in a surface scratch, telling them to *hit the road, Ja-Ja-Ja-Ja-Ja* . . .

'Awful sound.' Pip's mum, Leanne, entered with a dish of roasted potatoes, placing them on a trivet on the table. 'Skip to the next one, Pips,' she said, leaving the room again.

Pip set Barney down and prodded the button on the CD player; that last relic of the twentieth century that her mum was not ready to give up for touch screens and Bluetooth speakers. Fair enough; even watching her use the TV remote was painful.

'Have you carved, Vic?' Leanne shouted, backing into the room with a bowl of steaming broccoli and peas, a small knob of butter melting on top.

'The poultry is pared, my fair lady,' came his response.

'Josh! Dinner's ready,' Leanne called.

Pip went to help her dad carry in the plates and the roast chicken, Josh sidling in behind them.

'You finished your homework, sweetie?' Mum asked Josh as they all took their acknowledged seats at the table. Barney's place was on the floor beside Pip, a co-conspirator in her mission to drop small bits of meat when her parents weren't looking.

Pip nipped in and grabbed the potato dish before her dad could beat her to it. He, like Pip, was a spud connoisseur.

'Joshua, may you bestow the Bisto upon your father?'

When each of their plates were loaded up and everyone had dug in, Leanne turned to Pip, her fork pointed at her. 'When's the deadline for sending in your UCAS application then?'

'The fifteenth,' Pip said. 'I'm going to try to send it in a couple of days. Be a tad early.'

'Have you spent enough time on your personal statement? All you ever seem to be doing is that EPQ at the moment.'

'When am I ever not on top of things?' Pip said, spearing a particularly overgrown broccoli stump, the *Sequoiadendron giganteum* tree of the broccoli world. 'If I ever miss a deadline, it will be because the apocalypse has started.'

'OK, well, Dad and I can read it through after dinner if you want?'

'Yep, I'll print a copy.'

The train whistle of Pip's phone blared, making Barney jump and her mum scowl.

'No phones at the table,' she said.

'Sorry,' Pip said. 'I'm just putting it on silent.'

It could very well be the start of one of Cara's lengthy monologues sent line by line, where Pip's phone became a station out of hell, all the trains in a frenzied scram screaming over each other. Or maybe it was Ravi. She pulled out the phone and looked down at the screen in her lap to flick the ringer button.

She felt the blood drain from her face.

All the heat guttered down her back, slopping into her gut where it churned, pushing her dinner back up. Her throat constricted at the sudden drop into cold fear.

'Pip?'

'Uh . . . I . . . suddenly desperate for a wee,' she said, jumping up from her chair with her phone in hand, almost tripping over the dog.

She darted from the room and across the hall. Her thick woollen socks slipped out under her on the polished oak and she fell, catching the weight of the fall on one elbow.

'Pippa?' Victor's voice called.

'I'm OK,' she said, picking herself up. 'Just skidded.'

She shut the bathroom door behind her and locked it. Slamming down the toilet-seat lid, she turned shakily to sit on top of it. Her phone between both hands, she opened it and clicked on to the message.

You stupid bitch. Leave this alone while you still can.

From Unknown.

Production Log – Entry 24

I can't sleep.

School starts in five hours and I can't sleep.

There's no part of me that thinks this can be a joke any more. The note in my sleeping bag, this text. It's real. I've plugged all the leaks in my research since the camping trip; the only people who know what I've discovered are Ravi and those I've interviewed.

Yet someone knows I'm getting close and they are starting to panic. Someone who followed me into the woods. Someone who has my phone number.

I tried to message them back, a futile *who is this?* It errored. It couldn't send it. I've looked it up: there are certain websites and apps you can use to anonymize texts so I can neither reply nor find out who sent it.

They are fittingly named. Unknown.

Is Unknown the person who actually murdered Andie Bell? Do they want me to think they can get to me too?

I can't go to the police. I don't have enough evidence yet. All I have are unsworn statements from people who knew different fragments of Andie's secret lives. I have seven persons of interest but no one main suspect yet. There are too many people in Little Kilton who had motive to kill Andie.

I need tangible proof.

I need that burner phone.

And only then will I leave this alone, Unknown. Only when the truth is out there and you no longer are.

Twenty-Two

'Why are we here?' Ravi said when he caught sight of her.

'Shhh,' Pip hissed, grabbing his coat sleeve to pull him behind the tree with her. She peeked her head out past the trunk, watching the house across the street.

'Shouldn't you be at school?' he asked.

'I've pulled a sickie, OK?' Pip said. 'Don't make me feel worse about it than I already do.'

'You've never pulled a sickie before?'

'Only ever missed four days of school. Ever. And that was because of chickenpox,' she said quietly, her eyes on the large detached cottage. Its old bricks speckled from pale yellow to dark russet and were overrun with ivy that climbed up to the crooked roofline where three tall chimneys perched. A large white garage door behind the empty drive winked the morning autumn sunshine back at them. It was the last house on the street before the road climbed up to the church.

'What are we doing here?' Ravi said, tucking his head around the other side of the tree to see Pip's face.

'I've been here since just after eight,' she said, hardly pausing to breathe. 'Becca left about twenty minutes ago; she's interning over at the *Kilton Mail* office. Dawn left just as I was arriving. My mum says she works part-time at a charity head office in Wycombe. It's quarter past nine now, so she should still be out for a while. And there's no alarm on the front of the house.'

Her last word slipped into a yawn. She'd hardly slept last night, waking to stare again at the text from Unknown until the words were burned into the underside of her eyelids, haunting her every time she closed her eyes.

'Pip,' Ravi said, bringing her attention back to him. 'And, yet again, why are we here?' His eyes were wide in their telling-off way already. 'Tell me it's not what I think it is.'

'To break in,' Pip said. 'We have to find that burner phone.'

He groaned. 'How did I know you were going to say that?'

'It's actual evidence, Ravi. Actual physical evidence. Proof that she was dealing drugs with Howie. Maybe the identity of the secret older guy Andie was seeing. If we find it, we can phone an anonymous tip in to the police and maybe they'll reopen the investigation and actually find her killer.'

'OK, but here's a quick observation,' Ravi said, holding up his finger. 'You're asking me, the brother of the person everyone believes murdered Andie Bell, to break into the Bell house? Not to mention the amount of trouble I would be in anyway as a brown kid breaking into a white family's house.'

'Shit, Ravi,' Pip said, stepping back behind the tree, her breath catching in her throat. 'I'm so sorry. I wasn't thinking.'

She really hadn't been thinking; she was so convinced the truth was just waiting for them in this house that she hadn't considered the position this would put Ravi in. Of course he couldn't break in with her; this town already treated him like a criminal – how much worse would it be for him if they got caught?

Since Pip was a little girl, her dad had always taught her about their different experiences of the world, explaining whenever something happened: whenever someone followed him around a shop, whenever someone questioned him for being alone with a white kid, whenever someone presumed he worked security at his office, not as the firm's partner. Pip grew up determined never to be blind to this, nor her invisible step up that she'd never had to fight for.

But she'd been blind this morning. She was angry at herself, her stomach twisting in uncomfortable hurricane turns.

'I'm so sorry,' she said again. 'I was being stupid. I know you can't take the same risks I can. I'll go in alone. Maybe you can stay here, keep a lookout?'

'No,' he said thoughtfully, fingers burrowing through his hair. 'If this is how we're going to clear Sal's name, I have to be there for that. That's worth the risk. It's too important. I still think this is reckless and I'm crapping myself, but –' he paused, flashing her a small smile – 'we're partners in crime after all. That means partners no matter what.'

'Are you sure?' Pip shifted and the strap of her rucksack fell down to her elbow crook.

'I'm sure,' he said, reaching out and lifting the strap back up for her.

'OK.' Pip turned to survey the empty house. 'And if it's any consolation, I wasn't planning on us getting caught.'

'So what *is* the plan?' he said. 'Break a window?'

She gaped at him. 'No way. I was planning to use a key. We live in Kilton; everyone has a spare key outside somewhere.'

'Oh . . . right. Let's go and scope out the target, Sarge.' Ravi looked intently at her, pretending to do a complex sequence of military hand gestures. She flicked him to get him to stop.

Pip went first, walking briskly across the road and over the front lawn. Thank goodness the Bells lived right at the end of a quiet street; there was no one around. She reached the front door and turned to watch Ravi darting across, head down, to join her.

They checked under the doormat first, the place where Pip's family kept their spare key. But no luck. Ravi reached up and felt the frame above the front door. He pulled his hand back empty, fingertips covered in dust and grime.

'OK, you check that bush, I'll check this one.'

There was no key under either, nor hidden around the fitted lanterns nor on any secret nail behind the creeping ivy.

'Oh, surely not,' Ravi said, pointing at a chrome wind chime mounted beside the front door. He snaked his hand through the metal tubes, gritting his teeth when two knocked tunefully together.

'Ravi,' she said in an urgent whisper, 'what are you –'

He pulled something off the small wooden platform that hung in the middle of the chimes and held it up to her. A key with a little nub of old Blu-Tack attached.

'Aha,' he said, 'student becomes master. You may be the sarge, Sarge, but I am chief inspector.'

'Zip it, Singh.'

Pip swung her bag off and lowered it to the ground. She rustled inside and immediately found what she was looking for, her fingers alighting on their smooth vinyl texture. She pulled them out.

'Wh– I don't even want to ask,' Ravi laughed, shaking his head as Pip pulled on the bright yellow rubber gloves.

'I'm about to commit a crime,' she said. 'I don't want to leave any fingerprints. There's a pair in here for you too.'

She held out her florescent yellow palm and Ravi placed the key into it. He bent to rifle through her bag and stood up again, his hands gripped round a pair of purple flower-patterned gloves.

'What are these?' he said.

'My mum's gardening gloves. Look, I didn't have long to plan this heist, OK?'

'Clearly,' Ravi muttered.

'They're the bigger pair. Just put them on.'

'*Real* men wear floral when trespassing,' Ravi said, slipping them on and clapping his gloved hands together.

He nodded that he was ready.

Pip shouldered her bag and stepped up to the door. She took a breath and held it in. Gripping her other hand to steady it, she guided the key into the lock and twisted.

Twenty-Three

The sunlight followed them inside, cracking into the tiled hallway in a long, glowing strip. As they stepped over the threshold, their shadows carved through the beam of light, both of them together as one stretched silhouette, with two heads and a tangle of moving arms and legs.

Ravi closed the door and they walked slowly down the hallway. Pip couldn't help but tiptoe, even though she knew no one was home. She'd seen this house many times before, pictured at different angles with police in black and high-vis swarming outside. But that was always outside. All she'd ever seen of the inside were snippets when the front door was open and a press photographer clicked the moment into forever.

The border between outside and in felt significant here.

She could tell Ravi felt it too, the way he held his breath. There was a heaviness to the air in here. Secrets captured in the silence, floating around like invisible motes of dust. Pip didn't even want to think too loudly, in case she disturbed it. This quiet place, the place where Andie Bell was last seen alive when she was only a few months older than Pip. The house itself was part of the mystery, part of Kilton's history.

They moved towards the stairs, glancing into the plush living room on the right and the huge vintage-style kitchen on the left, fitted with duck-egg blue cabinets and a large wood-top island.

And then they heard it. A small thump upstairs.

Pip froze and Ravi grabbed her gloved hand with his.

Another thump, closer this time, just above their heads.

Pip looked back at the door; could they make it in time?

The thumps became a sound of frantic jingling and a few seconds later a black cat appeared at the top of the stairs.

'Holy crap,' Ravi said, dropping his shoulders and her hand, his relief like an actual blast of air rippling through the quiet.

Pip sniffed a hollow, anxious laugh, her hands starting to sweat inside the rubber. The cat bounded down the stairs, stopping halfway to meow in their direction. Pip, born and raised a dog person, wasn't sure how to react.

'Hi, cat,' she whispered as it padded down the rest of the stairs and slinked over to her. It rubbed its face on her shins, curling in and out of her legs.

'Pip, I don't like cats,' Ravi said uneasily, watching with disgust as the cat started to press its fur-topped skull into his ankles. Pip bent down and patted the cat lightly with her rubber-gloved hand. It came back over to her and started to purr.

'Come on,' she said to Ravi.

Unwinding her legs from the cat, Pip headed for the stairs. As she took them, Ravi following behind, the cat meowed and raced after them, darting round his legs.

'Pip . . .' Ravi's voice trailed nervously as he tried not to step on it. Pip shooed the cat and it trotted back downstairs and into the kitchen. 'I wasn't scared,' he added unconvincingly.

Gloved hand on the banister, she climbed the rest of the stairs, almost knocking off a notebook and a USB stick that were balanced on the post at the very top. Strange place to keep them.

When they were both upstairs, Pip studied the various doors that opened on to the landing. That back bedroom on the right couldn't be Andie's; the floral bedspread was ruffled and slept in, paired socks on the chair in the corner. Nor could it be the bedroom at the front where a dressing gown was strewn on the floor and a glass of water on a bedside table.

Ravi was the first to notice. He tapped her gently on the arm and pointed. There was only one door up here that was closed. They crossed over to it. Pip grasped the gold handle and pushed open the door.

It was immediately obvious this was *her* room.

Everything felt staged and stagnant. Though it had all the props of a teenage girl's bedroom – pinned-up photos of Andie standing between Emma and Chloe as they posed with their fingers in Vs, a picture of her and Sal with a candyfloss between them, an old brown teddy tucked into the bed with a fluffy hot-water bottle beside it, an overflowing make-up case on the desk – the room didn't feel quite real. A place entombed in five years of grief.

Pip took a first step on to the plush cream carpet.

Her eyes flicked from the lilac walls to the white wooden furniture; everything clean and polished, the carpet showing recent vacuum tracks. Dawn Bell must still clean her dead daughter's room, preserving it as it had been when Andie left it for the final time. She didn't have her daughter but she still had the place where she'd slept, where she'd woken, where she'd dressed, where she'd screamed and shouted and slammed the door, where her mum whispered goodnight and turned off the light. Or so Pip imagined, reanimating the empty room with the life that might have been lived here. This room, perpetually waiting for someone who was never coming back while the world ticked on outside its closed door.

She looked back at Ravi and, by the look on his face, she knew there was a room just like this in the Singhs' house.

And though Pip had come to feel like she knew Andie, the one buried under all those secrets, this bedroom made Andie a real person to her for the first time. As she and Ravi crossed over to the wardrobe, Pip silently promised the room that she would find the truth. Not just for Sal, but for Andie too.

The truth that could very well be hidden right here.

'Ready?' Ravi whispered.

She nodded.

He opened the wardrobe on to a rack bulging with dresses and jumpers on wooden hangers. At one end hung Andie's old Kilton Grammar uniform, squashed against the wall by skirts and tops, no room to part even an inch of space between the clothes.

Struggling with the rubber gloves, Pip pulled her phone out of her jeans pocket and swiped up to turn on the torch. She got down on her knees, Ravi beside her, and they crawled under the clothes, the torch lighting up the old floorboards inside. They started prodding the boards, tracing their fingers round the shape of them, trying to prise up their corners.

Ravi found it. It was the one against the back wall, on the left.

He pushed down one corner and the other side of the board kicked up. Pip shuffled forward to pull up the floorboard, sliding it behind them. With her phone held up, Pip and Ravi leaned over to look inside the dark space below.

'No.'

She moved the torch down inside the small space to be absolutely sure, pivoting the light into each corner. It illuminated only layers of dust, gusting out in whirlwinds now because of their picked-up breath.

It was empty. No phone. No cash. No drug stash. Nothing.

'It's not here,' Ravi said.

The disappointment was a physical sensation gouging through Pip's gut, leaving a space for the fear to fill in.

'I really thought it would be here,' he said.

Pip had too. She thought the phone screen would light up the killer's name for them and the police would do the rest. She thought she'd be safe from Unknown. It was supposed to be over, she thought, her throat constricting the way it did before she cried.

She slid the floorboard back in place and inched backwards out of the wardrobe after Ravi, her hair getting briefly tangled in the zip of a long dress. She stood, closed the doors and turned to him.

'Where could the burner phone be then?' he said.

'Maybe Andie had it on her when she died,' Pip said, 'and now it's buried with her or otherwise destroyed by the killer.'

'Or,' Ravi said, studying the items on Andie's desk. 'Or someone knew where it was hidden and they took it after her disappearance, knowing that it would lead the police to them if it was found.'

'Or that,' Pip agreed. 'But that doesn't help us now.'

She joined Ravi at the desk. On top of the make-up case was a paddle hairbrush with long blonde hairs still wound round the bristles. Beside it, Pip spotted a Kilton Grammar academic planner for the year 2011/2012, almost identical to the one she owned for this year. Andie had decorated the title page of her planner under the plastic with doodled hearts and stars and small printouts of supermodels.

She flipped through some of the pages. The days were filled with scribbled homework and coursework assignments. November and December had various university open days listed. The week before Christmas there was a note to herself to *maybe get Sal a Christmas present*. Dates and locations of calamity parties, school deadlines, people's birthdays. And, strangely, random letters with times scribbled in next to them.

'Hey.' She held it up to show Ravi. 'Look at these weird initials. What do you think they mean?'

Ravi stared for a moment, resting his jaw in his gardening-gloved hand. Then his eyes darkened as he tensed his brows.

He said, 'Do you remember that thing Howie Bowers said to us? That he'd told Andie to use codes instead of names.'

'Maybe these are her codes,' Pip finished his sentence for him, tracing her rubber finger over the random letters. 'We should document these.'

She laid the planner down and pulled out her phone again. Ravi helped her tug one of her gloves off and she thumbed on to the camera. Ravi skipped the pages back to February 2012 and Pip took pictures of each double page, as they flicked right through to that week in April just after the Easter holidays, where the last thing Andie had written on the Friday was: *Start French revision notes soon.* Eleven photos in all.

'OK,' Pip said, pocketing her phone and slipping back into the glove. 'We –'

The front door slammed below them.

Ravi's head snapped round, terror pooling in the pupils of his eyes.

Pip dropped the planner in its place. She nodded her head towards the wardrobe. 'Get back in,' she whispered.

She opened the doors and crawled inside, looking for Ravi. He was on his knees now just outside the cupboard. Pip shuffled aside to give him space to crawl back in. But Ravi wasn't moving. Why wasn't he moving?

Pip reached forward and grabbed him, pulling him into her against the back wall. Ravi snapped back into life then. He grasped the wardrobe doors and quietly swung them closed, shutting them inside.

They heard sharp-heeled steps in the hallway. Was it Dawn Bell, back from work already?

'Hello, Monty.' A voice carried through the house. It was Becca.

Pip felt Ravi shaking beside her, right through into her own bones. She took his hand, the rubber gloves squeaking as she held it.

They heard Becca on the stairs then, louder with each step, the jingling collar of the cat behind her.

'Ah, that's where I left them,' she said, footsteps pausing on the landing.

Pip squeezed Ravi's hand, hoping he could feel how sorry she was. Hoping he knew she would take the fall if she could.

'Monty, have you been in here?' Becca's voice drew nearer.

Ravi closed his eyes.

'You know you're not supposed to go in this room.'

Pip buried her face into his shoulder.

Becca was in the room with them now. They could hear her breathing, hear the ticking of her tongue as she moved it around her mouth. More steps, stifled by the thick carpet. And then the sound of Andie's bedroom door clicking shut.

Becca's words were muffled through it now as she called, 'Bye, Monty.'

Ravi opened his eyes slowly, squeezing Pip's hand back, his panicked breaths rippling through her hair.

The front door slammed again.

<u>Production Log – Entry 25</u>

Well, I thought I'd need about six coffees to keep me awake for the rest
of the day. Turns out that close call with Becca more than did the trick.
Ravi still wasn't quite himself by the time he had to leave for work. I can't
believe how close we came to getting caught. And the burner phone
wasn't there . . . but it might not all have been for nothing.

I emailed the photos of Andie's planner to myself so I could see them
bigger on my laptop screen. I've trawled through each one dozens of
times and I think there are some things to pick up on here.

This is the week after the Easter holidays, the week Andie
disappeared. There's quite a lot to note on this page alone. I can't ignore

Week Beginning: 16th A

Monday 16th

French – do passage translation
for friday

Drama – do blocking notes on Act
scene 4

Shopping with Chlo Chlo after school.

Tuesday 17th

In double free do
translation today !!!
↑
Or get Sal's one
Rehearsal with Jamie and Lex @

Fat da Silva 0-3

Wednesday 18th

– Geog – read and do notes on
river chapter

→ CP @ 7:30

that *Fat da Silva 0–3 Andie* scorecard comment. This was just after Andie had posted the nude video of Nat online. And I know from Nat that she only returned to school on Wednesday 18th April and Andie called her a slut in the corridor, prompting the death threat stuffed in Andie's locker.

But, judging this comment at face value, it seems Andie was gloating over three victories she'd had over Nat in her twisted high-school games. What if the topless video accounts for one of these goals and Andie blackmailing Nat to drop out of *The Crucible* was another? What was the third thing Andie did to Nat da Silva that she's revelling in here? Could that have been what made Nat snap and turned her into a killer?

Another significant entry on that page is on Wednesday 18th April. Andie wrote: *CP @ 7:30.*

If Ravi is right, and Andie is noting things down in code, I think I've just cracked this one. It's so simple.

Thursday 19th

- get translation from Chris Parks
· Drama -get Lex to get fake cigar
  props - oba
Free p 5+6 -go back to Em's

Friday 20th

Start French revision notes soon

Saturday/Sunday 21st/22nd

CP = car park. As in the train station car park. I think Andie was reminding herself that she had a meeting with Howie in the car park that evening. I know that she *did*, in fact, meet Howie that evening, because Sal wrote Howie's number plate in his phone at 7:42 p.m. on the very same Wednesday.

There are many more instances of CP with an accompanying time in the photos we took. I think I can confidently say that these refer to Andie's drug trades with Howie and that she was following Howie's instruction to use codes, to keep her activities hidden from any prying eyes. But, as all teenagers, she was prone to forgetting things (especially her schedule) so she wrote the meetings down on the one item she would have looked at once every lesson at least. The perfect memory prompt.

So now that I think I've cracked Andie's code, there are some other initialized entries with times written in the planner.

Week Beginning: 12th Ma

Monday 12th

~~Ge~~ Read Chap 9 in encore tricolore ☐

Drama - read Revenger's tragedy

→ CP @ 6

Tuesday 13th

AndieBell   AndieBell   Andie
AndieBell   AndieBell
· read Revenger's Tragedy ☐

Wednesday 14th

Read frickin' Revengers

- order presents for EH + CB

During this mid-March week, Andie wrote on Thursday the 15th: *IV @ 8.*

This one I'm stumped on. If it follows the same code pattern, then IV = *I . . . V . . .*

If, like CP, IV refers to a place, I have absolutely no idea what it is. There's nowhere in Kilton I can think of with those initials. Or what if IV refers to somebody's name? It only appears three times in the pages we photographed.

There's a similar entry that appears much more frequently: HH @ 6. But on this March 17th entry, Andie has also written 'before Calam' underneath it. Calam presumably means Calamity Party. So maybe HH actually just means Howie's House and Andie was picking up drugs to take to the party.

---

ursday 15th

- Wiki the plot of Revenger's tragedy
- french questions
→ I V @ 8

iday 16th

!!! Mock-mock Geography Exam !!!

urday/Sunday 17th/18th

Sat: HH @ 6
^ before Calam

Monday 5th

- Pick either Revenger's Tragedy or Maccy Bee for drama exam

   go to Sal's later

Tuesday 6th

- Watch Macbeth on youtube

- Chap 6 of French textbook

Wednesday 7th

Geography - Essay plan for Friday ☑

→ CP @ 6:30

An earlier spread in March caught my eye too. Those numbers scrawled in and scribbled out on the Thursday 8th March are a phone number. 11 digits starting with 07; it has to be. Thinking out loud here: why would Andie be writing down a phone number in her planner? Of course the planner would have been on her at most times, both in school and afterwards, just as mine is a permanent fixture in my bag. But if she was taking a new number, why not enter it straight into her phone? Unless, perhaps, she didn't want to put that number into her *actual* phone. Maybe she wrote it down because she didn't have her burner phone on her at the time and that's where she wanted the number to go. Could this be Secret Older Guy's number? Or maybe a new phone number for Howie? Or a new client wanting to buy drugs from her? And after she entered it into her second phone, she must have scribbled over it to hide her tracks.

ursday 8th ~~07700900~~

- Start reading the Revenger's
  Tragedy for drama

day 9th

  Extra free period 3 - go out for
  ★ lunch with galsssss
  · French questions ☐

urday/Sunday 10th/11th

  Car in for MOT
      grrrrrrr

I've been staring at the scribble for a good half an hour. It looks
to me like the first eight digits are: 07700900. It's possible those last
two numbers are a double 8 instead, but I think that's just the way the
scribble crosses them. And then, for the last three digits, it gets a bit
tricky. The third final digit looks like a 7 or a 9, the way it seems to have a
leg and a hooked line at the top. The next number I'm pretty confident is
either a 7 or a 1, judging by that straight upward line. And then bringing
up the rear is a number with a curve in it, so either a 6, a 0 or an 8.

This leaves us with twelve possible combinations:

07700900776	07700900976	07700900716	07700900916
07700900770	07700900970	07700900710	07700900910
07700900778	07700900978	07700900718	07700900918

I've tried ringing the first column. I got the same robotic response to each call: *I'm sorry, the number you have dialled has not been recognized. Please hang up and try again.*

In the second column, I got through to an elderly woman up in Manchester, who'd never been to or even heard of Little Kilton. Another *not recognized* and a *no longer in service*. The third column racked up two *not recognized* and a generic phone provider voicemail. In the final three numbers, I got through to the voicemail for a boiler engineer called Garrett Smith with a thick Geordie accent, one *no longer in service* and a final straight to a generic voicemail.

Chasing this phone number is another dud. I can hardly make out those last three digits and the number is over five years old now and probably out of use. I'll keep trying the numbers that went to generic voicemails, just in case anything comes of it. But I really need a) a proper night's sleep and b) to finish my Cambridge application.

Persons of Interest

Jason Bell

Naomi Ward

Secret Older Guy

Nat da Silva

Daniel da Silva

Max Hastings

Howie Bowers

Pippa Fitz-Amobi
EPQ   11/10/2017

<u>Production Log – Entry 26</u>

Application to Cambridge sent off this morning. And school has registered me for the pre-interview ELAT exam on 2nd November for Cambridge English applicants. In my free periods today I started looking back through my literature essays to send into admissions. I like my Toni Morrison one, I'll send that off. But nothing else is good enough. I need to write a new one, about Margaret Atwood, I think.

I should really be getting on with it now, but I've found myself dragged back into the world of Andie Bell, clicking on to my EPQ document when I should be starting a blank page. I've read over Andie's planner so many times that I can almost recite her February-to-April schedule by heart.

One thing is abundantly clear: Andie Bell was a homework procrastinator.

Two other things are quite clear, leaning heavily on assumption: CP refers to Andie's drug deal meetings with Howie at the station car park and HH refers to those at his house.

I still haven't managed to work out IV at all. It appears only three times in total: on Thursday 15th March at 8p.m., Friday 23rd March at 9p.m. and Thursday the 29th March at 9p.m.

Unlike CPs or HHs, which jump around at all different times, IV is once at eight and twice at nine.

Ravi's been working on this too. He just sent me an email with a list of possible people/places he thinks IV could refer to. He's spread the search further afield than Kilton, looking into neighbouring towns and villages as well. I should've thought to do that.

His list:

Imperial Vault Nightclub in Amersham

The Ivy House Hotel in Little Chalfont

Ida Vaughan, aged ninety, lives in Chesham

The Four Cafe in Wendover (IV = four in Roman numerals)

OK, on to Google I go.

Imperial Vault's website says that the club was opened in 2010. From its location on the map it looks like it's just in the middle of nowhere, a concrete slab nightclub and car park amid a mass of green grass pixels. It has student nights every Wednesday and Friday and holds regular events like 'Ladies' Night'. The club is owned by a man called Rob Hewitt. It's possible that Andie was going there to sell drugs. We could go and look into it, ask to speak to the owner.

The Ivy House Hotel doesn't have its own website but it has a page on TripAdvisor, only two and a half stars. It's a small family-run B&B with four available rooms, right by Chalfont station. From the few pictures on the site it looks quaint and cosy, but it's 'right on a busy road and loud when you're trying to sleep' according to Carmel672. And Trevor59 wasn't happy with them at all; they'd double-booked his room and he'd had to find other accommodation. T9Jones said 'the family were lovely' but that the bathroom was 'tired and filthy – with dirt tracked all round the tub.' She's even posted some pictures on her review to bolster her point.

CRAP.

Oh my god, oh my god, oh my god. I've been saying, oh my god, out loud for at least thirty seconds but it's not enough; it needs to be typed as well. Oh My God.

And Ravi isn't picking up his damn phone!

My fingers can't keep up with my brain. T9Jones posted two close-up pictures of the bathtub at different angles. And then she has a long shot of the entire bathroom. Beside the bath is a huge full-length mirror on the wall; we can see T9Jones and the flash of her phone reflected in it. We can see the rest of the bathroom too, from its cream ceiling with circle spotlights down to its tiled floor. *A red and white tiled floor.*

I'll eat my fluffy fox-head hat if I'm wrong, BUT I'm almost certain it is the very same tiled floor from a grainy printed photo pinned up behind a *Reservoir Dogs* poster in Max Hastings' bedroom. Andie naked but for a small pair of black pants, pouting at a mirror, this mirror . . . in the Ivy House Hotel, Little Chalfont.

If I'm right, then Andie went to that hotel at least three times in the span of three weeks. Who was she there to meet? Max? Secret Older Guy?

Looks like I'm going to Little Chalfont after school tomorrow.

Twenty-Four

There were a few moments of muffled shrieking as the train pulled off and started to gain speed. It jerked and jogged Pip's pen, scribbling a line down the page from her essay introduction. She sighed, ripped the piece of paper from the pad and screwed it into a ball. It was no good anyway. She shoved the paper ball into the top of her rucksack and readied her pen again.

She was on the train to Little Chalfont. Ravi was meeting her there, straight from work, so she thought she could put the eleven minutes there to good use, get a chunk of her Margaret Atwood essay drafted. But reading her own words back, nothing felt right. She knew what she wanted to say, each idea perfectly formed and moulded but the words got muddled and lost on the way from brain to fingers. Her mind stuck in Andie Bell sidetracks.

The recorded voice on the tannoy announced that Chalfont was the next stop and Pip gratefully looked away from the thinning A4 pad and shoved it back in her rucksack. The train slackened and came to a stop with a sharp mechanical sigh. She skipped down on to the platform and fed her ticket into the barriers.

Ravi was waiting for her outside.

'Sarge,' he said, flicking his dark hair out of his eyes. 'I was just coming up with our crime-fighting theme tune. So far, I've got chilled strings and a pan flute when it's me, and then you come on with some heavy, Darth Vader-ish trumpets.'

'Why am I the trumpets?' she said.

'Because you stomp when you walk; sorry to be the one to tell you.'

Pip pulled out her phone and typed the Ivy House Hotel address into her maps app. The line appeared on screen and they followed the three-minute-long walking directions, Pip's blue circle avatar sliding along the route in her hands.

She looked up when her blue circle collided with the red destination pin. There was a small wooden sign just before the drive that read *Ivy House Hotel* in fading carved letters. The drive was sloped and pebbled, leading to a red-brick house almost wholly covered in creeping ivy. It was so thick with the green leaves that the house itself seemed to shiver in the gentle wind.

Their footsteps crunched up the drive as they headed for the front door. Pip clocked the parked car, meaning someone must be in. Hopefully it was the owners and not a guest.

She jabbed her finger on to the cold metal doorbell and let it ring out for one long note.

They heard a small voice inside, some slow shuffled steps and then the door swung inward, sending a tremor through the ivy around the frame. An old woman with fluffy grey hair, thick glasses and a very premature Christmas-patterned jumper stood before them and smiled.

'Hello, dears,' she said. 'I didn't realize we were expecting someone. What name did you make the booking under?' she said, ushering Pip and Ravi inside and closing the door.

They stepped into a dimly lit squared hallway, with a sofa and coffee table on the left and a white staircase running along the far wall.

'Oh, sorry,' Pip said, turning back to face the woman, 'we haven't actually got a booking.'

'I see, well, lucky for you two we aren't booked up so –'

'– Sorry,' Pip cut in, looking awkwardly at Ravi, 'I mean, we're not looking to stay here. We're looking for . . . we have some questions for the owners of the hotel. Are you . . .?'

'Yes, I own the hotel,' the woman smiled, looking unnervingly at a point just left of Pip's face. 'Ran it for twenty years with my David; he was in charge of most things, though. It's been hard since my David passed a couple of years ago. But my grandsons are always here, helping me get by, driving me around. My grandson Henry is just upstairs cleaning the rooms.'

'So five years ago, you and your husband were running the hotel?' Ravi said.

The woman nodded and her eyes swayed over to him. 'Very handsome,' she said quietly, and then to Pip, 'lucky girl.'

'No, we're not . . .' Pip said, looking to Ravi. She wished she hadn't. Out of the old lady's wandering eyeline, he shimmied his shoulders excitedly and pointed to his face, mouthing 'very handsome' at Pip.

'Would you like to sit down?' the woman said, gesturing to a green-velvet sofa beneath a window. 'I know I would.' She shuffled over to a leather armchair facing the sofa.

Pip walked over, intentionally treading on Ravi's foot as she passed. She sat down, knees pointed towards the woman, and Ravi slotted in beside her, still with that stupid grin on his face.

'Where's my . . .' the woman said, patting her jumper and her trouser pockets, a blank look falling over her face.

'Um, so,' Pip said, drawing the woman's attention back to her. 'Do you keep records of people who have stayed here?'

'It's all done on the, err . . . that, um . . . the computer now, isn't it?' the woman said. 'Sometimes by the telephone. David always sorted all the bookings; now Henry does it for me.'

'So how did you keep track of the reservations you had?' Pip said, guessing already that the answer would be lacking.

'My David did it. Had a spreadsheet printed out for the week.' The woman shrugged, staring out of the window.

'Would you still have your reservation spreadsheets from five years ago?' asked Ravi.

'No, no. The whole place would be flooded in paper.'

'But do you have the documents saved on a computer?' Pip said.

'Oh no. We threw David's computer out after he passed. It was a very slow little thing, like me,' she said. 'My Henry does all the bookings for me now.'

'Can I ask you something?' Pip said, unzipping her rucksack

and pulling out the folded bit of printer paper. She straightened out the page and handed it to the woman. 'Do you recognize this girl? Has she ever stayed here?'

The woman stared down at the photo of Andie, the one that had been used in most newspaper reports. She lifted the paper right to her face, then held it at arm's length, then brought it close again.

'Yes,' she nodded, looking from Pip to Ravi to Andie. 'I know her. She's been here.'

Pip's skin prickled with nervous excitement.

'You remember that girl stayed with you five years ago?' she said. 'Do you remember the man she was with? What he looked like?'

The woman's face muddied and she stared at Pip, her eyes darting right and left, a blink marking each change in direction.

'No,' she said shakily. 'No, it wasn't five years ago. I saw this girl. She's been here.'

'In 2012?' Pip said.

'No, no.' The woman's eyes settled past Pip's ear. 'It was just a few weeks ago. She was here, I remember.'

Pip's heart sank a few hundred feet, a drop tower back into her chest.

'That's not possible,' she said. 'That girl has been dead for five years.'

'But, I –' the woman shook her head, the wrinkled skin around her eyes folding together – 'but I remember. She was here. She's been here.'

'Five years ago?' Ravi prompted.

'No,' the woman said, anger creeping into her voice. 'I remember, don't I? I don't –'

'Grandma?' A man's voice called from upstairs.

A set of heavy boots thundered down the stairs and a fair-haired man came into view.

'Hello?' he said, looking at Pip and Ravi. He walked over and proffered his hand. 'I'm Henry Hill,' he said.

Ravi stood and shook his hand. 'I'm Ravi, this is Pip.'

'Can we help you with something?' he asked, darting concerned looks over at his grandmother.

'We were just asking your grandma a couple of questions about someone who stayed here five years ago,' said Ravi.

Pip looked back to the old woman and noticed that she was crying. Tears snaking down her tissue-paper skin, dropping from her chin on to the printout of Andie.

The grandson must have noticed as well. He walked over and squeezed his grandma's shoulder, taking the piece of paper out of her shaking grip.

'Grandma,' he said, 'why don't you pop the kettle on and make us a pot of tea? I'll help out these people here, don't worry.'

He helped her up off the chair and steered her towards a door to the left of the hall, handing the photo of Andie to Pip as they passed. Ravi and Pip looked at each other, questions in their eyes, until Henry returned a few seconds later, closing the kitchen door to muffle the sound of the boiling kettle.

'Sorry,' he said with a sad smile. 'She gets upset when she

gets confused. The Alzheimer's . . . it's starting to get quite bad. I'm actually just cleaning up to put the place on the market. She keeps forgetting that.'

'I'm sorry,' Pip said. 'We should have realized. We didn't mean to upset her.'

'No, I know, course you didn't,' he said. 'Can I help with whatever it is?'

'We were asking about this girl.' Pip held up the paper. 'Whether she stayed here five years ago.'

'And what did my grandma say?'

'She thought she'd seen her recently, just weeks ago,' she swallowed. 'But this girl died in 2012.'

'She does that quite often now,' he said, looking between the two of them. 'Gets confused about times and when things happened. Sometimes still thinks my grandad is alive. She's probably just recognizing your girl from five years ago, if that's when you think she was here.'

'Yeah,' Pip said, 'I guess.'

'Sorry I can't be of more help. I can't tell you who stayed here five years ago; we haven't kept the old records. But if she recognized her, I guess that gives you your answer?'

Pip nodded. 'It does. Sorry for upsetting her.'

'Will she be OK?' said Ravi.

'She'll be fine,' Henry said gently. 'Cup of tea will do the trick.'

They strolled out of Kilton station, the town just dimming

as it ticked into the hour of six and the sun slumped off to the west.

Pip's mind was a centrifuge, spinning over the shifting pieces of Andie, separating them and putting them back together in different combinations.

'Weighing it up,' she said, 'I think we can confirm that Andie stayed at the Ivy House Hotel.' She thought the bathroom tiles and the woman's time-confused recognition were proof enough of that. But this confirmation loosened and rearranged certain pieces.

They turned right into the car park, heading for Pip's car down at the far end, speaking in harmonized *if*s and *so*s as they walked.

'If Andie was going to that hotel,' Ravi said, 'must be because that's where she met Secret Older Guy and they were both trying to avoid getting caught.'

Pip nodded in agreement. 'So,' she said, 'that means that whoever Secret Older Guy was, he couldn't have Andie over at his house. And the most likely reason for that would be that he lived with his family or a wife.'

This changed things.

Pip carried on. 'Daniel da Silva lived with his new wife in 2012 and Max Hastings was living with his parents who knew Sal well. Both of them would have needed to be away from home to carry on a secret relationship with Andie. And, let's not forget, Max has a naked photo of Andie taken inside the Ivy House Hotel, a photo he supposedly "found",' she said,

243

using fingered air quotes.

'Yeah,' Ravi said, 'but Howie Bowers lived alone then. If it was him Andie was secretly seeing, they wouldn't have needed to stay in a hotel.'

'That's what I was thinking,' Pip said. 'Which means, we can now rule Howie out as a candidate for Secret Older Guy. Although that doesn't mean he can't still be the killer.'

'True,' Ravi agreed, 'but at least it starts to clear the picture a little. It wasn't Howie who Andie was seeing behind Sal's back in March, and it wasn't him she spoke of ruining.'

They had deduced all the way over to her car. Pip fiddled in her pocket and blipped the key. She opened the driver door and shoved her rucksack inside, Ravi taking it on his lap in the passenger seat. But as she started to climb in she looked up and noticed a man leaning against the far fence, about sixty feet away, in a green parka coat with bright orange lining. Howie Bowers, furred hood up, obscuring his face, nodding at the man beside him.

A man whose hands were gesticulating wildly as he mouthed silent and angry-looking words. A man in a smart wool coat with floppy blonde hair.

Max Hastings.

Pip's face drained. She dropped into her seat.

'What's wrong, Sarge?'

She pointed out of his window to the fence where the two men stood. 'Look.'

Max Hastings, who had lied to her yet again, saying he

244

never bought drugs in Kilton after Andie disappeared, that he had no clue who her dealer was. And here he was, shouting at that very drug dealer, the words lost and blown apart in the distance between them all.

'Oh,' Ravi said.

Pip started the engine and pulled out, driving away before either Max or Howie could spot them, before her hands started to shake too much.

Max and Howie knew each other.

Yet another tectonic shift in the world of Andie Bell.

Production Log – Entry 27

Max Hastings. If anyone should go on the persons of interest list in bold, it's him. Jason Bell has been downgraded as number-one suspect and Max has now stepped up to take the title. He's lied twice now in Andie-related matters. You don't lie unless you have something to hide.

Let's recap: he's an older guy, he has a naked picture of Andie taken in a hotel he could very well have been meeting her in in March 2012, he was close to both Sal and Andie, he regularly bought Rohypnol from Andie and he knows Howie Bowers pretty well from the looks of it.

This also opens up the possibility of another pair who could have colluded together in Andie's murder: Max and Howie.

I think it's time to pick up the Rohypnol trail and run with it. I mean, it's no normal nineteen-year-old that buys roofies for school parties, is it? It's the thing that links this messy Max/Howie/Andie triangle.

I'll message some 2012 Kilton Grammar schoolers and see if I can shed some light on what was going on at calamity parties. And if I find that what I'm suspecting is true, could Max and Rohypnol be key players in what happened to Andie that night? Like the missing cards on a Cluedo board.

Persons of Interest

Jason Bell

Naomi Ward

Secret Older Guy

Nat da Silva

Daniel da Silva

Max Hastings

Howie Bowers

Production Log – Entry 28

Emma Hutton replied to my text while I was at school. This is what she said:

> Yeah, maybe. I do remember girls saying they thought their drinks
> had been spiked. But tbh everyone used to get really really drunk
> at those parties, so they were probably just saying it because they
> didn't know their limits or for attention. I never had mine spiked.

Chloe Burch replied forty minutes ago, when I was watching *The Fellowship of the Ring* with Josh:

> No, I don't think so. I never heard any rumours like that. But girls
> sometimes say that when they've drunk too much, don't they?

Last night, I messaged a few people who were tagged in photos with Naomi at calamities in 2012 and helpfully had their email addresses on their profiles. I lied slightly, told them I was a reporter for the BBC called Poppy because I thought it would encourage them to talk. If they had anything to say, that is. One of them just responded.

**From: pfa20@gmail.com
to: handslauraj116**   Oct 12 (1 day ago)

Dear Laura Hands,

    I'm a reporter working on an independent news story for the BBC about underage house parties and drug use. From my research, I can see that you used to attend certain house parties that were nicknamed 'Calamities' in the Kilton area in 2012. I wonder if you can offer any comment as to whether you ever heard any rumours or saw any instances of girls having their drinks spiked at these events?

    I would be extremely grateful if you can provide any information regarding this matter and please know that any comments you offer will be anonymized and treated with the upmost discretion.

Thank you for your time.

Yours sincerely,

                             9:22 PM (2 minutes ago)

**From: handslauraj116@yahoo.com
to: pfa20@gmail.com**

Hi Poppy,

    No worries at all, I'm happy to help.

    Actually I do remember there being talk of drinks being spiked. Of course everyone used to drink to excess at these parties so the issue was a little confused.

    But I did have a friend, called Natalie da Silva, who thought she'd had her drink spiked at one of those parties. She said she couldn't remember anything of the night and she'd only had one drink. I think that was in early 2012, if I remember correctly.

    I might still have her phone number if you wanted to get in contact with her?

    Good luck with your report. Could you let me know when it airs? I'd be interested to see it.

Best wishes,

Laura

Pippa Fitz-Amobi
EPQ   14/10/2017

<u>Production Log – Entry 29</u>

Two more responses this morning while I was out at Josh's football match. The first one said she didn't know anything about it and didn't want to offer any comment. The second one said this:

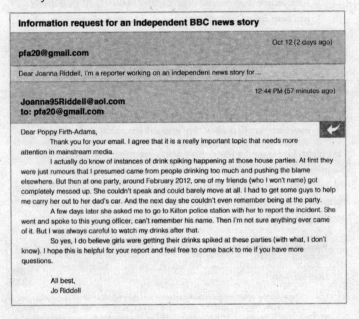

Information request for an independent BBC news story

Oct 12 (2 days ago)

pfa20@gmail.com

Dear Joanna Riddell, I'm a reporter working on an independent news story for...

12:44 PM (57 minutes ago)

**Joanna95Riddell@aol.com
to: pfa20@gmail.com**

Dear Poppy Firth-Adams,
    Thank you for your email. I agree that it is a really important topic that needs more attention in mainstream media.
    I actually do know of instances of drink spiking happening at those house parties. At first they were just rumours that I presumed came from people drinking too much and pushing the blame elsewhere. But then at one party, around February 2012, one of my friends (who I won't name) got completely messed up. She couldn't speak and could barely move at all. I had to get some guys to help me carry her out to her dad's car. And the next day she couldn't even remember being at the party.
    A few days later she asked me to go to Kilton police station with her to report the incident. She went and spoke to this young officer, can't remember his name. Then I'm not sure anything ever came of it. But I was always careful to watch my drinks after that.
    So yes, I do believe girls were getting their drinks spiked at these parties (with what, I don't know). I hope this is helpful for your report and feel free to come back to me if you have more questions.

        All best,
        Jo Riddell

The plot just keeps on thickening.

I think I can safely assume that drinks *were* being spiked at calamity parties in 2012, though the fact wasn't widely known to partygoers. So, Max was buying Rohypnol from Andie and girls were getting their drinks spiked at the parties he started. It doesn't take a genius to put the two together.

Not only that, Nat da Silva may very well have been one of the girls he spiked. Could this be relevant to Andie's murder? And did anything happen to Nat the night she thought she'd been drugged? I can't ask her: she's what I would call an *exceptionally hostile witness.*

And finally, to top it all off, Joanna Riddell said that her friend thought she was spiked and reported it to the Kilton police. To a 'young' male officer. Well, I've done my research and the only young and male officer in 2012 was (yep, DING DING DING) Daniel da Silva. The next youngest male officer was forty-one in 2012. Joanna said that nothing came of the report. Was that just because the unnamed girl reported it after any drug would have shown up in her system? Or was Daniel involved somehow . . . trying to cover something up? And why?

I think I've just stumbled on another link between entries on the persons of interest list, between Max Hastings and the two Da Silvas. I'll call Ravi later and we can brainstorm what this possible triangle could mean. But my focus needs to be on Max right now. He's lied enough times and now I have real reason to believe he was spiking girls' drinks at parties and secretly seeing Andie behind Sal's back at the Ivy House Hotel.

If I had to stop the project right now and point my finger, it would be pointing at Max. He is suspect number one.

But I can't just go and talk to him about all this; he's another hostile witness and now possibly one with a history of assault. He won't talk without leverage. So I have to find some the only way I know how: by way of serious cyber-stalking.

I need to find a way to get on to his Facebook profile and hound him through every post and picture, looking for anything that connects him to Andie or the Ivy House Hotel or drugging girls. Something I can use to make him talk or, even better, go straight to the police with.

I need to get round Nancy Tangotits' (aka Max's) privacy settings.

Twenty-Five

Pip ceremoniously placed her knife and fork across her plate with exaggerated precision.

'*Now* may I leave the table?' She looked at her mum, who was scowling.

'I don't see what the rush is,' her mum said.

'I'm just right in the middle of my EPQ and I want to hit my targets before bed.'

'Yes, off you pop, pickle,' her dad smiled, reaching over to scrape Pip's leftovers on to his own plate.

'Vic!' Her mum now turned the scowl on him as Pip stood and tucked in her chair.

'Oh, darling, some people have to worry about their kids rushing off from dinner to inject heroin into their eyeballs. Be thankful it's homework.'

'What's heroin?' Josh's small voice said as Pip left the room.

She took the steps two at a time, leaving her shadow Barney at the foot of the stairs, his head tilting in confusion as he watched her go to that dog-forbidden place.

She'd had the chance to think over all things Nancy Tangotits at dinner, and now she had an idea.

Pip closed her bedroom door, pulled out her phone and dialled.

'Hello, *muchacha*,' Cara chimed down the line.

'Hey,' Pip said, 'are you busy bingeing *Downton* or do you have a few minutes to help me be sneaky?'

'I'm always available for sneakiness. What d'you need?'

'Is Naomi in?'

'No, out in London. *Why?*' Suspicion crept into Cara's voice.

'OK, sworn to secrecy?'

'Always. What's up?'

Pip said, 'I've heard rumours about old calamity parties that might give me a lead for my EPQ. But I need to find proof, which is where the sneakiness comes in.'

She hoped she'd played it just right, omitting Max's name and downplaying it enough that Cara wouldn't worry about her sister, leaving just enough gaps to intrigue her.

'Oooh, what rumours?' she said.

Pip knew her too well.

'Nothing substantial yet. But I need to look through old calamity photos. That's what I need your help with.'

'OK, hit me.'

'Max Hastings' Facebook profile is a decoy, you know for employers and universities. His actual one is under a fake name and has really strict privacy settings. I can only see things that Naomi is tagged in as well.'

'And you want to log in as Naomi so you can look through Max's old photos?'

'Bingo,' Pip said, sitting down on her bed and dragging

251

the laptop over.

'Can do,' Cara's voice trilled. 'Technically we're not snooping on Naomi, like that time when I just *had* to know whether ginger Benedict Cumberbatch-alike was her new boyfriend. So this doesn't technically break any rules, *Dad*. Plus, Nai should learn to change her password sometime; she has the same one for everything.'

'Can you get on to her laptop?' Pip said.

'Just opening it now.'

A pause filled with the tapping of keys and a clicking mousepad. Pip could picture Cara now with that ridiculously oversized topknot she always wore on her head when she was dressed in pyjamas. Which was, in Cara's case, as often as physically possible.

'OK, she's still signed in here. I'm on.'

'Can you click on to security settings?' asked Pip.

'Yep.'

'Uncheck the box next to log-in alerts so she won't know I'm logging in from a new machine.'

'Done.'

'OK,' Pip said, 'that's all the hacking I need from you.'

'Shame,' Cara said, 'that was much more thrilling than my EPQ research.'

'Well, you shouldn't have chosen to do yours on mould,' Pip said.

Cara read out Naomi's email address and Pip typed it into the Facebook log-in page.

'Her password will be Isobel0610,' Cara said.

'Excellent.' Pip typed it in. 'Thanks, comrade. Stand down.'

'Loud and clear. Although if Naomi finds out, I'm dobbing you in it straight away.'

'Understood,' said Pip.

'All right, Plops, Dad's yelling. Tell me if you find out anything interesting.'

'OK,' Pip said, even though she knew she couldn't.

She dropped the phone and, leaning over her laptop, pressed the Facebook log-in button.

Glancing quickly at Naomi's newsfeed, she noticed that, like her own, it was filled with cats doing silly things, quick-time recipe videos and posts with ungrammatical motivational quotes over pictures of sunsets.

Pip typed *Nancy Tangotits* into the search bar and clicked on to Max's profile. The spinning loading circle on the tab disappeared and the page popped up, a timeline full of bright colours and smiling faces.

It didn't take long for Pip to realize why Max had two profiles. There's no way he would have wanted his parents to see what he got up to away from home. There were so many photos of him in clubs and bars, his blonde hair stuck down on his sweaty forehead, jaw tensed and his eyes reeling and unfocused. Posing with his arms round girls, sticking his stippled tongue out at the camera, drops from spilled drinks splattered on his shirts. And those were just the recent ones on his timeline.

Pip clicked on to Max's photos and began the long scroll down towards 2012. Every eighty or so photos down, she had to wait for the three loading bars to take her further into Nancy Tangotits' past. It was all much of the same: clubs, bars, bleary eyes. There was a brief respite from Max's nocturnal activities with a series of photos from a ski trip, Max standing in the snow wearing just a Borat mankini.

The scrolling took so long that Pip propped up her phone and pressed play on the true crime podcast episode she was halfway through. She finally reached 2012 and took herself right back to January before looking through the photos properly, studying each one.

Most photos were of Max with other people, smiling in the foreground, or a crowd laughing as Max did something stupid. Naomi, Jake, Millie and Sal were his main co-stars. Pip lingered for a long time on a picture of Sal flashing his brilliant smile at the camera while Max licked his cheek. Her gaze flicked between the two drunk and happy boys, looking for any pixelated imprint of the possible and tragic secrets that existed between them.

Pip paid particular attention to those photos with a crowd of people, searching for Andie's face in the background, searching for anything suspicious in Max's hand, for him lurking too close to any girl's drink. She clicked forward and back through so many photos of calamity parties that her tired eyes, scratchy from the laptop's drying white light, turned them into flipbook moving pictures. Until she right arrowed on to the photos from *that* night and everything became sharp and static again.

Pip leaned forward.

Max had taken and uploaded ten photos from the night Andie disappeared. Pip immediately recognized everyone's clothes and the sofas from Max's house. Added to Naomi's three and Millie's six, that made a total of nineteen photos from that night, nineteen snapshots of time that existed alongside Andie Bell's last hours of life.

Pip shivered and pulled the duvet over her feet. The photos were of a similar nature to the ones Millie and Naomi had taken: Max and Jake gripping controllers and staring out of frame, Millie and Max posing with funny filters superimposed over their faces, Naomi in the background staring down at her phone unaware of the posed photo going on behind her. Four best friends without their fifth. Sal out allegedly murdering someone instead of goofing around with them.

That's when Pip noticed it. When it had been just Millie and Naomi it was simply a coincidence, but now that she was looking at Max's too it made a pattern. All three of them had uploaded their photos from *that* night on Monday the 23rd, all between 9:30 and 10:00 p.m. Wasn't it a little strange that, in the midst of all the craziness of Andie's disappearance, they all decided to post these photos at almost the exact same time? And why upload these photos at all? Naomi said she and the others had decided on the Monday night to tell the police the truth about Sal's alibi; was uploading these photos the first step in that decision? To stop hiding Sal's absence?

Pip typed up some notes about this upload coincidence, then she clicked save and closed the laptop. She got ready for bed, wandering back from the bathroom with her toothbrush in mouth, humming as she scribbled her to-do list for tomorrow. *Finish Margaret Atwood essay* was underlined three times.

Tucked up in bed, she read three paragraphs of her current book before tiredness started meddling with the words, making them strange and unfamiliar in her head. She only just managed to hit the light before sleep took her.

It was with a sniff and a jerk of the leg that Pip sat bolt upright in bed. She leaned against the headboard and rubbed her eyes as her mind stirred into wakefulness. She pressed the home button on her phone, the screen light blinding her. It was 4:47 a.m.

What had woken her? Was it a screaming fox outside? A dream?

Something stirred then, on the tip of her tongue and the tip of her brain. A vague thought: too fluffy, spiky and morphing to put into words, beyond the span of just-awake comprehension. But she knew where it was drawing her.

Pip slid quickly out of bed. The cold room stung her exposed skin, turning her breath into ghosts. She grabbed her laptop from the desk and took it back to bed, wrapping the duvet round her for warmth. Opening the computer, she was

256

blinded again by the silvery backlight. Squinting through it, she opened up Facebook, still signed in as Naomi, and navigated her way back to Nancy Tangotits and the photos from *that* night.

She looked through them all once and then back again a little slower. She stopped on the second-to-last picture. All four of the friends were captured within it. Naomi was sitting with her back to the camera, looking down. Though she was in the background, you could see her phone in her hands lighting up its lock screen with small white numbers, her eyes down on it. The main focus of the photo was on Max, Millie and Jake, the three of them standing by the near side of the sofa, smiling as Millie rested her arms over both the boys' shoulders. Max was still holding a controller in his outside hand and Jake's disappeared out of shot on the right.

Pip shivered, but it wasn't from the cold.

The camera must have been at least five feet in front of the grinning friends to get that much in the frame.

And in the dead silence of the night Pip whispered, 'Who's taking the picture?'

Twenty-Six

It was Sal.

It had to be.

Despite the cold, Pip's body was a flume of racing blood, warm and fast, hammering through her heart.

She moved mechanically, her mind adrift in waves of thoughts shouting unintelligibly over each other. But her hands somehow knew what to do. A few minutes later, she'd downloaded the trial version of Photoshop to her computer. She saved Max's photo and opened the file up in the programme. Following an online tutorial by a man with a silky Irish accent, she enlarged the photo and then sharpened it.

Her skin flashed cold to hot. She sat back and gasped.

There was no doubt about it. The little numbers projected on Naomi's phone read 00:09.

They said Sal left at half ten but there they were, all four of the friends at nine minutes past midnight, encased in the frame, and not one of them could have taken the photo themselves.

Max's parents were away that night and no one else had been there, that's what they'd always said. It was just the five of them until Sal left at ten thirty to go and kill his girlfriend.

And here, right in front of Pip's eyes, was proof that that was a lie. There was a fifth person there after midnight. And who could it have been but Sal?

Pip scrolled up to the topmost strip of the enlarged photo. Behind the sofa on the far wall was a window. And in its very centre pane was the flash of the phone camera. You couldn't distinguish the figure holding the phone from the darkness of outside. But, just beyond the streaks of bright white, there was a faint halo of reflected blue, only just visible against the surrounding black. The very same blue as the corded shirt Sal was wearing that night, the one Ravi still wore sometimes. Her stomach flipped as she thought his name, as she imagined the look in his eyes when he saw this photo.

She extracted the enlarged image to a document and cropped it to show only Naomi with her phone on one page and the flash in the window on another. Along with the original saved photo, she sent each page over to the wireless printer on her desk. She watched from her bed as the printer sputt-sputtered each page, making that gentle steam train rattle as it did. Pip closed her eyes for just a moment, listening to the soft chugging sound.

'Pips, can I come in and vacuum?'

Pip's eyes snapped open. She pulled herself up from her slumped position, the whole right side of her body aching from hip to neck.

'You're still in bed?' her mum said, opening the door. 'It's half one, lazy. I thought you were already up.'

'No . . . I,' Pip said, her throat dry and scratchy, 'was just tired, not feeling so well. Could you do Josh's room first?'

Her mum paused and looked at her, her warm eyes staining with worry.

'You're not overworking yourself, are you, Pip?' she said. 'We've talked about this.'

'No, I promise.'

Her mum closed the door and Pip climbed out of bed, almost knocking her laptop off. She got ready, pulling her dungarees on over a dark green jumper, fighting to get the brush through her hair. She picked up the three photo printouts, placed them in a plastic folder and slid them inside her rucksack. Then she scrolled to the recent calls list in her phone and dialled.

'Ravi!'

'What's up, Sarge?'

'Meet me outside your house in ten minutes. I'll be in the car.'

'OK. What's on the menu today, more blackmailing? Side order of breaking and enteri–'

'It's serious. Be there in ten.'

Sitting in her passenger seat, his head almost touching the roof of the car, Ravi stared down open-mouthed at the printed photo in his hands.

It was a long while before he said anything. They sat in silence, Pip watching as Ravi traced his finger over the fuzzy blue reflection in the far window.

'Sal never lied to the police,' he said eventually.

'No, he didn't,' Pip said. 'I think he left Max's at twelve fifteen, just like he originally said. It was his friends who lied. I don't know why, but on that Tuesday they lied and they took away his alibi.'

'This means he's innocent, Pip.' His big round eyes fixed on hers.

'That's what we're here to test, come on.'

She opened her door and stepped out. She'd picked Ravi up and driven him straight here, parking on the grass verge off Wyvil Road, her hazard lights flashing. Ravi closed the car door and followed as Pip started up the road.

'How are we testing that?'

'We need to be sure, Ravi, before we accept it as truth,' she said, making her steps fall in time with his. 'And the only way to be sure is to do an Andie Bell murder re-enactment. To see, with Sal's new time of departure from Max's, whether he would still have had enough time to kill her or not.'

They turned left down Tudor Lane and traipsed all the way to just outside Max Hastings' sprawling house, where this had all begun five and a half years ago.

Pip pulled out her phone. 'We should give the pretend prosecution the benefit of the doubt,' she said. 'Let's say that Sal left Max's just after that photo was taken, at ten minutes past midnight. What time did your dad say Sal got home?'

'Around twelve fifty,' he replied.

'OK. Let's allow for some misremembering and say it was more like twelve fifty-five. Which means that Sal had forty-five minutes door to door. We have to move fast, Ravi, use the minimum possible time it might have taken to kill her and dispose of her body.'

'Normal teenagers sit at home and watch TV on a Sunday,' he said.

'Right, I'm starting the stopwatch . . . now.'

Pip turned on her heels and marched back up the road the way they'd come, Ravi at her side. Her steps fell somewhere between a fast walk and a slow jog. Eight minutes and forty-seven seconds later, they reached her car and her heart was already pounding. This was the intercept point.

'OK.' She turned the key in the ignition and pulled back on to the road. 'So this is Andie's car and she has intercepted Sal. Let's say that she was driving for a faster pick-up time. Now we go to the first quiet spot where the murder theoretically could have taken place.'

She hadn't been driving long before Ravi pointed.

'There,' he said, 'that's quiet and secluded. Turn off here.'

Pip pulled off on to the small dirt road, packed in by tall hedgerows. A sign told them that the winding single-track road led down to a farm. Pip stopped the car where a widened passing place was cut into the hedge and said, 'Now we get out. They didn't find any blood in the front of the car, just the boot.'

Pip glanced at the ticking stopwatch as Ravi was crossing round the bonnet to meet on her side of the car: 15:29, 15:30 . . .

'OK,' she said. 'Let's say that right now they are arguing. It's starting to get heated. Could have been about Andie selling drugs or about this secret older guy. Sal is upset, Andie's shouting back.' Pip hummed tunelessly, rolling her hands to fill the time of the imaginary scene. 'And right about now, maybe Sal finds a rock on the road, or something heavy from Andie's car. Maybe no weapon at all. Let's give him at least forty seconds to kill her.'

They waited.

'So now Andie's dead.' Pip pointed down at the gravel road. 'He opens the boot –' Pip opened her boot – 'and he picks her up.' She bent down and held out her arms, taking enough time to lift the invisible body. 'He puts her inside the boot where her blood was found.' Pip laid her arms down on the carpeted boot floor and stepped back to shut it.

'Now back in the car,' Ravi said.

Pip checked the timer: 20:02, 20:03 . . . She put the car in reverse and swung back out on to the main road.

'Sal's driving now,' she said. 'His fingerprints get on the steering wheel and around the dashboard. He'd be thinking of how to dispose of her body. The closest possible forest-y area is Lodge Wood. So, maybe he'd come off Wyvil Road here,' she said, turning, the woods appearing on their left.

'But he would have needed to find a place to get the car up close to the woods,' said Ravi.

They chased the woods for several minutes searching for such a place, until the road grew dark under a tunnel of trees pressing in on either side.

'There.' They spotted one together. Pip indicated and pulled off on to the grassy verge that bordered the forest.

'I'm sure the police searched here a hundred times, as these are the closest woods to Max's house,' she said. 'But let's just say Sal managed to hide the body here.'

Pip and Ravi got out of the car once more.

26:18.

'So he opens the boot and drags her out.' Pip recreated the action, noticing the muscles in Ravi's jaw clench and release. He'd probably had nightmares about this very scene, his kind older brother dragging a dead and bloodied body through the trees. But maybe, after today, he'd never have to picture it again.

'Sal would have had to take her quite far in, away from the road,' she said.

Pip mimicked dragging the body, her back bent, staggering slowly backwards.

'Up here's pretty hidden from the road,' Ravi said once Pip had dragged her about 200 feet through the trees.

'Yep.' She let go of Andie.

29:48.

'OK,' she said, 'so the hole has always been a problem, how he could have had enough time to dig one deep enough anyway. But, now that we're here,' she glanced around the sun-dappled trees, 'there are quite a few downed trees in these woods. Maybe he didn't need to dig much at all. Maybe he

264

found a shallow ditch ready made for him. Like there.' She pointed to a large mossy dip in the ground, a tangle of old dry roots creeping through it, still attached to a long-fallen tree.

'He would've needed to make it deeper,' Ravi said. 'She's never been found. Let's allow three or four minutes for digging.'

'Agreed.'

When the time came she dragged Andie's body into the hole. 'Then he would have needed to fill it again, cover her with dirt and debris.'

'Let's do it then,' Ravi said, his face determined now. He stabbed the toe of his boot into the dirt and kicked a spray of soil into the hole.

Pip followed suit, pushing mud, leaves and twigs in to fill the small ditch. Ravi was on his knees, sweeping whole armfuls of earth over and on top of Andie.

'OK,' Pip said when they were done, eyes on the once-hole that was now invisible on the forest floor. 'So now her body is buried, Sal would have headed back.'

37:59.

They jogged back to Pip's car and climbed inside, kicking mud all over the floor. Pip three-point turned, swearing when a horn screamed at them from an impatient four-by-four trying to pass, her ears ringing with it all the way.

When they were back on Wyvil Road she said, 'Right, now Sal drives to Romer Close, where Howie Bowers happens to live. And he ditches Andie's car.'

They pulled into it a few minutes later and Pip parked out of sight of Howie's bungalow. She blipped the car behind them.

'And now we walk to my house,' Ravi said, trying to keep up with Pip, her steps breaking into an almost-run. They were both concentrating too hard for words, their eyes down on their pounding feet, treading in *allegedly Sal*'s years-old footsteps.

They arrived outside the Singhs' house breathless and warm. A sheen of sweat was tickling Pip's upper lip. She wiped it on her sleeve and pulled out her phone.

She pressed the stop button on the timer. The numbers rushed through her, dropping all the way to her stomach, where they began to flutter. She looked up at Ravi.

'What?' His eyes were wide and searching.

'So,' Pip said, 'we gave Sal an upper-limit forty-five-minute time window between locations. And our re-enactment worked with the closest possible locations and in an almost inconceivably prompt manner.'

'Yes, it was the speediest of murders. And?'

Pip held her phone out to him and showed him the timer.

'Fifty-eight minutes, nineteen seconds,' Ravi read aloud.

'Ravi.' His name fizzed on her lips and she broke into a smile. 'Sal couldn't possibly have done it. He's innocent; the photo proves it.'

'Shit.' He stepped back and covered his mouth, shaking his head. 'He didn't do it. Sal's innocent.'

He made a sound then, one that grew slowly in his throat, gravelly and strange. It burst out of him, a quick bark of laughter shaded with the breathiness of disbelief. The smile stretched so slowly across his face, it was as though it were unfolding muscle by muscle. He laughed again, the sound pure and warm, Pip's cheeks flushing with the heat of it.

And then, the laughter still on his face, Ravi looked up at the sky, the sun on his face, and the laugh became a yell. He roared up into the sky, neck strained, eyes screwed shut.

People eyed him from across the street and curtains twitched in houses. But Pip knew he didn't care. And neither did she, watching him in this raw, confusing moment of happiness and grief.

Ravi looked down at her and the roar cracked into laughter again. He lifted Pip from her feet and something bright whirred through her. She laughed, tears in her eyes, as he spun her round and round.

'We did it!' he said, putting her down so clumsily that she almost fell over. He stepped back from her, looking suddenly embarrassed, wiping his eyes. 'We actually did it. Is it enough? Can we go to the police with that photo?'

'I don't know,' Pip said. She didn't want to take this away from him, but she really didn't know. 'Maybe it's enough to convince them to reopen the case, maybe it isn't. But we need answers first. We need to know why Sal's friends lied. Why they took his alibi away from him. Come on.'

Ravi took one step and hesitated. 'You mean, ask Naomi?'

She nodded and he drew back.

'You should go alone,' he said. 'Naomi won't talk if I'm there. She physically can't talk. I bumped into her last year and she burst into tears just looking at me.'

'Are you sure?' Pip said. 'But you, out of everyone, deserve to know why.'

'It's the way it has to be, trust me. Be careful, Sarge.'

'OK. I'll ring you straight after.'

Pip wasn't quite sure how to leave him. She touched his arm and then walked past and away, carrying that look on Ravi's face with her.

Twenty-Seven

Pip walked back towards her car on Romer Close, her tread much lighter on this, the return journey. Lighter because now she knew for sure. And she could say it in her head. Sal Singh did not kill Andie Bell. A mantra to the beat of her steps.

She dialled Cara's number.

'Well, hello, sugar,' Cara answered.

'What are you doing now?' Pip asked.

'I'm actually doing homework club with Naomi and Max. They're doing job applications and I'm cracking on with my own EPQ. You know I can't focus alone.'

Pip's chest tightened. 'Both Max and Naomi are there now?'

'Yep.'

'Is your dad in?'

'Nah, he's over at my Auntie Lila's for the afternoon.'

'OK, I'm coming over,' Pip said. 'Be there in ten.'

'Wicked. I can leech some of your focus.'

Pip said goodbye and hung up. She felt an ache of guilt for Cara, that she was there and would now be involved in whatever was about to come out. Because Pip wasn't bringing focus to the homework club. She was bringing an ambush.

Cara opened the front door to her, wearing her penguin

269

pyjamas and bear-claw slippers.

'*Chica*,' she said, rubbing Pip's already messy hair. 'Happy Sunday. *Mi club de homeworko es su club de homeworko.*'

Pip closed the front door and followed Cara towards the kitchen.

'We've banned talking,' Cara said, holding the door open for her. 'And no typing too loudly, like Max does.'

Pip stepped into the kitchen. Max and Naomi were sitting next to each other at the table, laptops and papers splayed out in front of them. Steaming mugs of just-made tea in their hands. Cara's place was on the other side: a mess of paper, notebooks and pens strewn across her keyboard.

'Hey, Pip,' Naomi smiled. 'How're you doing?'

'Fine thanks,' Pip said, her voice suddenly gruff and raw.

When Pip looked at Max, he turned his gaze away immediately, staring down at the surface of his taupe-coloured tea.

'*Hi*, Max,' she said pointedly, forcing him to look back at her.

He raised a small closed-mouth smile, which might have looked like a greeting to Cara and Naomi, but she knew it was meant as a grimace.

Pip walked over to the table and dropped her rucksack on to it, just across from Max. It thumped against the surface, making the lids of all three laptops wobble on their hinges.

'Pip loves homework,' Cara explained to Max. 'Aggressively so.'

270

Cara slid back into her chair and wiggled the mousepad to bring her computer back to life. 'Well, sit,' she said, using her foot to pull a chair out from under the table. Its feet scraped and shrieked against the floor.

'What's up, Pip?' Naomi said. 'Do you want a tea?'

'What are you looking at?' Max cut in.

'Max!' Naomi hit him roughly on the arm with a pad of paper.

Pip could see Cara's confused face in her periphery. But she didn't take her eyes away from Naomi and Max. She could feel the anger pulsing through her, her nostrils flaring with its surge. She hadn't known until she saw their faces that this was how she would feel. She thought she would be relieved. Relieved that it was all over, that she and Ravi had done what they set out to do. But their faces made her seethe. These weren't just small deceits and innocent gaps in memory any more. This was a calculated, life-changing lie. A momentous treachery unburied from the pixels. And she would not look away or sit until she knew why.

'I came here first just as a courtesy,' she said, her voice shaking. 'Because, Naomi, you've been like a sister to me nearly my whole life. Max, I owe you nothing.'

'Pip, what are you talking about?' Cara said, her voice strained with the beginnings of worry.

Pip unzipped her bag and pulled out the plastic folder. She opened it and, leaning across the table, laid the three printed pages out in the space between Max and Naomi.

'This is your chance to explain before I go to the police. What do you have to say, Nancy Tangotits?' She glared at Max.

'What are you on about?' he scoffed.

'That's your photo, Nancy. It's from the night Andie Bell disappeared, isn't it?'

'Yes,' Naomi said quietly. 'But, why –'

'The night Sal left Max's house at ten thirty to go and kill Andie?'

'Yes, it is,' Max spat. 'And what point are you trying to make?'

'If you stop blustering for one second and look at the photo, you'll see my point,' Pip snapped back. 'Obviously you're no stickler for detail or you wouldn't have uploaded it in the first place. So I'll explain. Both you and Naomi, Millie and Jake are in this picture.'

'Yeah, so?' he said.

'So, Nancy, who took that picture of the four of you?'

Pip noticed Naomi's eyes widen, her mouth hanging slightly open as she stared down at the photo.

'Yeah, OK,' Max said, 'so maybe Sal took the photo. It's not like we said he wasn't there at all. He must have taken this earlier on in the night.'

'Nice try,' Pip said, 'but –'

'My phone.' Naomi's face fell. She reached up to hold it in her hands. 'The time is on my phone.'

Max went quiet, looking down at the printouts,

a muscle tensing in his jaw.

'Well, you can hardly see those numbers. You must have doctored this photo,' he said.

'No, Max. I got it from your Facebook as it is. Don't worry, I've researched this: the police can access it even if you delete it now. I'm sure they'd be very interested to see it.'

Naomi turned to Max, her cheeks reddening. 'Why didn't you check properly?'

'Shut up,' he said quietly but firmly.

'We're going to have to tell her,' Naomi said, pushing back her chair with a scrape that cut right through Pip.

'Shut up, Naomi,' Max said again.

'Oh my god.' Naomi stood and started pacing the length of the table. 'We have to tell her –'

'Stop talking!' Max said, getting to his feet and grabbing Naomi by the shoulders. 'Don't say anything else.'

'She'll go to the police, Max. Won't you?' Naomi said, tears pooling in the grooves around her nose. 'We have to tell her.'

Max took in a deep and juddering breath, his eyes darting between Naomi and Pip.

'Fuck,' he shouted abruptly, letting go of Naomi and kicking out at the table leg.

'What the hell is going on?' Cara said, pulling at Pip's sleeve.

'Tell me, Naomi,' Pip said.

Max fell back into his chair, his blonde hair in wilting

clumps across his face. 'Why have you done this?' He looked up at Pip. 'Why didn't you just leave everything alone?'

Pip ignored him. 'Naomi, tell me,' she said. 'Sal didn't leave Max's at ten thirty that night, did he? He left at twelve fifteen, just like he told the police. He never asked you all to lie to give him an alibi; he actually had one. He was with you. Sal never once lied to the police; you all did on that Tuesday. You lied to take away his alibi.'

Naomi squinted as tears glazed her eyes. She looked at Cara and then slowly over to Pip. And she nodded.

Pip blinked. 'Why?'

Twenty-Eight

'Why?' Pip said again when Naomi had stared wordlessly down at her feet long enough.

'Someone made us,' she sniffed. 'Someone made us do it.'

'What do you mean?'

'We – me, Max, Jake and Millie – we all got a text on that Monday night. From an unrecognized number. It told us we had to delete every picture of Sal taken on the night Andie disappeared and to upload the rest as normal. It told us that at school on Tuesday we had to ask the head teacher to call in the police so we could make a statement. And we had to tell them that Sal actually left Max's at half ten and that he'd asked us to lie before.'

'But why would you do that?' asked Pip.

'Because –' Naomi's face cracked as she tried to hold back her sobs – 'because they knew something about us. About something bad we'd done.'

She couldn't hold them back anymore. She slapped her hands to her face and bawled into them, the cries strangled against her fingers. Cara jumped up from her seat and ran over, wrapping her arms round her sister's waist. She looked over at Pip as she held the quaking Naomi, her face pale with the touch of fear.

'Max?' Pip said.

Max cleared his throat, his eyes down on his fiddling hands. 'We, um . . . something happened on New Year's Eve 2011. Something bad, something we did.'

'We?' Naomi spluttered. 'We, Max? It all happened because of you. You got us into it and you're the one who made us leave him there.'

'You're lying. We all agreed at the time,' he said.

'I was in shock. I was scared.'

'Naomi?' Pip said.

'We . . . um, we went out to that crappy little club in Amersham,' she said.

'The Imperial Vault?'

'Yeah. And we had all had a lot to drink. And when the club closed it was impossible to get a taxi; we were like seventieth in the queue and it was freezing outside. So Max, who'd driven us all there, he said that actually he hadn't drunk that much and was OK to drive. And he convinced me, Millie and Jake to get in the car with him. It was so stupid. Oh god, if I could go back and change one thing in my life, it would be that moment . . .' She trailed off.

'Sal wasn't there?' Pip asked.

'No,' she said. 'I wish he had been because he'd never have let us be that stupid. He was with his brother that night. So Max, who was just as drunk as the rest of us, he was driving too fast up the A413. It was like four o' clock and there were no other cars on the road. And then –' the tears came again – 'and then . . .'

'This man comes out of nowhere,' Max said.

'No, he didn't. He was standing well back on the shoulder, Max. I remember you losing control of the car.'

'Well, then we remember very differently,' Max snapped defensively. 'We hit him and spun. When we came to a stop I pulled off the road and we went to see what had happened.'

'Oh god, there was so much blood,' Naomi cried. 'And his legs were bent out all wrong.'

'He looked dead, OK?' Max said. 'We checked to see if he was breathing and we thought he wasn't. We decided it was too late for him, too late to call an ambulance. And because we'd all been drinking, we knew how much trouble we'd be in. Criminal charges, prison. So we all agreed and we left.'

'Max made us,' Naomi said. 'You got inside our heads and scared us into agreeing, because you knew you were the one really in trouble.'

'We *all* agreed, Naomi, all four of us,' Max shouted, a red flush creeping to the surface of his face. 'We drove back to mine 'cause my parents were in Dubai. We cleaned off the car and then crashed it again into the tree just before my driveway. My parents never suspected a thing and got me a new one a few weeks later.'

Cara was now crying too, wiping the tears before Naomi could see them.

'Did the man die?' Pip said.

Naomi shook her head. 'He was in a coma for a few weeks, but he pulled through. But . . . but . . .' Naomi's face creased in agony. 'He's paraplegic. He's in a wheelchair. We did that to him. We should never have left him.'

They all listened as Naomi cried, struggling to suck in air between the tears.

'Somehow,' Max eventually said, 'someone knew what we had done. They said that if we didn't do everything they asked, they would tell the police what we did to that man. So we did it. We deleted the pictures and we lied to the police.'

'But how could someone have found out about your hit-and-run?' said Pip.

'We don't know,' Naomi said. 'We all swore to never tell anyone, ever. And I never did.'

'Me neither,' Max said.

Naomi looked over at him with a weepy scoff.

'What?' he stared back at her.

'Me, Jake and Millie have always thought you were the one who let it slip.'

'Oh, really?' he spat.

'Well, you're the one who used to get completely plastered almost every night.'

'I never told anyone,' he said, turning back to Pip now. 'I have no idea how someone found out.'

'There's a pattern of you letting things slip,' said Pip. 'Naomi, Max accidentally told me you were M.I.A. for a while the night Andie disappeared. Where were you? I want the truth.'

'I was with Sal,' she said. 'He wanted to talk to me upstairs, alone. About Andie. He was angry at her about something she'd done; he wouldn't say what. He told me she was a different person when it was just the two of them, but he could no longer ignore the way she treated other people. He decided that night that he was going to end things with her. And he seemed . . . almost relieved after he came to that decision.'

'So let's be clear,' Pip said. 'Sal was with you all at Max's until twelve fifteen the night Andie disappeared. On the Monday, someone threatens you to go to the police and say he left at ten thirty and to delete all trace of him from that night. The next day Sal disappears and is found dead in the woods. You know what this means, don't you?'

Max looked down, picking at the skin around his thumbs. Naomi covered her face again.

'Sal was innocent.'

'We don't know that for sure,' Max said.

'Sal was innocent. Someone killed Andie and then they killed Sal, after making sure he'd look guilty beyond reasonable doubt. Your best friend was innocent, and you've all known it for five years.'

'I'm sorry,' Naomi wept. 'I'm so, so sorry. We didn't know what else to do. We were in too deep. We never thought that Sal would end up dead. We thought if we just played along, the police would catch whoever had hurt Andie, Sal would be cleared and we'd all be OK. We told ourselves it was just a small lie at the time. But we know now what we did.'

'Sal died because of your *small* lie.' Pip's stomach twisted with a rage quieted with sadness.

'We don't know that,' Max said. 'Sal might still have been involved in what happened to Andie.'

'He didn't have time to be,' said Pip.

'What are you going to do with the photo?' he said quietly.

Pip looked over at Naomi, her red puffy face etched with pain. Cara was holding her hand, staring at Pip, tears trickling down her cheeks.

'Max,' Pip said. 'Did you kill Andie?'

'What?' He stood up, scraping the messy hair out of his face. 'No, I was at my house the whole night.'

'You could have left when Naomi and Millie went to bed.'

'Well, I didn't, OK?'

'Do you know what happened to Andie?'

'No, I don't.'

'Pip,' Cara spoke up now. 'Please don't go to the police with that photo. Please. I can't have my sister taken away as well as Mum.' Her bottom lip trembled and she scrunched her face, trying to hold back the sobs. Naomi wrapped her arms round her.

Pip's throat ached with a helpless, hollow feeling, watching them both in so much pain. What should she do? What could she do? She didn't know whether the police would take this photo seriously anyway. But if they did, Cara would be left all alone and it would be Pip's fault. She couldn't do that to her. But what about Ravi? Sal was innocent and there was no question of her abandoning him now. There was only one way through this, she realized.

'I won't go to the police,' she said.

Max heaved a sigh and Pip eyed him, disgusted, as he tried to hide a faint smile crossing his mouth.

'Not for you, Max,' she said. 'For Naomi. And everything your mistakes have done to her. I doubt the guilt has played much on your mind, but I hope you pay in some way.'

'They're my mistakes too,' Naomi said quietly. 'I did this too.'

Cara walked over to Pip and hugged her from the side, tears soaking into her jumper.

Max left then, without another word. He packed up his laptop and notes, swung his bag on his shoulder and took off towards the front door.

The kitchen was silent as Cara went to splash her face in the sink and filled up a glass of water for her sister. Naomi was the first to break the silence.

'I'm so sorry,' she said.

'I know,' Pip said. 'I know you are. I won't go to the police with the photo. It would be far easier, but I don't need Sal's alibi to prove his innocence. I'll find another way.'

'What do you mean?' Naomi sniffed.

'You're asking me to cover for you and what you did. And I will. But I will not cover up the truth about Sal.' She swallowed and it grated all the way down her tight and scratchy throat. 'I'm going to find who really did all this, the person who killed Andie and Sal. That's the only way to clear

Sal's name and protect you at the same time.'

Naomi hugged her, burying her tear-stained face in Pip's shoulder. 'Please do,' she said quietly. 'He's innocent and it's killed me every day since.'

She stroked Naomi's hair and looked over at Cara, her best friend, her sister. Pip's shoulders slumped as a weight settled there. The world felt heavier than it had ever been before.

PART III

Production Log – Entry 31

He's innocent.

All day at school those two words have ticker-taped around my head. This project is no longer the hopeful conjecture it started life as. It's no longer me indulging my gut instinct because Sal was kind to me when I was small and hurting. It's no longer Ravi hoping against hope that he really knew the brother he loved. It's real, no shred of *maybe/possibly/allegedly* left. Sal Singh did not kill Andie Bell. And he did not kill himself.

An innocent life was taken and everyone in this town turned it ugly in their mouths, turned him into a villain. But if a villain can be made, then they can be unmade. Two teenagers were murdered in Little Kilton five and a half years ago. And we hold the clues to finding the killer: me and Ravi and this ever-expanding Word document.

I went to meet Ravi after school – I've only just got home. We went to the park and talked for over three hours, well into darkness. He was angry when I told him why Sal's alibi had been taken away. A quiet kind of angry. He said it wasn't fair that Naomi and Max Hastings got to walk away from everything without punishment when Sal, who never hurt anyone, was killed and framed as a murderer. Of course it's not fair; nothing about any of this is fair. But Naomi never meant to hurt Sal, it's clear from her face, clear from the way she's tiptoed through life since. She acted out of fear and I can understand that. Ravi does too, though he's not sure he can forgive her.

His face fell when I said I didn't know whether the photo was enough for the police to reopen the case; I'd bluffed to get Max and Naomi to talk. The police might think I doctored the image and refuse to apply for a warrant to check Max's profile. He's deleted the photo already, of course. Ravi thinks I'd have more credibility with the police than him, but I'm not so sure; a teenage girl rabbiting on about photo angles and tiny white numbers on a phone screen, especially when the evidence against Sal is so solid. Not to mention Daniel da Silva on the force, shutting me down.

And the other thing: it took Ravi a long time to understand why I wanted to protect Naomi. I explained that they are family, that Cara and Naomi are both sisters to me and though Naomi may have played her part in what happened, Cara is innocent. It would kill me to do this to her, to make her lose her sister after her mum too. I promised Ravi that this wouldn't be a setback, that we don't need Sal to have an alibi to prove his innocence; we just have to find the real killer. So we came to a deal: we are giving ourselves three more weeks. Three weeks to find the killer or solid evidence against a suspect. And if we have nothing after that deadline, Ravi and I will take the photo to the police, see if they'll even take it seriously.

So that's it. I have just three weeks now to find the killer or Naomi's and Cara's lives get blown apart. Was it wrong of me to ask Ravi to do this, to wait when he's waited so long already? I'm torn, between the Wards and the Singhs and what's right. I don't even know what's right any more – everything is so muddied. I'm not sure I'm the good girl I once thought I was. I've lost her along the way.

But there's no time to waste thinking about it. So from the persons of interest list, we now have five suspects. I've taken Naomi off the list. My reasons for suspecting her have now been explained away: the M.I.A. thing and her being so awkward when answering questions about Sal.

A spider diagram recap on all the suspects:

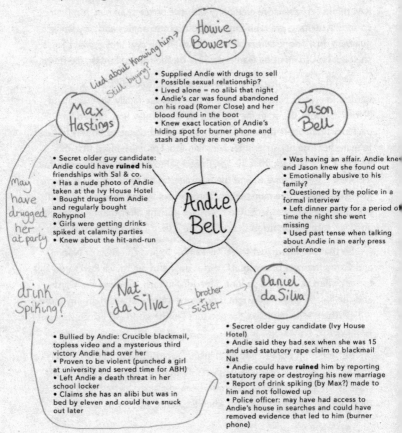

Howie Bowers
- Supplied Andie with drugs to sell
- Possible sexual relationship?
- Lived alone = no alibi that night
- Andie's car was found abandoned on his road (Romer Close) and her blood found in the boot
- Knew exact location of Andie's hiding spot for burner phone and stash and they are now gone

Lied about knowing him →
Still buying?

Max Hastings
- Secret older guy candidate: Andie could have **ruined** his friendships with Sal & co.
- Has a nude photo of Andie taken at the Ivy House Hotel
- Bought drugs from Andie and regularly bought Rohypnol
- Girls were getting drinks spiked at calamity parties
- Knew about the hit-and-run

May have drugged her at party

drink spiking?

Andie Bell

Jason Bell
- Was having an affair. Andie knew and Jason knew she found out
- Emotionally abusive to his family?
- Questioned by the police in a formal interview
- Left dinner party for a period of time the night she went missing
- Used past tense when talking about Andie in an early press conference

Nat da Silva ← *brother + sister* → **Daniel da Silva**

Nat da Silva
- Bullied by Andie: Crucible blackmail, topless video and a mysterious third victory Andie had over her
- Proven to be violent (punched a girl at university and served time for ABH)
- Left Andie a death threat in her school locker
- Claims she has an alibi but was in bed by eleven and could have snuck out later

Daniel da Silva
- Secret older guy candidate (Ivy House Hotel)
- Andie said they had sex when she was 15 and used statutory rape claim to blackmail Nat
- Andie could have **ruined** him by reporting statutory rape or destroying his new marriage
- Report of drink spiking (by Max?) made to him and not followed up
- Police officer: may have had access to Andie's house in searches and could have removed evidence that led to him (burner phone)

Along with the note and text I received, I now have another lead straight to the killer: the fact that they knew about the hit-and-run. First up and most obviously, Max knew about it because he was the one who did it. He could have pretended to threaten himself along with his other friends so he could pin Andie's murder on Sal.

But, as Naomi said, Max has always partied a lot. Drinking and taking drugs. He could have let slip about the hit-and-run to someone while in that state. Someone he knew, like Nat da Silva or Howie Bowers. Or maybe even Andie Bell who then, in turn, could have told any of the names above. Daniel da Silva was a working policeman who responded to traffic accidents; maybe he put two and two together? Or could one of them have been on the same road that night and watched it all happen? It's feasible then that any of the five could have learned about the accident and used it to their advantage. But Max remains the strongest option in that respect.

I know Max technically has an alibi for the majority of the Andie disappearance window but I do not trust him. He could have left when Naomi and Millie went to bed. As long as he intercepted Andie before 12:45, when she was expected to pick her parents up, it's still possible. Or maybe he went to help finish something that Howie started? He said he didn't leave his house but I don't trust his answers. I think he called my bluff. I think he knew it was so unlikely I would turn Naomi in to the police, so he didn't have to be honest with me. I'm in a bit of a Catch 22 here: I can't protect Naomi without simultaneously protecting Max too.

The other lead this new information gives me is that the killer somehow had access to the phone numbers of Max, Naomi, Millie and Jake (as well as mine). But again, this doesn't really narrow it down. Max obviously had them and Howie could have had access that way. Nat da Silva probably had all their numbers, especially as she was good friends with Naomi; Daniel could have got them through her. Jason Bell may seem like the black sheep in this matter, BUT if he did kill Andie and had her phone, she probably had each of their numbers saved on it.

Agh. I haven't narrowed anything down and I'm running out of time. I need to pursue every open lead, find the loose threads that, when pulled, can unravel this writhing and confusing ball of string. AND finish my bloody Margaret Atwood essay!!!

Twenty-Nine

Pip unlocked the front door and shunted it open. Barney bounded down the hall and escorted her back as she moved towards the familiar voices.

'Hello, pickle,' Victor said as Pip popped her head into the living room. 'We only just beat you home. I'm about to sort some dinner for Mum and me; Joshua ate at Sam's house. Did you eat at Cara's?'

'Yeah, I did,' she said. They'd eaten but they hadn't talked much. Cara had been quiet all week at school. Pip understood; this project had sent the foundations of her family spinning, her life as it was was dependent on Pip finding the truth. She and Naomi had asked on Sunday, after Max left, who Pip thought had done it. She didn't tell them anything, only warned Naomi to stay away from Max. She couldn't risk sharing Andie's secrets with them in case they came hand in hand with threats from the killer. That was her burden to bear.

'So how was parents' evening?' Pip asked.

'Yeah, good,' Leanne said, patting Josh's head. 'Getting better in science and maths, aren't you, Josh?'

Josh nodded, fumbling Lego bricks together on the coffee table.

'Although Miss Speller did say you have a proclivity for being the class clown.' Victor threw a mock-serious face in Josh's direction.

'I wonder where he gets that from,' Pip said, throwing the same face right back at her dad.

He hooted and slapped his knees. 'Don't sass me, girl.'

'I don't have time to,' she replied. 'I'm going to get a few hours' work done before bed.' She stepped back into the hallway and towards the stairs.

'Oh, sweetie,' Mum sighed, 'you work too hard.'

'There's no such thing,' Pip said, waving from the stairs.

On the landing, she stopped just outside her bedroom and stared. The door was open slightly and the sight jarred with Pip's memory of this morning before school. Joshua had taken two bottles of Victor's aftershave and – wearing a cowboy hat – held one in each hand, squirting as he sashayed along the upstairs hallway, saying: 'I'm rooty-tooty-perfume-booty and this house ain't big enough for the both of us, Pippo.' Pip had escaped, closing her door behind her, so that her room wouldn't later smell of a sickly amalgamation of Brave and Pour Homme. Or maybe that had been yesterday morning? She hadn't slept well this week and the days were sticking to each other.

'Has someone been in my room?' she called downstairs.

'No, we just got in,' her mum replied.

Pip went inside and dumped her rucksack on the bed. She walked over to her desk and knew with only half a glance that something wasn't right. Her laptop was open, the screen tilted right back. Pip always, always closed the lid when she left it for the day. She clicked the on button and as it burred back into life she noticed that the neat stack of printouts beside her computer had been fanned out. One had been picked up and placed at the top of the pile.

It was *the* photograph. The evidence of Sal's alibi. And it wasn't where she'd left it.

Her laptop sang two welcome notes and loaded her home screen up. It was just as she'd left it; the Word document of her most recent production log in the task bar beside a minimized Chrome tab. She clicked into her log. It opened on the page below her spider diagram.

Pip gasped.

Below her final words, someone had typed: *YOU NEED TO STOP THIS, PIPPA.*

Over and over again. Hundreds of times. So many that it filled four entire A4 pages.

Pip's heart became a thousand drumming beetles scattering under her skin. She drew her hands away from the keyboard and stared down at it. The killer had been here, in her room. Touching her things. Looking through her research. Pressing the keys on her laptop.

Inside her home.

She pushed away from the desk and bounded downstairs.

'Um, Mum,' she said, trying to speak normally over the breathless terror in her voice, 'did anyone come over to the house today?'

'I don't know, I've been at work all day and went straight

290

to Josh's parents' evening. Why?'

'Oh, nothing,' Pip said, improvising. 'I ordered a book and thought it would turn up. Um . . . actually, one more thing. There was a story going round school today. A couple of people's houses have been broken into; they think they're using people's spare keys to get in. Maybe we shouldn't keep ours out until they're caught?'

'Oh, really?' Leanne said, looking up at Pip. 'No, I suppose we shouldn't then.'

'I'll get it,' Pip said, trying not to skid as she hurried for the front door.

She pulled it open and a blast of cool October night air prickled her burning face. She bent to her knees and pulled over one corner of the outside doormat. The key winked the hallway light back at her. It was sitting not in, but just next to its own imprint in the dirt. Pip reached forward and grabbed it and the cold metal stung her fingers.

She laid under her duvet, arrow-straight and shivering. She closed her eyes and focused her ears. There was a scraping sound somewhere in the house. Was someone trying to get inside? Or was it just the willow tree that sometimes scuffed against her parents' window?

A thud from the front. Pip jumped. A neighbour's car door slamming or someone trying to break in?

She got out of bed for the sixteenth time and went to the window. She moved a corner of the curtain and peeked through. It was dark. The cars on the front drive were dusted with pale silver moon-streaks but the navy blush of night hid everything else. Was someone out there, in the darkness? Watching her? She watched back, waiting for a sign of movement, for a ripple of darkness to shift and become a person.

Pip let the curtain fall again and got back into bed. The duvet had betrayed her and lost all the body heat she'd filled it with. She shivered under it again, watching the clock on her phone tick through 3:00 a.m. and onwards.

When the wind howled and rattled her window and Pip's heart jumped to her throat she threw the duvet off and climbed out again. But this time she tiptoed across the landing and pushed open the door into Josh's room. He was sound asleep, his peaceful face lit up by his cool blue star nightlight.

Pip crept over to the foot of his bed. She climbed up and crawled over to the pillow end, avoiding the sleeping lump of her brother. He didn't wake but moaned a little when she flicked his duvet over herself. It was so warm inside. And Josh would be safe, if she was here to watch him.

She lay there, listening to his deep breaths, letting her brother's sleep-heat thaw her. Her eyes crossed and tripped over each other as she stared ahead, transfixed by the soft blue light of spinning stars.

Thirty

'Naomi's been a bit jumpy since . . . you know,' Cara said, walking Pip down the corridor to her locker. There was still something awkward between them, a solid thing only just starting to melt around the edges, though they both pretended it wasn't there.

Pip didn't know what to say.

'Well, she's always been a bit jumpy but even more now,' Cara continued anyway. 'Yesterday, Dad called her from the other room and she jumped so hard that she threw her phone across the kitchen. Completely smashed it up. Had to send it off this morning to get fixed.'

'Oh,' Pip said, opening up her locker and stacking her books inside. 'Um, does she need a spare phone? My mum just upgraded and still has the old one.'

'Nah, it's fine. She found an old one of hers from years ago. Her SIM didn't fit but we found an old pay-as-you-go one with some credit left. That'll do her for now.'

'Is she OK?' Pip said.

'I don't know,' Cara replied. 'Don't think she's been OK for a long while. Not since Mum died, really. And I'd always thought there was something more she was struggling with.'

Pip closed the locker and followed her. She hoped Cara hadn't noticed the make-up pasted dark circles under her eyes, or the bloodshot spider legs of veins running through them. Sleep wasn't really an option any more. Pip had sent off her Cambridge admission essays and started studying for her ELAT entrance exam. But her deadline for keeping Naomi and Cara out of everything was ticking down every second. And when she did sleep there was a dark figure in her dreams just out of sight, watching her.

'It'll be OK,' Pip said. 'I promise.'

Cara gave her hand a squeeze as they turned their separate ways down the corridor.

A few doors down from her English classroom, Pip stopped sharply, her shoes squeaking against the floor. Someone was trudging down the hall towards her, someone with pixie-cut white hair and black-winged eyes.

'Nat?' Pip said with a small wave.

Nat da Silva slowed and came to stop just in front of her. She didn't smile and she didn't wave. She barely looked at her.

'What are you doing in school?' Pip said, noticing Nat's electronic ankle tag was a sock-covered bulge above her trainers.

'I forgot all details of my life were suddenly your business, Penny.'

'Pippa.'

'Don't care,' she spat, her top lip arching in a sneer. 'If you must know, for your perverted project, I've officially hit rock bottom. My parents are cutting me off and no one will hire me. I just begged that slug of a head teacher for my brother's old caretaker job. They can't hire violent criminals, apparently. There's an after-Andie effect for you to analyse. She really played the long game with me.'

'I'm sorry,' Pip said.

'No.' Nat picked up her feet and strode away, the gust of her sudden departure ruffling Pip's hair. 'You're not.'

After lunch Pip returned to her locker to grab her Russia textbook for double history. She opened the door and the paper was just sitting there on top of her book pile. A folded piece of printer paper that had been pushed through the top slit.

A flash of cold dread dropped through her. She checked over both shoulders that no one was watching her and reached in for the note.

This is your final warning, Pippa. Walk away.

She read the large black printed letters only once, folded the page back up and slipped it inside the cover of her history textbook. She pulled out the book – a two-handed job – and walked away.

It was clear now. Someone wanted her to know that they could get to her at home and at school. They wanted to scare her. And she was; terror chased away her sleep, made her watch out of the dark window these last two nights. But daytime Pip was more rational than the one at night. If this person was really prepared to hurt her or her family, wouldn't they have done it by now? She couldn't walk away from this, from Sal and Ravi, from Cara and Naomi. She was in too deep and the only way was down.

There was a killer hiding in Little Kilton. They'd seen her last production log entry and now they were reacting. Which meant that Pip was on the right track somewhere. A warning was all it was, she had to believe that, had to tell herself that when she lay sleepless at night. And although Unknown might be closing in on her, she was also closing in on them.

Pip pushed the classroom door with the spine of her textbook and it swung open much harder than she'd meant.

'Ouch,' Elliot said as the door crashed into his elbow.

The door bounded back into Pip and she tripped, dropping her textbook. It landed with a loud thwack.

'Sorry, El– Mr Ward,' she said. 'I didn't know you were right there.'

'That's OK,' he smiled. 'I'll interpret it as your eagerness for learning rather than an assassination attempt.'

'Well, we are learning about 1930s Russia.'

'Ah, I see,' he said, bending to pick up her book, 'so it was a practical demonstration?'

The note slipped out from the cover and glided to the floor. It landed on its crease and came to rest, partly open. Pip lunged for the paper, scrunching it up in her hands.

'Pip?'

She could see Elliot trying to make eye contact with her. But she stared straight ahead.

'Pip, are you OK?' he asked.

'Yep,' she nodded, flashing a closed-mouth smile, biting back that feeling you get when someone asks if you're OK and you're anything but. 'I'm fine.'

'Listen,' he said gently, 'if you're being bullied, the worst thing to do is keep it to yourself.'

'I'm not,' she said, turning to him. 'I'm fine, really.'

'Pip?'

'I'm good, Mr Ward,' she said as the first group of chattering students slipped in the door behind them.

She took her textbook from Elliot's hands and wandered over to her seat, knowing his eyes were following her as she went.

'Pips,' Connor said as he shoved his bag down on the place beside her. 'Lost you after lunch.' And then, in a whisper, he added, 'So why are you and Cara acting all frosty? You fallen out or something?'

'No,' she said, 'we're all fine. Everything's fine.'

Production Log – Entry 33

I'm not ignoring the fact that I saw Nat da Silva in school just a few hours
before I found the note in my locker. Especially considering her history
with death threats in lockers. And although her name has now climbed to
the top of the suspect list, it is in no way definitive. In a small town like
Kilton, sometimes things that seem connected are entirely coincidental,
and vice versa. Running into someone in the only high school in town
does not a murderer make.

Almost everyone on my suspect list has a connection with that
school. Both Max Hastings and Nat da Silva went there, Daniel da Silva
used to work there as a caretaker, both of Jason Bell's daughters went
there. I actually don't know if Howie Bowers went to Kilton Grammar
or not; I can't seem to find any information online about him. But all of
these suspects would know I go there; they could have followed me, could
have been watching me on Friday morning when I was at my locker with
Cara. It's not like there's any security at the school; anyone can walk in
unchallenged.

So maybe Nat, but maybe the others too. And I've just talked myself
back round to square one. Who is the killer? Time is running out and I'm
still no closer to pointing my finger.

From everything Ravi and I have learned I still consider Andie's burner
phone as the most important lead. It's missing but if we can find it or
the person who has it then our job here is done. The phone is physical,
tangible evidence. Exactly what we need if we're going to find a way to
bring the police in on this. A printed photo with blurry details they might
sneer at, but no one could ignore the secret second phone of the victim.

Yes, I've mused before that maybe the burner phone was on Andie
when she died and it's lost forever with her body. But let's pretend it
wasn't. Let's say that Andie was intercepted as she drove away from home.
Let's say that she was killed and disposed of. And then the killer thinks
to themselves: oh no, the burner phone could lead to me and what if the
police find it in their searches?

So they have to go and get it. There are two people on my list that I've confirmed knew about the burner phone: Max and Howie. If Daniel da Silva was Secret Older Guy, then he surely knew about it too. Howie, in particular, knew where it was hidden.

What if one of them went to the Bell house and removed the burner phone after killing Andie, before it could be found? I have some more questions for Becca Bell. I don't know if she'll answer them but I have to try.

Thirty-One

She felt the nerves as barbs sticking in her gut as she walked up to the building. It was a tiny glass-fronted office building with a small metallic sign reading *Kilton Mail* beside the main door. And although it was a Monday morning the place looked and felt abandoned. No sign of life or movement in any of the lower windows.

Pip pressed the button on the wall next to the door. It made a tinny whining sound that grated in her ears. She let it go and, seconds later, a muffled robotic voice came through the speaker.

'Hello?'

'Err, hi,' Pip said. 'I'm here to see Becca Bell.'

'OK,' the voice said, 'I'll buzz you in. Give the door a good push 'cause it's sticky.'

A harsh buzz sounded. Pip pushed the door and barged it with her hip and, with a clacking noise, the door unstuck and swung inwards. She closed it behind her and stood there in a small and cold room. There were three sofas and a couple of coffee tables but no people.

'Hello?' she called.

A door opened and a man strolled through, flicking the collar up on his long beige coat. A man with straight dark hair pushed to the side and grey-tinged skin. It was Stanley Forbes.

'Oh.' He stopped when he saw Pip. 'I'm just on my way out. I . . . who are you?'

He stared at her with narrowed eyes, his lower jaw jutted out, and Pip felt goosebumps crawling down her neck. It was cold in here.

'I'm here to see Becca,' she said.

'Oh, right.' He smiled without showing his teeth. 'Everyone's working in the back room today. Heating's busted at the front. That way.' He pointed at the door he'd come through.

'Thank you,' she said, but Stanley wasn't listening. He was already halfway out of the front door. It banged shut, drowning out the 'ooo' in her thanks.

Pip walked over to the far door and pushed through it. A short corridor opened up into a larger room, with four paper-laden desks pushed against each wall. There were three women in here, each typing away at the computers on their desks, jointly creating a pitter-patter song that filled the room. None of them had noticed her over the sound of it.

Pip walked towards Becca Bell, her short blonde hair scraped back in a stubby ponytail, and cleared her throat.

'Hi, Becca,' she said.

Becca spun around in her chair and the other two women looked up. 'Oh,' she said, 'it's you that's here to see me? Shouldn't you be at school?'

'Yeah, sorry. It's half-term,' Pip said, shifting nervously under Becca's gaze, thinking of how close she and Ravi had been to getting caught by her in the Bell house. Pip looked instead over Becca's shoulder, at the computer screen full of typed words.

Becca's eyes followed hers and she turned back to minimize the document.

'Sorry,' she said, 'it's the first piece I'm writing for the newspaper and my first draft is absolutely awful. My eyes only,' she smiled.

'What's it about?' Pip asked.

'Oh, um, it's just about this old farmhouse that's been uninhabited for eleven years now, just off the Kilton end of Sycamore Road. They can't seem to sell it.' She looked up at Pip. 'A few of the neighbours are thinking about pitching in to buy it, trying to apply for change of use and doing it up as a pub. I'm writing about why that's a terrible idea.'

One of the women across the room cut in: 'My brother lives near there and he doesn't think it's such a terrible idea. Beer on tap just down the road. He's ecstatic.' She gave a hacking foghorn laugh, looking to her other colleague to join in.

Becca shrugged, glancing down at her hands as she picked at the sleeve of her jumper. 'I just think the place deserves to be a home for a family again one day,' she said. 'My dad almost bought and restored it years ago, before everything happened. He changed his mind, in the end, but I've always wondered what things would be like if he hadn't.'

The other two keyboards fell silent.

'Oh, Becca, sweetheart,' the woman said, 'I had no idea that was the reason. Well, I feel terrible now.' She slapped her forehead. 'I'll do the tea rounds for the rest of the day.'

'No, don't worry.' Becca gave her a small smile.

The other two women turned back to their computers.

'Pippa, isn't it?' Becca spoke quietly. 'What can I help you with? If it's about what we discussed before, you know I don't want to be involved.'

'Trust me, Becca,' Pip said, her voice dipping into whispers. 'This is important. Really important. Please.'

Becca's wide blue eyes stared up at hers for a few lingering moments.

'Fine.' She stood up. 'Let's go out to the front room.'

The room felt colder the second time around. Becca took a seat on the nearest sofa and crossed her legs. Pip sat at the other end and turned to face her.

'Um . . . so . . .' She tapered off, not quite sure how to phrase it, nor how much she should tell her. She stalled, staring into Becca's Andie-like face.

'What is it?' Becca said.

Pip found her voice. 'So, while researching, I found out that Andie might have been dealing drugs and selling at calamity parties.'

Becca's neat brows drew down to her eyes as she cast a distrustful look at Pip. 'No,' she said, 'there's no way.'

'I'm sorry, I've confirmed it with multiple sources,' Pip said.

'She can't have done.'

'The man who supplied her gave her a secret second phone, a burner phone, to use in her deals,' Pip carried on over Becca's protests. 'He said that Andie hid the phone along with her stash in her wardrobe.'

'I'm sorry but I think someone's been playing a trick on you,' Becca said, shaking her head. 'There's no way my sister was selling drugs.'

'I understand it must be hard to hear,' Pip said, 'but I'm learning that Andie had a lot of secrets. This was one of them. The police didn't find the burner phone in her room and I'm trying to find out who might have had access to her room after she went missing.'

'Wh . . . but . . .' Becca sputtered, still shaking her head. 'No one did; the house was cordoned off.'

'I mean, before the police arrived. After Andie left the house and before your parents discovered she was missing. Was there any way someone could have broken into your house without you knowing? Had you gone to sleep?'

'I . . . I –' her voice cracked – 'no, I don't know. I wasn't asleep, I was downstairs watching TV. But you –'

'Do you know Max Hastings?' Pip said quickly before Becca could object again.

Becca stared at her, confusion glassing over her eyes. 'Um,' she said, 'yeah, he was Sal's friend, wasn't he? The blonde guy.'

'Did you ever notice him hanging round near your house

after Andie disappeared?'

'No,' she said quickly. 'No, but why –'

'What about Daniel da Silva? Do you know him?' Pip said, hoping this quick-fire questioning was working, that Becca would answer before she thought not to answer.

'Daniel,' she said, 'yeah, I know him. He was close with my dad.'

Pip's eyes narrowed. 'Daniel da Silva was close to your dad?'

'Yeah,' Becca sniffed. 'He worked for my dad for a while, after he quit that caretaker's job at school. My dad owns a cleaning company. But he took a shine to Daniel and promoted him to a job in the office. He was the one who convinced Daniel to apply to be a police officer, supported him through the training. Yeah. I don't know if they're still close; I don't speak to my dad.'

'So did you see a lot of Daniel?' asked Pip.

'Quite a bit. He often popped round, stayed for dinner sometimes. What has this got to do with my sister?'

'Daniel was a police officer when your sister went missing. Was he involved in the case at all?'

'Well, yeah,' Becca replied, 'he was one of the first responding officers when my dad reported it.'

Pip felt herself tilting forward, her hands against the sofa cushion, leaning into Becca's words. 'Did he do a search of the house?'

'Yeah,' Becca said. 'He and this policewoman took our

statements and then did their primary search.'

'Could Daniel have been the one that searched Andie's room?'

'Yeah, maybe.' Becca shrugged. 'I don't really see where you're going with this. I think you've been misled by someone, really. Andie was not involved in drugs.'

'Daniel da Silva was the first to access Andie's room,' Pip said, more to herself than to Becca.

'Why does that matter?' said Becca, annoyance starting to stir in her voice. 'We know what happened that night. We know Sal killed her, regardless of what Andie or anyone else was up to.'

'I'm not sure he did,' Pip said, widening her eyes in what she hoped was a meaningful way. 'I'm not so sure Sal did it. And I think I'm close to proving it.'

<u>Production Log – Entry 34</u>

Becca Bell did not respond well to my suggestion that Sal might be innocent. I think asking me to leave was proof enough of that. It's not surprising. She's had five and a half unwavering years of knowing that Sal killed Andie, five and a half years to bury the grief for her sister. And here I come, kicking up the dirt and telling her she's wrong.

But she'll have to believe it soon, along with the rest of Kilton, when Ravi and I find out who really killed both Andie and Sal.

And after my conversation with Becca I think the front runner has changed again. Not only have I unearthed a strong connection between two names on my suspect list (another possible murder team: Daniel da Silva and Jason Bell?) but I've confirmed my suspicions about Daniel. He not only had access to Andie's room after she went missing, but he was probably the first person to search it! He would have had the perfect opportunity to take and hide the burner phone, and remove any trace of himself from Andie's life.

Web searches bring up nothing useful about Daniel. But I have just seen this on the Thames Valley Police Kilton area page:

Have Your Say Meetings

Meet your local neighbourhood officers and
<u>have a say</u> on policing priorities in your local area.

Upcoming events:

Type: Have Your Say Meeting
Date: Tuesday 24th October, 2017
Time: 12:00 - 1:00
Venue: Library, Little Kilton

Kilton has only five designated police officers and two police community support officers. I like my odds that Daniel will be there. I don't like my odds that he'll tell me anything.

Thirty-Two

'And there are still too many youths loitering on the common in the evenings,' an old woman croaked, her arm raised beside her head.

'We spoke about this at a previous meeting, Mrs Faversham,' a female police officer with ringlet-sprung hair said. 'They aren't engaging in any anti-social behaviour. They are just playing football after school.'

Pip was sitting on a bright yellow plastic chair in an audience of just twelve people. The library was dark and stuffy and the air filled her nostrils with that wonderful cosmic smell of old books and the fusty smell of old people.

The meeting was slow and dreary, but Pip was alert and sharp-eyed. Daniel da Silva was one of the three officers taking the meeting. He was taller than she'd expected, standing there in his black uniform. His hair was light brown and wavy, styled back from his forehead. He was clean-shaven, with a narrow up-turned nose and wide rounded lips. Pip tried to not watch him for long stretches of time, in case he noticed.

There was another familiar face here too, sitting just three seats down from Pip. He stood up suddenly, flashing his open palm at the officers.

'Stanley Forbes, *Kilton Mail*,' he said. 'Several of my readers have complained that people are still driving too fast down the high street. How do you intend to tackle this issue?'

Daniel stepped forward now, nodding for Stanley to retake his seat. 'Thanks, Stan,' he said. 'The street already has several traffic-calming measures. We have discussed performing more speed checks and, if it's a concern, I am happy to reopen that conversation with my superiors.'

Mrs Faversham had two more complaints to drawl through and then the meeting was finally over.

'If you have any other policing concerns,' the third officer said, noticeably avoiding eye contact with old Mrs Faversham, 'please fill out one of the questionnaires behind you,' she gestured. 'And if you'd prefer to talk to any of us in private, we will be sticking around for the next ten minutes.'

Pip held back for a while, not wanting to appear too eager. She waited as Daniel finished talking to one of the library volunteers and then she pushed up from her chair and approached him.

'Hi,' she said.

'Hello,' he smiled, 'you seem a few decades too young for a meeting like this.'

She shrugged. 'I'm interested in law and crime.'

'Nothing too interesting in Kilton,' he said, 'just loitering kids and slightly fast cars.'

Oh, if only.

'So you've never made an arrest over suspicious salmon handling?' she said, laughing nervously.

Daniel stared blankly at her.

'Oh, it's . . . that's an actual British law.' She felt her cheeks redden. Why didn't she just play with her hair or fiddle like normal people do when nervous? 'The Salmon Act of 1986 made it illegal to . . . uh, never mind.' She shook her head. 'I had a couple of questions I wanted to ask you.'

'Shoot,' he said, 'as long as it's not about salmon.'

'It's not.' She coughed lightly into her fist and looked up. 'Do you remember reports being made, about five or six years ago, of drug use and drinks being spiked at house parties thrown by Kilton Grammar students?'

He tensed his chin and his mouth sank into a thoughtful frown.

'No,' he said, 'I don't remember that. Are you wanting to report a crime?'

She shook her head. 'No. Do you know Max Hastings?' she said.

Daniel shrugged. 'I know the Hastings family a bit. They were my very first call-out alone after I finished training.'

'For what?'

'Oh, nothing big. Their son had crashed his car into a tree in front of the house. Needed to file a police report for the insurance. Why?'

'No reason,' she said faux-nonchalantly. She could see Daniel's feet starting to turn away from her. 'Just one more thing I'm interested to know.'

'Yep?'

'You were one of the first responding officers when Andie

Bell was reported missing. You conducted the primary search of the Bell residence.'

Daniel nodded, lines tightening around his eyes.

'Was that not some sort of conflict of interest, seeing as you were so close to her father?'

'No,' he said, 'it wasn't. I'm a professional when I have this uniform on. And I have to say, I don't really like where these questions are going. Excuse me.' He shuffled a few inches away.

Just then, a woman appeared behind Daniel and stepped in beside him and Pip. She had long fair hair and a freckled nose, and a giant belly pushing out the front of her dress. She must have been at least seven months pregnant.

'Well, hi,' she said in a forced pleasant tone to Pip. 'I'm Dan's wife. How entirely unusual for me to catch him talking to a young girl. Must say you aren't his usual type.'

'Kim,' Daniel said, placing his arm on her back, 'come on.'

'Who is she?'

'Just some kid who came to the meeting. I don't know.' He led his wife away to the other side of the room.

At the library's exit Pip took one more look over her shoulder. Daniel stood with his wife, talking to Mrs Faversham, deliberately not looking over at her. Pip pushed the door and went outside, huddling further into her khaki coat as the cold air enclosed her. Ravi was waiting for her just up the road, opposite the cafe.

'You were right not to come in,' she said when she arrived at his side. 'He was pretty hostile to just me.

And Stanley Forbes was there too.'

'Lovely guy,' Ravi said sarcastically, dipping his hands in his pockets to hide them from the bitter wind. 'So you didn't learn anything?'

'Oh, I didn't say that,' Pip said, stepping in closer to him to shield herself from the wind. 'He let one thing slip; don't even know if he realized it.'

'Stop pausing for dramatic effect.'

'Sorry,' she said. 'He said he knew the Hastings, that he was the one who filed the police report when Max crashed his car into the tree by their house.'

'Oh,' Ravi's lips opened around the sound. 'So he . . . maybe he could have known about the hit-and-run?'

'Maybe he could.'

Pip's hands were so cold now that they started to curl into claws. She was about to suggest going back to hers when Ravi stiffened, his eyes fixed on a point behind her.

She turned.

Daniel da Silva and Stanley Forbes had just left the library, the door banging behind them. They were deep in hushed conversation, Daniel explaining something with gestured hands. Stanley's head did a half-owl spin, checking around them and that's when he spotted Pip and Ravi.

Stanley's eyes cooled, and his gaze was a cold blast in the wind as it flicked between the two of them. Daniel looked over and stared, but his eyes were just on Pip, sharp and blistering.

Ravi took her hand. 'Let's go,' he said.

Thirty-Three

'All right, puppuccino,' Pip said to Barney, bending down to unclip the lead from his tartan collar. 'Off you go.'

He looked up at her with his sloped and smiling eyes. And when she straightened up he was off, bounding up the muddy track ahead and winding between the trees in that forever-puppy way that he ran.

Her mum had been right; it was a little too late to be going out on a walk. The woods were darkening already, the sky a churned grey peeking through the gaps between the autumn-speckled trees. It was quarter to six already and her weather app told her that sunset was in two minutes. She wouldn't stay out long; she just needed a quick jaunt to get her away from her workstation. She needed air. Needed space.

All day she had flitted between studying for her exam next week and staring hard at the names in her suspect list. She would stare for so long that her gaze went cross-eyed, drawing imaginary and thorny lines that budded from the letter-tips of one name to wrap round the others until the list was just a chaotic mess of swaddled names and tangled bonds.

She didn't know what to do. Perhaps try to talk to Daniel da Silva's wife; there certainly was palpable friction between the couple. And why, what possible secrets had caused it? Or should she focus back on the burner phone, consider breaking into the homes of those suspects that knew about the phone and searching for it there?

No.

She had come on this walk to forget Andie Bell and to clear her head. She reached into her pocket and unwound her headphones. Tucking them into her ears, she pressed play on her phone, resuming the true crime podcast episode she was on. She had to turn the volume right up, struggling to hear the episode over the crunch of her wellies on the path of fallen leaves.

Listening to the voice in her ears, to the story of another murdered girl, Pip tried to forget her own.

She took the short circuit through the woods, her eyes on the shadows from scraggy branches above, shadows that grew lighter as the world around was growing darker. When the twilight took a turn towards darkness Pip walked off the path, dipping into the trees to get to the road faster. She called Barney when the gate to the road was visible, thirty feet in front of her.

When she reached it she paused her podcast and spooled the headphones back round her phone.

'Barney, come on,' she called, slipping it into her pocket.

A car flew by on the road, the full beam of its headlights blinding Pip when she looked into them.

'Doggo!' she called, louder and higher this time. 'Barney, come!'

The trees were dark and still.

Pip wet her lips and whistled.

'Barney! Here, Barney!'

No sound of paws trampling through the fallen leaves. No golden flash among the trees. Nothing.

Cold fear began to creep up her toes and down her fingers.

'Bar-ney!' she shouted and her voice cracked.

She ran back the way she'd come. Back into the dark engulfing trees.

'Barney,' she screamed, crashing along the path, the dog lead swinging in wide empty arcs from her hand.

Thirty-Four

'Mum, Dad!' She shoved open the front door, tripping on the doormat and falling to her knees. The tears stung, pooling at the crack between her lips. 'Dad!'

Victor appeared at the kitchen door.

'Pickle?' he said. And then he saw her. 'Pippa, what is it? What happened?'

He hurried forward as she picked herself up from the floor.

'Barney's gone,' she said. 'He didn't come when I called. I went around the whole woods, calling him. He's gone. I don't know what to do. I've lost him, Dad.'

Her mum and Josh were in the hallway now too, watching her silently.

Victor squeezed her arm. 'It's OK, pickle,' he said in his bright and warm voice. 'We'll find him; don't you worry.'

Her dad grabbed his thick padded coat from the understairs cupboard and two torches. He made Pip put on a pair of gloves before he handed one of them to her.

The night was dark and heavy by the time they were back in the woods. Pip walked her dad round the path she'd taken. The two white torch beams cut through the darkness.

'Barney!' her dad called in his booming voice, thrown forward and sideways as echoes through the trees.

It was two hours later and two hours colder that

Victor said it was time to go home.

'We can't go home until we find him!' she sniffed.

'Listen.' He turned to her, the torch lighting them from below. 'It's too dark now. We will find him in the morning. He's wandered off somewhere and he'll be OK for one night.'

Pip went straight up to bed after their late and silent dinner. Her parents both came up to her room and sat on her bedspread. Her mum stroked her hair as she tried not to cry.

'I'm sorry,' she said. 'I'm so sorry.'

'It's not your fault, sweetie,' Leanne said. 'Don't worry. He'll find his way home. Now try to get some sleep.'

She didn't. Not much at least. One thought crept into her head and burrowed there: what if this really was her fault? What if this was because she'd ignored her final warning? What if Barney wasn't just lost, what if he'd been taken? Why had she not been paying attention?

They sat in the kitchen, eating an early breakfast none of them were hungry for. Victor, who looked like he hadn't slept much either, had already called in to work to take the day off. He listed their plan of action between cereal bites: he and Pip would go back to the woods. Then they would widen the search and start knocking on doors, asking after Barney. Mum and Josh would stay back and make some missing posters. They would go and put them up in the high street and pass them out. When they were done, they would all meet up and search the other woodland areas near town.

317

They heard barking in the woods and Pip's heart picked up, but it was just a family walking with two beagles and a labradoodle. They said they hadn't seen a golden retriever lone and wandering but they would look out for one now.

Pip's voice was hoarse by the time they'd circled the woods for the second time. They knocked on their neighbours' houses up Martinsend Way; no one had seen a lost dog.

Early afternoon, and Pip's train whistle text tone blared in the quiet forest.

'Is that Mum?' her dad said.

'No,' Pip said, reading the message. It was from Ravi. *Hey,* it said, *I've just seen missing posters for Barney up in town. Are you OK? Do you need help?*

Her fingers were too numb from the cold to type a response.

They stopped briefly for sandwiches and then carried on, her mum and Josh joining them now, traipsing through trees and across private farmland, choral shouts of 'Barney' carrying on the wind.

But the world turned on them and darkness fell again.

Back home, drained and quiet, Pip picked through the Thai takeaway Victor had collected from town. Her mum had put a Disney film on in the background to lighten the mood, but Pip was just staring down at the noodles, wrapped like tightening worms round her fork.

She dropped the fork when a train whistle sounded, vibrating in her pocket.

She placed her plate on the coffee table and pulled out her phone. The screen glared up at her.

Pip tried her hardest to blink the terror from her eyes, to force her jaw closed. She fought a blank look on to her face and put the phone face down on the sofa.

'Who's that?' her mum asked.

'Just Cara.'

It wasn't. It was Unknown: *Want to see your dog again?*

Thirty-Five

The next text didn't come until eleven in the morning.

Victor was working from home. He came into Pip's bedroom at around eight and told her that they were going off on another search and would be back at lunchtime.

'You should stay here and get on with your revision,' he said. 'This exam is very important. Leave Barney to us.'

Pip nodded. She was relieved in a way. She didn't think she could walk alongside her family, calling out his name, knowing that he wasn't there to be found. Because he wasn't lost, he was taken. By Andie Bell's killer.

But there was no time to waste hating herself, asking why she hadn't listened to the threats. Why she'd been stupid enough to think herself invincible. She just had to get Barney back. That was all that mattered.

Her family had been gone for a couple of hours when her phone screeched, making her flinch and slosh coffee over her duvet. She grabbed the phone and read the text over several times.

Take your computer and any USBs or hard drives that your project is saved on. Bring them to the tennis club car park with you and walk 100 paces into the trees on the right side. Do not tell anyone and come alone. If you follow these instructions, you will get your dog back.

Pip jumped up, spattering more coffee on her bed.

She moved fast, before the fear could congeal and paralyse her. She stepped out of her pyjamas and into a jumper and jeans. She grabbed her rucksack, undid the zips and upturned it, spilling her schoolbooks and academic planner on to the floor. She unplugged her laptop and piled both it and the charger into the bag. The two memory sticks she'd saved her project on were in the middle drawer of her desk. She scooped them out and shoved them in on top of the computer.

She ran down the stairs, almost stumbling as she swung the heavy bag up on to her back. She slipped on her walking boots and coat and grabbed her car keys from the side table in the hall. There was no time to think this through. If she stopped to think, she'd falter and lose him forever.

Outside, the wind was cold against her neck and fingers. She ran to the car and climbed in. Her grip was sticky and shaky on the steering wheel as she pulled out of the drive.

It took her five minutes to get there. She would have been quicker if she hadn't got stuck behind a slow driver, tailgating and flashing them to hurry up out of the way.

She turned into the car park beyond the tennis courts and pulled into the nearest bay. Grabbing her rucksack from the passenger seat, she left her car and headed straight for the trees that bordered the car park.

Before stepping from concrete on to mud, Pip paused for just a moment to look over her shoulder. There was some kids' club on the tennis courts, shrieking and whacking balls into the fence. A couple of mums with young and squawking toddlers standing beside a car, chatting away. There was no one there with their eyes fixed on her. No car she recognized. No person. If she was being watched, she couldn't tell.

She turned back to the trees and started to walk. She counted in her head each step she took, panicking that her strides were either too long or too short and she wouldn't end up where they wanted her to.

At thirty paces her heart throbbed so hard that it jolted her breath.

At sixty-seven the skin on her chest and under her arms prickled as sweat broke the surface.

At ninety-four she started muttering, 'Please, please, please,' under her breath.

And then she stopped one hundred steps into the trees. And she waited.

There was nothing around her, nothing but the stippled shade from half-bare trees and leaves from red to pale yellow padding the mud.

A long, high whistling sounded above her, trailing into four short bursts. She looked up to see a red kite flying over her, just a sharp wide-winged outline against the grey sun. The bird flew out of sight and she was alone again.

It was almost a whole minute later that her phone shrieked from her pocket. Fumbling, she pulled it out and looked down at the text.

Destroy everything and leave it there. Do not tell anyone what you know. No more questions about Andie. This is finished now.

Pip's eyes flicked over the words, forward and back. She forced a deep breath down her throat and put away the phone. Her skin seared under the gaze of the killer's eyes, watching her from somewhere unseen.

On her knees, she slid her rucksack to the ground, took out the laptop, its charger and the two memory sticks. She laid them out on the autumn leaves and pulled open the laptop lid.

She got to her feet and, as her eyes filled and the world blurred, she stamped down on the first memory stick with her boot heel. One side of the plastic casing cracked and sprang away. The metal connector part dented. She stamped again and then turned her left boot on to the other stick, jumping on them both as their parts cracked and splintered off.

Then she turned to her laptop, the screen looking at her with a line of dim sunlight glinting back. She watched her dark silhouette reflected in the glass as she drew up her leg and kicked out at it. The screen flattened over its hinge, lying in the leaves prone with its keyboard, a large crack webbed across it.

The first tear dropped to her chin as she kicked again, at the keyboard this time. Several letters came away with her boot, scattering into the mud. She stamped and her boots cracked right through the glass on the screen, pushing out into the metal casing.

She jumped and jumped again, tears chasing each other as they snaked down her cheeks.

The metal around the keyboard was cracked now, showing

the motherboard and the cooling fan below. The green circuit board snapped into pieces beneath her heel, and the little fan severed and flew away. She jumped again and stumbled on the mangled machine, falling on her back in the soft and crackling leaves.

She let herself cry there for a few short moments. Then she sat upright and picked up the laptop, its broken screen hanging limply from one hinge, and hurled it against the trunk of the nearest tree. With another thud, it came to rest on the ground in pieces, lying dead among the tree roots.

Pip sat there, coughing, waiting for the air to return to her chest. Her face stinging from the salt.

And she waited.

She wasn't sure what she was supposed to do now. She'd done everything they asked; was Barney about to be released to her here? She should wait and see. Wait for another message. She called his name and she waited.

More than half an hour passed. And nothing. No message. No Barney. No sound of anyone but the faint screams of the kids on the tennis court.

Pip pushed on to her feet, her soles sore and lumpy against the boots. She picked up her empty rucksack and wandered away, one last lingering look back at the destroyed machine.

'Where did you go?' Dad said when she let herself back into the house.

Pip had sat in the car for a while in the tennis car park.

To let her rubbed-red eyes settle before she returned home.

'I couldn't concentrate here,' she said quietly, 'so I went to do my revision in the cafe.'

'I see,' he said with a kind smile. 'Sometimes a change of scenery is good for concentration.'

'But, Dad . . .' She hated the lie that was about to come out of her mouth. 'Something happened. I don't know how. I went to the toilet for just a minute and when I came back my laptop was gone. No one there saw anything. I think it was stolen.' She looked down at her scuffed boots. 'I'm sorry, I shouldn't have left it.'

Victor shushed her and folded her into a hug. One she really, really needed. 'Don't be silly,' he said, 'things are not important. They are replaceable. I only care if you're OK.'

'I'm OK,' she said. 'Any sign this morning?'

'None yet, but Josh and Mum are going back out this afternoon and I'm going to ring round the local shelters. We will get him back, pickle.'

She nodded and stepped back from him. They were going to get Barney back; she'd done everything she had been told to do. That was the deal. She wished she could say something to her family, to take some of the worry out of their faces. But it wasn't possible. It was another of those Andie Bell secrets Pip had found herself trapped inside.

As for giving up on Andie now, could she really do that? Could she walk away, knowing that Sal Singh wasn't guilty? Knowing a killer walked the same Kilton streets as her?

She had to, didn't she? For the dog she'd loved for ten years, the dog who loved her back even harder. For her family's safety. For Ravi too. How would she convince him to give up on this? He had to, or his could be the next body in the woods. This couldn't go on; it wasn't safe any more. There was no choice. The decision felt like a shard from the shattered laptop screen had stuck through her chest. It stabbed and cracked every time she breathed.

Pip was upstairs at her desk, looking through past papers for the ELAT exam. The day had grown dark and Pip had just flicked on her mushroom-shaped desk lamp. She was working to the *Gladiator* soundtrack playing through her phone speakers, flicking her pen in time with the strings. She paused the music when someone knocked on the door.

'Yep,' she said, spinning in her desk chair.

Victor came in and closed the door behind him. 'You working hard, pickle?'

She nodded.

He walked over and propped his back against her desk, his legs crossed out in front of him.

'Listen, Pip,' he said gently. 'Someone just found Barney.'

Pip's breath stuck halfway down her throat. 'Wh-why don't you look happy?'

'He must have fallen in somehow. They found him in the river.' Her dad reached down and took her hand. 'I'm sorry, darling. He drowned.'

Pip wheeled away from her dad, shaking her head.

'No,' she said. 'He can't have done. That's not what . . . No, he can't be . . .'

'I'm sorry, pickle,' he said, his bottom lip trembling. 'Barney died. We're going to bury him tomorrow, in the garden.'

'No, he can't be!' Pip jumped to her feet now, pushing Victor away as he stepped forward to hug her. 'No, he isn't dead. That's not fair,' she cried, the tears hot and fast down to the dimple in her chin. 'He can't be dead. It's not fair. It's not . . . it's not . . .'

She dropped to her knees and sat back on the floor, hugging her legs into her chest. A chasm of unspeakable pain opened inside, glowing black.

'This is all my fault.' Her mouth pressed into her knee, stifling her words. 'I'm so sorry. I'm so, so sorry.'

Her dad sat down beside her and tucked her into his arms. 'Pip, I don't want you to blame yourself, not even for a second. It's not your fault he wandered away from you.'

'It's not fair, Dad,' she cried into his chest. 'Why is this happening? I just want him back. I just want Barney back.'

'Me too,' he whispered.

They sat that way for a long time on her bedroom floor, crying together. Pip didn't even hear when her mum and Josh came into the room. She didn't know they were there until they slotted themselves in, Josh sitting on Pip's lap, his head on her shoulder.

'It's not fair.'

Thirty-Six

They buried him in the afternoon. Pip and Josh planned to plant sunflowers over his grave in the spring, because they were golden and happy, just like him.

Cara and Lauren came over for a while, Cara laden with cookies she'd baked for them all. Pip couldn't really talk; every word almost stumbled into a cry or a scream of rage. Every word stirred that impossible feeling in her gut, that she was too sad to be angry but too angry to be sad. They didn't stay for long.

It was evening now and there was a high ringing sound in her ears. The day had hardened her grief and Pip felt numb and dried out. He wasn't coming back and she couldn't tell anyone why. That secret, and the guilt in its wake, was the heaviest thing of all.

Someone knocked lightly at her bedroom door. Pip dropped her pen on to the blank page.

'Yes,' she said, her voice hoarse and small.

The door pushed open and Ravi stepped into the room.

'Hi,' he said, flicking his dark hair back from his face. 'How are you doing?'

'Not good,' she said. 'What are you doing here?'

'You weren't replying and I got worried. I saw the posters were gone this morning. Your dad just told me what happened.'

328

He closed the door and leaned back against it. 'I'm so sorry, Pip. I know it doesn't help when people say that; it's just something you say. But I am sorry.'

'There's only one person who needs to be sorry,' she said, looking down at the empty page.

He sighed. 'It's what we do when someone we love dies; blame ourselves. I did it too, Pip. And it took me a long time to work out that it wasn't my fault; sometimes bad things just happen. It was easier after that. I hope you get there quicker.'

She shrugged.

'I also wanted to say to you –' he cleared his throat – 'don't worry about the Sal thing for a bit. This deadline we made for taking the photo to the police, it doesn't matter. I know how important it is to you to protect Naomi and Cara. You can have more time. You already overstretch yourself and I think you need a break, you know, after what's happened. And there's your Cambridge exam coming up.' He scratched the back of his head and the long hair at the front trailed back into his eyes. 'I know that my brother was innocent now, even if no one else does yet. I've waited over five years; I can wait a little longer. And in the meantime I'll keep looking into our open leads.'

Pip's heart knotted, voiding itself of everything. She had to hurt him. It was the only way. The only way to make him give up, to keep him safe. Whoever murdered Andie and Sal, they'd shown her they were prepared to kill again. And she couldn't let it be Ravi.

She couldn't look at him. Couldn't look at his kind-without-trying face, or at the perfect smile he shared with his brother, or his eyes so brown and deep you could fall right into them. So she didn't look.

'I'm not doing the project any more,' she said. 'I'm done.'

He straightened up. 'What do you mean?'

'I mean I'm done with the project. I've emailed my supervisor telling her I'm changing topic or dropping out. It's over.'

'But . . . I don't understand,' he said, the first wounds opening up in his voice. 'This isn't just a project, Pip. This is about my brother, about what really happened here. You can't just stop. What about Sal?'

It was Sal she was thinking of. How, above all other things, he would've wanted his little brother not to die in the woods as he had.

'I'm sorry, but I'm done.'

'I don't . . . wh . . . look at me,' he said.

She wouldn't.

He came over to the desk and crouched in front of it, looking up at her in the chair.

'What's wrong?' he said. 'Something's wrong here. You wouldn't do this if –'

'I'm just done, Ravi,' she said. She looked down at him and knew immediately that she shouldn't have. This was so much harder now. 'I can't do it. I don't know who killed them. I can't work it out. I'm finished.'

'But we will,' he said, desperation sculpting his face. 'We *will* work it out.'

'I can't. I'm just some kid, remember.'

'An idiot said that to you,' he said. 'You're not *just* some anything. You're Pippa fricking Fitz-Amobi.' He smiled and it was the saddest thing she'd ever seen. 'And I don't think there's anyone in this world quite like you. I mean, you laugh at my jokes, so there must be something wrong with you. We're so close to this, Pip. We know Sal's innocent; we know someone framed him for Andie and then killed him. You can't stop. You swore to me. You want this just as much as I do.'

'I've changed my mind,' she said flatly, 'and you won't change it back. I'm done with Andie Bell. I'm done with Sal.'

'But he's innocent.'

'It's not my job to prove that.'

'You made it your job.' He pushed against his knees and stood over her, his voice rising now. 'You barged your way into my life, offering me this chance I never had before. You can't take that away from me now; you know I need you. You can't give up. This isn't you.'

'I'm sorry.'

A twelve-heartbeat silence fell between them, Pip's eyes on the floor.

'Fine,' he said coldly. 'I don't know why you're doing this but fine. I'll go to the police with Sal's alibi photo on my own. Send me the file.'

'I can't,' Pip said. 'My laptop got stolen.'

Ravi shot a look at the surface of her desk. He charged over to it, spreading her stack of papers and exam notes, eyes desperate and searching.

'Where's the printout of the photo?' he said, turning to her, notes clutched in his hand.

And now for the lie that would break him.

'I destroyed it. It's gone,' she said.

The look in his eyes set her on fire and she withered away.

'Why would you do that? Why are you doing this?' The papers dropped from his hands, gliding like severed wings to the floor. They scattered around Pip's feet.

'Because I don't want to be a part of this any more. I never should have started it.'

'This isn't fair!' Tendons stuck out like vines up his neck. 'My brother was innocent, and you just got rid of the one small bit of evidence we had. If you stand back now, Pip, you're just as bad as everyone else in Kilton. Everyone who painted the word *scum* on our house, who smashed our windows. Everyone who tormented me at school. Everyone who looks at me that way they look at me. No, you'll be worse; at least they think he's guilty.'

'I'm sorry,' she said quietly.

'No, I'm sorry,' he said, his voice breaking. He ran his sleeve over his face to catch the angry tears and reached for the door. 'I'm sorry for thinking you were someone you're clearly not. You are just a kid. A cruel one, like Andie Bell.'

He left the room, hands to his eyes as he turned

to the stairs.

Pip watched him walk away for the last time.

When she heard the front door open and close she clenched her hand into a fist and punched her desk. The pen pot juddered and fell, scattering pens across the surface.

She screamed herself empty into her cupped hands, holding on to the scream, trapping it with her fingers.

Ravi hated her, but he would be safe now.

Thirty-Seven

The next day, Pip was in the living room with Josh, teaching him how to play chess. They were finishing their first practice match and, despite her best efforts to let him win, Josh was down to just his king and two pawns. Or prawns, as he called them.

Someone knocked on the front door and the absence of Barney was an immediate punch to the gut. No skittering claws on the polished wood racing to stand and greet.

Her mum pattered down the hall and opened the door.

Leanne's voice floated into the living room. 'Oh, hello, Ravi.'

Pip's stomach leaped into her throat.

Confused, she put her knight back down and wandered out of the room, her unease ramping into panic. Why would he come back after yesterday? How could he bear to look at her ever again? Unless he was desperate enough to come and ambush her parents, tell them everything they knew and try to force Pip to go to the police. She wouldn't; who else would die if she did?

When the front door came into view she saw Ravi unzipping a large sports rucksack and dipping his hands inside.

'My mum sends her condolences,' he said, pulling out two large Tupperware boxes. 'She made you a chicken curry, you know, in case you didn't feel like cooking.'

'Oh,' Leanne said, taking the boxes from Ravi's offered hands. 'That's very thoughtful. Thank you. Come in, come in. You must give me her number so I can thank her.'

'Ravi?' Pip said.

'Hello, trouble,' he said softly. 'Can I talk to you?'

In her room, Ravi closed the door and dropped his bag on the carpet.

'Um . . . I,' Pip stuttered, looking for clues in his face. 'I don't understand why you've come back.'

He took a small step towards her. 'I thought about it all night, literally all night; it was light outside when I finally slept. And there's only one reason I can think of, only one thing that makes sense of this. Because I do know you; I wasn't wrong about you.'

'I don't –'

'Someone took Barney, didn't they?' he said. 'Someone threatened you and they took your dog and killed him so you would stay quiet about Sal and Andie.'

The silence in the room was buzzy and thick.

She nodded and her face cracked with tears.

'Don't cry,' Ravi said, closing the distance between them in one swift step. He pulled her into him, locking his arms round her. 'I'm here,' he said. 'I'm here.'

Pip leaned into him and everything – all the pain, all the secrets she'd caged inside – came free, radiating out of her like heat. She dug her nails into her palms, trying to

335

hold back the tears.

'Tell me what happened,' he said when he finally let her go.

But the words got lost and tangled in Pip's mouth. Instead she pulled out her phone and clicked on to the messages from Unknown, handing it to him. She watched Ravi's flitting eyes as he read through.

'Oh, Pip,' he said, looking at her wide-eyed. 'This is sick.'

'They lied,' she sniffed. 'They said I'd get him back and then they killed him.'

'That wasn't the first time they contacted you,' he said, scrolling up. 'The first text here is from the eighth of October.'

'That wasn't the first,' she said, pulling open the bottom drawer of her desk. She handed Ravi the two sheets of printer paper and pointed at the one on the left. 'That one was left in my sleeping bag when I camped in the woods with my friends on the first of September. I saw someone watching us. That one –' she pointed to the other – 'was in my locker last Friday. I ignored it and I carried on. That's why Barney's dead. Because of my arrogance. Because I thought I was invincible and I'm not. We have to stop. Yesterday . . . I'm sorry, I didn't know how else to get you to stop, other than to make you hate me so you stayed away, away from danger.'

'I'm hard to get rid of,' he said, looking up from the notes. 'And this isn't over.'

'Yes, it is.' She took them back and dropped them on the desk. 'Barney's dead, Ravi. And who will be next? You? Me? The killer's been here, in my house, in my room. They read my research and typed a warning on my EPQ log. Here, Ravi, in the same house as my nine-year-old brother. We are putting too many people in danger if we carry on. Your parents could lose the only son they have left.' She broke off, an image of Ravi dead in the autumn leaves behind her eyes, Josh beside him. 'The killer knows everything we know. They've beaten us and we have too much to lose. I'm sorry that it means I have to abandon Sal. I'm so sorry.'

'Why didn't you tell me about the threats?' he said.

'At first I thought it might just be a prank,' she said, shrugging. 'But I didn't want you to know, in case you made me stop. And then I just got stuck, keeping it a secret. I thought they were just threats. I thought I could beat them. I was so stupid and now I've paid for my mistakes.'

'You're not stupid; you were right all along about Sal,' he said. 'He was innocent. We know that now but it's not enough. He deserves everyone to know that he was good and kind until the end. My parents deserve that. And now we don't even have the photo that proved it.'

'I still have the photo,' Pip said quietly, taking the printout from the bottom drawer and handing it to him. 'Of course I'd never destroy it. But it can't help us now.'

'Why?'

'The killer is watching me, Ravi. Watching us. If we take that photo to the police and they don't believe us, if they think we Photoshopped it or something, then it's too late. We would have played our final hand and it's not strong enough.

Then what happens? Josh gets taken? You do? People could die here.' She sat on her bed, picking at the lumps on her socks. 'We don't have our smoking gun. The photo isn't proof enough; it relies on massive interpretive leaps and it's no longer online. Why would they believe us? Sal's brother and a seventeen-year-old schoolgirl. *I* hardly believe us. All we have are tall stories about a murdered girl, and you know what the police here think of Sal, just like the rest of Kilton. We can't risk our lives on that photo alone.'

'No,' Ravi said, laying the photo on the desk and nodding. 'You're right. And one of our main suspects is a policeman. It's not the right move. Even if the police did somehow believe us and reopen the case, it would take them a long time to find the actual killer that way. Time we wouldn't have.' He wheeled the desk chair over to face her on the bed, straddling it. 'So I guess our only option is to find them ourselves.'

'We can't –' Pip started.

'Do you seriously think walking away is the best move here? How would you ever feel safe again in Kilton, knowing the person that killed Andie and Sal and your dog is still out there? Knowing they're watching you? How could you live like that?'

'I have to.'

'For such a clever person, you're being a real plonker right now.' He leaned his elbows on the back of the chair, chin against his knuckles.

'They murdered my dog,' she said.

338

'They murdered my brother. And what are we going to do about it?' he said, straightening up, a daring glint in his dark eyes. 'Are we going to forget everything, curl up and hide? Live our lives knowing a killer is out there watching us? Or do we fight? Do we find them and punish them for what they've done to us? Put them behind bars so they can't hurt anyone ever again?'

'They'll know we haven't stopped,' she said.

'No they won't, not if we're careful. No more talking to the people on your list, no more talking to anyone. The answer must be somewhere in everything we've learned. You'll say you've given up your project. Only you and I will know.'

Pip didn't say anything.

'If you need more persuasion,' Ravi said, walking over to his rucksack, 'I brought my laptop for you. It's yours until this is done.' He pulled it out and brandished it.

'But –'

'It's yours,' he said. 'You can use it to revise for your exam and to type up what you remember of your log, your interviews. I took some notes myself on there. I know you've lost all your research but –'

'I haven't lost my research,' she said.

'Huh?'

'I always email everything to myself, just in case,' she said, watching Ravi's face twitch into a smile. 'Who do you think I am, some Reckless Ruth?'

'Oh no, Sarge. I know you're a Cautious Carol. So are you

saying yes or should I have brought some bribery muffins too?'

Pip reached out for the laptop.

'Come on then,' she said. 'We have a double homicide to solve.'

They printed everything: every entry from her production log, every page from Andie's academic planner, a picture of each suspect, the car park leverage photos of Howie with Stanley Forbes, Jason Bell and his new wife, the Ivy House Hotel, Max Hastings' house, the newspapers' favourite photo of Andie, a picture of the Bell family dressed up in black tie, Sal winking and waving at the camera, Pip's catfish texts to Emma Hutton, her emails as a BBC reporter about drink spiking, a printout of the effects of Rohypnol, Kilton Grammar school, the photo of Daniel da Silva and other police searching the Bell house, an online article about burner phones, Stanley Forbes' articles about Sal, Nat da Silva next to information about *Assault occasioning actual bodily harm*, a picture of a black Peugeot 206 beside a map of Romer Close and Howie's house, newspaper reports of a hit-and-run on New Year's Eve 2011 on the A413, screen grabs of the texts from Unknown and scans of the threat notes with their dates and location.

They looked down, together, at the reams of paper on the carpet.

'It's not environmentally friendly,' Ravi said, 'but I've always wanted to make a murder board.'

'Me too,' Pip said. 'And I'm well prepared, stationery wise.'

From the drawers in her desk she pulled out a pot of coloured drawing pins and a fresh bundle of red string.

'And you just happen to have red string ready to go?' Ravi said.

'I have every colour of string.'

'Of course you do.'

Pip took down the corkboard hanging over her desk. It was currently covered with pinned-up photos of her and her friends, Josh and Barney, her school timetable and quotes from Maya Angelou. She removed it all and they started sorting.

Working on the floor, they pinned the printed pages to the board with flat silver pins, organizing each page around the relevant person in huge colliding orbits. Andie and Sal's faces in the middle of it all. They had just started making the connection lines with the string and multicoloured pins when Pip's phone started ringing. A number not saved in her phone.

She pressed the green button. 'Hello?'

'Hi, Pip, it's Naomi.'

'Hi. That's weird: you're not saved in my phone.'

'Oh, it's 'cause I smashed mine,' Naomi said. 'I'm using a temp until it's fixed.'

'Oh yeah, Cara said. What's up?'

'I was at my friend's house this weekend, so Cara only just told me about Barns. I'm really sorry, Pip. I hope you're OK.'

'Not yet,' Pip said. 'I'll get there.'

'And I know you may not want to think about this right now,' she said, 'but I found out my friend's cousin studied

341

English at Cambridge. I thought maybe I could see if he'd email you about the exam and interview and stuff, if you wanted.'

'Actually, yeah, yes please,' Pip said. 'That would help. I'm a bit behind on my revision.' She looked pointedly at Ravi hunched over the murder board.

'OK, cool, I'll ask her to contact him. The exam's on Thursday, right?'

'Yep.'

'Well, if I don't see you before, good luck. You'll smash it.'

'Right, so,' Ravi said when Pip had hung up the phone, 'our open leads right now are the Ivy House Hotel, the phone number scribbled out of Andie's planner –' he pointed to its page – 'and the burner phone. As well as knowledge of the hit-and-run, access to Sal's friends' phone numbers and yours. Pip, maybe we are over-complicating this.' He stared up at her. 'As I see it, these are all pointing to one person.'

'Max?'

'Let's just focus on the definites here,' he said. 'No ifs or maybes. He's the only one with direct knowledge of the hit-and-run.'

'True.'

'He's the only one here who had access to Naomi, Millie and Jake's phone numbers. And his own.'

'Nat and Howie could have.'

'Yeah, "could" have. We're looking at definites.' He shuffled over to the Max side of the board. 'He says he just

342

found it, but he has a naked picture of Andie from the Ivy House. So he was probably the one meeting her there. He bought Rohypnol from Andie and girls were getting spiked at calamities; he probably assaulted them. He's clearly messed up, Pip.'

Ravi was going through the very same thoughts she'd struggled with and Pip knew he was about to run into a wall.

'Also,' he carried on, 'he's the only one here we know definitely has your phone number.'

'Actually, no,' she said. 'Nat has it from when I tried to phone-interview her. Howie has it too: I rang him when trying to identify him, and forgot to withhold my number. I got Unknown's first text soon after.'

'Oh.'

'And we know that Max was at school giving a statement to the police at the time when Sal disappeared.'

Ravi slumped back. 'We must be missing something.'

'Let's go back to the connections.' Pip shook the pot of pins at him. He took them and cut off a measure of red string.

'OK,' he said. 'The two Da Silvas are obviously connected. And Daniel da Silva with Andie's dad. And Daniel also with Max, because he filed the report on Max's crashed car and might have known about the hit-and-run.'

'Yes,' she said, 'and maybe covered up drink spiking.'

'OK,' Ravi said, wrapping the string round a pin and pressing it in. He hissed when he stabbed himself in the thumb, a tiny bubble of blood bursting through.

'Can you stop bleeding all over the murder board, please?' Pip said.

Ravi pretended to throw a pin at her. 'So Max also knows Howie and they were both involved in Andie's drug dealing,' he said, circling his finger round their three faces.

'Yep. And Max knew Nat from school,' Pip said, pointing, 'and there's a rumour she had her drink spiked as well.'

Lines of red fraying string covered the board now, webbing and criss-crossing each other.

'So, basically –' Ravi looked up at her – 'they are all indirectly connected with each other, starting with Howie at one end and Jason Bell at the other. Maybe they all did it together, all five of them.'

'Next you'll be saying someone has an evil twin.'

Thirty-Eight

All day at school her friends handled her like she would shatter, never once mentioning Barney, talking around it in wide circles. Lauren let Pip have her last Jaffa Cake. Connor gave up his middle seat at the cafeteria table so Pip didn't have to sit ignored at the end. Cara stayed by her side, knowing just when to talk to her and when to stay quiet. And none of them laughed too hard, checking her way whenever they did.

She spent most of the day working silently through past papers for the ELAT exam, trying to push everything else out of her head. She practised, creating brain-scribed essays in her head while pretending to listen to Mr Ward in history and Miss Welsh in politics. Mrs Morgan cornered her in the corridor, her pudgy face stern as she listed the reasons why it wasn't really possible to change an EPQ title this late. Pip just mumbled, 'OK,' and drifted away, hearing Mrs Morgan tut, 'Teenagers,' under her breath.

As soon as she got home from school, she went straight to her workstation and opened up Ravi's laptop. She would revise more later, after dinner and into the night, even though her eyes were already set inside dark planetary rings. Her mum thought she wasn't sleeping because of Barney. But she wasn't sleeping because there wasn't time to.

Pip opened the browser and pulled up the TripAdvisor

345

page for the Ivy House Hotel. This was her designated lead; Ravi was working on the phone number scribble from the planner. Pip had already messaged some Ivy House reviewers who'd posted around March and April 2012, asking if they remembered seeing a blonde girl at the hotel. But no responses yet.

Next she navigated to the website that had actually processed the bookings for the hotel. On the *contact us* page, she found their phone number and the friendly adage: *Call us anytime!* Perhaps she could pretend to be a relative of the old woman who owned the hotel and see whether she could access their old booking information. Probably not, but she had to try. Secret Older Guy's identity could be at the end of this line.

She unlocked her mobile and clicked on to the phone app. It opened on her recent calls list. She pressed over to the keypad and started to type in the company's number. Then her thumbs slackened and stopped. She stared down at them, her head whirring as the thought overturned and became conscious.

'Wait,' she said aloud, thumbing back on to her recent calls list.

She gazed at the entry right at the top, from when Naomi called her yesterday. On her temporary number. Pip's eyes traced the digits, a feeling both dreadful and strange curdling in her chest.

She jumped out of her chair so fast that it whirled and crashed into the desk. With her phone in hand she dropped to her knees and pulled the murder board out from its hiding place under her bed. Her eyes darted straight to the Andie section, and to the trajectory of printed pages around her smiling face.

She found it. The page from Andie's school planner. The scribbled-out phone number and her log entry beside it. She held out her phone, looking from Naomi's temporary number to the scribble.

07700900476

It wasn't one of the twelve combinations she had written out. But it very nearly was. She'd thought that the third last digit had to be a 7 or a 9. But what if that was just a loopy scribble? What if it was really a 4?

She slumped back on the floor. There was no way to be absolutely certain, no way to unscribble the number and see it for what it was. But it would be one unbelievable pigs-flying hell-freezing-over coincidence if Naomi's old SIM just happened to have a number that similar to the one Andie wrote in her planner. It had to be the same number, just had to.

And what did this mean, if anything? Wasn't this now an irrelevant lead, just Andie copying down the phone number of her boyfriend's best friend? The number was unrelated and could be discarded as a clue.

Then why did she have that sinking feeling in her gut?

Because if Max was a strong contender, then Naomi was even more so. Naomi knew about the hit-and-run. Naomi had access to the phone numbers of Max, Millie and Jake.

347

Naomi had Pip's number. Naomi could have left Max's house while Millie slept and intercepted Andie before 12:45. Naomi had been the closest to Sal. Naomi knew where Pip and Cara were camping in the woods. Naomi knew which woods Pip walked Barney in, the same ones Sal died in.

Naomi already had a lot to lose because of the truths Pip had uncovered. But what if there was even more to it than that? What if she was involved in Andie and Sal's deaths?

Pip was getting ahead of herself, her tired brain running off and tripping her up. It was just a phone number Andie wrote down; it didn't tie Naomi to anything else. But there was something that could she realized when she caught up with her brain.

Since taking Naomi off the Persons of Interest list, she'd received another printed note from the killer: the one in her locker. At the start of term, Pip had set up Cara's laptop to record everything that came through the Wards' printer.

If Naomi was involved in this, Pip now had a sure way to find out.

Thirty-Nine

Naomi had a knife and Pip stepped back.

'Be careful,' she said.

'Oh no!' Naomi shook her head. 'The eyes are uneven.'

She spun the pumpkin round so Pip and Cara could see its face.

'Looks a bit like Trump,' Cara cackled.

'It's supposed to be an evil cat.' Naomi placed her knife down next to the bowl of pumpkin innards.

'Don't give up the day job,' Cara said, wiping pumpkin goo from her hands and sauntering over to the cupboard.

'I don't have a day job.'

'Oh, for god's sake,' Cara grumbled, on tiptoes looking through the cupboard. 'Where have those two packets of biscuits gone? I was literally with Dad two days ago when we bought them.'

'I don't know. I haven't eaten them.' Naomi came over to admire Pip's pumpkin. 'What on earth is yours, Pip?'

'Sauron's eye,' she said quietly.

'Or a vagina on fire,' Cara said, grabbing a banana instead.

'Now that is scary,' Naomi laughed.

No, this was.

Naomi had had the pumpkins and knives laid out and ready for when Cara and Pip got in from school. Pip hadn't had a chance to sneak off yet.

'Naomi,' she said, 'thanks for ringing me the other day. I got that email from your friend's cousin about the Cambridge exam. It was very helpful.'

'Oh good,' she smiled. 'No worries.'

'So when will your phone be fixed?'

'Tomorrow actually, the shop says. It's taken bloody long enough.'

Pip nodded, tensing her chin in what she hoped was a sympathetic look. 'Well, at least you had your old phone with a SIM that still worked. Lucky you held on to them.'

'Well, lucky Dad had a spare pay-as-you-go micro SIM kicking around. And bonus: eighteen pounds credit on it. There was just an expired contract one in my phone.'

The knife almost fell from Pip's hand. A climbing hum in her ears.

'Your dad's SIM card?'

'Yeah,' Naomi said, scoring the knife along her pumpkin face, her tongue out as she concentrated. 'Cara found it in his desk. At the bottom of his bits and bobs drawer. You know that drawer every family has, full of old useless chargers and foreign currency and stuff.'

The hum split into a ringing sound, shrieking and shrieking and stuffing her head. She felt sick, the back of her throat filling with a metallic taste.

Elliot's SIM card.

Elliot's old phone number scribbled out in Andie's planner.

Andie calling Mr Ward an arsehole to her friends the week she disappeared.

Elliot.

'You OK, Pip?' Cara asked as she dropped the lit candle into her pumpkin and it glowed into life.

'Yeah.' Pip nodded too hard. 'I'm just, um . . . just hungry.'

'Well, I would offer you a biscuit, but they seem to have disappeared, as always. Toast?'

'Err . . . no thanks.'

'I feed you because I love you,' Cara said.

Pip's mouth filled, all tacky and sickly. No, it might not mean what she was thinking. Maybe Elliot was just offering to tutor Andie and that's why she wrote his number down. Maybe. It couldn't be him. She needed to calm down, try to breathe. This wasn't proof of anything.

But she had a way to find proof.

'I think we should have spooky Halloween music on while we do this,' Pip said. 'Cara, can I go get your laptop?'

'Yeah, it's on my bed.'

Pip closed the kitchen door behind her.

She raced up the stairs and into Cara's room. With the laptop tucked under her arm she crept back downstairs, her heart thudding, fighting to be louder than the ringing in her ears.

She slipped into Elliot's study and gently closed the door, staring for a moment at the printer on Elliot's desk. The rainbow-coloured people from Isobel Ward's paintings watched her as she put Cara's laptop down on the oxblood leather chair and pulled open the lid, kneeling on the floor before it.

When it awoke she clicked on to the control panel and into *Devices and Printers*. Hovering the mouse over *Freddie Prints Jr,* she right-clicked and, holding her breath, clicked the top item in the drop-down menu: *See what's printing.*

A small blue-bordered box popped up. Inside was a table with six columns: Document Name, Status, Owner, Pages, Size and Date Submitted.

It was filled with entries. One yesterday from Cara called *Personal Statement second draft.* One a few days ago from *Elliot Comp: Gluten free cookies recipe.* Several in a row from *Naomi: CV 2017, Charity Job application, Cover letter, Cover letter 2.*

The note was put in Pip's locker on Friday the 20th October. With her eyes on the *Date Submitted* column, she scrolled down.

Her fingers drew up. On the 19th October at twenty to midnight, *Elliot Comp* had printed *Microsoft Word – Document 1.*

An unnamed, unsaved document.

Her fingers left sweaty tracks on the mousepad as she right-clicked on the document. Another small drop-down menu appeared. Her heart in her throat, she bit down on her tongue and clicked the *Restart* option.

The printer clacked behind her and she flinched.

Pivoting on the balls of her feet, she turned as it hissed, sucking in the top piece of paper.

She straightened up as it started to *sputt-sputt-sputt* the page through.

She moved towards it, a step between each *sputt*.

The paper started to push through, a glimpse of fresh black ink, upside down.

The printer finished and spat it out.

Pip reached for it.

She turned it round.

This is your final warning, Pippa. Walk away.

Forty

Words left her.

She stared down at the paper and shook her head.

It was something primal and wordless, the feeling that took her. Numb rage blackened with terror. And a betrayal that gored through every part of her.

She staggered back and looked away, out of the darkening window.

Elliot Ward was Unknown.

Elliot was the killer. Andie's killer. Sal's. Barney's.

She watched the half-deadened trees beckoning in the wind. And in her reflection in the glass she recreated the scene. Her bumping into Mr Ward in the history classroom, the note gliding to the floor. This note, the one he'd left for her. His deceitful kind face as he asked whether she was being bullied. Cara dropping round cookies she and Elliot had baked to cheer up the Amobis about their dead dog.

Lies. All lies. Elliot, the man she'd grown up looking to as another father figure. The man who'd made elaborate scavenger hunts for them in the garden. The man who bought Pip matching bear-claw slippers to wear at their house. The man who told knock-knock jokes with an easy high laugh. And he was the murderer. A wolf in the pastel shirts and thick-rimmed glasses of a sheep.

She heard Cara call her name.

She folded the page and slipped it in her blazer pocket.

'You've been ages,' Cara said as Pip pushed open the door to the kitchen.

'Toilet,' she said, placing the laptop down in front of Cara. 'Listen, I'm not feeling so great. And I should really be studying for my exam; it's in two days. I think I'm going to head off.'

'Oh,' Cara frowned. 'But Lauren's gonna be here soon and I wanted us all to watch *Blair Witch*. Dad even agreed and we can all laugh at him 'cause he's such a wimp with scary films.'

'Where is your dad?' Pip said. 'Tutoring?'

'How often are you here? You know tutoring is Mondays, Wednesdays and Thursdays. Think he just had to stay late at school.'

'Oh yeah, sorry, the days are blurring.' She paused, thinking. 'I've always wondered why your dad does tutoring; surely he doesn't need the money.'

'Why,' Cara said, 'because my mum's side of the family are minted?'

'Exactly.'

'I think he just enjoys it,' Naomi said, placing a lit tea light through the mouth of her pumpkin. 'He'd probably be willing to pay his tutees just to let him garble on about history.'

'I can't remember when he started,' Pip said.

'Um.' Naomi looked up to think. 'He started just before I was about to leave for university, I think.'

'So, just over five years ago?'

'Think so,' Naomi said. 'Why don't you ask him? His car's just pulled up.'

Pip stiffened, a million bumps flaring up out of her skin.

'OK, well, I'm going to head off now anyway. Sorry.' She grabbed her rucksack, watching the headlights flick off to darkness through the window.

'Don't be silly,' Cara said, concern lining around her eyes, 'I get it. Maybe you and I can redo Halloween when you have less on?'

'Yeah.'

A key scraping. The back door shoved open. Footsteps crossing the utility room.

Elliot appeared in the doorway. The lenses in his glasses steamed up around the edges as he entered the warm room, smiling at the three of them. He placed his briefcase and a plastic bag down on the counter.

'Hello, all,' he said. 'Gosh, teachers do love the sound of their own voices. Longest meeting of my life.'

Pip forced a laugh.

'Wow, look at these pumpkins,' he said, eyes flicking between them, a wide smile splitting his face. 'Pip, are you here for dinner? I've just picked up some spooky Halloween potato shapes.'

He held up the frozen packet and waved it, singing a haunted ghost-like howl.

Forty-One

She got home just as her parents were leaving to take a Harry-Pottered Josh out trick-or-treating.

'Come with us, pickle,' Victor said as Leanne zipped him into his Ghostbusters Stay Puft Marshmallow Man costume.

'I should stay in and study,' she said. 'And deal with any trick-or-treaters.'

'Can't give yourself the night off?' Leanne asked.

'Can't. Sorry.'

'OK, sweetie. The sweeties are by the door.' Her mum giggled at her own joke.

'Got it. See you later.'

Josh stepped outside waving his wand and shouting, '*Accio* candy.'

Victor grabbed his marshmallow head and followed. Leanne paused to kiss the top of Pip's head and then closed the door behind them.

Pip watched through the glass pane in the front door. When they reached the end of the drive, she pulled out her phone and texted Ravi: *COME TO MY HOUSE RIGHT NOW!*

He stared down at the mug clasped between his fingers.

'Mr Ward.' He shook his head. 'It can't be.'

'It can, though,' Pip said, her knee rattling against the

underside of the table. 'He doesn't have an alibi for the night Andie disappeared. I know he doesn't. One of his daughters was at Max's house all night and the other one was sleeping round mine.'

Ravi exhaled and it rippled through the surface of his milky tea. It must have been cold by now, like hers.

'And he has no alibi for the Tuesday when Sal died,' she said. 'He called in sick to work that day; he told me himself.'

'But Sal loved Mr Ward,' Ravi said in the smallest voice she'd ever heard from him.

'I know.'

The table suddenly seemed very wide between them.

'So is he the secret older man Andie was seeing?' Ravi said after a while. 'The one she was meeting at the Ivy House?'

'Maybe,' she said. 'Andie spoke of ruining this person; Elliot was a teacher in a position of trust. He would have been in a lot of trouble if she told someone about them. Criminal charges, jail time.' She looked down at her own untouched tea and the shaky reflection of herself in it. 'Andie called Elliot an arsehole to her friends in the days before she went missing. Elliot said it was because he found out Andie was a bully and contacted her father about the topless video. Maybe that's not what it was about.'

'How did he find out about the hit-and-run? Did Naomi tell him?'

'I don't think so. She said she's never told anyone. I don't know how he knew.'

'There are still some gaps here,' Ravi said.

'I know. But he's the one who threatened me and killed Barney. It's him, Ravi.'

'OK.' Ravi locked his wide and drained eyes on hers. 'So how do we prove it?'

Pip moved her mug away and leaned on the table. 'Elliot tutors three times a week,' she said. 'I'd never really thought it was weird until tonight. The Wards don't need to worry about money; his wife's life insurance paid out a lot and Isobel's parents are still alive and are super rich. Plus Elliot is head of department at school; he's probably on a really good salary. He only started tutoring just over five years ago, in 2012.'

'OK?'

'So what if he's *not* tutoring three times a week?' she said. 'What if he . . . I don't know, goes to the place where he buried Andie? Visiting her grave as some kind of penance?'

Ravi pulled a face, lines of doubt crossing his forehead and nose. 'Not three times every week.'

'Yeah OK,' she conceded. 'Well, what if he's visiting . . . *her*?' She only thought it for the first time as the word formed in her throat. 'What if Andie is alive and he's keeping her somewhere? And he goes to see her three times a week.'

Ravi pulled the same face again.

A handful of near-forgotten memories elbowed their way into her head. 'Disappearing biscuits,' she muttered.

'Sorry?'

Her eyes darted left and right, grappling with the thought.

'Disappearing biscuits,' she said again louder. 'Cara keeps finding food missing from their house. Food she just saw her dad buy. Oh my god. He has her and he's feeding her.'

'You might be slightly jumping to conclusions here, Sarge.'

'We have to find out where he goes,' Pip said, sitting straighter as something prickled up her backbone. 'Tomorrow's Wednesday, a tutoring day.'

'And what if he's actually tutoring?'

'And what if he's not?'

'You think we should tail him?' said Ravi.

'No,' she said as an idea dragged itself to the fore. 'I have a better idea. Give me your phone.'

Wordlessly Ravi rummaged in his pocket and pulled out his phone. He slid it across the table to her.

'Passcode?' she said.

'One one two two. What are you doing?'

'I'm going to enable Find My Friends between our phones.' She clicked on to the app and sent an invitation to her own phone. She swiped it open and accepted. 'Now we are sharing our locations indefinitely. And just like that,' she said, shaking her phone in the air, 'we have a tracking device.'

'You scare me a little bit,' he said.

'Tomorrow, at the end of school, I need to find a way to leave my phone in his car.'

'How?'

'I'll think of something.'

'Don't go anywhere alone with him, Pip.' He leaned

forward, eyes unwavering. 'I mean it.'

Just then there was a knock on the front door.

Pip jumped up and Ravi followed her down the hall. She picked up the bowl of sweets and opened the door.

'Trick or treat?!' a chorus of small voices screeched.

'Oh, wow,' Pip said, recognizing two vampires as the Yardley children from three doors down. 'Don't you all look scary?'

She lowered the bowl and the six kids swarmed towards her, grabby hands first.

Pip smiled up at the group of adults behind as their kids argued and cherry-picked the sweets. And then she noticed their eyes, dark and glaring, fixed on a point past Pip's shoulder, where Ravi stood.

Two of the women drew together, staring at him as they muttered small, unheard things behind their hands.

Forty-Two

'What have you done?' Cara said.

'I don't know. I tripped coming down the stairs from politics. I think I've sprained it.'

Pip fake-limped over to her.

'I walked to school this morning; I don't have my car,' she said. 'Oh crap, and Mum has a late viewing.'

'You can get a lift with me and Dad,' Cara said, slipping her arm under Pip's to help her to her locker. She took the textbook from Pip's hand and placed it on the pile inside. 'Don't know why you'd willingly choose to walk when you have your own car. I never get to use mine now Naomi's home.'

'I just fancied a walk,' Pip said. 'I don't have Barney as an excuse any more.'

Cara gave her a pitying look and closed the locker door. 'Come on then,' she said, 'let's hobble out to the car park. Lucky for you I'm Muscles McGee; I did nine whole press-ups yesterday.'

'Nine whole ones?' Pip smiled.

'I know. Play your cards right and you might win a ticket to the gun show.' She flexed and growled.

Pip's heart broke for her then. She hoped, thinking *please please please* over and again, that Cara wouldn't lose her happy, silly self after whatever was to come.

Propped up against her, they staggered up the corridor and out of the side door.

The cold wind bit at her nose and she narrowed her eyes against it. They made their way, slowly, round the back and towards the teachers' car park, Cara filling the journey with details from her Halloween film night. Pip tensed every time she mentioned her dad.

Elliot was there already, waiting by his car.

'There you are,' he said, spotting Cara. 'What's happened here?'

'Pip's sprained her ankle,' Cara said, opening the back door. 'And Leanne's working late. Can we give her a lift?'

'Yes, of course.' Elliot darted forward to take Pip's arm and help her into the car.

His skin touched hers.

It took all her strength not to recoil from him.

Rucksack settled beside her, Pip watched as Elliot closed her door and climbed in the driver's seat. When Cara and Pip had clicked in their seat belts, he started the engine.

'So what happened, Pip?' he asked, waiting for a group of kids to cross the road before pulling out of the car park and on to the drive.

'I'm not sure,' she said. 'I think I just landed on it funny.'

'You don't need me to take you to A&E, do you?'

'No,' she said, 'I'm sure it'll be fine in a couple of days.' She pulled out her phone and checked it was on silent.

She'd had it turned off most of the day and the battery was almost full.

Elliot batted Cara's hand away when she started flicking through the radio stations.

'My car, my cheesy music,' he said. 'Pip?'

She jumped and almost dropped the phone.

'Is your ankle swollen?' he said.

'Um . . .' She bent forward and reached down to feel it, the phone in her hand. Pretending to knead her ankle, she twisted her wrist and pushed the phone far underneath the back seat. 'A little bit,' she said, straightening up, her face flushed with blood. 'Not too bad.'

'OK, that's good,' he said, winding through the traffic up the high street. 'You should sit with it raised up this evening.'

'Yeah, I will,' she said and caught his eye in the rear-view mirror. And then: 'I've just realized it's a tutoring day. I'm not going to make you late, am I? Where do you have to get to?'

'Oh, don't worry,' he said, indicating left down Pip's road. 'I've only got to get over to Old Amersham. It's no bother.'

'Phew, OK.'

Cara was asking what was for dinner as Elliot slowed and swung into Pip's drive.

'Oh, your mum *is* home,' he said, nodding towards Leanne's car as he pulled to a stop.

'Is she?' Pip felt her heart doubling, scared that the air around her was visibly throbbing. 'Her viewing must have been cancelled last minute. I should have checked, sorry.'

364

'Don't be silly.' Elliot turned round to her. 'Do you need help to the door?'

'No,' she said quickly, grabbing her rucksack. 'No, thank you, I'll be fine.'

She pushed open the car door and started to shuffle out.

'Wait,' Cara said suddenly.

Pip froze. *Please say she hasn't seen the phone. Please.*

'Will I see you before your exam tomorrow?'

'Oh,' Pip said, breathing again. 'No, I have to register at the office and go to the room first thing.'

'OK, well, goooooooood luuuuuuuck,' she said, drawing out the words in sing-song bursts. 'You'll do amazing, I'm sure. I'll come find you after.'

'Yes, best of luck, Pip,' Elliot smiled. 'I would say break a leg but I think the timing is a little off for that.'

Pip laughed, so hollow it almost echoed. 'Thanks,' she said, 'and thanks for the lift.' She leaned into the car door and pushed it shut.

Limping up to the house, her ears pricked, listening to the rumble of Elliot's car as it drove away. She opened her front door and dropped the limp.

'Hello,' Leanne called from the kitchen. 'Do you want the kettle on?'

'Um, no thanks,' she said, loitering in the doorway. 'Ravi's coming over for a bit to help me study for my exam.'

Her mum gave her a look.

'What?'

'Don't think I don't know my own daughter,' she said, washing mushrooms in the colander. 'She only works alone and has a reputation for making other children cry in group projects. Studying, indeed.' She gave her the look again. 'Keep your door open.'

'Jeez, I will.'

Just as she was starting up the stairs a Ravi-shaped blur knocked at the front door.

Pip let him in and he called, 'Hello,' to her mum as he followed her upstairs to her room.

'Door open,' Pip said when Ravi went to close it.

She sat cross-legged on her bed and Ravi pulled the desk chair over to sit in front of her.

'All good?' he said.

'Yep, it's under the back seat.'

'OK.'

He unlocked his phone and opened the Find My Friends app. Pip leaned in closer and, heads almost touching, they stared down at the map on screen.

Pip's little orange avatar was parked outside the Wards' house on Hogg Hill. Ravi clicked refresh but there it stayed.

'He hasn't left yet,' Pip said.

Shuffled footsteps drew along the corridor and Pip looked up to see Josh standing in her doorway.

'Pippo,' he said, fiddling with his springy hair, 'can Ravi come down and play *FIFA* with me?'

Ravi and Pip turned to look at each other.

366

'Um, not now, Josh,' she said. 'We're quite busy.'

'I'll come down and play later, OK, bud?' Ravi said.

'OK.' Josh dropped his arm in defeat and padded away.

'He's on the move,' Ravi said, refreshing the map.

'Where?'

'Just down Hogg Hill at the moment, before the roundabout.'

The avatar did not move in real time; they had to keep pressing refresh and wait for the orange circle to jump across its route. It stopped just at the roundabout.

'Refresh it,' Pip said impatiently. 'If he doesn't turn left, then he's not heading to Amersham.'

The refresh button spun with fading lines. Loading. Loading. It refreshed and the orange avatar disappeared.

'Where's it gone?' said Pip.

Ravi scrolled around the map to see where Elliot had jumped to.

'Stop.' Pip spotted it. 'There. He's heading north up the A413.'

They gazed at each other.

'He's not going to Amersham,' Ravi said.

'No, he is not.'

Their eyes followed for the next eleven minutes as Elliot drove up the road, jumping incrementally whenever Ravi pressed his thumb on the refresh arrow.

'He's near Wendover,' Ravi said and then, seeing Pip's face, 'What?'

'The Wards used to live in Wendover before they moved to a bigger house in Kilton. Before we met them.'

'He's turned,' Ravi said and Pip leaned in again. 'Down somewhere called Mill End Road.'

Pip watched the orange dot motionless on the white pixel road. 'Refresh,' she said.

'I am,' said Ravi, 'it's stuck.' He pressed refresh again; the loading spool spun for a second and stopped, leaving the orange dot in the same place. He pressed it again and it still didn't move.

'He's stopped,' Pip said, clutching Ravi's wrist and turning it to get a better look at the map. She stood up, grabbed Ravi's laptop from her desk and settled it on her lap. 'Let's see where he is.'

She opened the browser and pulled up Google Maps. She searched for *Mill End Road, Wendover* and clicked on to the satellite mode.

'How far down the road would you say he is? Here?' she pointed at the screen.

'I'd say a bit more to the left.'

'OK.' Pip dropped the little orange man on to the road and the street view popped up.

The narrow country road was enclosed by trees and tall shrubbery that glittered in the sun as Pip clicked and dragged the screen to get a full view. The houses were just on one side, set back a little from the road.

'You think he's at this house?' She pointed at a small brick house with a white garage door, barely visible behind the trees and telephone pole that bordered it.

'Hmm . . .' Ravi looked from his phone to his laptop screen. 'It's either that one or the one to the left of it.'

Pip looked up the street numbers. 'So he's either at number forty-two or forty-four.'

'Is that where they used to live?' Ravi asked. Pip didn't know. She shrugged, and he said, 'But you can find out from Cara?'

'Yes,' she said. 'I've had a lot of practise with pretending and lies.' Her gut churned and her throat tightened. 'She's my best friend and this is going to destroy her. It's going to destroy everyone, everything.'

Ravi slipped his hand into hers. 'It's nearly over, Pip,' he said.

'It's over now,' she said. 'We need to go there tonight and see what Elliot's hiding. Andie could be alive in there.'

'That's just a guess.'

'This whole thing has been guesswork.' She took her hand away so she could hold her aching head. 'I need this to be over.'

'OK,' Ravi said gently. 'We are going to end this. But not tonight. Tomorrow. You find out from Cara which address he's going to, if it's their old house. And after you finish school tomorrow, we can go there at night, when Elliot's not there, and see what he's up to. Or we call the police with an anonymous tip and send them to that address, OK?

But not now, Pip. You can't upend your whole life tonight, I won't let you. I won't let you throw away Cambridge. Right now, you are going to study for your exam and you are going to get some bloody sleep. OK?'

'But –'

'No buts, Sarge.' He stared at her, his eyes suddenly sharp. 'Mr Ward has already ruined too many lives. He's not ruining yours as well. OK?'

'OK,' she said quietly.

'Good.' He took her hand, pulled her off the bed and into her chair. He wheeled her over to the desk and put a pen in her hand. 'You are going to forget about Andie Bell and Sal for the next eighteen hours. And I want you in bed and sleeping by ten thirty.'

She looked up at Ravi, at his kind eyes and his serious face, and she didn't know what to say, didn't know what to feel. She was on a high cliff edge somewhere between laughing and crying and screaming.

Forty-Three

The following poems and extracts from longer texts all offer representations of guilt. They are arranged chronologically by date of publication. Read all the material carefully, and then complete the task below.

The ticking of the clock was a snare-drum echo in her head. She opened her answer booklet and looked up one last time. The exam invigilator was sitting with his feet up on a table, his face stuck into a paperback with a craggy spine. Pip was on a small and wobbling desk in the middle of an empty classroom made for thirty. And three minutes had already ticked by.

She looked down, brain talking to block out the sound of the clock, and pressed her pen on to the page.

When the invigilator called stop, Pip had already been finished for forty-nine seconds, her eyes following the second hand of the clock as it strutted on in a near-complete circle. She closed the booklet and handed it to the man on her way out.

She'd written about how certain texts manipulate the placing of blame by using the passive voice during the character's guilty act. She'd had almost seven hours' sleep and she thought she'd done OK.

It was nearly lunchtime and, turning into the next corridor, she heard Cara calling her name.

'Pip!'

She remembered only at the last second to put the limp back into her tread.

'How did it go?' Cara caught up with her.

'Yeah, fine I think.'

'Yay, you're free,' she said, waving Pip's arm in celebration for her. 'How's your ankle?'

'Not too bad. Think it'll be better by tomorrow.'

'Oh, and,' Cara said, shuffling around in her pocket, 'you were right.' She pulled out Pip's phone. 'You *had* somehow left it in Dad's car. It was wedged under the back seat.'

Pip took it. 'Oh, don't know how that happened.'

'We should celebrate your freedom,' Cara said. 'I can invite everyone round mine tomorrow and have a game night or something?'

'Yeah, maybe.'

Pip waited and when there was finally a lull she said, 'Hey, you know my mum's doing a viewing of a house in Mill End Road in Wendover today. Isn't that where you used to live?'

'Yeah,' Cara said. 'How funny.'

'Number forty-four.'

'Oh, we were forty-two.'

'Does your dad still go there?' Pip asked, her voice flat and disinterested.

'No, he sold it ages ago,' Cara said. 'They kept it when we moved because Mum had just got a huge inheritance from her grandma. They rented it out for extra income while Mum did her painting. But Dad sold it a couple of years after Mum died, I think.'

Pip nodded. Clearly Elliot had been telling lies for a long time. Over five years, in fact.

She sleepwalked through lunch. And when it was over and Cara was heading off the other way, Pip limped up and hugged her.

'All right, clingy,' Cara said, trying to wriggle out. 'What's up with you?'

'Nothing,' said Pip. The sadness she felt for Cara was black and twisting and hungry. How was any of this fair? Pip didn't want to let her go, didn't think she could. But she had to.

Connor caught her up and helped Pip up the stairs to history, even though she told him not to. Mr Ward was already in the classroom, perched on his desk in a pastel green shirt. Pip didn't look at him as she staggered past her usual seat at the front and went to sit right at the back.

The lesson would not end. The clock mocked her as she sat watching it, looking anywhere but at Elliot. She would not look at him. She couldn't. Her breath felt gummy, like it was trying to choke her.

'Interestingly,' Elliot said, 'about six years ago, the diaries of one of Stalin's personal doctors, a man called Alexander Myasnikov, were released. Myasnikov wrote that Stalin suffered from a brain illness that might have impaired his decision-making and influenced his paranoia. So –'

The bell rang and interrupted him.

Pip jumped. But not because of the bell. Because something had clicked when Elliot said 'diaries', the word repeating around her head, slowly slotting into place.

The class packed up their notes and books and started to file towards the door. Pip, hobbling and at the back, was the last to reach it.

'Hold on, Pippa.' Elliot's voice dragged her back.

She turned, rigid and unwilling.

'How did the exam go?' he said.

'Yeah, it was fine.'

'Oh good,' he smiled. 'So now you can relax.'

She returned an empty smile and limped out into the corridor. When she was out of Elliot's sight she dropped the limp and started to run. She didn't care that she had a final period of politics now. She ran, that one word in Elliot's voice chasing her as she went. *Diaries*. She didn't stop until she slammed into the door of her car, fumbling for the handle.

Forty-Four

'Pip, what are you doing here?' Naomi stood in the front doorway. 'Shouldn't you still be at school?'

'I had a free period,' she said, trying to catch her breath. 'I just have one question I need to ask you.'

'Pip, are you OK?'

'You've been going to therapy ever since your mum died, haven't you? For anxiety and depression,' Pip said. There was no time to be delicate.

Naomi looked at her strangely, her eyes shining. 'Yes,' she said.

'Did your therapist tell you to keep a diary?'

Naomi nodded. 'It's a way to manage the stress. It helps,' she said. 'I've done it since I was sixteen.'

'And did you write about the hit-and-run?'

Naomi stared at her, lines webbing around her eyes. 'Yes,' she said, 'of course I did. I had to write about it. I was devastated and I couldn't talk to anyone. No one ever sees them but me.'

Pip exhaled, cupping her hands around her mouth to catch it.

'You think that's how the person found out?' Naomi shook her head. 'No, it's not possible. I always lock my diaries and keep them hidden in my room.'

'I have to go,' Pip said. 'Sorry.'

She turned and charged back to her car, ignoring when Naomi shouted, 'Pip! Pippa!'

Her mum's car was parked at home when Pip pulled into the drive. But the house was quiet and Leanne didn't call out when the front door opened. Walking down the hallway, Pip heard another sound over her throbbing pulse: the sound of her mother crying.

At the entrance to the living room Pip stopped and watched the back of her mum's head over the rim of the sofa. She was holding her phone up in both hands and small recorded voices were playing from it.

'Mum?'

'Oh, sweetie, you scared me,' she said, pausing her phone and wiping her eyes quickly. 'You're home early. So, the exam went well?' She patted the cushion beside her eagerly, trying to rearrange her tear-stained face. 'What was your essay about? Come and tell me.'

'Mum,' Pip said, 'why are you upset?'

'Oh, it's nothing, really nothing.' She gave Pip a teary smile. 'I was just looking through old pictures of Barney. And I found the video from that Christmas two years ago, when Barney went round the table giving everyone a shoe. I can't stop watching it.'

Pip walked over and hugged her from behind. 'I'm sorry you're sad,' she whispered into her mum's hair.

'I'm not,' she sniffed. 'I'm happy-sad. He was such a good dog.'

Pip sat with her, swiping through their old photos and videos of Barney, laughing as he jumped in the air and tried to eat the snow, as he barked at the vacuum cleaner, as he splayed on the floor with his paws up, little Josh rubbing his belly while Pip stroked his ears. They stayed like that until her mum had to go and pick up Josh.

'OK,' Pip said. 'I think I'm going to nap upstairs for a bit.'

It was another lie. She went to her room to watch the time, pacing from bed to door. Waiting. Fear burned to rage and if she didn't pace, she would scream. It was Thursday, a tutoring day, and she wanted him to be there.

When Little Kilton was the other side of five o'clock, Pip tugged the charger out of her phone and pulled on her khaki coat.

'I'm going to Lauren's for a few hours,' she called to her mum who was in the kitchen helping Josh with his maths homework. 'See you later.'

Outside, she unlocked the car, climbed in and tied her dark hair on top of her head. She looked down at her phone, at the lines and lines of messages from Ravi. She replied: *It went OK, thanks. I'll come to yours after dinner and we'll phone the police then.* Yet another lie, but Pip was fluent in them now. He would only stop her.

She opened the map app on her phone, typed in the search bar and pressed *Go* on the directions.

The harsh mechanical voice chanted up at her: *Starting route to 42 Mill End Road, Wendover.*

Forty-Five

Mill End Road was narrow and overgrown, a tunnel of dark trees pushing in on all sides. She pulled off on to the grass verge just after number forty and flicked off her headlights.

Her heart was a hand-sized stampede, and every hair, every layer of skin was alive and electric.

She reached down for her phone, propped up in the cupholder, and dialled 999.

Two rings and then: 'Hello, emergency operator, which service do you require?'

'Police,' Pip said.

'I'll just connect you now.'

'Hello?' A different voice came through the line. 'Police emergency, can I help?'

'My name is Pippa Fitz-Amobi,' she said shakily, 'and I'm from Little Kilton. Please listen carefully. You need to send officers to forty-two Mill End Road in Wendover. Inside is a man named Elliot Ward. Five years ago, Elliot kidnapped a girl called Andie Bell from Kilton and he's been keeping her in this house. He murdered a boy called Sal Singh. You need to contact DI Richard Hawkins, who led the Andie Bell case, and let him know. I believe Andie is alive and she's being kept inside. I'm going in now to confront Elliot Ward and I might be in danger. Please send officers quickly.'

'Hold on, Pippa,' the voice said. 'Where are you phoning from now?'

'I'm outside the house and I'm about to go in.'

'OK, stay outside. I'm dispatching officers to your location. Pippa, can you –'

'I'm going in now,' Pip said. 'Please hurry.'

'Pippa, do not go inside the house.'

'I'm sorry, I have to,' she said.

Pip lowered the phone, the operator's voice still calling her name, and hung up.

She got out of the car. Crossing from the grass verge on to the driveway down to number forty-two, she saw Elliot's car parked in front of the small red-brick house. The two downstairs windows glowed, pushing away the thickening darkness.

As she started towards the house a motion sensor flood light picked her up and filled the drive with a garish and blinding white light. She covered her eyes and pushed through, a tree-giant shadow stitched to her feet behind her as she walked towards the front door.

She knocked. Three loud thumps against the door.

Something clattered inside. And nothing.

She knocked again, hitting the door over and over with the soft side of her fist.

A light flicked on behind the door and in the now yellow-lit frosted glass she saw a blurred figure walking towards her.

A chain scraped against the door, a sliding lock, and it was pulled open with a damp clacking sound.

Elliot stared at her. Dressed in the same pastel green shirt from school, a pair of dark oven mitts slung over his shoulder.

'Pip?' he said in a voice breathy with fear. 'What are you . . . what are you doing here?'

She looked into his lens-magnified eyes.

'I'm just . . .' he said. 'I'm just . . .'

Pip shook her head. 'The police are going to be here in about ten minutes,' she said. 'You have that time to explain it to me.' She stepped one foot up over the threshold. 'Explain it to me so I can help your daughters through this. So the Singhs can finally know the truth after all this time.'

All the blood left Elliot's face. He staggered back a few steps, colliding into the wall. Then he pressed his fingers into his eyes and blew out all of his air. 'It's over,' he said quietly. 'It's finally over.'

'Time's running out, Elliot.' Her voice was much braver than she felt.

'OK,' he said. 'OK, do you want to come in?'

She hesitated, her stomach recoiling inside to push back against her spine. But the police were on their way; she could do this. She had to do this. 'We'll leave the front door open, for the police,' she said, then she followed him in and down the hall, keeping a three-step distance.

He led her right and into a kitchen. There was no furniture in it, none at all, but the counters were laden with food packets and cooking instruments, even a spice rack. There was a small

380

glinting key on the counter beside a packet of dried pasta. Elliot bent to turn off the hob and Pip walked to the other side of the room, putting as much space between them as she could.

'Stand away from the knives,' she said.

'Pip, I'm not going to –'

'Stand away from them.'

Elliot moved away, stopping by the wall opposite her.

'She's here, isn't she?' Pip said. 'Andie's here and she's alive?'

'Yes.'

She shivered inside her warm coat.

'You and Andie Bell were seeing each other in March 2012,' she said. 'Start at the beginning, Elliot; we don't have long.'

'It wasn't like th-th–' he stuttered. 'It . . .' He moaned and held his head.

'Elliot!'

He sniffed and straightened. 'OK,' he said. 'It was late February. Andie started . . . paying attention to me at school. I wasn't teaching her; she didn't take history. But she'd follow me in the halls and ask me about my day. And, I don't know, I guess the attention felt . . . nice. I'd been so lonely since Isobel died. And then Andie starts asking to have my phone number. Nothing had happened at this point, we hadn't kissed or anything, but she kept asking. I told her that that would be inappropriate. And yet, soon enough, I found myself in the phone shop, buying another SIM card so I could talk to her and no one would find out. I don't know why I did it; I suppose it felt like a distraction from missing Isobel. I just wanted someone to talk to. I only put the SIM in at night, so Naomi would never see anything, and we started texting. She was nice to me; let me talk about Isobel and how I worried about Naomi and Cara.'

'You're running out of time,' Pip said coldly.

'Yes,' he sniffed, 'and then Andie started suggesting we meet somewhere outside of school. Like a hotel. I told her absolutely not. But in a moment of madness, a moment of weakness, I found myself booking one. She could be very persuasive. We agreed a time and date, but I had to cancel last minute because Cara had chickenpox. I tried to end it, whatever it was we had at this point, but then she asked again. And I booked the hotel for the next week.'

'The Ivy House Hotel in Chalfont,' said Pip.

He nodded. 'That's when it happened the first time.' His voice was quiet with shame. 'We didn't stay the night; I couldn't leave the girls for a whole night. We stayed just a couple of hours.'

'And you slept with her?'

Elliot didn't say anything.

'She was seventeen!' Pip said. 'The same age as your daughter. You were a teacher. Andie was vulnerable and you took advantage of that. You were the adult and should have known better.'

'There's nothing you can say that will make me more

382

disgusted at myself than I already am. I said it couldn't happen again and tried to call it off. Andie wouldn't let me. She started threatening to turn me in. She interrupted one of my lessons, came over and whispered to me that she'd left a naked picture of herself hidden in the classroom somewhere and that I should find it before someone else did. Trying to scare me. So, I went back to the Ivy House the next week, because I didn't know what she'd do if I didn't. I thought she would tire of whatever this was soon enough.'

He stopped to rub the back of his neck.

'That was the last time. It only happened twice and then it was the Easter holidays. The girls and I spent a week at Isobel's parents' house and, with time away from Kilton, I came to my senses. I messaged Andie and I said it was over and I didn't care if she turned me in. She texted back, saying that when school started again she was going to ruin me if I didn't do what she wanted. I didn't know what she wanted. And then, by complete chance, I had an opportunity to stop her. I found out about Andie cyber-bullying that girl and so I called her dad, as I told you, and said that if her behaviour didn't improve, I would have to report her and she'd be expelled. Of course Andie knew what it really meant: mutually assured destruction. She could have me arrested and jailed for our relationship, but I could have her expelled and ruin her future. We were at a stalemate and I thought it was over.'

'So why did you kidnap her on Friday the twentieth of April?' Pip said.

'That's not . . .' he said. 'It didn't happen like that at all. I was home alone and Andie turned up, I think around ten-ish. She was irate, just so angry. She screamed at me, telling me I was sad and disgusting, that she'd only touched me because she needed me to get her a place at Oxford, like I'd helped Sal. She didn't want him to leave without her. Screaming that she had to get away from home, away from Kilton because it was killing her. I tried to calm her down but she wouldn't. And she knew exactly how to hurt me.'

Elliot blinked slowly.

'Andie ran to my study and started tearing those paintings Isobel made when she was dying, my rainbow ones. She smashed up two of them and I was shouting for her to stop and then she went for my favourite one. And I . . . I just pushed her to get her to stop, I wasn't trying to hurt her. But she fell back and hit her head on my desk. Hard. And,' he sniffed, 'she was on the floor and her head was bleeding. She was conscious but confused. I rushed off to get the first-aid kit and when I came back Andie had gone and the front door was open. She hadn't driven to mine, there was no car in the drive and no sound of one. She walked out and vanished. Her phone was on the floor in the study, she must have dropped it in the scuffle.

'The next day,' he continued, 'I heard from Naomi that Andie was missing. Andie was bleeding and left my house with a head injury and now she was missing. And as the weekend passed I started to panic: I thought I'd killed her. I thought she must have wandered out of my house and then, confused and hurt, got lost somewhere and died from her injuries. That she was lying in a ditch somewhere and it would only be a matter of time until they found her. And when they did there might be evidence on her body that would lead back to me: fibres, fingerprints. I knew the only thing I could do was to give them a stronger suspect to protect myself. To protect my girls. If I got taken away for Andie's murder, I didn't think Naomi would survive it. And Cara was only twelve at the time. I was the only parent they had left.'

'There's no time for your excuses,' Pip said. 'So then you framed Sal Singh. You knew about the hit-and-run because you'd been reading Naomi's therapy diaries.'

'Of course I'd read them,' he said. 'I had to make sure my little girl wasn't thinking of hurting herself.'

'You made her and her friends take Sal's alibi away. And then, on the Tuesday?'

'I called in sick to work and dropped the girls at school. I waited outside and when I saw Sal alone in the car park, I went up to talk to him. He wasn't coping well with her disappearance. So I suggested that we go back to his house and have a chat about it. I'd planned to do it with a knife from the Singhs' house. But then I found some sleeping pills in the bathroom, and I decided to take him to the woods; I thought it would be kinder. I didn't want his family to find him. We had tea and I gave him the first three pills; said they were for his headache. I convinced him that we should go out in the woods and look for Andie ourselves; that it would help his feeling of helplessness. He trusted me. He didn't wonder why I was wearing leather gloves inside. I took a plastic bag from their kitchen and we walked out into the woods. I had a penknife, and when we were far enough in I held it up to his neck. Made him swallow more pills.'

Elliot's voice broke. His eyes filled and a lone tear snaked down his cheek. 'I said I was helping him, that he wouldn't be a suspect if it looked like he'd been attacked too. He swallowed a few more and then he started to struggle. I pinned him down and forced him to take more. When he started to get sleepy, I held him and I talked to him about Oxford, about the amazing libraries, the formal hall dinners, how beautiful the city looked in spring. Just so he would fall asleep thinking about something good. When he was unconscious, I put the bag around his head and held his hand as he died.'

Pip had no pity for this man before her. Eleven years of memories dissolved from him, leaving a stranger standing in the room with her.

'Then you sent the confession text from Sal's phone to his dad.'

Elliot nodded, staunching his eyes with the heels of his hands.

'And Andie's blood?'

'It had dried under my desk,' he said. 'I'd missed some when I first cleaned, so I placed some of it under his nails with tweezers. And the last thing, I put Andie's phone in his pocket and I left him there. I didn't want to kill him. I was trying to save my girls; they'd already been through so much pain. He didn't deserve to die, but neither did my girls. It was an impossible choice.'

Pip looked up to try to push her tears back in. There was no time to tell him how wrong he was.

'And then as more days passed,' Elliot cried, 'I realized what a grave mistake I'd made. If Andie had died somewhere from her head injury, they would have found her by now. And then her car turns up and they find blood in the boot; she must have been well enough to drive somewhere after leaving mine. I'd panicked and thought it was fatal when it wasn't. But it was too late. Sal was already dead and I'd made him the killer. They closed the case and everything settled down.'

'So how do we get from there to you imprisoning Andie in this house?'

He flinched at the anger behind her words.

'It was the end of July. I was driving home and I just saw her. Andie was walking on the side of the main road from Wycombe, heading towards Kilton. I pulled over and it was obvious she'd got herself messed up in drugs . . . that she'd been sleeping rough. She was so skinny and dishevelled. That's how it happened. I couldn't let her return home because if she did, everyone would know Sal had been murdered. Andie was high and disoriented but I pulled over and got her in the car. I explained to her why I couldn't let her go home but that I would take care of her. I'd just put this place up for sale, so I brought her here and took it off the market.'

'Where had she been all those months? What happened to her the night she went missing?' Pip pressed, feeling the minutes escaping from her.

'She doesn't remember all the details; I think she was concussed. She says she just wanted to get away from everything. She went to a friend of hers who was involved in drugs and he took her to stay with some people he knew. But she didn't feel safe there, so she ran away to come home. She doesn't like talking about that time.'

'Howie Bowers,' Pip thought aloud. 'Where is she, Elliot?'

'In the loft.' He looked over at the small key on the counter. 'We made it nice up there for her. I insulated it, put in plywood walls and proper flooring. She picked out the wallpaper. There aren't any windows but we put in lots of lamps. I know you must think I'm a monster, Pip, but I've never touched her, not since that last time at the Ivy House. It's not like that. And she's not like she was before. She's a different person; she's calm and grateful. She has food up there but I come round to cook for her three times during the week, once at the weekend, and let her down to shower. And then we just sit together in her loft, watching TV for a while. She's never bored.'

'She's locked up there and that's the key?' Pip pointed to it. Elliot nodded.

And then they heard the sound of wheels crackling on the road outside.

'When the police interrogate you,' Pip said, hurrying now, 'do not tell them about the hit-and-run, about taking Sal's alibi away. He doesn't need one when you've confessed. And Cara does not deserve to lose her entire family, to be all alone. *I'm* going to protect Naomi and Cara now.'

The sound of car doors slamming.

'Maybe I can understand why you did it,' she said. 'But you will never be forgiven. You took Sal's life from him to save your own. You destroyed his family.'

A shout of, 'Hello, police,' came from the open front door.

'The Bells have grieved for five whole years. You threatened me and my family; you broke into my house to scare me.'

'I'm sorry.'

Heavy footsteps down the hallway.

'You killed Barney.'

Elliot's face crumpled. 'Pip, I don't know what you're talking about. I didn't –'

'Police,' the officer said, stepping into the kitchen. The skylights glittered against the rim on his hat. His partner walked in behind, her eyes darting from Elliot to Pip and back, her tightly scraped ponytail flicking as she did.

'Right, what's going on here?' she said.

Pip looked over at Elliot and their eyes met. He straightened up and held out his wrists.

'You're here to arrest me for the abduction and false imprisonment of Andie Bell,' he said, not taking his eyes off her.

'And the murder of Sal Singh,' said Pip.

The officers looked at each other for a long moment and

one of them nodded. The woman started towards Elliot and the man pressed something on the radio strapped to his shoulder. He moved back out to the hallway to speak into it.

With both their backs turned Pip darted forward and snatched the key from the counter. She ran out into the hall and bounded up the stairs.

'Hey!' the male officer shouted after her.

At the top she saw the small white loft hatch in the ceiling. A large padlock was fitted through the catch and a metal ring that was screwed into the wooden frame. A small two-step ladder was placed beneath it.

Pip stepped up and reached, slotting the key into the padlock and letting it fall, clattering loudly to the floor. The policeman was coming up the stairs after her. She twisted the catch and ducked to let the reinforced hatch swing down and open.

Yellow light filled the hole above her. And sounds: dramatic music, explosions and people shouting in American accents. Pip grabbed the loft ladder and pulled it down to the floor just as the officer thundered up the last few steps.

'Wait,' he shouted.

Pip stepped up on to it and climbed, her hands clammy and sticky on the metal rungs.

She poked her head up through the hatch and looked around. The room was lit by several floor lamps and the walls were decorated with a white and black floral design. On one side of the loft there was a mini-fridge with a kettle and a microwave on top, shelves of food and books. There was a fluffy pink rug in the middle of the room and behind it was a large flat-screen TV that was just being paused.

And there she was.

Sitting cross-legged on a single bed piled high with coloured cushions. Wearing a pair of blue penguin-patterned pyjamas, the same that both Cara and Naomi had. She stared over at Pip, her eyes wide and wild. She looked a little older, a little heavier. Her hair was mousier than it had been before and her skin much paler. She gaped at Pip, the TV remote in her hand and a packet of Jammie Dodger biscuits on her lap.

'Hi,' Pip said. 'I'm Pip.'

'Hi,' she said, 'I'm Andie.'

But she wasn't.

Forty-Six

Pip stepped closer, into the yellow glow of the lamplight. She took a quieting breath, trying to think over the screeching that filled her head. She screwed her eyes and studied the face before her.

Now that she was closer, she could see the obvious differences, the slight differing slope to her plump lips, the downturn to her eyes where they should flick up, the swell of her cheekbones lower than they should be. Changes that time couldn't make to a face.

Pip had looked at the photographs so many times these past months, she knew every line and groove of Andie Bell's face.

This wasn't her.

Pip felt unattached to the world, floating away, empty of all sense.

'You're not Andie,' she said quietly, just as the policeman climbed up the ladder behind and placed a hand on her shoulder.

The wind was screaming in the trees and 42 Mill End Road was lit up with flashes of blue, rippling in and out of darkness. Four police cars in a broken square filled the drive now, and Pip had just seen DI Richard Hawkins – in the same black coat he'd worn in all those press conferences five years ago – step into the house.

Pip stopped listening to the policewoman taking her statement. She heard her words only as a rockslide of falling syllables. She concentrated on breathing in the fresh and whistling air and that's when they brought Elliot out. Two officers on either side, his hands cuffed behind. He was weeping, the blue lights blinking on his wet face. The wounded sounds he made woke some ancient, instinctive fear inside her. This was a man who knew his life was finished. Had he really believed the girl in his loft was Andie? Had he clung to that belief this whole time? They ducked Elliot's head for him, put him in a car and took him away. Pip watched it go until the tunnel of trees swallowed all the car's edges.

As she finished dictating her contact number to the officer she heard a car door slamming behind her.

'Pip!' The wind carried Ravi's voice to her.

She felt the pull in her chest and then she was running after it. At the top of the driveway she ran into him and Ravi caught her, his arms tight as they anchored themselves together against the wind.

'Are you OK?' he said, holding her back to look at her.

'Yes,' she said. 'What are you doing here?'

'Me?' He tapped his chest. 'When you didn't turn up at mine, I looked for you on Find My Friends. Why did you come here alone?' He eyed the police cars and officers behind her.

'I had to come,' she said. 'I had to ask him why. I didn't

know how much longer you'd have to wait for the truth if I didn't.'

Her mouth opened once, twice, three times before the words found their way, and then she told Ravi everything. She told him how his brother had died, standing under shivering trees, blue light undulating all around them. She said she was sorry when the tears broke down Ravi's face, because that's all there was to say; a blanket stitch sent to mend a crater.

'Don't be sorry,' he said with a half-laugh, half-cry. 'Nothing can bring him back, I know that. But we have, in a way. Sal was murdered, Sal was innocent, and now everyone will know.'

They turned to watch as DI Richard Hawkins walked the girl out of the house, a lilac blanket wrapped round her shoulders.

'It's really not her, is it?' Ravi said.

'She looks a lot like her,' said Pip.

The girl's eyes were wide and spinning and free as she looked around at everything, relearning what outside was. Hawkins led her to a car and climbed in beside her as two uniformed officers got in the front.

Pip didn't know how Elliot had come to believe this girl he found on the side of the road was Andie. Was it delusion? Did he need to believe Andie hadn't died as some kind of atonement for what he did to Sal in her name? Or was it fear that blinded him?

That's what Ravi thought: that Elliot was terrified Andie

Bell was alive and would come back home and then he'd go down for Sal's murder. And in that heightened state of fear, all it took was a blonde girl who looked similar enough to convince himself he'd found Andie. And he'd locked her up, so he could lock up that terrible fear of being caught right along with her.

Pip nodded in agreement, watching the police car drive away. 'I think,' she said quietly, 'I think she was just a girl with the wrong hair and the wrong face when the wrong man drove past.'

And that other itching question that Pip couldn't yet give voice to: what had happened to the real Andie Bell after she'd left the Wards' house that night?

The officer who'd taken her statement approached them with a warm smile. 'Do you need someone to take you home, darling?' she asked Pip.

'No, it's OK,' she said, 'I have my car.'

She made Ravi get in the car with her; there was no way she'd let him drive home on his own – he was shaking too hard. And, secretly, she didn't want to be alone either.

Pip turned the key in the ignition, catching sight of her face in the rear-view mirror before the lights dimmed. She looked gaunt and grey, her eyes glowing inside sunken shadows. She was tired. So unutterably tired.

'I can finally tell my parents,' Ravi said when they were back on the main road out of Wendover. 'I don't know how to even start.'

Her headlights lit up the *Welcome to Little Kilton* sign, the letters thickening with side shadows as they moved past and crossed into town. Pip drove down the high street, heading towards Ravi's house. She drew to a stop at the main roundabout. There was a car waiting on the cusp of the roundabout at the other side, its headlights a bright and piercing white. It was their right of way.

'Why aren't they moving?' Pip said, staring at the dark boxy car ahead, lines of yellow light across its body from the street lamp above.

'Don't know,' Ravi said. 'You just go.'

She did, pulling forward slowly across the roundabout. The other car had still not moved. As they drew closer and out of the glare of the oncoming headlights, Pip's foot eased up on the pedal as she looked curiously out of her window.

'Oh shit,' Ravi said.

It was the Bell family. All three of them. Jason was in the driver seat, his face red and striped with tear trails. It looked like he was shouting, smacking his hand against the steering wheel, his mouth moving with angry words. Dawn Bell was beside him, shrinking away. She was crying, her body heaving as she tried to breathe through the tears, her mouth bared in confused agony.

Their cars drew level and Pip saw Becca in the back seat on this side. Her face was pale, pushed up against the cold touch of the window. Her lips were parted and her brows furrowed, her eyes lost in some other place as she stared quietly ahead.

And as they passed Becca's eyes snapped into life, landing on Pip. There was a flicker of recognition in them. And something heavy and urgent, something like dread.

They drove away down the street and Ravi let out his held breath.

'You think they've been told?' he said

'Looks like they just have,' said Pip. 'The girl kept saying her name was Andie Bell. Maybe they have to go and formally identify that she isn't.'

She looked into her rear-view mirror and watched as the Bells' car finally rolled away across the roundabout, towards the snatched promise of a daughter returned.

Forty-Seven

Pip sat at the end of her parents' bed well into the night. Her and the albatross on her shoulders and her story. The telling of it was almost as hard as the living of it.

The worst part was Cara. As the clock on her phone had ticked past 10:00 p.m., Pip knew she couldn't avoid it any longer. Her thumb had hovered over the blue call button but she couldn't do it. She couldn't say the words aloud and listen as her best friend's world changed forever, as it turned dark and strange. Pip wished she was strong enough, but she'd learned that she wasn't invincible; she too could break. She clicked over to messages and started to type.

I should be ringing to tell you this but I don't think I could get through the telling, not with your little voice at the end of the line. This is the coward's way out and I'm truly sorry. It was your dad, Cara. Your dad is the one who killed Sal Singh. He was keeping a girl he believed was Andie Bell in your old house in Wendover. He's been arrested. Naomi will be safe, I give you my word. I know why he did it when you're ready to hear it. I'm so sorry. I wish I could save you from this. I love you.

She'd read it over, in her parents' bed, and pressed send, tears falling against the phone as she cradled it into her cupped hands.

Her mum made Pip breakfast when she finally woke at two in the afternoon; there'd been no question of her going into school. They didn't talk about it again; there was nothing more to say, not yet. But still the question of Andie Bell played on Pip's mind, how Andie had one last mystery left in her yet.

Pip tried to call Cara seventeen times but it rang out each time. Naomi's phone too.

Later that afternoon, Leanne drove round to the Wards' house after picking up Josh. She came back saying that no one was home and their car was gone.

'They've probably gone to their auntie Lila's,' Pip said, pressing redial again.

Victor came home early from work. They all sat in the living room, watching old runs of quiz shows that would usually be punctuated by Pip and her dad racing to shout out the answer. But they watched silently, exchanging furtive looks over Josh's head, the air bloated with a sad and *what-now* tension.

When someone knocked at the front door Pip jumped up to escape the strangeness that smothered the room. In her tie-dye pyjamas she pulled open the door and the air stung her toes.

It was Ravi, standing in front of his parents, the spaces between them perfect like they'd pre-arranged the pose.

'Hello, Sarge,' Ravi said, smiling at her bright and garish pyjamas. 'This is my mum, Nisha.' He gestured like a game-show host and his mum smiled at Pip, her black hair in two loose plaits. 'And my dad, Mohan.' Mohan nodded and his chin tickled the top of the giant bouquet of flowers he held, a box of chocolates tucked under the other arm. 'Parents,' Ravi said, 'this is *the* Pip.'

Pip's polite 'Hello' got muddled in with theirs.

'So,' Ravi said, 'they called us in to the police station earlier. They sat us down and told us everything, everything we already knew. And they said they'd be holding a press conference once they've charged Mr Ward, and will release a statement about Sal's innocence.'

Pip heard her mum and heavy-footed dad walking up the hallway to stand behind her. Ravi did the introductions again for Victor's sake; Leanne had met them before, fifteen years ago when she'd sold them their house.

'So,' Ravi continued, 'we all wanted to come over and thank you, Pip. This wouldn't have happened without you.'

'I don't quite know what to say,' Nisha said, her Ravi-Sal round eyes beaming. 'Because of what the two of you did, you and Ravi, we now have our boy back. You've both given Sal back to us, and there are no words for how much that means.'

'These are for you,' Mohan said, leaning forward and handing over the flowers and chocolates to Pip. 'I'm sorry, we weren't quite sure what you're supposed to get for someone who's helped vindicate your dead son.'

'Google had very few suggestions,' said Ravi.

'Thank you,' Pip said. 'Do you want to come in?'

'Yes, do come in,' Leanne said, 'I'll put on a pot of tea.'

But as Ravi stepped into the house he took Pip's arm and

pulled her back into a hug, crushing the flowers between them, laughing into her hair. When he let her go Nisha stepped up and folded her into a hug; her sweet perfume smelled to Pip like homes and mothers and summer evenings. And then, not sure why or how it happened, they were all hugging, all six of them swapping and hugging again, laughing with tears in their eyes.

And just like that, with crushed flowers and a carousel of hugs, the Singhs had come and taken away the suffocating and confused sadness that had taken over the house. They'd opened the door and let out the ghost, for at least a while. Because there was one happy ending in all of this: Sal was innocent. A family set free from the grave weight they'd carried all these years. And through all the hurt and doubt that would come, it was worth hanging on to.

'What *are* you guys doing?' said Josh in a small and baffled voice.

In the living room they sat around a full afternoon tea spread that Leanne had improvised.

'So,' Victor said, 'are you going to the fireworks tomorrow night?'

'Actually,' Nisha said, looking from her husband to her son, 'I think we should go this year. It'll be the first time since . . . you know. But things are different now. This is the start of things being different.'

'Yeah,' Ravi said. 'I'd like to go. You can never really see them from our house.'

'Awesome sauce,' Victor said, clapping his hands. 'We could meet you there? Let's say seven, by the drinks tent?'

Josh stood up then, hurrying to swallow his sandwich so he could recite: 'Remember remember the fifth of November, the gunpowder treason and plot. I know of no reason why the gunpowder treason should ever be forgot.'

Little Kilton hadn't forgot, they'd just decided to move it to the fourth instead because the barbecue boys thought they'd get a better turnout on a Saturday. Pip wasn't sure she was ready to be around all those people and the questions in their eyes.

'I'll go and refill the pot,' she said, picking up the empty teapot and carrying it through to the kitchen.

She flicked on the kettle and stared at her warped reflection in its chrome frame until a distorted Ravi appeared in it behind her.

'You're being quiet,' he said. 'What's going on in that big brain of yours? Actually, I don't even need to ask, I already know what you're going to say. It's Andie.'

'I can't pretend like it's over,' she said. 'It's not finished.'

'Pip, listen to me. You've done what you set out to do. We know Sal was innocent and what happened to him.'

'But we don't know what happened to Andie. After she left Elliot's house that night, she still disappeared and was never found.'

'It's not your job any more, Pip,' he said. 'The police have reopened Andie's case. Let them do the rest. You've done enough.'

'I know,' she said and it wasn't a lie. She was tired. She needed to finally be free of all this. She needed the weight on her shoulders to be just her own. And that last Andie Bell mystery wasn't hers to chase any more.

Ravi was right; their part was over.

Forty-Eight

She had meant to throw it out.

That's what she'd told herself. The murder board needed to be thrown out because she was finished here. It was time to dismantle the Andie Bell scaffolding and see what remained of the Pip beneath. She'd made a good start, unpinning some of the pages and putting them in piles by a bin bag she'd brought up.

And then, without realizing what she was doing or how it happened, she'd found herself looking through it all again: re-reading log entries, tracing her finger across the red string lines, staring into the suspects' photos, searching for the face of a killer.

She'd been so sure she was out. She hadn't let herself think about it all day as she'd played board games with Josh, as she'd watched back-to-back episodes of American sitcoms, as she'd baked brownies with Mum, sneaking dollops of raw batter into her mouth when unwatched. But with half a second and an unplanned glance Andie had found a way to suck her in again.

She was supposed to be getting dressed for the fireworks but now she was on her knees hunched over the murder board. Some of it really did go in the bin bag: all the clues that had pointed to Elliot Ward. Everything about the Ivy House Hotel, the phone number in the planner, the hit-and-run, Sal's stolen alibi, Andie's nude photo that Max found at the back of a classroom and the printed notes and texts from Unknown.

But the board also needed adding to, because she now knew more about Andie's whereabouts on the night she disappeared. She grabbed a printout of a map of Kilton and started scribbling in a blue marker pen.

Andie went to the Wards' house and left not long after with a potentially serious head injury. Pip circled the Wards' house on Hogg Hill. Elliot had said it was around ten-ish, but he must have been slightly off with that guess. His and Becca Bell's statements of time did not match, yet Becca's was backed up by CCTV: Andie had driven up the high street at 10:40 p.m. That's when she must have headed to the Wards' house. Pip drew a dotted line and scribbled in the time. Yes, Elliot had to be mistaken, she realized, otherwise it meant that Andie had returned home with an injured head before leaving again. And if that had been the case, Becca would have told the police those details. So Becca was no longer the last person to see Andie alive, Elliot was.

But then . . . Pip chewed the end of the pen, thinking. Elliot said that Andie hadn't driven to his house; he thought she'd walked. And, looking at the map, Pip saw why that made sense. The Bells' and the Wards' houses were very close; on foot you just had to cut through the church and over the pedestrian bridge. It was probably a quicker walk than a drive. Pip scratched her head. But that didn't fit: Andie's car was picked up by CCTV so she must have driven. Maybe she'd parked somewhere near Elliot's but not near enough for him to notice.

So how did Andie go from that point into non-existence? From Hogg Hill to her blood in the boot of her car ditched near Howie's house?

Pip tapped the end of the pen against the map, her eyes flitting from Howie to Max to Nat to Daniel to Jason. There had been two different killers in Little Kilton: one who thought he'd killed Andie and then murdered Sal to cover it up, and another who'd actually killed Andie Bell. And which of these faces staring up at her could it be?

Two killers, and yet only one of them had tried to get Pip to stop which meant that . . .

Wait.

Pip held her face as she closed her eyes to think, thoughts firing off and then coming back altered and new and smoking. And one image: Elliot's face, just as the police stepped in. His face when Pip said she'd never forgive him for killing Barney. It had crumpled, his brows tensed. But, picturing it now, it hadn't been remorse on his face. No, it was confusion.

And the words he'd spoken, Pip finished them off for him now: Pip, I don't know what you're talking about. I didn't – *kill Barney.*

Pip swore under her breath, scrabbling over to the slumped bin bag. She pulled out the discarded pages and hunted through them, scattering paper all around her. And then they were in her hands; the notes from the camping trip and her locker in one hand, the printed texts from Unknown in the other.

They were from two different people. It was so obvious now, looking at them.

The differences weren't only in form, it was in their tone. In the printed notes, Elliot had referred to her as Pippa and the threats were subtle, implied. Even the one typed into her EPQ log. But Unknown had called her a 'Stupid bitch,' and the threats weren't just implied: they'd made her smash her laptop up and then they'd killed her dog.

She sat back and let out her too-full breath. Two different people. Elliot wasn't Unknown and he hadn't killed Barney. No, that had been Andie's real killer.

'Pip, come on! They'll have already lit the bonfire,' her dad called upstairs.

She bounded over to her door and opened it a crack. 'Um, you guys go on ahead. I'll find you there.'

'What? No. Get down here, Pipsy.'

'I'm just . . . I just want to try to call Cara a few more times, Dad. I really need to speak to her. I won't be long. Please. I'll find you there.'

'OK, pickle,' he called.

'I'll leave in twenty minutes, I promise,' she said.

'OK, call me if you can't find us.'

As the front door crashed shut Pip sat back beside the murder board, the texts from Unknown shaking in her hands. She scanned through her log entries, trying to work out when in her investigation she had received them. The first had come just after she found Howie Bowers, after she and Ravi had spoken to him and learned about Andie's dealing, about Max buying Rohypnol. And then Barney had been taken in half-term week. A lot had happened just before that: she'd bumped into Stanley Forbes twice, she'd gone to see Becca, and she'd spoken to Daniel at the police meeting.

She scrunched up the pieces of paper and threw them across the room with a growl she'd never heard from herself. There were just too many suspects still. And now that Elliot's secrets were out and Sal was to be exonerated, would the killer be looking for revenge? Would they make good on their threats? Should Pip really be in the house on her own?

She scowled down at all their photos. And with the blue marker she drew a big cross through Jason Bell's face. It couldn't be him. She'd seen the look on his face in the car, once the detective must have called them. Both he and Dawn: crying, angry, confused. But there'd been something else in both of their eyes too, the smallest glimmer of hope alongside their tears. Maybe, even though they'd been told she wasn't, some small part of them had hoped it would still be their daughter. Jason couldn't have faked that reaction. The truth was in his face.

The truth was in the face . . .

Pip picked up the photo of Andie with her parents and Becca, and she stared at it. Into those eyes.

It didn't come all at once.

It came in little blips, lighting up across her memory.

The pieces dropped and fell in a line.

From the murder board she grabbed all the relevant pages. Log entry 3: the interview with Stanley Forbes. Entry 10: the first interview with Emma Hutton. Entry 20: the interview with Jess Walker about the Bells. 21 about Max buying drugs from Andie. 23 about Howie and what he supplied her with. Entry 28 and 29 about drink spiking at calamities. The paper on which Ravi had written: *who could have taken the burner phone???* in large, capital letters. And the time Elliot said Andie left his house.

She looked them over and she knew who it was.

The killer had a face and a name.

The last person to see Andie alive.

But there was just one last thing to confirm. Pip pulled out her phone, scrolled down her contacts and dialled the number.

'Hello?'

'Max?' she said. 'I'm going to ask you a question.'

'I'm not interested. See, you were wrong about me. I've heard what happened, that it was Mr Ward.'

'Good,' Pip said, 'then you know that right now I have a lot of credibility with the police. I told Mr Ward to cover up the hit-and-run, but if you don't answer my question, I will ring the police now and tell them everything.'

'You wouldn't.'

'I will. Naomi's life is already destroyed; don't think that will stop me any more,' she bluffed.

'What do you want?' he spat.

Pip paused. She put the phone on speaker and scrolled to her recording app. She pressed the red record button and sniffed loudly to hide the beep.

'Max, at a calamity party in March 2012,' she said, 'did you drug and rape Becca Bell?'

'What? No, I fucking didn't.'

'MAX,' Pip roared down the phone, 'do not lie to me or I swear to god I will ruin you! Did you put Rohypnol in Becca's drink and have sex with her?'

He coughed.

'Yes, but, like . . . it wasn't rape. She didn't say no.'

'Because you drugged her, you vile rapist gargoyle,' Pip shouted. 'You have no idea what you've done.'

She hung up, stopped the recording and pressed the lock button. Her sharp eyes encased in the darkened screen stared right back into her.

The last person to see Andie alive? It had been Becca. It had always been Becca.

Pip's eyes blinked back at her and the decision was made.

Forty-Nine

The car jerked as Pip pulled roughly on to the kerb. She stepped out into the darkened street and up to the front door.

She knocked.

The wind chimes beside it were swaying and singing in the evening breeze, high and insistent.

The front door opened and Becca's face appeared in the crack. She looked at Pip and pulled it fully open.

'Oh, hi, Pippa,' she said.

'Hi, Becca. I'm . . . I came to see if you were OK, after Thursday night. I saw you in the car and –'

'Yeah,' she nodded, 'the detective told us it was you who found out about Mr Ward, what he'd done.'

'Yeah, sorry.'

'Do you want to come in?' Becca said, stepping back to clear the threshold.

'Thanks.'

Pip walked past her and into the hallway she and Ravi had broken into weeks ago. Becca smiled and gestured her through into the duck-egg blue kitchen.

'Would you like a tea?'

'Oh, no thanks.'

'Sure? I was just making one for myself.'

'OK then. Black please. Thanks.'

Pip took a seat at the kitchen table, her back straight, knees rigid, and watched as Becca grabbed two flowery mugs from a cupboard, dropped in the teabags and poured from the just-boiled kettle.

'Excuse me,' Becca said, 'I just need to get a tissue.'

As she left the room the train whistle sounded from Pip's pocket. It was a message from Ravi: *Yo, Sarge, where are you?* She flicked the phone on to silent and zipped it back into her coat.

Becca re-entered the room, tucking a tissue into her sleeve. She brought over the teas and put Pip's down in front of her.

'Thank you,' Pip said, taking a sip. It wasn't too hot to drink. And she was glad for it now; something to do with her quaking hands.

The black cat came in then, strutting over with its tail up, rubbing its head into Pip's ankles until Becca shooed it away.

'How are your parents doing?' Pip asked.

'Not great,' Becca said. 'After we confirmed she wasn't Andie, my mum booked herself into rehab for emotional trauma. And my dad wants to sue everyone.'

'Do they know who the girl is yet?' Pip said into the rim of her mug.

'Yeah, they called my dad this morning. She was on the missing persons register: Isla Jordan, twenty-three, from Milton Keynes. They said she has a learning disability and the mental age of a twelve-year-old. She came from an abusive home and had a history of running away and possession of

412

drugs.' Becca fiddled with her short hair. 'They said she's very confused; she lived like that for so long – being Andie because it's what pleased Mr Ward – that she actually believes she's a girl called Andie Bell from Little Kilton.'

Pip took a large gulp, filling the silence while the words in her head shivered and readjusted. Her mouth felt dry and there was an awful tremor in her throat, echoing back her doubled heartbeat. She raised the mug and finished off the tea.

'She did look like her,' Pip finally said. 'I thought she was Andie for a few seconds. And I saw in your parents' faces that hope that maybe it would be Andie after all. That me and the police could be wrong. But you already knew, didn't you?'

Becca put her own mug down and stared at her.

'Your face wasn't like theirs, Becca. You looked confused. You looked scared. You knew for sure it couldn't be your sister. Because you killed her, didn't you?'

Becca didn't move. The cat jumped up on the table beside her and she didn't move.

'In March 2012,' Pip said, 'you went to a calamity party with your friend, Jess Walker. And while you were there, something happened to you. You don't remember but you woke up and you knew something felt wrong. You asked Jess to go and get the morning-after pill with you and when she asked who you'd slept with, you didn't tell her. It wasn't, as Jess presumed, because you were embarrassed, it's because you didn't know. You didn't know what happened or with who. You had anterograde amnesia because someone had

413

slipped Rohypnol into your drink and then assaulted you.'

Becca just sat there, inhumanly still, like a small fleshed-out mannequin too scared to move in case she ruffled the dark side of her sister's shadow. And then she started to cry. Tears like silent minnows chased down her cheeks, the muscles twitching in her chin. Something hurt inside Pip, something congealed and cold that closed round her heart as she looked into Becca's eyes and saw the truth in them. Because the truth was no victory here; it was just sadness, deep and decaying.

'I can't imagine how horrible and lonely it was for you,' Pip said, feeling unsteady. 'Not being able to remember but just knowing that something bad had happened. You must have felt like no one could help you. You did nothing wrong and you had nothing to be ashamed of. But I don't think you felt that way at first and you ended up in hospital. And then what happened? Did you decide to find out what had happened to you? Who was responsible?'

Becca's nod was almost imperceptible.

'I think you realized someone had drugged you, so is that where you started looking? Started asking around about who bought drugs at calamities and who from. And the questions led you back to your own sister. Becca, what happened on Friday the twentieth of April? What happened when Andie walked back from Mr Ward's house?'

'All I'd found out was someone bought weed and MDMA off her once,' Becca said, looking down and catching her tears. 'So when she went out and left me alone I looked in her room.

414

I found the place where she hid her other phone and the drugs. I looked through the phone: all the contacts were saved with just one letter names, but I read through some messages and I found the person who bought Rohypnol from her. She'd used his name in one of the texts.'

'Max Hastings,' said Pip.

'And I thought,' she cried, 'I thought that now I knew, we would be able to fix everything and put it right. And I thought that when Andie got home, I'd tell her and she'd let me cry on her and tell me she was so sorry and that we, me and her, were going to set this right and make him pay. All I wanted was my big sister. And just the freedom of finally telling someone.'

Pip wiped her eyes, feeling shaky and drained.

'And then Andie came home,' Becca said.

'With a head injury?'

'No, I didn't know that at the time,' she said. 'I didn't see anything. She was just here, in the kitchen and I couldn't wait any longer. I had to tell her. And –' Becca's voice broke – 'when I did she just looked at me and said she didn't care. I tried to explain and she wouldn't listen. She just said I wasn't allowed to tell anyone or I'd get her in trouble. She tried to leave the room and I stood in her way. Then she said I should be grateful that someone had actually wanted me, because I was just the fat, ugly version of her. And she tried to push me out of the way. I just couldn't believe it, I couldn't believe she could be so cruel. I pushed her back and tried to explain again and we were both shouting and shoving and then . . . it was so fast.

'Andie fell back on the floor. I didn't think I'd pushed her that hard. Her eyes were closed. And then she was being sick. It was all over her face and in her hair. And,' Becca sobbed, 'then her mouth was full and she was coughing and choking on it. And I . . . I just froze. I don't know why, I was just so angry at her. When I look back now I don't know whether I made any decision or not. I don't remember thinking anything at all, I just didn't move. I must have known she was dying and I stood there and did nothing.'

Becca shifted her gaze then, to a place on the kitchen tiles by the door. That must have been where it happened.

'And then she went still and I realized what I'd done. I panicked and tried to clear her mouth but she was already dead. I wanted to take it back so badly. I've wanted to every day since. But it was too late. Only then did I see the blood in her hair and thought I must have hurt her; for five years I've thought that. I didn't know until two days ago that Andie had injured her head before with Mr Ward. That must be why she lost consciousness, why she was sick. Doesn't matter, though. I was still the one who let her choke to death. I watched her die and did nothing. And because I'd thought it was me who hurt her head, and there were scratches on her arms from me, signs of a struggle, I knew everyone – even my parents – would think I'd meant to kill her. Because Andie was always so much better than me. My parents loved her more.'

'You put her body in the boot of her car?' Pip said, leaning forward to hold her head because it was too heavy.

'The car was in the garage and I dragged her inside. I don't know how I found the strength to do it. It's all a blur now. I cleaned everything up; I'd watched enough documentaries. I knew which type of bleach you have to use.'

'Then you left the house at just before 10:40 p.m.,' said Pip. 'It was you the CCTV picked up, driving Andie's car up the high street. And you took her . . . I think you took her to that old farmhouse on Sycamore Road, the one you were writing an article about, because you didn't want the neighbours to buy it and restore it. And you buried her there?'

'She's not buried,' Becca sniffed. 'She's in the septic tank.'

Pip nodded gently, her fuzzy head grappling with Andie's final fate. 'Then you dumped her car and you walked home. Why did you leave it on Romer Close?'

'When I looked through her second phone, I saw that that was where her dealer lived. I thought if I left the car there, the police would make the connection and he'd be the main suspect.'

'What must you have thought when suddenly Sal was the guilty one and it was all over?'

Becca shrugged. 'I don't know. I thought maybe it was some kind of sign, that I'd been forgiven. Though I've never forgiven myself.'

'And then,' Pip said, 'five years later, I start digging. You got my number from Stanley's phone, from when I interviewed him.'

'He told me some kid was doing a project, thinking Sal was

innocent. I panicked. I thought that if you proved his innocence, I'd need to find another suspect. I'd kept Andie's burner phone and I knew she was having a secret relationship; there were some texts to a contact named *E* about meeting up at this hotel, the Ivy House. So I went there to see if I could find out who this man was. I didn't get anywhere, the old woman who owned it was very confused. Then weeks later I saw you hanging round the station car park and I knew that's where Andie's dealer worked. I watched you, and as you followed him I followed you. I saw you go to his house with Sal's brother. I just wanted to make you stop.'

'That's when you first texted me,' Pip said. 'But I didn't stop. And when I came to talk to you at your office, you must have thought I was so close to figuring out it was you, talking about the burner phone and Max Hastings. So you killed my dog and made me destroy all my research.'

'I'm sorry.' She looked down. 'I didn't mean for your dog to die. I let him go, I really did. But it was dark; he must have got confused and fallen in the river.'

Pip's breath stuttered. But accident or not, it wouldn't bring Barney back.

'I loved him so much,' Pip said, feeling dizzy, unjoining from herself. 'But I choose to forgive you. That's why I came here, Becca. If I've worked all this out, the police won't be far behind me, not now they've reopened the case. And Mr Ward's story starts to poke holes in yours.' She spoke fast, slurring, her tongue tripping up over the words. 'It's not right what you

418

did, Becca, letting her die. I know you know that. But it's also not fair what happened to you. You didn't ask for any of this. And the law lacks compassion. I came to warn you. You need to leave, get out of the country and find a life for yourself somewhere. Because they will be coming for you soon.'

Pip looked at her. Becca must have been talking, but suddenly all the sound in the world disappeared, there was just the buzz of a beetle's wings trapped inside her head. The table was mutating and fizzing between them and some ghost-drawn weight started to drag down Pip's eyelids.

'I-I . . .' she stuttered. The world dimmed, the only bright thing was the empty mug in front of her, wavering, its colours dripping up into the air. 'You put somethi– My drink?'

'There were a few of Max's pills left in Andie's hiding place. I kept them.'

Becca's voice came to Pip loud and garish, a shrieking clown-laugh echo, switching from ear to ear.

Pip pushed up from her chair but her left leg was too weak. It gave out under her and she crashed into the kitchen island. Something smashed and the pieces were flying around like jagged clouds and up and up as the world spun around her.

The room lurched and Pip stumbled over to the sink, leaned into it and rammed her fingers down her throat. She vomited, and it was dark brown and stinging and she vomited again. A voice came to her from somewhere near and somewhere far.

'I'll work something out, I have to. There's no evidence. There's just you and what you know. I'm sorry. I don't want to do this. Why couldn't you just leave it alone?'

Pip staggered back and wiped her mouth. The room reeled again and Becca was in front of her, her shaking hands outstretched.

'No,' Pip tried to scream but her voice got lost somewhere inside. She hurtled back and side-stepped around the island. Her fingers bit into one of the stools to keep her on her feet. She grabbed it and launched it behind her. There was a head-split echo of clattering as it took out Becca's legs.

Pip ran into the wall in the hallway. Ears ringing and shoulder throbbing, she leaned into it so it wouldn't morph away from her and scaled her way to the front door. It wouldn't open but then she blinked and it vanished and she was outside somehow.

It was dark and spinning and there was something in the sky. Bright and colourful mushrooms and doomclouds and sprinkles. The fireworks with a ripping-the-earth sound from the common. Pip picked up her feet and ran towards the bright colours, into the woods.

The trees were walking in a wooden two-step and Pip's feet went numb. Missing. Another sparkling sky-roar and it made her blind.

Her hands out in front to be her eyes. Another crack and Becca was in her face.

She pushed and Pip fell on her back in the leaves and mud. And Becca was standing over her, hands splayed and reaching down and . . . a rush of energy came back to her.

420

She forced it down her leg and kicked out hard. And Becca was on the ground too, lost in the dark leaves.

'I was tr-trying to h-help you,' Pip stammered.

She turned and crawled and her arms wanted to be legs and her legs, arms. She scrabbled up to her missing feet and ran from Becca. Towards the churchyard.

More bombs were bursting and it was the end of the world behind her. She grasped at the trees to help push her on as they danced and twirled at the falling sky. She grabbed a tree and it felt like skin.

It lunged out and gripped her with two hands. They fell on the ground and they rolled. Pip's head smashed into a tree, a snaking trail of wet down her face, the iron-bite of blood in her mouth. The world went dark again as the redness pooled by her eyes. And then Becca was sitting on her and there was something cold round Pip's neck. She reached up to feel and it was fingers but her own wouldn't work. She couldn't prise them off.

'Please.' The word squeezed out of her and the air wouldn't come back.

Her arms were stuck in the leaves and they wouldn't listen to her. They wouldn't move.

She looked up into Becca's eyes. *She knows where to put you where they'll never find you. In a dark as dark place, with the bones of Andie Bell.*

Her arms and legs were gone and she was following.

'I wish someone like you had been there for me,'

Becca cried. 'All I had was Andie. She was my only escape from my dad. She was my only hope after Max. And she didn't care. Maybe she never had. Now I'm stuck in this thing and there's no way out except this. I don't want to do this. I'm sorry.'

Pip couldn't remember now what it felt like to breathe.

Her eyes were splitting and there was fire in the cracks.

Little Kilton was being swallowed by an even bigger dark. But those rainbow sparks in the night were nice to look at. One last nice thing to send you on before it all goes black.

And as it did, she felt the cold fingers loosen and come away.

The first breath ripped and snagged as she sucked it down. The blackness pulled back and sounds grew out of the earth.

'I can't do it,' Becca said, moving her hands back to hug herself. 'I can't.'

Then a crash of rustling footsteps and a shadow leaped over them and Becca was dragged off. More sounds. Shouting and screaming and, 'You're OK, pickle.'

Pip turned her head and her dad was here with her, pinning Becca down on the ground while she struggled and cried.

And there was another person behind her, sitting her up, but she was a river and couldn't be held.

'Breathe, Sarge,' Ravi said, stroking her hair. 'We're here. We're here now.'

'Ravi, what's wrong with her?'

'Hypnol,' Pip whispered, looking up at him. 'Rohypnol

422

in . . . tea.'

'Ravi, call an ambulance now. Call the police.'

The sounds went away again. It was just the colours and Ravi's voice vibrating in his chest and through her back to the outer edge of all sense.

'She let Andie die,' Pip said or she thought she said. 'But we have to let her go. It's not fair. Not fair.'

Kilton blinked.

'I might not remember. I might get mm . . . nesia. She's in septic tank. Farmhouse . . . Sycamore. That's where . . .'

'It's OK, Pip,' Ravi said, holding her so she didn't fall off the world. 'It's over. It's all over now. I've got you.'

'How didddu find me?'

'Your tracking device is still on,' Ravi said, showing her a fuzzy, jumping screen with an orange blip on the Find My Friends map. 'As soon as I saw you here, I knew.'

Kilton blinked.

'It's OK, I've got you, Pip. You're going to be OK.'

Blink.

They were talking again, Ravi and her dad. But not in words she could hear, in the scratching of ants. She couldn't see them any more. Pip's eyes were the sky and fireworks were rupturing inside. Flower sprays of Armageddon. All red. Red glows and red shines.

And then she was a person again, on the cold damp ground, Ravi's breath in her ear. And through the trees were flashing blue lights spewing black uniforms.

Pip watched them both, the flashes and the fireworks.

No sound. Just her rattlesnake breath and the sparks and the lights.

Red and blue. Red

        and blue. Bled a n

                d rue. B e

                      ll a n

                              n

                                  d

Three Months Later

'There are a *lot* of people out there, Sarge.'

'Really?'

'Yeah, like, two hundred.'

She could hear them all; the chattering and the clattering of chairs as people took their seats in the school hall.

She was waiting in the wings, her presentation notes clutched in her hands, the sweat from the bulbs of her fingers smudging the printed ink.

Everyone else in her year had done their EPQ presentations earlier in the week, to small classrooms of people and the modulators. But the school and the exam board thought it would be a good idea to turn Pip's presentation into '*a bit of an event*,' as the head teacher had put it. Pip had been given no choice in the matter. The school had advertised it online and in the *Kilton Mail*. They'd invited members of the press to attend; Pip had seen a BBC van pull up earlier and the equipment and cameras unpacked.

'Are you nervous?' Ravi said.

'Are you asking obvious questions?'

When the Andie Bell story broke it had been in the national newspapers and on TV stations for weeks. It was in the height of all that craziness that Pip had had her interview for Cambridge. The two college fellows had recognized her from the news, gawping at her, yapping questions about the case. Her offer was one of the very first to come in.

Kilton's secrets and mysteries had followed Pip so closely in those weeks she'd had to wear them like a new skin.

Except that one that was buried deep down, the one she'd keep forever to save Cara. Her best friend who'd never once left Pip's side in the hospital.

'Can I come over later?' Ravi asked her.

'Sure. Cara and Naomi are round for dinner too.'

They heard a sharp patter of clip-clop heels and Mrs Morgan appeared, fighting through the curtain.

'I think we're just about ready when you are, Pippa.'

'OK, I'll be out in a minute.'

'Well,' Ravi said when they were alone again, 'I'd better go and take my seat.'

He smiled, put his hands on the back of her neck, fingers in her hair, and leaned in to press his forehead against hers. He'd told her before that he did it to take away half her sadness, half her headache, half her nerves as she'd got on the train to Cambridge for her interview. Because half less of a bad thing meant there was room for half good.

He kissed her, and she glowed with that feeling. The one with wings.

'You bring the rain down on them, Pip.'

'I will.'

'Oh, and,' he said, turning one last time before the door, 'don't tell them the only reason you started this project was because you fancied me. You know, think of a more noble reason.'

'Get out of here.'

'Don't feel bad. You couldn't help yourself, I'm ravishing,'

427

he grinned. 'Get it? Ravi-shing. Ravi Singh.'

'Sign of a great joke, having to explain it,' she said. 'Now go.'

She waited another minute, muttering the first lines of her speech under her breath. And then she walked out on stage.

People weren't quite sure what to do. About half the audience started clapping politely, the news cameras panning to them, and the other half sat deadly still, a poppy field of eyes stalking her as she moved.

From the front row, her dad stood up and whistled with his fingers, shouting: 'Get 'em, pickle.' Her mum swiftly pulled him back down and exchanged a look with Nisha Singh, sitting beside her.

Pip strode over to the head teacher's lectern and flattened her speech down on top.

'Hi,' she said, and the microphone screeched, cutting through the silent room. Cameras clicked. 'My name is Pip and I know many things. I know that *typewriter* is the longest word that can be made with just one row of the keyboard. I know that the Anglo-Zanzibar war was the shortest in history, lasting only thirty-eight minutes. I also know that this project put myself, my friends and my family in danger and has changed many lives, not all for the better. But what I don't know,' she paused, 'is why this town and the national media still don't really understand what happened here. I am not the "prodigy student" who found the truth for Andie Bell in long articles where Sal Singh and his brother Ravi are relegated to

428

small side notes. This project began with Sal. To find the truth.'

Pip's eyes uncovered him then. Stanley Forbes in the third row, scribbling away in an open notebook. She still wondered about him, him and the other names on her persons of interest list, the other lives and secrets that had criss-crossed this case. Little Kilton still had its mysteries, unturned stones and unanswered questions. But this town had too many dark corners; Pip had learned to accept that she couldn't shine a light into each and every one.

Stanley was sitting just behind her friends, Cara's face absent among them. As brave as she had been through everything, she'd decided today would have been too hard for her.

'I couldn't have fathomed,' Pip continued, 'that when this project was over, it would end with four people in handcuffs and one being set free after five years in her own prison. Elliot Ward has pleaded guilty to the murder of Sal Singh, to the kidnap of Isla Jordan and perverting the course of justice. His sentencing hearing is next week. Becca Bell will face trial later this year for the following charges: manslaughter by gross negligence, preventing a lawful burial and perverting the course of justice. Max Hastings has been charged with four counts of sexual assault and two counts of rape, and will also be tried later this year. And Howard Bowers has pleaded guilty to the charge of supplying a controlled drug and possession with intent to sell.'

429

She shuffled her notes and cleared her throat.

'So, why did the events of Friday the twentieth of April 2012 happen? The way I see it, there are a handful of people who carry some of the blame for what happened that night and the days following, morally if not all criminally. These are: Elliot Ward, Howard Bowers, Max Hastings, Becca Bell, Jason Bell and, do not forget, Andie herself. You have cast her as your beautiful victim and wilfully overlook those more shaded layers of her character, because it doesn't comfortably fit your narrative. But this is the truth: Andie Bell was a bully who used emotional blackmail to get what she wanted. She sold drugs without care or regard for how they might be used. We will never know if she knew she was facilitating drug-assisted sexual assault, but certainly when confronted with this truth by her own sister she could not find it in herself to show compassion.

'And yet, when we look closer, what do we find behind this true Andie? We find a girl, vulnerable and self-conscious. Because Andie grew up being taught by her father that the only value she had was in the way she looked and how strongly she was desired. Home for her was a place where she was bullied and belittled. Andie never got the chance to become the young woman she might have been away from that house, to decide for herself what made her valuable and what future she wanted.

'And though this story does have its monsters, I've found that it is not one that can be so easily cleaved into the good and the bad. In the end, this was a story about people and their different shades of desperation, crashing up against each other. But there was one person who was good until the very end. And his name was Sal Singh.'

Pip looked up then, her eyes flicking straight to Ravi, sitting between his parents.

'The thing is,' she said, 'I didn't do this project alone, as the guidelines require. I couldn't have done it on my own. So, I guess you're going to have to disqualify me.'

A few people gasped in the audience, Mrs Morgan loudly among them. A few titters of laughter.

'I couldn't have solved this case without Ravi Singh. In fact, I wouldn't have survived it. So, if anyone should speak about how kind Sal Singh was now that you're all finally listening, it's his brother.'

Ravi stared at her from his seat, his eyes wide in that telling-off way that she loved. But she knew he needed this. And he knew it too.

She beckoned with a tilt of her head and Ravi got to his feet. Victor stood up too, whistling with his fingers again and smacking his big hands loudly together. Some of the students in the audience joined in, clapping as Ravi jogged up the steps to the stage and walked over to the lectern.

Pip stepped back from the microphone as Ravi joined her. He winked at her and Pip felt a flash of pride as she watched him step up to the lectern, scratching the back of his head. He'd told her just yesterday that he was going to retake his school exams so he could go on to study law.

'Erm . . . hi,' Ravi said, and the microphone screeched for him too. 'I wasn't expecting this, but it's not every day a girl throws away a guaranteed A star for you.' There was a quiet ripple of warm laughter. 'But, I guess, I didn't need preparation to talk about Sal. I've been preparing for that nearly six years now. My brother wasn't just a good person, he was one of the best. He was kind, exceptionally kind, always helping people and nothing was ever too much trouble. He was selfless. I remember this one time when we were kids, I spilt Ribena all over the carpet and Sal took the fall for me so I wouldn't get in trouble. Oops, sorry, Mum, guess you had to find out some time.'

More laughter from the audience.

'Sal was cheeky. And he had the most ridiculous laugh; you couldn't help but join in. And, oh yeah, he used to spend hours drawing these comics for me to read in bed because I wasn't a great sleeper. I still have them all. And damn was Sal clever. I know he would have done incredible things with his life, if it hadn't been taken away from him. The world will never be as bright without him in it,' Ravi's voice cracked. 'And I wish I'd been able to tell him all this when he was alive. Tell him he was the best big brother anyone could ever wish for. But at least I can say it now on this stage and know that this time everyone will believe me.'

He looked back at Pip, his eyes shining, reaching for her. She drew forward to stand with him, leaning into the

432

microphone to say her final lines.

'But there was one final player in this story, Little Kilton, and it's us. Collectively we turned a beautiful life into the myth of a monster. We turned a family home into a ghost house. And from now on we must do better.'

Pip reached down behind the lectern for Ravi's hand, sliding her fingers between his. Their entwined hands became a new living thing, her finger pads perfect against the dips in his knuckles like they'd grown just that way to fit together.

'Any questions?'

Acknowledgements

This book would have remained an abandoned Word document or an unexplored idea in my head if it weren't for a whole list of amazing humans. Firstly, to my super-agent, Sam Copeland, it is incredibly annoying that you're always right. Thank you for being so cool and calm, you're the best person anyone could have on their team and I will be forever grateful that you took a chance on me.

A Good Girl's Guide to Murder found its perfect home with Farshore and I'm so happy it did. To Ali Dougal, Lindsey Heaven and Soraya Bouazzaoui: thank you for your tireless enthusiasm, for seeing the heart of this story and for helping me to find it. Special thanks to my amazing editor, Lindsey, for guiding me through. To Amy St Johnston for being the first to read and champion the book; I'm so grateful you did. To Sarah Levison for her hard work whipping this book into shape and to Lizzie Gardiner for my beautiful cover design; I couldn't have dreamed up one more perfect. To Melissa Hyder, Jennie Roman and to everyone in the marketing and publicity team: Heather Ryerson for the gorgeous proof, Siobhan McDermott for all her hard work at YALC and beyond, Emily Finn and Dannie Price for the genius YALC campaign and Jas Bansal for being the social media queen. And to Tracy Phillips and the rights team for an incredible job bringing this story to other parts of the world.

To my 2019 debut group for all their support, with special mentions to Savannah, Yasmin, Katya, Lucy, Sarah, Joseph and my agency/publisher twin, Aisha. This whole publishing thing is far less scary when you go through it with friends.

To my Flower Huns (what a useless WhatsApp group name, and now it's in a published book so we can't ever get rid of it) thank you for being my friends for more than a decade and for understanding when I disappear into my writer's hole. Thanks to Elspeth, Lucy and Alice for being early readers.

To Peter and Gaye, thank you for your unwavering support; for reading the earliest version of this book and for letting me live somewhere so nice while I write the next one. And to Katie for championing this book from the start and for giving me the first spark of Pip.

To my big sister, Amy, thanks for letting me sneak into your room to watch *Lost* when I was too young – my love of mysteries has grown from there. To my little sister, Olivia, thank you for reading every single thing I've ever written, from that red notebook of scribbled stories to Elizabeth Crowe, you were my very first reader and I'm so grateful. To Danielle and George – oh hey look, you've made it into the acknowledgements just for being cute. You better not read this book until you are an appropriate age.

To Mum and Dad, thank you for giving me a childhood filled with stories, for raising me alongside books and films and games. I wouldn't be here without all those years of *Tomb Raider* and *Harry Potter*. But thank you mostly for always saying I could when others said I couldn't. We did it.

And to Ben. You are my constant through every tear, tantrum, failure, worry and victory. Without you, I couldn't have done it at all.

Finally, thank *you* for picking up this book and reading to the end. You'll never know how much it means.

Holly Jackson started writing stories from a young age, completing her first (poor) attempt at a novel aged fifteen. She graduated from the University of Nottingham with an MA in English, where she studied literary linguistics and creative writing. She lives in London and aside from reading and writing, she enjoys playing video games and watching true crime documentaries so she can pretend to be a detective. *A Good Girl's Guide to Murder* is her first novel. You can follow Holly on Twitter and Instagram @HoJay92.

'Nail-biting, taut and pacy'
Guardian

Good Girl, Bad Blood

HOLLY JACKSON

The No.1 *New York Times* bestselling author of
A Good Girl's Guide to Murder

The sequel to the bestselling
A Good Girl's Guide to Murder

'A taut, compulsively readable,
elegantly plotted thriller.'

Guardian on *A Good Girl's Guide to Murder*

The thrilling final book in the bestselling,
award-winning series.

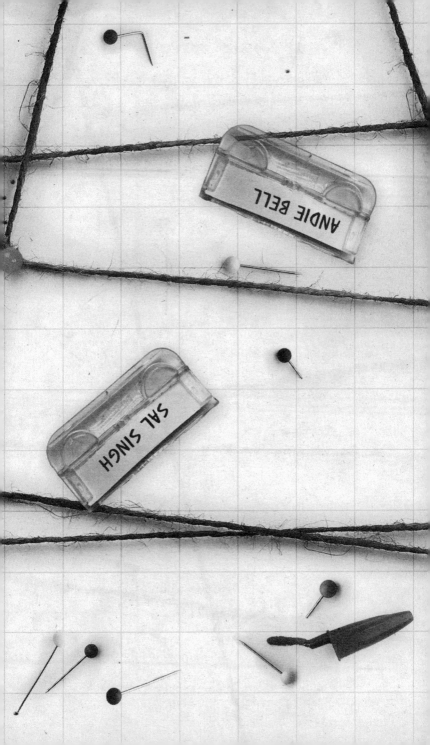

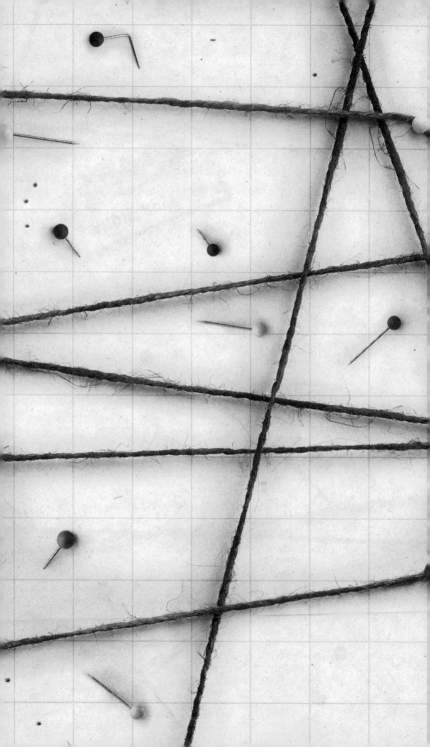